13 DAYS OF TERROR

DWAYNE CLAYDEN

BAD ALIBI PRESS

dwayneclayden@gmail.com

DwayneClayden.com

Published in Canada by Bad Alibi Press

Printed and Bound in Canada

Cover Graphic by Travis Miles, Pro Book Covers

Editing by Taija Morgan

Proofing by Jonas Saul

Formatting by Dwayne Clayden

13 Days of Terror / Dwayne Clayden—1st print ed.

ISBN: 978-1-989912-02-7 (pbk), 978-1-989912-03-4 (e-book)

Created with Vellum

For Calgary Police Service
Recruit Class 74

My career started with great friends.

ALSO BY DWAYNE CLAYDEN

The Brad Coulter Thrillers

Crisis Point

Outlaw MC

Wolfman is Back

13 Days of Terror

The Brad Coulter Thrillers Continue in 2021

Goddess of Justice

Bonded Labor

The Speargrass Thriller Series

Speargrass Opioid

Speargrass Casino

Short Story

Hell Hath No Fury

AB Negative. An Anthology of Alberta Crime

CHAPTER ONE

Wednesday Day One

GUNFIRE ECHOED ALONG THE FORESTRY CUTLINE. TALL EVERGREENS and golden-red deciduous trees lined the makeshift gun range. Massive towers held sagging transmission lines. Shafts of wild grass, sapped of life by the fall frost, formed a golden carpet.

Marvin Pittman and Logan Hirsch stood side by side, rifles at their shoulders as they fired at targets a hundred yards away. They reloaded and shot again. When they emptied their magazines, they set the guns down and jogged to the targets.

Pittman, at thirty-five, was seven years older than Hirsch, but he ran like he was sixty. Where Pittman had a stocky build, Hirsch was slim, on the verge of scrawny.

Pittman stopped at the targets, hands on his knees, gasping for breath. Finally, he stood, wiped his hand across his sweating forehead and balding scalp, and stared at his target. "Shit."

Hirsch glanced over and laughed. "Looks like you used a shotgun, not a rifle."

"Jeez," Pittman said. "You put twenty shots in the chest from a hundred yards. Where did you learn to shoot like this?"

"I grew up in Grande Prairie. From about the time I was six, I went hunting with my dad and uncles. We hunted everything—deer, elk, moose. Bear, sometimes. Dad said I was a natural shooter."

"I'd say so. Put up some new targets and let's go again."

An hour later they sat on some tree stumps and cleaned the guns. Pittman wandered over to his truck and came back with a cooler. He pulled out two beers, handed one to Hirsch, and they guzzled.

"That hit the spot," Hirsch said. "You plan for everything."

"I try," Pittman said. "I needed that."

"No, shit." Hirsch stretched his long legs and yawned.

"Shooting is cleansing, peaceful." Pittman closed his eyes and let the sun warm his face. "I love fall. I could sit here all day."

"A lot better than employment training. If I have to attend another week, I might blow my brains out." Hirsch mimicked the instructor in a high-pitched voice, saying, "Now that you know what to put in a résumé, it's time to put that into practice. Use the notebook to create your résumé. Just put up a hand if you need my help." Hirsch drained his beer and threw the bottle into the trees. "Treating us like stupid kids."

"Have another beer, or three. You'll feel better."

"It will take more than beer," Hirsch said. "The economy is in the shitter and my life is worse than that."

"What's happening with your family?"

"When the bank foreclosed on the house, the wife and kids

went to stay with her parents in Whitecourt. We were talking by phone every day for about a month. But when I didn't find work, she stopped talking. Like it was my fault. She filed for divorce two months ago. Wants full custody of the kids."

"Shit, that hurts. You gonna fight it?"

"Sure, I'll just take money out of my savings account and hire a good lawyer. Other than the cash they pay us for retraining, I don't have two nickels to rub together. Even if I fought it, I have no job and no prospects. The lawyers would get rich. I'd still be divorced and still not see my kids. The system is screwed."

"How do you feel about this re-training?"

"It doesn't matter how I feel," Hirsch said. "It's all bullshit. You and me know how to drill an oil well. I don't want to be some parts guy in an automotive store or a stock boy in some hardware chain."

Pittman emptied his beer, tossed it into the trees next to Hirsch's, and grabbed another. Pittman's leg vibrated. He had to be patient and lead Hirsch to the solution. "Don't know what to say. The oil industry is dying. Maybe it will come back in a few years. That doesn't help us today."

"That's the problem," Hirsch said. "No one is helping us. The bank didn't give me a break or time to figure things out. I missed three payments and boom, they're in court and taking the house. Fuckin' Ford dealership took my truck."

"We get laid off with one month's pay while the oil executives keep their jobs, get their high salaries and bonuses," Pittman said. "How can they earn bonuses when the industry is in shambles? Then they lay off half their staff. The big wigs need to feel *our* pain." Pittman glanced at Hirsch, watching for a reaction. Hirsch didn't take the bait.

"Fat chance of that happening. They've closed ranks. They have the money to wait this out. We don't." Hirsch grabbed another beer and stared at the targets. "You got family?"

Pittman shook his head. "Not no more. I've been through this before. About ten years ago, things got really bad. I got laid off, but I got a job at a well-servicing company in Calgary. Did that for about five years. I hated it, but it paid the bills. Then my old lady found religion. She was off to church meetings all the time, Bible study at our house. I had to drink beer in the garage. Then she took off with a bus driver she met at church. He promised he'd *save* her and give her everything she wanted."

"Jeez, I didn't know." Hirsch scratched the patchy blond stubble on his face. "Sorry."

"They hate each other and he's dirt poor. But God will provide. That'll teach her." Pittman twirled his beer, then took a long pull. "Jobs were opening up here again, so I came back. Just in time for another fuckin' collapse."

"Neither of us got any luck." Hirsch finished his beer.

Pittman picked at the beer label. He grabbed two beers out of the cooler and handed one to Hirsch. It was now or never. "What if we could strike back?"

Hirsch cocked his head, eyebrows scrunched. "You have an idea?"

Pittman picked up his rifle and pointed it down the meadow. "I've been planning this for a long time."

CHAPTER TWO

BRAD COULTER SAT BACK IN THE RECLINER, ARMS ACROSS HIS CHEST, and stared at the stupid paintings on the wall. Why did shrinks think abstract pictures of nothing but color on a canvas was soothing? Or maybe that wasn't the point. Perhaps they just had shitty taste in art. How about a beautiful sunset? Lovely white sand beach and deep blue water? Dogs playing poker?

He glared at the man seated opposite.

Twice a week Brad met with a psychologist appointed by the police service. If he had any hope of getting back on the street as a detective in Homicide, this guy would make the decision.

"Brad," Dr. Hans Keller said. "Sitting there, arms crossed and ignoring me, won't get you to work any faster."

Brad hardened his glare.

Keller leaned back. "Fine. I can sit here for the next hour and watch you pout. They pay me either way."

The two men stared at each other for several moments.

Brad leaned forward. "I don't know what you want from me.

I've made it clear I want back on the street. You've made it clear you don't think I'm ready. I've taken every psychological test invented. They don't say I'm violent. They don't say I'm a danger to myself or others. They say I'm depressed. No kidding. Because of me, my girlfriend and our unborn baby died. You never get over that."

Keller steepled his fingers in front of his face. "No, you don't get over it. You move ahead."

"Being a cop, that's what I need. Do some good for others, not just me." Brad had been a cop in Calgary since he was twenty-four. Starting as a street cop, he quickly worked his way up the ranks through the tactical support unit, to sergeant in charge of a tactical team, and at thirty-two, a detective. He didn't know how to sit at home doing nothing, and after two-and-a-half months it was taking its toll.

"Tell me how you felt when you killed Wolfe."

Brad rolled his eyes. "We've been over this story a hundred times. I felt nothing. I'd wasted a piece of shit hell-bent on killing people. People close to me."

"You weren't glad he was dead?"

"I was glad he couldn't hurt anyone ever again. But I was wrong."

Keller cocked his head. "How so?"

"He was dead, but it didn't end there. Maggie and the baby died. It was like he was mocking me from hell. In the end, he won."

"Do you always think in terms of winning and losing?"

"I lost Maggie and the baby." Brad leaned forward and stabbed a finger at Keller. "That's losing."

"You're competitive."

"That makes me good at what I do. That's why you need to end these stupid sessions and clear me to go back to work."

"You think you're mentally prepared to return to duty?"

Keller's monotone voice did nothing to calm Brad. "Damn right."

"How about physically?"

"My wounds have healed. I did physiotherapy and I work out every day."

"Yes. I see the results of your workout. You lost some weight, too?"

Brad had always been athletic and played university football. On the tactical support unit, he'd worked out with the team and was in excellent physical condition. But over the last two months he'd taken workouts to a new level. His six-foot-one body was defined and fat free.

"Sure, but what does that have to do with going back to work?"

"I need to be sure you aren't using your workouts as a crutch, as an escape."

"I give up." Brad threw up his hands and leaned back. "No matter what I do, it's not good enough or the right thing." He stood. "Tell me, Doc, was your wife murdered? The woman you love? How about your kids? Any of them murdered by a psychopathic killer?" Brad glared at Keller. "Didn't think so. Keep your textbook psychobabble to yourself. I'm outta here."

"If you leave, I have to put it in my report."

Brad stopped at the door. "Doc, it would help if I knew what your objective is—this seems like playing games—mind games. If you want to toss around a football, give me a call. That I understand."

Keller leaned back in his chair, his face expressionless.

Brad shook his head and yanked the door closed behind him.

Brad unlocked the door and found Lobo sitting on a mat, tail wagging. Brad knelt. "Hello, buddy. I missed you. I had another fun hour with Dr. Keller. I think I screwed up today."

Lobo cocked his head to the side and barked.

"Apparently, there are things you should merely think, not say out loud. Getting back to work will be a challenge. I'll just spend extra time with you."

Lobo licked his face, then lifted a paw.

"Most people would think you were happy to see me. But I know you want a treat."

Lobo raced to the pantry and sat by the door. Brad opened the door and pulled out two treats. Lobo sat and lifted his paw again. Brad knelt and gave Lobo a biscuit. Brad tried to get Lobo to lift his other paw. Nope. Lobo was a right-pawed dog. Brad shook the paw and offered a second treat.

Brad stood and noticed the flashing light on the answering machine. The counter showed eight messages.

"Hey, Brad, it's Sam. I'm sure you're there listening. Just pick up the phone. Okay, ignore me. Look, Charlie and I are worried about you. Time to get together for drinks. Charlie even said he'd buy. Don't be a jerk. At least call me."

Brad erased the message. His best friend, Sam Steele, had been calling all week. He knew Sam meant well and was concerned. For the first few weeks, it had been okay hanging out with Sam and Charlie Zerr. They had become friends four years ago when the Tactical Support Unit was created, and they'd been inseparable. But something changed—Maggie was killed.

And because of that, Brad had changed, he'd aged. He was thirty-two but mentally felt fifty. Sam at twenty-eight and Charlie at twenty-six seemed too young to hang around with. Or maybe he just didn't want to be around people, even his friends. He liked the solitude and didn't want the company. He was okay with it just being Lobo and him.

He hit the button and the next recording started. "Dipshit. It's Devlin. Call me or I'll come over and kick in the door. And no, I'm not afraid of your mutt. Call me, jackass."

Jeez. Brad erased that message and stared at the machine. Tommy Devlin was another of the original TSU, but his real love was the narcotics unit. Earlier this year they'd battled a psychotic ex-biker named Jeter Wolfe—Wolfman. He severely injured Devlin and kidnapped and murdered his partner Tina Davidson the same night. Devlin was still recovering. He'd never work on the street again, but Deputy Chief Archer had sent him to Quantico to learn hostage negotiation.

At least Tommy understood recovery.

The next five calls were hang ups.

Brad stared at the answering machine and then the phone. A quick call to each of them, a quick chat, and they'd leave him alone.

Not now.

"Lobo, let's head to the barn."

Lobo jumped to his feet, tail wagging, and bounded to the back door. He sprinted ahead as they crossed the yard to the old-fashioned barn.

After the battle with Wolfe in Brad's house, where Wolfe killed Maggie, Brad moved out. A month and a half ago, he found this farm for sale. On the outskirts of the city, the one-thousand-square-foot farmhouse with a garage, a barn, and ten acres was perfect. No neighbors close by. The road wasn't on the way to anywhere. Brad bought it outright with some of his stock dividends.

The house was nothing special, but it worked. Eighty-years old and haunted.

The bonus was that Brad and Lobo could jog from the farm, down the hill to Bearspaw Dam, through a thick forest of Douglass Firs, then to the seventy-four-acre woods of Bowness Park. The park comprised two islands in the Bow River. They dammed a channel flowing on the south bank to create a lagoon.

In the middle of the park, surrounded by towering evergreens, was a large grass field. Brad grew up in Bowness and his friends played football on that field day and night.

There wouldn't be a jog today. He slid the heavy barn door open and Lobo raced past. Brad had set the barn up as his gym. He'd cleaned out the moldy straw and manure and given it a thorough scrubbing. He'd replaced the dim lightbulbs with a string of fluorescent lights. Instead of the usual weights and stationary bike, he'd created his own workout plan. He used a large tractor tire he flipped over and over. He repurposed some bales for a bench press and curls. He attached a bale to the pulley over the loft and pulled the bale up to the loft, let it descend slowly, then pulled it up again. In one stall, he'd hung a heavy punching bag and a speed bag.

Lobo took on the role of gym supervisor and occasionally gave Brad a bark of encouragement, or maybe he was egging him on.

Through the hell since Maggie's death, Lobo had been a constant companion. There when Brad needed him, and sometimes when Brad didn't know he needed him.

Forty-five minutes later, Brad was soaked in sweat. Lobo was asleep and having a chasing-the-rabbit dream.

Brad did fifteen minutes on the speed bag until his arms and shoulders ached. He took a break, drank a bottle of water, and toweled off. Then he started on the heavy bag—quick jabs at first, then faster and harder punches. He felt the anger, felt it flow through his arms to his hands, and his fists flew as though he could punch through the bag.

The punches weakened, and his arms tired until he collapsed on the barn floor. His breath came in gasps and an unseen weight pressed down on his body. He rolled onto his side with his face against the cold floor. He glanced at the torn flesh on his knuckles and the dried blood. It wasn't the first time.

CHAPTER THREE

Thursday Day Two

Pittman and Hirsch huddled over a tray of draft beers in the nearly empty Drayton Valley bar. It was the class routine to head out for beers after the retraining classes. The bar had been popular among the oil workers in the area. Back then, most nights it was only standing room. Now, a year into the crash of the oil industry, you could get a seat anytime, any day. The jobs were gone and so were most of the oil workers. The few reminders of the thriving economy were the pictures on the wall of oil wells gushing with the workers covered in oil, towering derricks and pumping stations. The out of work oilmen sat at ten of the fifty tables.

Early that morning they had gone back to the transmission line. The sun was at their backs and provided perfect shooting conditions. With the new scope on the rifle, Hirsch lay on the ground and lined up the target. Then he fired five shots in rapid succession—a tight grouping.

Hirsch took a long pull of his beer. "The scope is fuckin' amazing."

"I thought that might help," Pittman said. "At two-hundred yards all five shots were in the X."

"Hard to miss."

Pittman pointed his beer at Hirsch. "The five in the target's nuts was mighty fine shooting. Remind me not to get you pissed at me."

"If I were, you'd never hear the shot." Hirsch grinned.

"If we do this, you've got to be all in," Pittman said.

"I'm in."

"Today, we leave this shithole behind. You're accurate shooting targets, but it's different with a face in the sights."

"Don't worry about me."

"I'm not worried. Well, maybe a little, but we need a test before we get to Calgary."

"What do you have in mind?"

"I have several possibilites."

"I don't know about you, but I don't have much cash."

Pittman nodded and finished his beer. "I've got enough to keep us going for a week or so. Leave that to me."

That afternoon they drove the back roads in Pittman's truck from Drayton Valley toward Rocky Mountain House. Along the way, they passed several oil pumping stations. Some still at work, others sitting motionless.

Hirsch popped two beers and handed one to Pittman. "That church thing your wife got tied up in … did you go to church?"

"Why do you want to know?"

"Just making conversation. I went to church as a kid, but as soon as I was too strong for Mom to make me go, I hung out with my buddies instead."

Pittman drank some beer and nodded. "I was the same as a kid. But Marlene thought it was a good way to meet neighbors and make friends. I maybe lasted six months and then I stayed home, drank beer, and watched sports. That pissed her off. Religion did nothing for me. Some hypocrite was quoting Bible scriptures telling me I was a sinner. Screw that. I heard the same bullshit so many times I can still recite it. 'Yea though I walk through the valley of the shadow of death, I will fear no evil—'"

"Yeah. I know that one, too."

Pittman grinned. "Not my version. 'I will fear no evil, cuz I'm the meanest son of a bitch in the valley.'"

"I like that version." Hirsch tilted his bottle to Pittman, and they clinked bottlenecks.

"Amen to that."

Hirsch rubbed his chin as he stared out the window. "I like that. I'm tired of being at the bottom. I'm fed up with people looking down at me or thinking I'm stupid."

Pittman glanced over to Hirsch and smirked. "Not anymore, Hirsch. We're the meanest sons of bitches in the valley and any other place we want to be."

Just outside Rocky Mountain House, they passed several abandoned pumping stations. Then Pittman spotted one of their former company's pumping stations with a worker on site. Pittman slowed and stopped a few hundred yards past the pump.

"No better time than today," Pittman said. "You ready."

"I'm not sure," Hirsch said. "He's a grunt, just like us."

"Sure, but a grunt still employed. We're gonna have to make some tough decisions. If we want to make our point, we can't get emotional. This is about sending a message. This is war. There'll be collateral damage."

Hirsch nodded. "Okay. Back up to about a hundred yards." He stepped out of the truck, jammed his beer bottle under the seat, and slid the rifle out of the case. He chambered a round, leaned against the side of the truck, and focused the scope on the worker.

The worker's feet lifted off the ground, then he fell backward, unmoving. The air echoed with the sound of the shot a moment after.

Hirsch stared at the unmoving man, then at the rifle. He tossed the gun aside like it was on fire. He rubbed his hands on his jeans and fought back a dry heave. His hand covered his mouth and his jaw clenched. *What have I done?*

CHAPTER FOUR

Friday Day Three

Brad glared at Dr. Keller as he entered the room, then he flopped into the recliner. Keller was flipping through a file folder, so Brad's glare was wasted. He pursed his lips and glanced around the room. The artwork still sucked—the shrink was still a pompous ass. Brad felt he was in the right frame of mind to get through the next hour.

"Glad to have you back," Keller said.

Brad's eyes drifted from the kindergarten art to the shrink. "Like I had a choice. You ratted me out to Deputy Chief Archer."

"When you stormed out after our last session, I needed to let him know we weren't progressing."

"All the stuff about 'you can talk to me, it's all confidential' is bullshit."

Keller held out his hands. "Oh, no. I didn't give details, merely said we would need extra time."

"It seems to me he knew more than just that you wanted additional time."

"I may have mentioned you were somewhat volatile."

"Volatile? Because I called you out on your bullshit? I don't need your textbook theories."

"What happened to your hands?"

Brad tucked his hands into his lap. "Clearing dead bushes on the farm."

"No gloves?"

"Nope. I forgot." Brad's glare was back. "Too lazy to get them."

"So, you endured the pain." Keller rubbed his chin with his index finger. "I see. Any other pains you are dealing with?"

"How can you relate when you have no experience with death?" The heat rose on Brad's neck, and his shoulders tensed.

"I've had friends and relatives die."

Brad bent forward, his fists tight at his side. "Big difference between people dying and getting murdered in front of you. When you're helpless to stop it from happening. When you fail the woman you love and your unborn child. Absolutely helpless."

Hans reclined in his chair and steepled his fingers. "Tell me about this helplessness."

Brad slid back into the recliner. His mind drifted to Bowness Park and strolling along the lagoon with Maggie and Lobo. Watching Lobo fetch rocks in the river, then sleep and dry off in the sun. His happy place.

His voice slid into a monotone story he'd told Keller dozens of times. So many times, he could recite it without being mentally present.

Brad had no clue how much time passed. He was sitting next to Maggie, then suddenly he was staring at Keller.

"Brad, are you okay? You zoned out for a minute."

"Sorry."

"That's okay." Keller closed the file folder. "It was a good session. We made some progress today."

Brad's eyes darted around the room. "It's over?"

"Yes. Time flies when you're having fun." Keller stood. "I'm away for about ten days. We leave for Hawaii tomorrow. You have the numbers to call if you have an emergency. If not, I'll see you when I get back. Make an appointment with my receptionist."

Brad nodded and headed out the door. He heard it close. He stopped at the reception desk to make another appointment, but the receptionist wasn't there. He waited a couple of minutes, then decided to leave. A stack of letterheads on the desk caught his attention. He glanced around the room, then grabbed a handful of the letterheads and a few envelopes and headed out the door.

CHAPTER FIVE

PITTMAN BRAKED, VEERED OFF HIGHWAY 2, AND CRUISED THROUGH the City of Airdrie. Only ten minutes north of Calgary, but the RCMP did the policing here. That was important. During the drive, they'd discussed a plan for the second shooting. The problem was that if Hirsch had to get out of the truck every time he shot, there were sure to be witnesses. And those few seconds needed for Hirsch to get back in the truck might be too long. People would turn toward the sound of the shot. If the timing was wrong, they'd see Hirsch. To do the shooting and make a clean getaway, they needed a better system.

They drove through an industrial area until Pittman found what he was seeking—a dealership with a used car lot. He pulled in, and they wandered among the vehicles. In the back corner, they found what they needed: a nondescript sedan.

A salesman—dark dress pants, a white shirt, a loose tie, and a toothy grin—wandered over. "Can I help you, boys? It seems like you've something special in mind."

"You the only one here?" Pittman asked.

"Yeah. I'm here until nine. Can I help you?"

Pittman pointed to the car. "This one."

The salesman put his hand on the hood. "Oh, you'll like this one. We don't get many like it. Ford LTD. Only four-years old. Low mileage."

"I'm interested," Pittman said. "Would you get the keys?"

"No problem. I'll be right back."

Pittman glanced at Hirsch and jerked his head toward the building.

"Hey," Hirsch said. "We've been on the road for hours. Mind if I use your restroom?"

"Sure. Follow me."

Less than five minutes later, Hirsch and the salesman were back. As the salesman handed Pittman the car keys, Hirsch mouthed, *We're good.*

Pittman unlocked the car and popped the hood. He spent a few minutes examining the engine and then the tires. He slid into the driver's seat and started the car. He revved it a few times, shut it off, and stood. "How much?"

"I'm looking to make a deal today. Let's say three grand."

Pittman laughed. "That's hardly a deal. This vehicle saw some hard miles, even if the mileage is low. Who knows what the undercarriage is like?"

The salesman held up his hands. "Hey, I gotta start somewhere. What price range are you thinking?"

"I'll trade in my GMC truck," Pittman said. "I used it in the oil business, so it's seen some rough driving, but I took care of it. I didn't want to get stranded miles away in the backcountry. Take the truck and five hundred."

"No, that's a little too low. I can call my manager, but he'll never accept it. I can convince him to go with the truck and seven-fifty."

Pittman glanced at Hirsch, who shrugged.

Pittman held out his hand. "You've got a deal."

As the salesman reached for his hand, Pittman raised a pistol in the other hand and shot the salesman in the chest.

Hirsch jumped at the sound and staggered backward. "What the hell?" His words came in gasps and he stared blankly at the salesman.

Pittman slid the gun back into his coat pocket. "Back my truck in here, clean it out and put the truck plates on the car. No one will notice the switch for weeks."

Pittman lifted the salesman over his shoulder and headed to the office. He dropped the salesman behind the desk and opened the cash drawers. He tossed the credit card slips on the floor. In another drawer, he found a few thousand in cash. He searched the salesman and pulled out a set of keys with the dealership logo. On his way out, he flipped up the 'We're Closed' sign and locked the dealership door .

Pittman slid into the driver's seat and started the car. Hirsch threw their gear in the back seat and jumped in. At the hardware store across from the dealership, they picked up everything they needed, headed north out of Airdrie and back onto the highway. Pittman hit the gas and the front of the car rose slightly as the speedometer climbed.

Pittman pulled off the highway and headed east and then north on a narrow gravel road. After a few minutes, they spotted a barn surrounded by large pines on an abandoned farm. The grass was brown and overgrown with no signs anyone had driven there in the last year.

Hirsch jumped out and opened the barn's ancient doors. Pittman pulled in, then Hirsch closed the doors.

Pittman opened the trunk and pulled out a toolbox and a few two-by-fours. He opened the toolbox, selected a hammer, saw, and nails, and went to work.

Hirsch removed the back seat and adapted it so when he was shooting, part of it could be removed, thus allowing his legs to extend fully into the passenger compartment. After the shooting, they'd replace that section, cover the seat with blankets, and no one would be the wiser.

Hirsch struggled to get the seat out. Once he'd manhandled it out the door, he used a box cutter to slice through the cloth and foam, and then a hacksaw to cut through the frame. He reinstalled the larger portion of the seat on the passenger side and bolted it to the floor. He unrolled thick foam and laid it in the trunk, with one end extending to the back seat. Next, he set a sleeping bag on top. He climbed into the trunk and lay down.

Still too low. He pulled the sleeping bag out and placed another layer of foam on the first, then the sleeping bag. He climbed back into the trunk. Perfect height and comfortable. He had a flawless view through the scope with the trunk slightly open. Then he went to work, creating the hole for the rifle barrel just below the trunk lid.

Pittman set a wooden stand in front of Hirsch and handed him the sniper rifle. The short tripod sat level on the wooden stand and lined up perfectly.

When Pittman lowered the trunk lid, claustrophobia bore down on Hirsch. No way he'd ever tell Pittman, though.

Hirsch added the last piece, a green sock that matched the

car's paint. From the trunk, he stuffed the sock in the hole for the rifle barrel.

They stood outside the car, admiring their work. Unless you knew what you were seeking, and in precisely the right spot, the hole was invisible.

"A test?" Hirsch asked.

Pittman slowed as he drove past the pasture. A herd of cows grazed on the dry fall grass. He pulled off the road with the back of the car facing the cows. Hirsch climbed into the back seat and got set. Pittman watched the cows through his side mirror.

"What's happening?" Hirsch shouted.

"Not much," Pittman mumbled.

"What?"

"I said, not much."

"You gotta talk loud. It's like I'm in a metal barrel. Damned uncomfortable, too."

"Sure, after this, we'll get you a comfy lounge chair."

"You try this. No reason we can't put extra foam padding in here. Maybe some air holes, too."

"I'll get right on that."

"Don't be an ass."

The car rocked as Hirsch changed his position. "I'm staring at about fifty cows. Any cow in particular?"

"Take the one farthest away. Must be about three-hundred yards."

"I've got him."

Pittman saw the cow drop—then the car echoed with the sound of the shot. *Shit, that was loud.*

CHAPTER SIX

FRIDAY AFTERNOON BRAD SAT ACROSS FROM DEPUTY CHIEF ARCHER as he read and re-read the letter on his desk. Brad's mouth went dry. He waited. Archer had a fashionable office. Not the fake paneling common in lots of offices, but actual wood. The bookshelf appeared to be oak, and the desk was undoubtedly cherry wood. Of course, Brad made that up. He didn't know pine from pasteboard. Still, it was better than the detective bullpen with Second World War surplus desks. Above Archer's desk was a picture of the city at night. Maybe Archer could give Keller some art tips.

Archer slid the letter to the side of his desk and sighed. "This was a surprise." His gray eyes squinted and his jaw set. "Last week, Dr. Keller didn't think you were making progress, then this week, he says you're ready to return to work."

Brad held his arms wide. "This was a breakthrough for me. Dr. Keller said he'd seen nothing like it. It was like everything blocking me collapsed at the same time."

Archer nodded and tapped his finger on the letter. "Full return to duty."

"That's what he said."

Archer cocked his head. "No restrictions?"

"None." Brad maintained eye contact.

Archer pursed his lips and stared off to the far side of his office. "I'm thrilled you're doing well. If this was a breakthrough, I'm happy for you. But I wonder if returning to full duty is the best solution."

"Chief." Brad held his hands in front of him like he was saying a prayer. "I can't stay home anymore. I'm going crazy. I can only work out so often. I can only run so many miles. Lobo can only fetch so many rocks. I need to get back to work. I'm ready. Put me to work."

Archer scrutinized Brad. Seconds passed. "Aside from your mental health, how are you physically?"

"Never been in better shape. I jog every day. Work out for a few hours."

"You appear gaunt. Are you eating well?" Archer stared at Brad, then shook his head and sighed.

"Very well." Archer picked up his pen and signed the letter. "There's an opening in Homicide. You'll be back with Don Griffin. Nothing is happening, so you can ease back into things. Start Monday."

"I'm ready to start today," Brad said.

Archer sighed. "Tomorrow, then. Find out when Griffin is working." He rose, took one last glance at the letter, then extended his hand. "Brad, I'm so sorry for your loss, both Maggie and the baby. You're right. It's time for you to get back to work."

Brad took his hand. "Thank you, sir. You won't regret this."

CHAPTER SEVEN

BRAD STEPPED INTO THE DETECTIVE BULLPEN. *THIS PLACE WILL NEVER change.* A haze of smoke hung near the ceiling. Years of detectives' chain-smoking had stained the white ceiling tiles a yellowish brown. While not as strong as a locker room, the distinct smell of male sweat and cologne fought the tobacco for the dominant odor.

He headed toward the Homicide office at the back of the room. With a sharp knock on the door, Brad entered. Several heads popped up, like gophers in a spring field. Then just as quickly the heads dropped, interest gone. Brad wandered through the maze of desks until he found Don Griffin seated in a chair, leaning back, feet on the desk, eyes closed. Brad pulled out the chair opposite Griffin and sat, staring at him. There was no movement or acknowledgment that Brad was there.

Brad waited a few minutes, then leaned forward, arms extended to knock Griffin's feet off the desk.

"I wouldn't," Griffin growled. "You could be my first Homicide call of the day." He stretched, slid his feet to the floor, and glared at Brad. "You know the rules: eat when you can, pee when you can, sleep when you can. You never know when you'll be able to do any of the three."

"Seems to me you've got nothing but time to do all three. If I'd known it was a sleepover, I'd have brought my jammies and security blanket."

"Why am I not surprised you have a security blanket to curl up with at night?" Griffin grabbed his head in his hands. "I'm a dumbass. I'm sorry."

"Don't sweat it. You didn't mean anything by it, and I have to get used to it. I can't take everything personally."

"Yeah, well, sometimes I don't think before I put my mouth in motion."

"You were explaining the three rules of being on the street. I'm not sure you can teach me anything about that. Try lying face down on the ground as a sniper, beside a dumpster, when an icy February wind is trying to blow you into Montana. Trying to keep your fingers warm in case you need to take a shot and realizing if you peed your pants, you'd feel warmer. A least for a few seconds."

"Thanks for the visual."

"What are you working on?"

"I've got two cases that are going nowhere, but we'll talk about them tomorrow. There are a few changes that will interest you."

"Like our new mayor?"

Griffin nodded. "Shocked us all, that's for sure. Roger Kearse, reporter, TV celebrity—at least in his mind—is our mayor. No one saw that coming."

Brad grinned. "Yeah. That's a rags-to-riches story. Reporter drinking with cops in the St. Louis Hotel bar to running the city. Did everyone go crazy while I was away?"

"He still drinks with the cops in the St. Louis. The difference nowadays is he can order us to take him home."

"I fell asleep election night before they announced the winner. When I read the paper the next day, I thought I'd been transported to an alternate universe."

"Lots of people felt that way."

"Might be good for us," Brad said. "Kearse likes us, and he was always fair in his reporting."

"I heard you didn't get along with him."

"We had our moments. Kearse was always digging for inside information."

"That was his job as a reporter."

"True."

"He might need a driver full-time. Since you like to hang out in the St. Louis bar, and you two got along so well, he'll probably ask for you."

"Not on your life."

Griffin glanced at his watch. "Time for you to head upstairs."

"What for?"

"Before you can come back to the street, you need to pass your firearms qualifications."

"Are you kidding me? I'm qualified to teach those courses."

Griffin grinned. "Policy, my friend, policy. Enjoy shooting. I'll see you tommorow."

After qualifying on the range on five different guns, Brad and Lobo headed north on Fourth Street. The back window was open, and Lobo had his head out gulping the air, his jowls flopping, a lopsided grin on his face. Brad swung left and followed the laneway for about a quarter mile, then parked at the curb.

Lobo raced ahead of Brad, sniffing for the track of a squirrel. Brad maintained a slower pace, weaving around the tombstones. The visits were not getting easier. He had hoped to find peace after enough time had passed. He'd been wrong. He dropped to his knees and stared at the tombstone. He'd still been in the hospital when they held Maggie's funeral. He'd needed a second surgery to readjust the titanium plate in his shattered leg.

Lobo chased a squirrel, loped over, and lay down, his head in Brad's lap. Brad stared ahead, reliving the years with Maggie. Starting with the first time they'd met, on a dark highway outside Calgary the night his former partner, Curtis Young, was killed. He remembered little of that night. Only that Maggie had been there. The next time they met, Brad ended up in the back of the ambulance assisting Maggie with a drug dealer who'd been shot in the leg and was bleeding everywhere. Maggie was a rookie paramedic. Brad, a cocky cop. A fleeting smile quirked his lips. Lobo snored.

"Hey, Mags. I'm going back to work. I'm working with Griffin, and I'm excited about that. Homicide. I know you think it's about time. Me too. Kept hitting a wall convincing Dr. Bonkers—well, Dr. Keller, that I was ready. Some of us at the station call him Dr. Bonkers behind his back. He's such an ass. I ... did something I probably shouldn't have, but if I get in trouble ... I don't know, I'll make them understand. I need this. I'm going crazy at home."

He glanced at Lobo. "There's only so much Lobo and I can do. I'm in great shape. You'd love the six-pack abs." He swallowed hard. "I miss you. Sometimes I don't think I can go on without you. Then I remember you'd kick my ass for saying that and somehow I keep going." He sighed, pushed Lobo off his lap, and lay with his head on Lobo's side.

CHAPTER EIGHT

Saturday Day Four

Brad had two homocide files laid out on the metal desk. Even though he was in a building with detectives, he hated having his back to the room, but Griffin was senior and had claimed the better location. With the continual murmur of voices on the telephone or yelling across the room at each other, it was hard to concentrate.

The first was a drug deal. The dealer had used most of the product and couldn't pay. This wasn't the first time this had happened. Fed up with the dealer, an enforcer was hired, and they'd found the dealer with two bullets in his head. The enforcer bragged in a bar and was overheard by undercover drug cops. After the enforcer pled not guilty, they released him on his own recognizance and he promptly skipped town. There was a Canada-wide warrant for his arrest. It was a waiting game.

The second case was interesting. This one involved a drug dealer as well. He was selling in Victoria Park. The drug cops knew him but left him alone. They were after the shitheads further up the chain. And, occasionally, he was good for a tip or two.

The report said the dealer was stabbed and was dead on scene, although the paramedics tried to resuscitate and rushed him to the hospital where he was officially pronounced dead. Brad pulled out the envelope with the autopsy photos. Interesting. There were a half-dozen minor lacerations and then the one that killed him. The knife plunged from under his ribcage and up into his heart. Why the lacerations? Brad sat back and pondered that. He'd seen similar cuts before. In some suicide attempts by slashing wrists, the victim hesitates, leaving slight lacerations—commonly referred to as hesitation cuts. There were a few things of interest. First, the attacker controlled the victim during the hesitation stabs. Second, the attacker found the courage to follow through.

Brad set the files aside and yawned. *Not good.*

Griffin cuffed Brad on the head as he slipped by to his desk. "You got those files memorized?"

"Not a lot to remember."

"Too true."

"Seems like it's been slow," Brad said.

"What the heck did you say?"

Brad leaned back and held up his hands. "Sorry, I wasn't thinking."

"We never say that. That's a sure way to end a partnership." Griffin stood and straightened his suit coat. "I'll let you make it up to me. Buy me dinner."

Brad wheeled the unmarked sedan out of the police garage, onto Sixth Avenue, and headed into the setting sun. He merged with the last surge of downtown workers. They rolled down their windows and enjoyed the crisp fall air.

"Where to?" Brad asked.

"Pizza."

"Do you have a favorite place?"

Griffin stared out the window, watching pedestrians. "Yeah, one where the cooks don't spit in my food."

"That narrows it down." Brad turned right onto Seventeenth Avenue.

"Back in your former zone," Griffin said.

"Old habits." He crossed Fourteenth Street and stopped at Puccini's Pizza.

"You sure they won't spit on my pizza?"

Brad got out of the car and headed to the door. "Sure about mine. Yours, not so much." Brad stepped into the restaurant and was immediately hugged by a tall, distinguished man.

"Mr. Brad. So long since I've seen you. How are you?" He glanced over his shoulder. "This is not the beautiful Maggie. How is she?"

Griffin stepped forward and offered his hand. "I'm Don Griffin. Brad's partner."

"And I am Paul Puccini, owner," he said as he accepted Griffin's hand.

"Brad. Grab us a booth," Griffin said as he pulled Puccini aside.

Brad's stomach cramped and his jaw clenched. He'd been so focused on getting back to work, he hadn't thought of the awkward moments he'd experience, like this one. He better get used to it. He wouldn't always have Griffin or someone else to provide interference.

Brad was seated in a booth. He had no recollection of how he got here. His last conscious thought was standing at the door with Puccini. Brad reached for a glass and as he lifted it, his shaking hand slopped water on the table.

Griffin slid into the booth. Puccini set two menus on the table. Brad noticed the redness in his eyes. Puccini had a soft spot for Maggie.

Brad glanced briefly at the menu—it hadn't changed.

"What's good?" Griffin asked.

"Everything. I love the pizza, but the spaghetti and lasagna are to die for."

Griffin flipped through the menu on the table. "Pizza it is."

"Pizza it is."

Griffin leaned back in the passenger seat, his hands holding his stomach. "Okay, you were right. I won't say that again, but that was a damn good pizza. And filling. I'm gonna burst."

Brad struggled with the right words. They didn't come, so he blurted out what he was thinking. "Thanks for backing me with Puccini."

"Sure." Griffin ran his tongue over his teeth and stared out the window. "That's what partners do."

"I mean it. I hadn't given a thought to the fact some people wouldn't know."

"Dispatch, any unit in 2 District. Assault in progress, 519, Twenty-Third Avenue SW. Second floor. Neighbors say there was shouting and screaming and then what sounded like glass breaking."

Brad glanced at Griffin. "Two blocks away."

Griffin shook his head. "Quiet, my ass." He grabbed the mic. "Dispatch, Coulter and Griffin responding."

"Ah, sure. Backup is on the way. District sergeant is responding."

Brad grinned. "We don't need no stinking backup."

Griffin shook his head.

Brad double-parked on the crowded street and raced out of the car. Griffin rushed to catch up. Brad took the front steps two at a time and burst through the front door, then up the steps to the second level. As they ascended the stairs, the shouts and crashing got louder. Once on the second floor, it was apparent where the assault was happening. Without breaking stride, Brad shouldered the door—it popped open. As he entered the room, he drew his pistol. "Police. Hands where I can see them."

The apartment was tiny, one bedroom with a bathroom off to the left side. A skinny man in a dirty tank top stood over the bed, a handful of blond hair in his left hand, his right hand poised for a punch.

"Let her go, or I spray your brains across the room," Brad said.

"Doubt it," the skinny guy said as he punched the woman, snapping her jaw to the side.

He was drawing his arm back for another punch when Brad slammed into him, driving him into the wall. As they fell, Brad grabbed the suspect's hair. They hit the ground and Brad's first punch shattered his nose. The second opened a cut over the suspect's right eye. The third sent spit flying as Brad's fist connected with his jaw.

Brad drew back for a fourth punch. As he swung forward, an arm hooked his elbow. It felt like his shoulder was dislocating. Hands roughly grabbed him, dragged him away from the suspect, and shoved him against the wall by the door.

The rage overwhelmed him and he struggled to his feet, eyes set on the suspect. It wasn't over.

"It's over," a voice said.

"Screw that," Brad said. "Let me go."

Hands grabbed his shirt and shoved him hard into the wall.

Brad reached down, grabbed the hands, and stared into the blazing eyes of Sergeant Jerry Briscoe.

"Coulter," Briscoe said. "It's over."

Brad struggled against the hands, but Briscoe held tight. He might be short, but he was upper body strong. He shoved Brad into the wall again. "Enough."

Brad's head hit the wall with a *thunk*. Air escaped his lungs and his body went limp.

Briscoe. How many times had he saved Brad's ass? Too many to count.

Brad relaxed, then Briscoe released his grip. "What was that?"

Brad shrugged. Good question. What *was* that? "I kinda lost it."

"You think?"

"All I saw was the guy holding blond hair and punching her. I snapped."

"Blond hair, huh?" Briscoe let go of Brad's shirt. "I didn't know you were coming back to work. I called a few times, like a hundred. You sure you're ready?"

"Damn right."

"I'm not so sure." Briscoe leaned close and jabbed his finger into Brad's chest. "Your friends will cover for you, once. You've used up that card."

Brad nodded and stepped back. "I'm fine."

Paramedics rushed into the room and over to the bed. Brad recognized one paramedic, Amir Sharma. He'd been Maggie's partner for a long time.

Sharma nodded as he passed Brad, followed by a paramedic Brad didn't recognize. Though she couldn't be taller than five-foot-five, she entered the room with the confidence of experience. Her eyes scrutinized the scene, then stopped on Brad and Griffin.

She nodded toward them. "Who are you two?"

"Detectives." Griffin held out his badge. "Griffin and Coulter."

Her head snapped toward Brad when Griffin said *Coulter*. She stared for a few seconds, then focused on her patient, her dark ponytail swinging.

She knelt next to her patient. "I'm Jill. I'm going to take care of you with my partner, Amir."

Brad heard Jill's calm, caring voice with compassion for her patient. He headed out of the room and down the stairs into the refreshing fall air.

He leaned against a tree and closed his eyes. Maybe it was too soon. He'd gone from giddiness at being back at work to psychotic in a microsecond. There'd been no hesitation.

The paramedics and cops lifted the stretcher out the doorway and rolled it toward the ambulance. Behind them, two other cops escorted the suspect toward their cruiser. The suspect slowed as he neared the stretcher. "I'll finish this later, bitch." Then he kicked at the stretcher.

Brad lunged for the suspect, but a uniformed cop punched

the suspect in the gut and he collapsed to the ground, gasping for breath.

Briscoe stepped in front of Brad, hand on his chest. Brad backed away, hands held out, scowling at the suspect lying on the sidewalk.

Griffin grabbed Brad by the arm and shoved him to their car. "We'll call it a night. Take tomorrow off. We work dayshift Monday. Tomorrow, get your shit together, or this will be the shortest partnership in police history."

CHAPTER NINE

Sunday Day Five

AFTER A LONG WORKOUT IN THE BARN, BRAD HEADED FOR HIS house. Lobo padded alongside. They rounded the corner and saw a Honda Civic parked behind Brad's Firebird.

"Looks like we have company."

Lobo bounced with his front paws in the air.

"Okay, go," Brad said.

Lobo raced to the house. Brad caught up and opened the back door. Odors of cooking flowed over him. Roast beef? Apple pie?

Lobo pushed past. When Brad entered the kitchen, Lobo was excitedly licking Annie's face.

"Nice to see you," Brad said.

Annie glanced up. "I'm sorry your phone and answering machine don't work."

"What? They work just ... ah shit."

Annie stood, hands on her hips. "Ah ha, they do work. You're ignoring me. I called five times, but you didn't answer."

"I've been ignoring everyone." Brad smiled sheepishly. "I've been busy."

Two years ago, when Annie was sixteen, she was kidnapped by the vicious biker, Jeter Wolfe, who assaulted her. After a couple of months in captivity, Annie escaped.

Brad and Maggie had unofficially adopted her, with Brad as the big brother figure in her life. To say Brad was protective was an understatement.

Earlier this year when Wolfe escaped from prison, he swore revenge on everyone involved in his arrest and incarceration, including Annie, Maggie, Brad, Tina Davidson and the crown prosecutor, Jenni Blighe.

Wolfe broke into Brad's house and held Maggie and Annie hostage. When Brad came home, Wolfe was waiting. He was about to kill Brad when Lobo raced into the room, propelling Wolfe to the ground. In the subsequent gun battle, Brad killed Wolfe, but Maggie, Brad and Lobo were shot. Brad and Lobo recovered. Maggie didn't.

Now almost nineteen, Annie cared for Brad. But that was difficult when he rejected help and over a month ago, in frustration with Dr. Keller's refusal to let him go back to work, he'd shut out Annie and his friends.

"You're lucky Lobo was with me. There's no way he'd have let you break and enter."

"Oh, that's nonsense. Lobo has always loved me more than you. Besides, I didn't have to break in. I have a key."

He nudged her with his elbow. "Who's going to rob this decrepit house? If they tried, they'd have to deal with Lobo. Anyway, key or no key, it is still breaking and entering."

Annie laughed and headed to the stove. "I'd like to see that charge stick."

Brad glanced at the pots. "You've got a lot of food going. Are you expecting an army?"

"Maybe."

"That's a lot of food."

"There'll be leftovers. At least I'll know you have food in the fridge. Maybe you'll even eat some of it."

Lobo raced to the back door, barking. The barks became low growls, then silence.

"What the heck." Brad headed to the door, then halted. He scrubbed a hand down his face and chuckled. *Ambushed.* He should have known they wouldn't let him be a hermit forever.

Jerry Briscoe, short and built like a tank, pushed past Brad. "Thanks for inviting us, rookie."

Sam Steele and Charlie Zerr were kneeling and roughing up Lobo.

Brad shook his head, smirking. "I need a better guard dog. What are you doing here? What's going on?"

"We were invited for dinner," Sam said.

"What? By whom?"

"By Annie."

"Really?"

Sam stepped forward, jabbing his finger in Brad's chest. "Three reasons. One, Annie invited us. Two, we are hungry. Three, you've shut us out."

"I'm ... not shutting you out. Come in."

Charlie slipped past, heading into the kitchen. "Something smells good." He stood behind Annie as she stirred the gravy.

Sam stepped around Brad, Lobo at his heels. Brad followed them into the kitchen. "Annie."

"Yes, Brad." She kept her back to Brad as she continued stirring.

"Did you invite them over?"

"Yes." She rotated slightly and pointed the spoon at him. "It's an intervention."

Brad lifted an eyebrow. "I'm not an addict."

Sam put his arm around Brad's shoulder. "We all felt the pain of Maggie's murder—you most of all. We get that."

"I'm busy, that's all."

"Uh, sure," Sam said. "We know you're hurting, always will be. But you don't have to work through this alone."

Brad scowled at Sam. "I see a shrink. He said I could come back to work."

"That's good. I hope *Dr. Bonkers* is helping you." Sam paused and glanced at Annie and Charlie, then to the doorway to the living room where Briscoe stood. "Maybe you don't need us, buddy, but we need you."

"Not me." Briscoe popped the top on a beer. "They made me come."

"Jeez, Briscoe," Charlie said. "You're not helping."

Briscoe smirked at Brad and winked. "If the rookie wants to pout, fine. I'm here cuz Annie is a great cook." He patted his stomach. "Takes a lot of calories to keep this physique."

Sam rolled his eyes. "Thanks for being a caring human being."

Briscoe shrugged and set a case of beer on the counter—minus one bottle. Sam opened beers and handed them out. "Brothers in blue." They tapped bottles.

"What about me?" Annie asked.

"Future criminologist is close enough," Sam said.

"Is that a thing?" Briscoe asked.

"It is nowadays," Annie said. "Charlie. Help me finish dinner. The rest of you, out of the kitchen."

Brad flopped into his recliner, and Lobo lay at his feet. Briscoe and Sam grabbed the couch.

Brad glanced at Sam. "Was this your idea?"

Sam took a drink. "Sure, I'll take credit."

"How's Emma?" Brad asked.

"She's doing good," Sam said. "She thinks she's huge and doesn't want anyone to see her like that."

"She could have come tonight," Brad said.

"Nah. Her mom is with us this week, so she stayed home."

"Basically, you're saying you escaped for the night," Briscoe said.

Sam tapped his nose in acknowledgement.

"When is she due?" Briscoe asked.

"Two more months—mid-December."

Briscoe chugged his beer. "Then you can take some time off. You can be a lazy bum like Brad."

Brad shook his head. "Nope. I'm back at work."

"Are you serious?" Sam asked. "When did this happen?"

"Cleared on Thursday, started Friday with Griffin in Homicide. I aced the firearms qualifications."

"Well damn," Briscoe said. "If all you have to do is shoot, you'll be fine."

"Annie didn't say anything about this," Sam said.

"She doesn't know." Brad took a long drink.

"Should have been school resource officer," Briscoe said.

"Oh, hell, Briscoe," Sam said. "Can't you ever shut up? Just drink your beer."

"What? We pretend nothing happened last night?" Briscoe

leaned forward. "Your little episode where you punched the hell out of the suspect."

"He had it coming," Brad said.

"What are you talking about?" Sam asked.

Briscoe told the story of the assault and Brad's response.

Brad spun to see Annie and Charlie standing behind him. "A blond teen?" Annie asked.

Briscoe nodded.

She glared at Brad. "Did you think it was me?"

His hand dropped to Lobo's head, and he rubbed Lobo's ears.

Annie knelt beside his chair. "Brad, what happened?"

He absently peeled the label on the bottle. Finally, he glanced up. "Last night … last night, I saw you. Pent-up anger, frustration for failing Tina and Maggie. The suspect wasn't Wolfe, but it didn't matter."

"Are you sure you're ready to go back to work?" Annie asked.

Brad felt Briscoe staring, but couldn't meet his eyes. "It was one time. I'm good." He glanced at the kitchen. "I'm starving."

Again, the room was silent. Then Annie stood. "Charlie, help me finish dinner."

"Since when is Charlie a chef?" Brad asked.

Sam smiled, then took a drink. "You are really out of touch."

"What does that mean?"

Briscoe grunted.

Brad glanced from Sam to Briscoe and back. Then he peered toward the kitchen and his eyes lit up. "No way."

Sam stood. "I'll get us another beer and check on the kids."

Brad's eyes followed Sam to the kitchen.

Briscoe smirked. "Life happens when you've got your head

up your ass. You missed a budding romance right under your nose. Not like you. Not like you at all."

"No kidding." Brad drained his beer.

Annie peeked around the door. "Dinner is ready."

Brad headed to the kitchen, grabbing a beer from Sam on the way.

"I can carve the roast," Brad said.

"Charlie already did," Annie said.

"Uh, okay then." Brad pulled out a chair.

Charlie slid half a cow onto his plate and passed it to Brad. "What's with the old truck by the barn?"

"It came with the place," Brad said. "I'm trying to see if I can get it running."

"By yourself?" Charlie asked.

Brad poured gravy over his potatoes and roast. "Yeah, I'm doing it. Do you have a problem with that?"

Charlie laughed. "Only that you're the least mechanical person I know."

Brad pointed at fork at Charlie. "You'll eat crow when I get it running."

"Never happen," Charlie said.

"I'm with Charlie." Sam turned to Briscoe. "Hey, I didn't know sergeants got rookies."

Briscoe snorted. "Caterina Toscana. She's getting her opportunity to be an acting district sergeant. She'll work as 501 district sergeant downtown. Lucky me, I get to train her for a few weeks."

"You better hope she turns out better than some of your other rookies," Sam said.

"No kidding." Briscoe glanced at Brad, then gulped his beer.

"She's gung ho. You know, in-your-face intense. She wants to know everything and right f'n today."

"Isn't she the first female cop to get this opportunity?" Sam asked.

"Might be," Briscoe said. "Guess she wants to make a statement for all lady cops. On the good side, she's athletic, so I won't have to chase the bad guys. I can just send her and heaven help them when she catches them."

"Didn't she try out for our team?" Charlie asked. "She's built."

"Charlie," Annie said.

He raised his hands in defense. "Well, she is. She played rugby for the national team."

"Oh yeah," Sam said. "Now I know who you're talking about."

"If I remember right," Charlie said, "she bench pressed a heavier weight than Sam."

"Like that's hard to do," Brad said.

"Hey, I'm a shooter, not a bruiser."

"I gather she didn't make it," Annie said.

"No," Sam said. "But she did well."

"But not good enough to break into the boy's club." Annie glared at Sam and Charlie.

"Good luck with her." Brad glanced around the table. "Or should I be wishing her luck having you as a mentor?"

Briscoe flipped Brad the finger.

CHAPTER TEN

Monday Day Six

PITTMAN SLOWED IN THE MORNING RUSH-HOUR TRAFFIC. HE KNEW who he wanted shot. He didn't know where. There were several options. As the traffic crept toward downtown, he spotted the target.

"There."

"Another dealership?" Hirsch asked. "Car salesman aren't our mission."

"Not any dealership. Wasn't it a Ford dealership that took your truck?"

"Actually, the bank."

Pittman pulled the car into the parking lot of an office building. "Close enough."

"It's just a guy mowing grass."

"At a Ford dealership. It's not about who dies, it's the symbolism."

Hirsch glared at Pittman. "What the hell does that mean?"

Pittman shrugged. "Anyone who fucked with us is a target."

Hirsch stared at the bumper-to-bumper traffic. "I don't know. In rush hour?"

Pittman swung toward Hirsch. "Enough with your fucking excuses and whining. You said you were in—all in."

Hirsch bit his bottom lip and stared at the guy mowing the lawn. "Yeah. Let's do it."

Pittman turned away and smirked. His heart raced and his body shook with excitement. *Putty in my hands.*

Paramedics Willie Dixon and Pete Thompson were cruising downtown a little after 7:15 a.m., waiting for their first response of the day. Both veteran paramedics, they loved their work and believed being on the street increased their chances of stealing a response from another crew. Dixon, tall and slim with a dark drooping mustache, had a dry sense of humor and was a little burned out. Thompson, shorter than Dixon with white-blond hair and a constant smile, exuded enthusiasm. That was probably why paramedic students loved training with him.

"It's time we took another student," Thompson said.

Dixon grunted. "Too much work."

"Hell, train them right, and they carry the kits, do the messy stuff, and clean the ambulance. What's better than that?"

Dixon glared at this partner. "You left out the part where they're book smart and street stupid, and it's like three months of babysitting."

"We've had some outstanding students."

"Sure, by the end of the three months, they finally get it, then they're done."

"Maggie was an exceptional student."

They were quiet for a minute.

Thompson stared out the window.

"Became one of the best," Dixon said. "She was a royal pain when we first got her."

Thompson's voice caught in his throat. "I still can't believe she's gone."

"Have you talked to Brad lately?"

Thompson shook his head. "No. I heard he's still on leave."

"Do you think he'll come back to work?"

"If I was him, I wouldn't."

"This would be a perfect time for him to use his law degree," Dixon said.

Thompson shrugged. "He has that option, but I don't see him behind a desk or in court."

"I don't know," Dixon said. "I think he'd be an excellent prosecutor."

The radio came to life. "Medic 2, man down. Ford dealership, Ninth Avenue West. Unknown cause. We got a few calls. Some said heart attack and others say he's bleeding. Police on the way."

Thompson grabbed the mic. "Roger."

Dixon swung the ambulance in a U-turn and activated the lights and siren.

As they pulled up, several people pointed to a man on the ground.

Thompson grabbed the kits and followed Dixon across the lawn in front of the dealership.

A man in his thirties lay motionless on the lawn with blood

covering his chest. *Not a heart attack,* Thompson thought. He checked for a pulse—none.

Dixon started chest compressions. Several police cruisers arrived. Dixon told a cop to take over compressions and two others to get the stretcher.

While Thompson inserted an airway, Dixon applied bandages to several open chest wounds. When he checked the patient's back, he found additional wounds. "He's got lacerations to the back."

"We need to get going," Thompson said.

Dixon nodded. They lifted the patient and rushed to the ambulance.

"I need you to come with us and keep doing compressions," Dixon said to the cop attending to the patient. "We also need a driver."

A young cop immediately volunteered.

"Nice and easy," Dixon said.

He nodded and headed to the front of the ambulance.

As they pulled away, Dixon started two intravenous lines. Thompson ventilated the patient with a bagging unit. The cop did compressions. Once the IVs were in place and flowing, Dixon applied the leads for the cardiac monitor. He glanced at the display—flatline.

CHAPTER ELEVEN

Coffee in hand, Brad headed back to his black Firebird. Even when life was shitty, there were things to be thankful for. For Brad, it was coffee—and coffee from Gerry's to start the day never failed.

He drove with the light pre-rush-hour traffic and sipped the hot coffee. People were gathering at bus stops. Some stood, reading the paper, others collected on the benches, eyes forward, not acknowledging the person beside them. The traffic grew heavier closer to downtown.

His thoughts drifted back to the dinner the night before. He had loyal friends. He hadn't planned to shut them out, it just happened slowly. Ignoring a call here and there became a habit. His twisted brain thought if he didn't see his friends, then he wouldn't think about Maggie. He wouldn't think about work if he wasn't around Charlie and Sam and hearing their cop stories.

Maybe he needed extra time with Dr. Keller. Another sip of

coffee. He'd just parked in the police lot and was reaching for his suit jacket when Griffin radioed him.

Brad parked in the no-parking zone in front of the café. It was in the corner of an older sandstone building downtown, and if you didn't know it was there, you'd probably miss it. Brad found Griffin, appearing dapper in a charcoal gray suit, at a table by the window. The other twenty chairs were occupied. Two uniformed cops sat in the back corner.

The waitress swung by and filled Brad's cup. "Nectar of the gods."

"Some things never change." Griffin grinned. "You still need coffee to feel human."

"This is my second one." Brad raised the cup and took a drink. "It's in your best interest as my partner to make sure I get my coffee. If you don't, well, you don't want to find out."

Griffin grunted. "I'll keep that in mind."

Brad's portable radio announced, "Downtown units, EMS is responding to a man down, Ford dealership, Ninth Avenue West. Unknown cause. We got a few calls. Some said heart attack and others say he's bleeding."

Brad lowered the volume on the radio.

Griffin took a sip of coffee and leaned forward. "I'm glad you're back at work and I can live with you being my partner. But I gotta ask, you doing okay? Are you ready for work?"

Brad swirled the coffee and stared at the spinning liquid. He was already tired of the question. "I'm not okay. I never will be." His eyes were glued to the coffee. "People say time heals all wounds. That's bullshit. This will never heal. I need to live with it and move forward. A part of me died that day. Two parts. To my last breath I will think of Maggie and what could have been."

"That doesn't sound healthy."

"I screwed up and they died."

"Whoa, buddy." Griffin placed his hands on the table, leaned toward Brad. His voice deepened. "That's a lot of guilt to pack around. You were in an impossible situation, but you did more than any cop could."

Brad shook his head. "Not enough."

"Back to my second question. Are you ready for work?" Griffin paused and stared at Brad. "I gotta know you're dialed in. That you've got my back."

The waitress refilled their coffee. Brad set his cup on the table and stared at Griffin. "I'm ready. I'm focused and I will always have your back." He glanced down at the table, then lifted his head. "I'm glad Archer assigned me to work with you. I don't trust many people. But I trust you—with my life."

Griffin sipped his coffee as he scrutinized Brad. "So, I don't have to worry about the angry Brad from Saturday night showing up?"

"Won't happen again."

Griffin pointed his coffee cup at Brad. "You wouldn't want to get blood on your pretty suit."

Brad glanced at his clothes. "What?"

Griffin smirked. "That come directly from Italy?"

"Hey, your suit is lovely, too. Can't be one from the police association discount rack."

"I didn't want to seem like some court-appointed lawyer compared to you. It's just that this is the one tailored suit I have.

I won't be showing up in a different designer suit every day like you."

"You might be surprised to learn I have two faults—I like suits and I like fancy cars."

"You're selling yourself short." Griffin raised his coffee and peered over the rim. "You have way more than two faults."

When their pagers went off, they glanced at the message—*shooting at the Shell station on Seventeenth Avenue and Fifth Street SW.*

"Ah, damn." Brad glanced longingly at his coffee, then sprinted out the door.

"We'll take my company car," Griffin said. The tires squealed as he raced out of the parking lot behind the café, clipping the curb.

"I see your driving hasn't improved." Brad activated the lights and siren.

"Already with the sarcasm." Griffin accelerated through a red light and ignored the glares from drivers and the honking horns. "Maybe you are ready for work."

Brad grabbed the dash. "I haven't heard of a shooting for months."

"Yeah. It's been quiet while you were off." Griffin threw a quick glance toward Brad. "I wonder if there's a connection."

"Woo-hoo," Brad said. "A zinger right back. You know, I missed that."

CHAPTER TWELVE

Griffin followed an ambulance toward the gas station. Police cruisers coming from the other direction skidded to a stop in the parking lot. Griffin parked on the street and had barely stopped when Brad jumped out of the car and surveyed the scene. Bystanders were standing three deep around the gas pumps. Brad pushed into the crowd at the pumps. "Move away. Let the paramedics in."

Brad stepped back, giving Dixon and Thompson room to work. A thirty-year-old male was slumped against the pump. There was a tiny hole in his forehead with some blood—no active bleeding. Thompson checked for a pulse and shook his head. They rolled the patient onto his side. The entire back of the patient's head was blown off.

Thompson and Dixon glanced at each other and headed over to Brad and Griffin.

"Hey, Griffin," Dixon said. "Who's the new guy?"

"He appears familiar," Thompson said.

Brad smirked. "Real funny, guys. Nice to see you, too."

Griffin glanced at the body. "That's not good."

"Nope," Thompson said. "Not conducive to life."

"Mighty big word for a little man," Dixon said.

Thompson ignored his partner. "Only one thing does that. Gunshot."

Brad nodded. "A high-powered rifle."

"That's the second one this morning," Dixon said.

Brad's head swung to Dixon. "What?"

"Yeah. We just came from the hospital. About forty minutes ago, we got called to a man down. It appeared his lawnmower had exploded. He was cut up and we could see chunks of metal embedded in his body, chest and back. But at the hospital, when they examined him, they decided he was shot first. The mower was self-propelled and kept going when he dropped. When it hit the curb, the blade shredded on the concrete and sprayed shrapnel everywhere."

"Well, shit," Brad said.

"Damn." Griffin glared at Brad. "You're barely back a day and we got two homicides."

"You can thank me for the overtime we're going to get. Let's talk to the witnesses."

"All right," Griffin said. "Let's split up."

Brad spoke to the uniformed cops first on scene and they pointed to a lady sitting on the bumper of the ambulance. Brad headed over.

"Hi, I'm Detective Coulter. What's your name?"

"Naomi."

"Hi, Naomi. I understand you saw what happened."

"I'm not sure. I was filling my car, then I heard a sharp bang. I thought a car had backfired, or a tire blew. I peered toward the street where the sound came from, but saw just vehicles driving past. When I turned back, I saw a man slumped by the gas pump. I thought he'd fallen. I stopped filling my car and called to him. He didn't answer, so I headed over. That's when I saw the blood. I didn't know what to do, so I ran into the station and got the clerk to call 911. I stayed inside. I know I should have tried to help him, but I just couldn't."

"Don't worry about that. There was nothing you could have done for him. Calling 911 was the right thing to do."

"Was he … was he shot?"

"We think so."

"Oh my god. Why would someone do that? It could have been me."

"Naomi, can you think of anything that could help us?"

She shook her head.

"What about any vehicles speeding away?"

Again, she shook her head. "There were just lots of cars on the street. No one vehicle stood out. I just took a glance. Then I saw the man lying there. Well, after that I remember little. I've never seen anything like it."

CHAPTER THIRTEEN

Brad met up with Griffin at their car. "You get anything?"

"Nothing that's gonna help us. The clerk was reading the paper. He hears cars backfire all the time, so he doesn't check it out. He didn't know anything was wrong until your lady rushed in. No one else was at the pumps except the lady and the dead guy. I've got some uniformed guys checking other businesses. But I don't think they'll get anything we can use."

"This gas station got any cameras?"

"Nah. They run these stations on the cheap. Never get surveillance here."

The radio interrupted them. "All units, woman down. Gas station, Twelfth Avenue and Macleod Trail SE. The caller says a woman is under her car."

"That's about ten blocks away," Brad said.

They jumped into Griffin's car and raced off. Within fifty seconds, they were pulling in. There was one car at the pumps with a few people standing by the car. As Brad approached, he saw two young children in the back seat peering out the window. He turned to a man dressed in a shirt with the gas station logo.

"Police," Brad said. "What happened?"

"I'm not sure. She was pumping gas. When I glanced that way, I couldn't see her, but the hose was still in the car. I came out and found her under the car."

"Griffin, get the kids. I'll get her out from under the car." He dropped onto his belly and slid as far as he could under the car. A young woman, late twenties, lay under the vehicle. Blood was pooling around her head from a wound in her neck. Brad reached out to touch her neck. He felt for a pulse—he wasn't sure. He grabbed her shirt collar, then dragged her out. Brad glanced up. Griffin held the two children, both under the age of five. Then an ambulance pulled in beside them. Amir Sharma and Jill Cook jumped out.

Cook knelt beside the lady and began her assessment.

"I don't know if I felt a pulse," Brad said.

Sharma glanced at the lady and then the car. "What happened?"

"She was pumping gas, was injured, and crawled under the car."

"Why would she do that?" Sharma asked.

"She was scared," Brad said. "We've had two shootings this morning. Check for entry and exit wounds—she may have been hit once, then dove for cover."

"No way," Sharma said. "This can't be happening ... not here."

"Sharma, she's got a faint pulse," Cook said. "Get the stretcher. We've got to move."

Two police cruisers slid to a stop and four officers raced over.

"Help the paramedic with the stretcher," Brad shouted to the first two officers. He pointed to the second pair. "Get ready to escort the ambulance to the hospital."

Cook applied four-by-four bandages to the neck wound. She glanced at Brad. "Apply pressure to her neck. Don't ease up."

He knelt next to Cook and applied pressure from both sides of her neck. He knew the paramedics would do everything they could, but in his guts, he knew their effort was futile.

"Be careful not to—"

Brad nodded. "Collapse her airway. I know. Let's go."

CHAPTER FOURTEEN

GRIFFIN HAD PICKED BRAD UP AT THE HOSPITAL AND THEN DROPPED him off outside the café at ten. The plan was to meet at headquarters to put the pieces together. Brad yanked the parking ticket from under his windshield and slid into the car. He opened the glove box and stuffed the ticket in with a half-dozen others.

He rolled down the window and slipped in a Neil Diamond cassette. He half sang, half lip-synched to Hot August Night. It was good to take a break, even for a few minutes. He exhaled deeply through pursed lips. What a morning. Pick whatever metaphor you wanted, thrown into the fire, thrown into the deep end or just ghastly Coulter luck. Likely the last.

It started fine, coffee from Gerry's, then another coffee with Griffin. That's the way he liked to begin his days. Ease into it. The best thing about the day shift was there weren't murders—until today. Deaths were supposed to happen at night when the crazies roamed the streets.

They had little information on the first murder. Heck, no one had reported it *was* a murder. All they had was a name—Gregg Penner—Dixon's description of what happened at the scene, and what the emergency physician told them at the hospital. Griffin sent detectives to the hospital to get statements. Maybe he could talk Griffin into sending the detectives to get statements from the paramedics, too.

Penner was minding his business, mowing a lawn, and got shot in the chest. But no one knew that because he had lawnmower shrapnel embedded in his body. The gunshot wasn't discovered until he was in the emergency department. Witnesses are gone and it was unlikely anyone got their names.

At the second shooting, they found out about the first. This time a guy was pumping gas. One shot to the forehead. There are people at the scene, potential witnesses, but no one saw anything out of the ordinary.

They had barely got that crime scene under control, when there was a third shooting—again at a gas station. A dealership and two gas stations. Two men and one woman, Kellie Singer. Were the victims in the wrong place? Or were the victims targeted, and the locations were random? Just a coincidence? Not bloody likely. The first two shots, fatal. Singer was hanging in there. But with that neck wound, it wasn't promising. He shook his head. Too much to process. He started the car, pulled away from the curb, and headed toward Police Headquarters when the call came over the radio.

"All units, reports of a shooting. Sixteenth Avenue and Edmonton Trail. Northside bus bench. Possible suicide."

When Brad reached Centre Street, he turned north and stomped on the accelerator. The engine responded, and the speedometer passed sixty miles per hour.

What were the chances of a suicide on a bus bench on a morning when there'd been three shooting deaths? It made no sense. He braked and fishtailed onto Sixteenth Avenue. Ahead, to his left, people had gathered on the sidewalk. He drove across traffic, slammed the car into park and jumped out. He sprinted to the crowd. "Police. Let me through."

The crowd parted. He was facing a twentyish woman sitting on the bus bench, her head fully extended. There was a hole midpoint in her forehead. Blood had trickled back toward her hair. No blood trickled now. For someone who had experienced such a tragic death, she appeared surprisingly at peace. She'd never known what happened.

He tentatively reached to her neck and felt for a pulse. None. Her skin was already cool.

"Everyone, move back ten steps." At best, they took five steps."Did she commit suicide?" a woman asked.

"Did anyone see a gun?"

Several shook their heads. Brad stepped back and glanced around the bus bench and underneath. No gun.

"Did anyone see her collapse?"

Again, shaking of heads.

An ambulance, a dozen police vehicles, the EMS supervisor, and two firetrucks pulled up, jamming Sixteenth Avenue. They parked anywhere they could, then descended on the crime scene. There were cops, paramedics and firefighters everywhere. It was too late—the scene was contaminated.

Chaos.

He circled the victim. He didn't know what he was searching for but hoped he'd recognize it. If it was the same killer and he used a high-powered rifle, then based on where she sat, the shot had come from across the street, near the 7-Eleven or Peters'

Drive-In. Peters' was closed, so a sniper might not be seen there. 7-Eleven was busy, with cars and pedestrians moving in and out in a steady stream. Not from there.

He traced the path he thought the bullet would have followed. Then he headed across the street, to a point behind the drive-in. As he got close to the fence, he swerved to the right, hoping he didn't disturb evidence, then to the fence, rotated and glanced back at the victim. He nodded. Right here, give or take a foot, was where the shot came from. He knelt and examined the ground. Tire tracks crisscrossed each other, and it was hard to tell which tire mark was the most recent. Yet there were no recent footprints. His instinct said the shot had come from here. He flagged two officers standing outside their car and directed them to put up police tape in a wide arc around the tire prints.

While the cops rolled out the tape, he glanced back across the street.

This victim wasn't shot at a gas station, but there was one directly behind her. Was a pattern emerging or just another shooting of opportunity? He doubted they'd find a single link between the victims. That wasn't what this was about. Not victims, then. Locations? Why gas stations? Why three different companies? The car dealership was the exception. But it was the first. Was that significant? Too many things were spinning through his head. He wasn't going to solve this standing here.

More questions than answers. A car started to his right. He watched an unmarked police car leave the 7-Eleven parking lot. Too many cops anyway.

Was the shooting over? He hoped so. His gut told him otherwise. He wished his gut was wrong, but it seldom was. He headed back across the street.

Four scenes, four victims—three confirmed dead. Four shots

from a distance and a high-powered rifle. Another perfect shot, as sick as that sounded. Three out of four shots were instant killers. Three shots to the head and one to the chest. Not good shooting, expert shooting. The killer knew what he was doing. And with a high-powered rifle as the likely murder weapon ... did Calgary have a sniper on the loose?

CHAPTER FIFTEEN

Pittman and Hirsch sat in their car drinking coffee in the 7-Eleven parking lot across from the bus bench. For the first three shootings, they'd left the scene immediately, heading to their next location. This time they stayed to see the chaos from their actions.

Police cars, ambulances, and firetrucks parked at all angles. Cops, paramedics, and firefighters were walking around, seeking something to do. No one was in charge. Not that they'd left any evidence because they hadn't come within at least a hundred yards of the victim.

They watched a guy in a stylish suit head across the street. He had his eye on something behind the drive-in. They sipped their coffees and watched the cop about one-hundred yards west of them. He never wavered from the path he was taking until just before the fence. Then he circled wide around something and stared back at the park bench.

"Son of a bitch." Pittman held his coffee halfway to his mouth. "He figured out where we were parked."

"How'd he do that?" Hirsch asked.

"Hell if I know." Pittman sipped coffee as he watched the guy in the suit step about ten yards back from where Hirsch had fired.

"Shit," Hirsch said. "He figured out the line of the shot."

"He's a shooter," Pittman said. "A cop who knows his stuff."

The cop called two uniformed guys over and swung his arm in an arc around him.

"He wants them to protect that area." Pittman started the car and dropped it into gear. "Time to go."

CHAPTER SIXTEEN

As Brad headed back across Sixteenth Avenue, Briscoe caught up to him. "We need to talk."

"What's up?"

"I just heard on the radio that the lady, Kellie Singer, didn't make it. She was dead on arrival at the hospital."

"Shit." Brad stopped in the middle of the street and ran his fingers through his hair. "What is going on?"

Briscoe shook his head. "Beats the hell out of me."

"I'm having trouble processing this. A busy month would be four homicides. But four in two-and-a-half hours?"

"I've got someone you need to talk to. Maybe she can give you something to work with."

"I need to catch up with Griffin."

"That can wait. You need to talk to her this second."

Brad recognized the intensity in Briscoe's eyes and the set jaw. There was no sense arguing. He followed Briscoe to a cruiser. A lady sat on the back seat with her legs out onto the asphalt.

Brad knelt. "I'm Detective Coulter. What's your name?"

"Brenda."

Brad nodded. "Sergeant Briscoe wants me to talk to you."

"I think I saw something."

"The gunman?"

She shook her head. "No. After the shot. A white van raced away, hitting the curb. The tires squealed as he raced off."

"What kind of van?"

"I don't know anything about vans. It was all white. I guess it was like servicemen use. You know, like plumbers or electricians. Maybe larger than that."

"Did you see anything on the side? Writing? A logo?"

Again, she shook her head. "Just the back of it as he drove away."

"Which direction did he go?"

She pointed to Sixteenth Avenue. "He headed east."

"How long ago?"

"About fifteen minutes ago, I'd guess."

"Did you see the license plate?"

"Oh, no. I'm so sorry. I'm not much help."

Brad stood. "You've done a great job. Please give these officers your contact information, and they'll get you to write a witness statement."

Brad grabbed a Coke and Griffin a coffee from the 7-Eleven and then headed to the picnic tables behind Peters' drive-in. They sat on opposite sides of the table.

Griffin gazed to the east, absently sipping his coffee. They sat in silence for a few minutes. They needed to catch their breath. They had been on the go for a few hours, but it felt like days.

Brad stared at the scarred tabletop. For years, patrons had carved their names and dates in the wood. The usual hearts with initials. A few less appropriate words, too. Someone had taken the time to tout their superiority, carving in large, deep letters, "I am that I am." He shook his head and rubbed his thumb across the condensation on the Coke can. "What the hell is going on, Griffin?"

Griffin set down his empty coffee cup, then slammed his hand over the cup. He shook his head. "I don't have a clue. I've never seen anything like this. Not here. Not sure any city has. Not four shootings in two-and-a-half hours." He rubbed the back of his hand across his mouth several times, then shook his head again. "I just don't know."

"How do we piece something like this together?"

Griffin leaned back and sighed. "We start at the beginning and take one piece at a time."

"That will take a long time. What if we don't have a long time? If this is the same guy, what if he strikes again?"

Griffin shrugged. "We can't control what he does. Maybe he strikes in another hour. Then we'll know he's staying active. Maybe nothing happens in an hour, but two hours later someone else is shot. We can only control what we do. Each time he strikes we get closer to catching him. We'll have lots of help. Cops will bring us thousands of puzzle pieces. But it stops with us. We need to start with the first piece, then finish the puzzle. The sooner we do, the better."

"We will need a lot of room—phones, TVs, you name it."

Griffin stood. "Look, I need to call my wife and tell her I

won't be home, maybe not for a few days or for a few hours of sleep. Who's watching Lobo?"

"I'll get Annie to take care of him."

"After I talk to my wife, then I'll start working on getting us a command center." Griffin glanced across the street. "I'll leave you to deal with the deputy chief."

CHAPTER SEVENTEEN

BRAD STOPPED BESIDE A BLACK TOWN CAR PARKED AT THE CURB. THE back door opened, and Deputy Chief Archer stepped out. He surveyed the scene, then peered at Brad.

Archer's eyes were black disks of coal. "Bring me up to speed."

"We have a highly active shooter."

"I had that part figured out." Archer's eyes bored into Brad.

A cop in dress uniform stepped beside Archer and stared at Brad. "You're Coulter."

"That's right." Brad smirked. *That puts you on the fast track to detective.*

"I'm Llewelyn Carew. I am the Public Information Officer."

"The what—"

"Media relations—the guy who talks to the press."

"Another change?" Brad asked. "Give us a minute, Lew. I'm talking to the deputy chief."

"Not Lew, Llewelyn. I'm here with the deputy. We're going to do a press conference."

"At a crime scene? No frickin' way," Brad said. "There are too many people here as it is."

Archer held up his hand. "It is the wish of the mayor that the press is fully briefed on this situation."

Brad started to speak, then saw the glare from Archer.

"Please continue, Detective," Archer said.

Brad glanced at Carew. "Right. We have four murders. All were shot, likely from a high-powered rifle. We have no idea who is doing this or why he targeted these four people."

"Two were at gas stations," Carew said. "Are they targeting gas stations?"

"And two of them were not at gas stations," Brad said. "It's too early to speculate on anything. We'll keep interviewing witnesses, the Crime Scene Unit will gather evidence, and we'll analyze it."

"Do you have any leads?"

"None at this time."

"You haven't given me anything to tell the press."

"That's because there's nothing to tell." Brad's jaw clenched. "Look, Lew, this is four murders in two-and-a-half hours."

"The mayor will want more than this."

"When we have something, I'll let you and the mayor know."

"He won't like this."

"Mayor Kearse knows how this works. If he were here, I'd tell him myself. If you don't mind, we've got four murders to solve."

Carew huffed and stalked toward some cops gathered at a cruiser.

"Public Information Officer?" Brad asked.

Archer nodded. "It was the mayor's idea. He felt there were times when he was a reporter that cops were deliberately obstructive and kept things from the press that the public needed to know. You wouldn't know anything about that, would you?"

"I have the highest level of respect for the press. Even when they are drunk out of their minds."

Brad struck out with the witnesses other than the lady who saw the white van. In the last half hour, he'd seen perhaps a hundred white vans drive by. He leaned against his car and scrutinized the crime scene again.

Briscoe strode to the car. "We got a crowd gathering down the road. Lots of reporters and camera crews."

Brad stared at the gathering crowd. "They're doing the morning press conference."

"What the hell are they going to say?" Briscoe asked.

"Hell if I know. I told Archer it was too soon. That we had nothing. The media information guy—"

"Public Information Officer—"

"Yeah, the shithead PIO is a piece of work. Where did they get him?"

"He graduated as a cop about three years ago," Briscoe said. "He created press releases for the mayor's campaign and then convinced the mayor he wasn't getting good information from us. Kearse put the pressure on the chief, and voila, we have a media spokesman who is a direct conduit to the mayor, and he was promoted to sergeant."

"Sergeant? Nothing good will come from this."

Briscoe tugged Brad's arm. "Let's head over and see what he has to say."

They headed down the road and stood on the sidewalk. Sergeant Carew stepped in front of dozens of reporters with extended microphones and a half-dozen television cameras.

"Good morning. I am Sergeant Llewelyn Carew, Public Information Officer. I haven't had the pleasure of meeting all of you, but I will get to that. Thank you for gathering for this impromptu press conference. Deputy Chief Nick Archer is here with me. I want to bring you up to date on the events of this morning."

Carew gave brief descriptions of the four shootings and even had most of the facts straight. To his credit, he kept the information brief without many details.

"Carew is smooth," Brad said.

Briscoe smirked. "Slicker than pig shit."

Members of the press asked for clarification on the time of the shootings and the extent of injuries. They asked for the names of the victims, and Carew said they would not be released pending notification of the next of kin.

A reporter next to a camera raised his hand. "Sergeant Carew, I'm Angus Ferguson, CFCN."

Carew smiled. "Yes, your former reporter is my boss."

Ferguson chuckled. "Please give my regards to Mayor Kearse."

Brad's head swiveled toward Ferguson, and he did a double-take. He gave the impression of being a professor—salt-and-pepper hair and beard, tweed jacket with a green-and-blue tartan tie. All that was missing was the pipe. But he spoke in an annoying, high-pitched, whiny tone. Brad expected that voice with different clothing.

"Annoying voice, huh?" Briscoe said.

Brad ground his teeth. "Yeah."

Ferguson nodded at Carew and gave his best used-car-salesman smile.

"My question is: do the police have any leads?"

"Excellent question, Angus. Just before I stepped up here, I learned a credible witness saw a white van speed out of this parking lot immediately after the shooting. He bounced over the curb and the tires screeched as he raced away to the east. It is likely that the shooter was in the van and fired the fatal shot from there."

Ferguson frowned. "I'm confused. My understanding was that it was not known it was a shooting until at least ten minutes after the first officer arrived. How did she know the van was related to a shooting?"

"Again, excellent follow-up question. At the time, she did not know of the shooting, but after excellent interrogation by Detective Coulter,"—Carew pointed to his left—"our detective realized the connection."

"What the heck," Brad said. "You and Griffin are the two people I told about the van. Where did he get this from?"

"There's probably fifty cops here. Any one of them could have overheard. It's possible she was interviewed by another cop."

"It must have been the cops I asked to get a statement from her."

"What're their names?" Briscoe asked. "I'll have their asses."

"I don't have a clue. They were dressed in blue on blue."

They watched Carew conclude the press conference. "That's

all I have at this time. I will have frequent press conferences to keep you informed. If you have further questions, I'd suggest you talk with Detective Coulter."

Oh, damn.

Brad grabbed Briscoe. "Let's get out of here."

It was too late. The press flocked to Brad and Briscoe, circling them. They shoved microphones in front of Brad, and questions were coming from all directions.

Brad held up his hand. "Sergeant Carew has given you all the information we can release. As he said, when we have information, he will update you. We are early in this investigation and a lot has happened in the past two-and-a-half hours. Thank you."

He tried to push through the reporters, but they wouldn't move.

Angus Ferguson stepped in front of Brad and blocked his path. "Detective Coulter, I understand you are recently back from leave. How are you doing?"

"I'm fine," he replied tersely and again tried to push past Ferguson, who stepped to the side to block Brad again.

"After the tragic loss of your fiancée and child, it must be difficult to come back to work and face four murders. Are you sure you're up to this challenge?"

Brad stepped close to Ferguson and cocked his head to the side. "Nothing I like more than a challenge."

Ferguson tried to step back, but he had no room as other reporters pressed closer.

"I have some work to do. Have a great day." Brad headed down the block.

When they were well away from the reporters, Briscoe asked, "You okay?"

Brad shrugged and straightened his jacket. "I'm fine. He's a pushy son of a bitch."

"You handled it well. I'm not under scrutiny. You are."

"What do you mean?"

"Archer knows the Brad of earlier this year," Briscoe said. "Not the Brad of today. Why do you think you're in Homicide with Griffin?"

"Back to my position before …"

Briscoe frowned. "Griffin asked for you because you're good. Well, you were. The jury is still out. Archer is watching. Hell, the entire department is watching. Understand?"

Brad nodded and stared at his feet. Steele strode over.

"Hey, you okay?" Steele cocked his head.

"Would you guys stop asking me that? I'm going to snap."

Steele stepped back a few paces. "I get it. Just concerned. What happened with the reporter?"

"Ferguson is an in-your-face kind of guy."

"Yeah, well, Kearse is the mayor and we've got to deal with Ferguson," Steele said. "Walk away. You always did with Kearse. I know he pissed you off every time. But you did what you do best, you outwitted him. You out-sarcasmed him, if that's a word."

Brad snorted. "I don't think it is."

"Well, it should be. Worth a lot in Scrabble. Don't take Ferguson's bait. Debate him, put him on the spot. Make him backtrack. You know, Kearse admired that about you."

"Sure."

"Kearse loved to verbally duel with you. Ferguson is no Kearse and no match for you."

Brad nodded. "I get it. Give me a few minutes." Brad headed over to the picnic tables behind the drive-in. He liked this spot.

He could think here. Sometimes the crowds were overwhelming. He felt suffocated and craved space.

The last thing he needed was Archer watching too closely. If Archer called Dr. Keller to check on Brad's progress, he'd be on permanent leave. Luckily, Keller was in Hawaii.

"Detective Coulter?" a soft voice called.

Brad swung around on the table. Standing about ten feet away was a lady, her brown eyes wide and flicking from side to side. Her slim body was twisted away from him for a fast escape. She appeared familiar. Long brown hair framing a heart-shaped face. She was dressed in smart business attire—skirt, jacket, and a pale-blue blouse. Lawyer? Maybe.

"Can I help you?" Then he saw the notepad, pen and a recorder. *Ah shit.* "You're a reporter."

"I'm Sadie Andrus. I work for CFAC TV. I have a few questions."

"I'm sorry, Ms. Andrus. I'm sure Sergeant Carew would be thrilled to talk to you."

She took a couple of steps back, then stopped. "We're not all like Ferguson."

"I'd hope not."

"Not me."

"What makes you different?"

She sighed. "Look. It's difficult for me. I'm a woman."

"I noticed."

"Reporting is cutthroat and a man's game. I have to work twice—three times as hard as they do. They do what's worked for them in the past; they bully stories out of people. They harass them. I'm not gonna scare anyone or get away with harassment. I'll treat you fair if you'll treat me fair."

"Forgive me ..."

"Sadie."

"Sadie. You seem like a pleasant person and like you're trying to do your job. I'm trying to do mine. I've got four murders to solve. That jackass Ferguson in my face isn't helping me catch bad guys."

He jumped off the picnic table. "Nice meeting you, Sadie. I wish you luck with your story."

Briscoe caught up to Brad as he headed away from Sadie. "What'd she want?"

"Reporter searching for the scoop of the century."

Briscoe nodded. "Did she get one?"

"What do you think?"

"Good. You've got a frickin' mess to sort out."

Brad nodded. "This is happening faster than we can keep up. We hadn't released that there was the first murder before the second occurred. Then the third. Now number four. Maybe we should have gone to the press right away."

"You didn't even know the first was a murder initially. It's just been a few hours—that's barely enough time to get to the crime scenes let alone address the press. You had no way of knowing there'd be more killings." Briscoe cleared his throat. "If you go to the press too soon, you create panic. It's easy to look back and think of a better way to do things. Hell, you don't even have a blurry picture of what's going on, let alone a clear one."

Brad faced the bus bench across the street. The Crime Scene Unit had the scene contained. The public pushed back, and a tarp blocked the bus bench from curious eyes. "I can't believe this lady was killed just because she was sitting at that bus stop."

Briscoe shrugged. "Happens. Wrong place, wrong time."

"Who's the next person in the wrong place?"

CHAPTER EIGHTEEN

THE DESK SERGEANT AT THE BACK COUNTER TOLD BRAD THAT Griffin was in the gym. Brad headed down the stairs. When he opened the gym door, there was a powerful odor of sweat—not from last night's basketball game, but from dozens of men working as fast as they could.

Griffin had been true to his word. The gym in the basement of Police Headquarters was buzzing with activity.

To Brad's left, men were unloading desks and chairs from large trolleys. To his right, a bank of six televisions on high stands were being connected to wires hanging down from the ceiling. Straight ahead, a dozen cork and whiteboards lined the wall.

Cables hung from the ceiling as telephone technicians pulled phone lines. The gym was the command center.

Griffin tapped Brad on the shoulder. "What do you think?"

"You work fast."

"Archer set it in motion. Follow me."

They exited the gym and headed to the left. Griffin opened the door to a racquetball court. The court held four desks with chairs and long tables.

"Welcome to our new office."

"Not too shabby." Brad glanced up. At the back of the court, the top one-third of the wall was all glass. "We might attract an audience."

Griffin glanced up. "The newest exhibit at the zoo. We'll worry about that later."

Brad pulled out a chair and sat. "What are your thoughts on our next steps?"

Griffin grabbed another chair, leaned back and put his feet on the desk. "The first mistake we can make is to get tunnel vision. We need to keep our assumptions and theories about why the crime was committed, why the victims were selected, and who we think might be suspects out of our minds. We don't make the evidence fit the scenario in our heads."

Brad leaned back. Was that what he was doing? Jumping ahead of the facts? But there had to be a reason, no matter how twisted, this was happening and to these people. How were they connected?

"With four murders over two-and-a-half hours, there's a need for urgency. We need to plan for additional shootings and structure our tactics on that. We need to provide patrol units with what to watch for. I see it as a two-pronged approach. One, how do we stop or prepare for the next shooting? Two, we need to be diligent and investigate each shooting. Solid police work will ultimately pay off."

"What if more people die?"

"Then we keep doing what we're doing," Griffin said.

"Gather evidence, interview witnesses, keep digging. We can't do this investigation based on what 'might' happen next."

Was it possible these people were collateral damage, that they were in the way of a shot meant for someone else? Targeted hits by street gangs or bikers that went wrong? It was beyond coincidence that they'd miss four targets but kill four innocent victims. Yet it was strange that these four seemingly unconnected people could all be targets of a gang. "What if we have a shooter on the loose and he's killing people at *random*, just because they are in the wrong place at the wrong time?"

Griffin nodded. "That would be the worst kind of scenario—a nightmare."

"If that's the case, it will be difficult to solve unless we find he's made a mistake."

Griffin swung his legs off the desk and rubbed his face with his palm. "Even worse is we don't find any clues, get any leads. In that case, we might need him to make a mistake at another shooting."

Shit, this isn't over.

Griffin returned to overseeing the set-up in the gym. Brad stayed in their new office, organizing the information they'd collected. He had an eerie feeling he was being watched. He glanced at the door—no one there. Then he glanced up. Standing at the glass overlooking the racquetball court were a half-dozen people, drinking coffee and watching. A few waved. *I'm in a freaking zoo.*

He called dispatch and asked them to bring him a city map. He used one wall to post what little information they had from each crime scene. He taped the name of each victim to the wall, then under each name added photos of the victims prior to the shooting—from driver's licenses, the victim's pictures at the scene, photos of the scene, witness interview statements, and what little forensic evidence had been analyzed.

He stood back and scrutinized the wall. He grabbed a pen and wrote a list of unanswered questions and a task list.

All four scenes had witnesses, but no one saw any of the shootings. No one saw a shooter. In most cases, a shot was heard, but they believed it to be a backfire or a tire blowing. No one could say what direction the sound came from. The few places that had security cameras showed the moment of the impact, but all faced toward the victim, not away. Not a single scrap of evidence was left to identify the shooter or his vehicle. The best lead so far was the white van, and that was sketchy.

Brad sat at his desk and penned his list.

Questions

- Victims targeted? Or victims random?
- Then who was the actual target?
- Significance of locations?
- Gang/Biker related?
- What is the underlying issue?
- Isolated to Calgary? Other cities experiencing this?
- One shooter?
- Different shooters per location?
- Experienced sniper?
- Experienced hunter?

- The gun?
- Scope?
- Vehicle: White Van?

Brad sat back and stared at the questions. The shootings appeared random, not related to gangs. No one was claiming credit for the killings yet, so not political.

The shooter was experienced, but was that military history or an expert hunter?

Until they got ballistics, which should be soon, it would be a wild-assed guess as to the caliber of ammunition and the make of the gun.

Brad's radio was continuous chatter from cops stopping white vans, running license plate numbers and driver's licenses. The focused stops of white vans were leading to a few arrests for outstanding warrants and drug possession when the vans were searched. The danger was Archer had decided to have one officer in each cruiser, instead of the usual two. It increased the visibility of police to double the number of cops on the street. But it also put those officers in danger at each traffic stop. They were alone without the usual backup of a partner. Although it appeared the cops were doing an excellent job of backing each other up when they heard about a traffic stop. Brad touched wood. Hopefully, backup didn't arrive too late.

There was a knock at the door. One of the 911 call takers came in. "I've got your map."

Brad grabbed the map. "Thanks. This will be handy."

He taped the map to the wall, then marked the site of each shooting and the time. It appeared the shooter could quickly get to each location, even in rush hour traffic.

The City of Calgary, Alberta, was home to 580,000 citizens

spread out over 250 square miles. The city itself was divided up into the four major quadrants of north, south, east and west, along with the downtown core at the city center. The first shooting took place on Ninth Avenue, west of the city center. The second shooting took place less than a mile south on Seventeenth Avenue in the southwest. Approximately four minutes driving in rush-hour traffic. The third, at Twelfth Avenue and Macleod Trail in the southeast, again four minutes from the second location and one minute from the downtown core. And the fourth shooting on Sixteenth Avenue and Centre Street northwest, occurred fifty minutes after the third, but was merely a ten-minute drive from the third shooting. Why the break in time? All were clustered around the perimeter of the city core.

Staring at the map was making him dizzy. Time to change his thinking. He went back to his desk and picked up the pen.

What do we know:

- Four shootings
- Two women
- Two men
- All killed
- Within two-and-a-half hours
- Shot from distance 100–200 yards
- Killed with one shot
- Three shots accurate, one not, but still did the job. (Double-check this one. Is it the ricochet? A different shooter or did the shooter mess up?)
- Locations? 1 Dealership, 2 gas stations and 1 bus bench, but a gas station immediately behind
- Were gas stations the target? Why?

His eyes roamed from one list back to the other. Killed with one shot from a distance means a high-powered rifle. That means a high-powered bullet. Which meant the ballistic vests cops and paramedics wore would not stop the bullet. The vests would just be another piece of clothing the paramedics had to remove at the scene, or worse, at the morgue. There had been nothing to suggest cops might be victims. But nothing to rule them out either.

He set down the pen, exhaled a deep breath, and stared at the map.

"Hey, buddy," a voice boomed. "Some of us are trying to solve the murders."

Brad's head swung, and the chair tipped back. He grabbed the desk to keep from falling. "Most people knock."

"Most cops don't sleep in the middle of four homicides," Sturgeon said.

Brad snorted. "Yeah, right. I'm going dizzy staring at this map trying to figure out a pattern."

"You don't need the map to appear dizzy. Anyway, I thought we needed some help with ballistics and guns, so I brought Ames with me."

Randy Ames stepped into the room. Brad jumped to his feet and held out his hand. "Damn good to see you, buddy."

Ames had been a sniper on Brad's TSU team three years ago during the biker war. He was an expert marksman with time in Vietnam. There wasn't anything he didn't know about snipers and high-powered rifles.

"I hope you two have something good to tell me."

"Nothing concrete yet," Sturgeon said. "But Ames collected bullet fragments from all four shootings—from the emergency department and the morgue."

"The first part won't be news to you," Ames said. "The shooter used a high-powered rifle with a high-velocity bullet, a long rifle or assault rifle, like the AR15. Preliminary examination shows bullet fragments are a .223 caliber round. It's gonna take some time for a full ballistics match, but I'm confident the round is .223. The wounds are similar with all victims. It's not a stretch to say the bullets recovered to this point likely came from the same rifle."

Brad nodded. "And the ballistic vest the street cops wear won't stop a .223."

"Might not even slow it down." Ames headed to the door. "I'm going to do the full ballistic assessment."

"Let me know as soon as you find anything."

"The tire tracks aren't any help. Too many on top of the other." Sturgeon headed to the door, then stopped. "I'll see what my teams have gathered from the crime scenes."

Brad went back to his lists, then his brain spun off in another direction. Was it crazy to think just one of these victims was the target? That the sniper killed four to disguise the one true target? To confuse us? One of the women? A nasty divorce? Who was the intended victim then? He remembered an Agatha Christie novel along these lines. His subconscious was messing with him.

Still, something to follow up. A business deal gone wrong? Brad made a note to check the victims for businesses and any in trouble.

Brad glanced at his watch—almost 2:00 p.m.—four hours

since the last shooting. Was it too early to relax? Maybe it was a brief spree of killings.

Perhaps the idea that he'd killed four to cover up the actual target wasn't so far-fetched. Unless they found a link between the victims, this theory was as good as any. His gut told him it *was* too early to relax—his brain said the immediate threat was over. Focus on solving the murders.

CHAPTER NINETEEN

Deputy Chief Archer ordered the afternoon shift which normally started at 3:00 p.m., to be at work at 2:00 p.m. So, when Brad and Briscoe arrived at the briefing room, close to seventy-five officers were crammed together. Already the odors of many competing colognes and sweat permeated the air. They pushed their way to the front of the room. Conversations buzzed.

"Okay, let's get started," Briscoe said.

The discussions continued.

"Quiet." Briscoe paused as he waited for the conversation to die down. "I'll make this quick. The shootings took place this morning over two-and-a-half hours. There have been no shootings since 9:58. The shooter may have accomplished what he'd planned to do. Other than the possibility the suspect or suspects were driving a white cargo van or a white box van, we don't have a lot to go on. A few things you need to know. There will be one officer in each cruiser. That's to maximize coverage."

A hand went up.

"Yes," Briscoe said. "I still expect you to stop white vans. Whenever possible, back up each other. The van is our best lead, so be cautious, but we have to stop every van. Second—I'm sure you've figured this out—our ballistic vests won't stop high-powered rifle bullets, which we suspect the shooter is using."

The officer lowered his hand.

"Last," Briscoe continued, "you see anything suspicious, get backup. Do not approach suspects on your own. Contact dispatch, they'll let Coulter know, and TSU will be dispatched to your location. Any questions?"

The cops murmured and glanced at each other, but no questions came.

One cop tentatively raised a hand. "How confident are you the shooter is done?"

Briscoe shook his head. "I wish I could say for sure he's stopped—I can't. Nothing is telling us that this is over. You should operate under the assumption we will hear from the shooter. Every hour there's not a shooting, provides optimism the worst is behind us. But we must stay prepared and vigilant in case the shooter is still active. I need you on the streets. Stay safe and go home tonight. Dismissed."

CHAPTER TWENTY

After the briefing, Brad returned to his office and started reading the dozens of witness statements detectives had collected. None had provided promising leads.

Griffin burst into the office. "We have our first lead."

Brad's head jerked up. "What?"

"A lady phoned dispatch. She's convinced her ex-husband, Garth Simpson, is the shooter."

Brad's shoulders slumped. "Maybe she just hates the guy. This is her way to get revenge."

"That's what I thought at first. But listen to this. He's a violent guy with a lengthy record of brutal assaults. He owns a bunch of firearms, including rifles. He wants to be a survivalist and is always talking about how the government is screwing him, and it's giant companies like the oil giants that are making money at the expense of the little guy. Now he's missing."

"If he's her ex, how does she know he's missing?"

"Because she rents the basement to him. She hasn't seen him

for at least three days. He said someday he'd go ballistic and make things right."

"Sounds promising."

"Better yet, he owns a white van."

Brad perked up. "We need to check him out if for no other reason than he sounds like a shithead."

Griffin waved a paper in the air. "Got his address."

Brad parked in front of the address in an older neighborhood. Most of the homes on this block had been neglected for years—decades, probably. The paint was dull and cracked, and the shingles were curled toward the sky. They headed up the uneven sidewalk, ducked under the hanging tree branches and up the steps. A welcome mat lay in front of the screen door. The lettering was faded, the worn corners curled. It was anything but welcoming. Brad stepped to the side as Griffin knocked.

The inside door opened and a lady, maybe late fifties but possibly as old as seventy, peered out the screen. "You the cops?"

"Mrs. Simpson?" Griffin held out his badge. "Can we come in?"

She opened the screen door and nodded toward the inside of the house. She followed them and pointed to the well-worn couch with knitted covers. Griffin sank deep into the couch. Brad stood. Mrs. Simpson sat in an armchair with knitting needles and yarn piled beside.

The room was clean and not cluttered. A stark contrast to the outside. Pictures lined the mantel of the electric fireplace, and several landscape prints were hung on the walls. A hallway to the left likely led to a bathroom and bedrooms. He figured the kitchen was to the back of the house.

Griffin pulled out a notebook and pen. "Tell us why you called?"

"Like I told the lady on the phone, my ex, Garth, is violent and has a record. Some fierce assaults. He thinks he's a survivalist. He hates the government and especially hates the oil companies."

"What's his problem with oil companies?"

"He believes the oil giants are making money at the expense of the little guy."

"Did he work for an oil company?"

Mrs. Simpson nodded. "Years ago, but he got fired."

"Why?"

"He was drunk and told the boss off," she said. "Then he couldn't get a job anywhere."

"You told the officer on the phone that your ex is missing," Brad said.

Mrs. Simpson shifted uncomfortably in her chair. "Well, not missing, he's just not here."

"What does that mean?" Brad asked.

"He goes on drinking binges, two, three, four days at a time."

"Does he have a favorite establishment?"

"What?"

"Bar," Griffin said. "What is his favorite bar?"

"Oh. Usually the Queens Hotel."

"Good to know," Brad said. "You mentioned guns?"

She nodded. "Oh, yeah. He's got lots of guns."

Brad glanced around the room. "Where are they?"

"In the basement. Go ahead and search. I never go down."

"Thank you." Griffin closed his notebook.

They headed down the rickety stairs to the basement.

Brad glanced around the unfinished room as he slid on examination gloves. A bed sat in the far corner, covers in a tangled mess, and clothes littered the floor.

"I'd feel better if I was in a full contamination suit." He kicked a few pizza boxes aside, then stumbled on an empty two-liter soda bottle. "I'm gonna twist an ankle. Some of this shit is knee-deep."

"Stop whining. If this is the guy, and we bust this case, it will be worth it."

"Not if we die of a disease." Brad pushed his way to a cabinet attached to a wall. A padlock held the doors closed. Like many such setups, the lock was sturdy, but the metal closures were held in place by four tiny screws. He pulled out his knife, wedged the blade under the metal and pried. After several attempts, the screws popped out. He pulled the door open and whistled. "Oh, my."

Griffin fought the surging garbage and headed to Brad. The cabinet stored guns and ammunition. Four long-guns were placed vertically in a homemade stand—a 12-gauge shotgun, a .22, a .308 and a Remington 700. On shelves beside the guns were boxes of ammunition for all four rifles, including .223 ammunition for the Remington 700. The boxes were three deep, four high, and six wide—seventy-two boxes on one shelf alone.

Brad opened the first of three drawers to find a half-dozen revolvers and ammunition. A mix of .38, .357 and .22.

The second drawer contained four pistols and ammunition.

The last drawer held camouflage clothing.

"Not enough to start a war," Brad said. "But enough to do a bunch of damage."

Griffin nodded. "We need to back out of here and call the Crime Scene Unit. Have them analyze the long-guns first."

"More work for Sturgeon," Brad said. "This might be a solid lead. He's got four crime scenes and add this one to process."

"We'll take the guns and a box of each type of ammunition to Ames. We'll get a cruiser here to seal the basement until Sturgeon has people to come back and do a thorough search."

"I've got Ames working on ballistics already. I'll tell him we're coming in with some guns."

They loaded the guns and ammunition into the trunk.

Brad swung the car away from the curb. "I gotta eat."

"Sure," Griffin said. "Peters' Drive-In is on the way back to headquarters. You call Ames and get a BOLO out on Garth Simpson. I'll get burgers and Cokes."

Brad was hanging up the payphone outside the 7-Eleven when Griffin sauntered over to the car. Brad glanced across the street to where the last shooting had occurred. CSU was still on scene, and they still blocked Sixteenth Avenue to traffic, making rush hour a complete mess with frequent honking.

Griffin passed Brad a burger and Coke and set a large bag of fries between them. "Got a paper, too."

"Fine dining." Brad grabbed a handful of fries and stuffed them into his mouth.

"Nothing but the best."

They wolfed down their meals in silence as cops and paramedics had learned to do. Unfortunately, that spilled over into personal life. Brad finished his burger, picked up the paper and flung it open.

The headline read: *Troubled Cop Investigating Shootings*

Below the headline was a photo of Brad sitting alone on the picnic table today next to a picture of his house surrounded by emergency vehicles the night Maggie was murdered. Brad scrubbed one hand down his face and swore.

"That's a shitty picture of you."

"Thanks. Ferguson is a piece of work."

Brad skimmed through the article. "He's rewritten the story of the night Maggie died and questions my ability to be on this case." Brad read some more. "Now he's done it."

"What?"

"He's got a second article—about the white van. In his version, from a high-level source in the police: 'Police think the shooter is a disgruntled tradesperson driving a white van. The public should be cautious of any tradespeople in their area. Do not open your doors and call the police immediately.'" Brad tossed the newspaper in the back seat.

"Shit. 911 is going to light up."

Brad's and Griffin's pagers buzzed at the same time. Brad glanced at the display. "Shit. Simpson was in the drunk tank from late Sunday night until one this afternoon. No way he did the shooting."

CHAPTER TWENTY-ONE

IT WAS CLOSE TO MIDNIGHT MONDAY NIGHT BY THE TIME HE HEADED home. The day rolled through his mind like a movie on fast forward. He knew he'd have to slow things down, but not tonight. Then the film stopped on the last shooting and the feeling he had that he was being watched—that the shooter was still there. Was he there for another shot? Or to watch how the cops responded to the shootings. Then his stomach rolled. Maybe the shooter was watching the paramedics. He shook his head. Now his mind was creating shit. There was no reason to think cops or paramedics were at risk. Right?

He'd been referring to this guy as the shooter and not a sniper. Why? There was nothing to point to gang executions, drive-by shooting, or a renewal of the biker war. The difference was a matter of opinion than definition. Add in the high-powered rifle with a scope and high-power bullets, and you had a sniper.

He sped out of the city toward his farm. Brad glanced at

the same spot where his partner was shot four years earlier. That empty feeling never went away. Once past that location, he relaxed. It was like there was a line between stress and peace.

Four miles farther, he exited to the right and looped back toward the city. He swung onto the dirt lane. The familiar Honda was parked in front of the house. A few lights flickered inside.

He slid out of the car and headed to the house. The screen door swung open and Lobo bounded toward him, barking excitedly. Brad knelt and Lobo smothered him with wet kisses. He roughed up Lobo's head and neck, then stepped into the house, Lobo at his side.

Annie met them at the door.

"Thanks for checking on Lobo." Brad hugged Annie.

"I saw the action on TV and read the newspaper. I figured you'd be late coming home."

"Thanks for staying with him, Annie. That's sweet of you. He's fine outside. He doesn't wander far, and he'll hunt if he needs food."

"Eeew. That's gross."

Brad shrugged. "He's made friends with a feral cat. I think they hunt together."

"That's still disgusting. I made some stew and cornmeal. You must be starving."

"I am. I had a burger with Griffin about six."

"That sounds healthy."

"Not a lot of options when you're on the run. It smells great. Let me wash up and change. Then I'll eat."

When Brad came back to the kitchen in a torn University of Calgary Dinos T-shirt and shorts, dinner was on the table.

He buttered a piece of cornbread and dug into the stew. "This is awesome." He sprayed cornbread crumbs as he spoke.

"Manners. You'd think you hadn't eaten for days."

"Seems like it." He scooped up a spoonful.

"You've forgotten about the roast beef meal last night?"

"That was a spectacular meal."

Annie handed him a napkin, and he wiped his mouth.

"Seems like days ago." He held a piece of cornbread close to his mouth. "You're not my mother, you know."

Annie put her hands to her face in mock surprise. "Really?"

"Funny. Why don't you tell me about you and Charlie while I eat?"

"Aren't you going to read me my rights first, Detective?" She held her hands out for handcuffs.

"It's not an interrogation. I'm curious."

Annie laughed. "When it comes to me and guys, you're a big brother protecting his little sister. There's no, 'just curious' about it."

"I'm not that unscrupulous."

"Hah."

"So?" He scooped a large portion of stew into his mouth, swallowed, then took a long drink of milk.

Annie shrugged. "When Charlie's girlfriend, Tina, was … murdered in the spring, and … when Maggie was killed, we had something in common. You were a fucking mess, and—"

"Language." He shoveled stew into his mouth, then shoved in a healthy portion of cornbread.

"You had your own issues. It wasn't something we could help each other with."

Brad frowned. "I wasn't there for you."

"Not then. You and I were both traumatized. Charlie was,

too. At first, we talked about you. We were worried about you. Then, I don't know when it happened, we started talking about how we were doing, how we were feeling. We were there for each other. At some point, it was more than friends, more than confidants."

"Okay, stop there." Brad wiped his lips again. "I don't need the details. You know I love Charlie. He'd take bullets for either of us. It sounds sappy, but I know that. I'd do anything for you. I'm sorry I wasn't there when you needed me. But I'm glad Charlie was. He's, um, older than you."

"Yes, Brad, he is. Seven years older."

"Closer to eight." Brad slurped some milk. "That's a lot."

"By chronological age, I'm nearly nineteen. But maturity-wise, I'm much older. You know that. How could I not be with what I've been through … what we've been through?"

Brad scooped up the last of the gravy with a piece of cornbread and stared at the bowl. "I will think about this. I'm not sure how I feel about it."

Annie grabbed his bowl and bread plate. "Don't think too long or hard about it. It's not your decision."

"I only mean—"

She wrapped her arms around his shoulders. "I know you're trying to protect me. Thank you. I'm a woman. You've got important things to worry about. Put your brainpower there." She kissed him on the cheek. "Don't stay up too late. I'm heading to bed." She headed down the hall to the spare room she'd made into her own.

The next morning Brad dressed in a dark-blue summer suit with a dress shirt and loose tie. From his gun safe in his bedroom, he pulled out his Browning Hi-Power and backup gun, a CZ75. He checked both guns and placed them in holsters.

The Browning on his left hip and CZ in an ankle holster on his inside right leg. He slid three magazines into the case on his right hip and handcuffs on his belt at his back. A gravity knife into his right pocket and a mini-Maglite into his left. He stepped out of the bedroom and headed to the back door. Lobo blocked his path and held his leash in his mouth.

"Sorry, boy. No time for a jog today."

Lobo continued his stare.

"No, I can't take you to work."

Lobo didn't move.

"Oh, what the hell. Let's go." Brad opened the back door and Lobo raced out. Halfway to the car Lobo stopped and marked his territory, then bounded to the open door, and jumped in.

CHAPTER TWENTY-TWO

Tuesday Day Seven

BRAD SAT TO THE SIDE OF THE PACKED BRIEFING ROOM AND DRANK coffee while Briscoe met with the cops coming on duty at 6:00 a.m. Lobo lay at Brad's feet.

The conversation in the room was hushed—respectful. Not the loud, enthusiastic conversations of yesterday.

Briscoe reviewed the four shootings and that while they were still searching for a white van, nothing had turned up during the night. They needed to be alert and watch for any vans or box trucks, not just white ones. They needed to stay high profile, especially at gas stations, grocery stores, and malls. On the good side, there hadn't been a shooting overnight.

It was hard to know if saturating the city with marked police vehicles had made a difference. Too soon to celebrate, but just maybe the heavy police presence would keep the killers lying low. Certainly, if they were driving a white van, it was in their best interest to keep it out of sight. With all the publicity, Brad wondered if the lead on the white van was worth the effort. If he was the sniper, he'd have dumped the white van the first time it was mentioned by the press.

Every minute, every hour, gave them time to sift through the crime scenes, to evaluate tips and to re-interview witnesses. They needed a break, some pieces that fit the puzzle and pointed them in a direction.

When the briefing cleared, Brad and Lobo headed to the zoo. Sturgeon and Ames were waiting by the door.

Sturgeon glanced at Lobo but said nothing.

"Got some information for you," Ames said.

"I hope it's good news."

"Depends on your perspective." Ames passed over a few sheets of paper. "I tested the guns you found yesterday at the suspect's house. None of them match the fragments we have. The .223 ammunition he has isn't a match either."

"It's good we can eliminate the guns. We'd already eliminated the suspect. He was in our jail cells." Brad sipped his coffee.

"That's a good alibi." Ames nodded. "How many people will know what .223 ammunition looks like or what kind of gun is used?"

"Excellent point," Brad said. "Let me work on that."

"I had my team working all night." Sturgeon slid a file folder over to Brad. "We believe two of the bullets recovered and fragments from the other two shootings came from the same gun. No cartridge cases were recovered at any of the crime scenes."

"We hold back the evidence from the two bullets. Just mention the fragments to the press." Brad peered at Ames. "Any leads on the gun?"

"Hard to say." Ames shrugged. "There are dozens of guns it could be. If it were me, I'd use a Bushmaster with a good scope. It's extremely accurate, and in the hands of a skilled shooter, deadly."

"Military?" Brad asked.

Ames shook his head. "No way to know. The best I can say is he has killed before. It's one thing to sight a target or use a scope on an unmoving piece of paper. It is different shooting something, human or animal, that moves. Harder to shoot a human, unless you've done it before."

"Back to the military angle?" Brad asked.

"Or he's killed before. Another city? Province? Country?"

"But not necessarily military."

Ames shook his head. "Nope. Might be a hunter."

Brad shoved the ballistics file to the corner of his desk. "That gives us nothing to go on."

CHAPTER TWENTY-THREE

The press conference was to take place in the alley behind Police Headquarters at 8:00 a.m.. A podium faced about a dozen chairs already filled with reporters. Others stood at the side.

Brad stood behind the reporters with Lobo at his side, scanning the crowd. Steele, Zerr, and Ames stood off to the side of the podium. Llewelyn Carew strode to the mic.

"Good Morning. I am Sergeant Llewelyn Carew, Public Information Officer."

The room quieted.

"There were four murders yesterday morning. Detectives worked through the night evaluating tips. We are following leads on several suspects but have not made an arrest. We have matched bullet fragments from two of the shootings and we can confirm the bullets are .223 and fired from a high-powered rifle. I'll turn the time over to Randall Ames, one of the Tactical Support Unit snipers."

Ames stepped up to the podium with rifles slung over his

shoulders. There were a few gasps from the reporters, then cameras clicked in rapid sequence.

Brad grinned. Show and tell was about to start.

"Good morning. I, uh, we thought it might be good to show you the type of rifle we are talking about and what kind of ammunition has been used." He held up a bullet. "This one might be familiar to some of you. This is a .22 bullet, commonly used in hunting gophers." Ames showed the reporters a .22 rifle.

He set the rifle aside and held up a longer bullet.

"This is the .223, the bullet used in the shootings yesterday." Ames held up two of the rifles he had slung over his shoulders. Zerr and Steele stepped beside Ames and held out rifles. "These are four of dozens of rifles that use the .223 bullet. After the news conference, we will be at our trucks and can show you the types of rifles we are talking about and you can examine the different bullets." Ames, Steele, and Zerr stepped away from the microphone and headed to their trucks.

Brad spotted Ferguson at the front of the pack of reporters. Maybe they had a seniority system. His pink shirt didn't go well with the tartan tie and tweed jacket. *Minus ten from the Russian judge.*

Carew stepped back to the microphone. "I would like to clarify a report in the media last night." Carew tugged at his shirt collar and licked his lips. He shuffled his papers, then glanced briefly at Ferguson. "We *are* searching for a white van, but we have no information that leads us to believe the driver or shooter is a tradesperson. That was reported in error."

Take that, Angus Ferguson.

"Using 911 last night to report suspicious persons or white vans overloaded our 911 system and emergency responses were delayed because of the volume of calls."

Like I said would happen.

"Instead, we have a dedicated Sniper Tip Line we ask the media to circulate, leaving our 911 dispatch to deal with emergencies."

An invitation for every crank and nutjob in the city to call.

"We want to keep this brief, but I can take a question or two." Carew surveyed the media. His eyes passed over, then swung back to Sadie Andrus. "Miss, you have a question?"

"Sadie Andrus, CFAC TV. This shooter is a ghost. He appears and shoots, then disappears. The shootings appear random. Witnesses have not seen where the shots have come from, let alone the shooter."

"Yes, the shooter appears to be a ghost, but we all know there's no such thing as ghosts. If he hasn't already, he will make a mistake. When he does, we will be ready to pounce."

"So, you expect additional shootings?" Andrus asked.

"Uh, no. Not at all. I mean that as we investigate, we may discover the shooter made a mistake—that we will find evidence or a witness leading to his arrest. I believe the sudden burst of shootings has taken its course, and it is unlikely there will be further incidents."

"Tony King, KL radio. Should citizens change their travel habits? Should they stay home?"

Carew gripped both sides of the podium and leaned toward the reporters. "Don't let this terror control your lives. Carry on as normal. We have saturated the city with uniformed officers in marked units. The gunman would be wise to stay in hiding."

No, no, no.

It was one thing to not panic the public, to not let the terror control their lives, but Carew was taunting the shooter.

"Another question?"

"Angus Ferguson, CFCN. If the police tactical unit uses a .223 rifle, are you sure they are all accounted for?"

"I can assure you all police weapons are where they should be."

Angus fired another question as Carew finished his previous reply. "Should citizens arm themselves? I mean, if they have a gun, at least they can shoot back."

No one can say where the shots came from. What will they shoot back at?

"This is not a time to arm yourselves. The gunman has not been seen in any of the shootings. Armed citizens pose an increased risk to everyone. Not to mention, it is a criminal code offense with jail time. As I have stated, we have this under control."

"Will you be asking the RCMP for help?" Ferguson pressed. "If the city police have no leads, perhaps they can help."

"Uh, there are no plans to, uh, request assistance from outside police enforcement."

"A follow-up question—"

Carew ignored Ferguson and scanned the gathered reporters. "The tip line phone number is in your information package. We ask that you ensure this number is widely publicized. That is all for today. We will keep you up to date."

The reporters broke away in a near stampede as they raced to the TSU trucks. Ames, Zerr, and Steele were swamped by reporters asking questions and surrounded by cameramen. One thing was for sure, by tonight, everyone would know about .223 ammunition and rifles.

"Aren't you going to help with the dog and pony show?"

Lobo growled. Brad spun and faced Sadie. "Those guys have it under control."

"Because you trained them well?" Sadie smiled.

"Because they're great tactical cops."

She glanced at Lobo. His eyes locked on her. "Is he friendly?"

Brad smirked. "Most of the time."

"Is he yours?"

Brad rubbed Lobo's ears. "He's my partner."

"Partner?"

"Long story."

She raised her eyebrows. "I'd like to hear that sometime."

Brad nodded toward the TSU trucks. "That doesn't interest you?"

Sadie shrugged. "My cameraman is there. I'll do a voice-over later. Do you miss it?"

"Miss what?"

"Do you miss tactical support? It must have been fun playing war games." She used her hands to draw guns and shoot with her fingers. "The everyman dream of good guys versus bad guys."

"It wasn't like that." Brad frowned and sighed. "I guess that's the image we have. We trained hard and worked on any scenario we could think of. We trained to be ready."

"Still, shooting, blowing up shit, no-holds-barred hide and seek."

Brad smirked. "There were fun times."

Sadie pulled out a pad and a pen. "Would you like to comment on Angus Ferguson's article on you yesterday? Your side of things?"

"Don't you dare." Brad cocked his head and glared.

"Worth a try." She slid the pen and pad into her handbag. "Do you think this will work—showing the guns and ammo?"

"You never turn it off, do you?"

Sadie shrugged. "Sometimes. The guns and ammo is the simple story. I need to dig deeper, find the underlying story."

Brad shook his head and glanced over at TSU. "Sometimes, the story is just the story. Someone is killing people. Only he knows why. For us to guess is just that, a guess. We won't know why until we stop him. Even then, his reasons might not make sense to us."

Sadie pouted. "Are you sure I can't quote you?"

"Go ahead." Brad held his hands out and grinned. "But never talk to me again."

"I'm not sure I'd like that."

CHAPTER TWENTY-FOUR

Brad and Lobo slipped past the reporters to an unmarked door and took the stairs to the basement. As they headed to the zoo office, Griffin met them. "We have to head to the interview rooms."

"Why?"

"A guy just came to the front desk. He says he witnessed a shooting."

"Which one?"

Griffin shrugged. "That's what we need to find out."

They took the stairs to the second floor. Brad said, "Did you hear about the tip line?"

"Yeah," Griffin said. "911 was going crazy after the shooting last night."

They stopped outside the interview rooms. Lobo lay down beside Brad. "We don't have the human resources to deal with that volume. Who's answering the tip line?"

Griffin smirked. "Today they've got support staff reassigned.

Tomorrow they're bringing in recruits."

Brad laughed. "Are you shitting me?"

"Good experience for them."

"They'll make every call a priority," Brad said. "Then who will follow up on the tips?"

Griffin slapped Brad on the back. "I volunteered you."

Lobo growled.

Brad glanced at Lobo, shook his head, then turned back to Griffin. "Ass. I'm serious."

Griffin winked. "Archer has reassigned some other detectives to give the tips a priority, then whoever is available will do the follow-up. If it is a solid tip, it'll be you or me."

Brad opened the door to an interview room—four bare gray walls, no windows, a table and three chairs. Lobo rushed past and lay in the corner. A man, mid-fifties, maybe older, with graying hair and a five-day stubble of beard, dressed in tattered clothes, sat at the table staring at his hands. When he realized Brad was there, he glanced up. "Are you detectives?"

"Griffin and Coulter," Griffin said.

Brad and Griffin stepped into the room and grabbed two chairs.

"What's your name?" Griffin asked.

"Mackenzie Poole. Everyone calls me Mac."

"Okay, Mac, you have something to tell us?" Griffin asked. Brad leaned back in his chair and folded his arms across his chest as Mac answered, scrutinizing the man's behavior, mannerisms, and speech patterns.

"Yeah." Mac's eyes glanced to Brad, then back to Griffin. "Yesterday I saw the shooter."

"Where?"

"On Sixteenth Avenue. By the 7-Eleven and the drive-in."

Griffin nodded. "Great, tell us what you saw."

"I was in the alley, scrounging for bottles and cans," Mac said. "I go down there every day. It's a good area."

"And you saw?"

"Right, well, I heard a noise in the bushes. I thought it was a cat, but I was worried it was a dog. I've been bitten a lot." Mac glanced at Lobo and held out his scarred arm. "So, I look for the cat or dog. At first, I don't see nothin'. But then I realize the guy is in the bushes. I couldn't see him at first because he's wearing camouflage and has his face painted black."

"What did you do?"

"I kept searching for bottles."

"You didn't think it was weird a guy in camo and face paint was in the middle of the city?" Griffin asked.

Mac shrugged. "I didn't. I see lots of weirdos. But then last night I heard the radio stories about the shootings. They said if anyone saw something, they should contact the police. That's when I remembered what I'd seen."

Griffin rubbed his chin. "Why didn't you contact us last night?"

"I live on the street. I ain't got no phone. I took the bus here this morning."

"How tall was he?" Griffin asked.

"I'm not sure. He was crouched in the bushes."

Griffin pointed at Brad. "My partner is over six feet. That tall?"

"No, I don't think so."

"Shorter."

"Yeah."

"What did he weigh?" Brad asked.

"That's hard, too."

Brad sighed. Like playing twenty questions.

"Skinny, fat?" Griffin asked.

"Not slim like your partner. But not as stocky as you."

Griffin scowled.

"What about his face?" Brad asked.

The man shrugged. "As I said, he was wearing camo. Had a camo beanie, too."

"Did you see a gun?"

"No. But about five minutes later, I heard the shot."

"What time was this?"

"I don't got no watch. Morning. The burger joint wasn't open yet."

Brad glanced at Griffin and nodded toward the door.

"We'll be right back," Griffin said. "Can I get you anything?"

"Yeah, maybe a sandwich and a Coke."

"You got it." Griffin followed Brad to the hall and closed the door. "So?"

Brad shrugged. "There's just enough there to make sense. But not enough to give us anything to work with."

"We could go back and check it out."

"Let's talk to him again before we chase this. I'll get him a Coke."

"And a sandwich."

Brad strode away.

When they entered the interview room, Brad set a Coke and a bag of chips on the table, then sat across from Mac.

Mac popped the Coke and took a drink, then glanced at Brad. "Sandwich?"

"Too early," Brad said. "Cafeteria hasn't made any yet. I hope the chips will do. We've got a few additional questions."

The man guzzled the Coke. "No problem. I want to help."

"Tell me again about the man in the bushes," Brad said. "I didn't take notes. Sorry to make you go through this again. What color was his hair?"

"Yeah, it was black."

"Facial hair?"

Mac shook his head. "Nope."

"What do you know about guns?"

"Not much. Shot a .22 as a kid."

"If you had to guess, what kind of gun?"

The man nodded. "Bigger than a .22."

"With a scope?"

Mac took a drink. "Yeah, I think so."

"What color was his camouflage?" Brad asked.

"You know, the usual, spotted green."

Brad nodded. "And he blended into the bushes?"

"Yeah, pretty much."

"We're gonna check on your sandwich." Brad stood.

"Hey, I got questions," Mac said.

Brad stopped at the door. "Fire away."

"Is there, like, some kind of reward for this information?"

"Yes, there is." Brad followed Griffin into the hall.

"His story is changing," Griffin said.

"Sure is," Brad said. "At first, I thought he was confused. But I was at the alley. The leaves have already fallen. Someone in green camouflage would stand out, not blend in."

Griffin nodded. "When he asked about the reward, I figured he was playing us. Frickin' waste of time."

"Let's kick him loose with a couple of sandwiches."

CHAPTER TWENTY-FIVE

DOWNTOWN CALGARY HAD A DOZEN BARS WITHIN A TWO-BLOCK radius—none of them five stars. And while it sounded fancy, like its Toronto namesake, the York Hotel in Calgary did not serve the elite. At one time, it did, but that was over fifty years ago. As it stood currently, in 1980, little of the glory days remained. The bonus was that if you were thrown out of one bar, you could crawl to the next. The choices appeared endless—the Legion, St. Regis, and the Calgarian. Or across the street to the Queens, the St. Louis, or King Eddy. All of them were close to the homeless shelter where they were staying. Dozens of reporter's hands shot into the air. Carew waved them off. "I will provide further information as we receive it.

This afternoon Pittman and Hirsch picked the Legion—cleaner and better lit than the others. The walls were decorated with armed forces memorabilia, Second World War pictures, and several displays of medals. Pittman had shown a card at the door and they were ushered in. The clientele was upscale, and it wasn't quite as loud as the other bars. The dinner crowd had shuffled in. A mix of food odors from the buffet filled the bar. Most patrons had stopped smoking to eat.

In the corner, they drank beer and played pool. Hirsch scratched on the eight ball and hung his head. "How much?"

"Five dollars a game," Pittman said.

"You know I don't have that."

"You're good for it." Pittman grabbed his beer and took a swig as he returned to the TV. "Hey, it's the cops." He headed to the bar. "Bartender, turn that up."

Hirsch grabbed his beer and joined Pittman.

Text at the bottom of the screen said this video was from the police press conference that morning. "There were four murders yesterday morning."

Pittman stared wide eyed at the TV.

"We playin' or not?" Hirsch asked.

"Fuck off," Pittman said. "I want to hear this."

Sergeant Llewelyn Carew said, "Detectives worked through the night evaluating tips. We are following leads on several suspects but have not made an arrest."

"Ha, no leads," Pittman said. "Breaks my heart."

"We have matched bullet fragments from some shootings, and we can confirm the bullets are .223 and fired from a high-powered rifle."

"How the hell did they do that?" Pittman asked.

Hirsch shook his head. "They're bluffing. All they have is pieces of bullets."

"Jeez. The police are doing a show and tell." Pittman downed the last of his beer.

"They're desperate," Hirsch said.

"I can't watch this. I'm getting another beer. Want one?"

"Yeah, sure." Hirsch stared at the TV.

A couple of minutes later, Pittman handed Hirsch a beer. "What'd I miss?"

Hirsch grabbed the beer and took a gulp. "He showed .223 ammunition and some rifles. He's going to let the reporters play with the guns."

They went back to their pool game and after a few shots each, Hirsch glanced up, slapped Pittman on the chest, and pointed to the TV.

"Who the hell is she?" Pittman blurted.

The camera had moved off Carew to a lady asking a question. "Sadie Andrus, CFAC TV. This shooter is a ghost. He appears and shoots, then disappears. The shootings appear random. Witnesses have not seen where the shots have come from, let alone the shooter."

"Ha. She says we're ghosts," Hirsch said.

"I ain't no ghost and I'd prove it to her—over and over." Pittman grabbed his crotch.

"Yes, the shooter appears to be a ghost, but we all know there's no such thing as ghosts," Carew replied. "If he hasn't already, he will make a mistake. When he does, we will be ready to pounce."

"Like I said, I'd pounce on her." Pittman grinned at the TV.

"So, you expect more shootings?" Andrus asked.

"Count on it, lady," Hirsch said.

"Uh, no. Not at all. I mean that as we investigate, we may discover the shooter made a mistake—that we will find evidence or a witness leading to his arrest. I believe the sudden burst of shootings has taken its course, and it is unlikely there will be further incidents."

Pittman's beer was halfway to his mouth. "Fuck you!"

"Hey, you guys, knock it off or get out." The bartender headed out from behind the bar, a baseball bat at this side. "We don't put up with that shit here. Go to one of the other bars."

Hirsch and held out his hands. "Sorry, buddy. We disagreed on a shot."

"Yeah, well, keep it down." He headed back behind the bar.

Hirsch grabbed Pittman and dragged him away from the TV. Carew droned on behind them. "We posted a reward for information that leads to the arrest and conviction of the sniper," Carew said. "The reward, raised by the community, is twenty-five-thousand dollars. Information on the sniper should be reported to the tip line, which we set up this morning."

Pittman shook free from Hirsch's grasp. "I should turn you in. I could use that money."

CHAPTER TWENTY-SIX

THE MORE PITTMAN DRANK, THE LOUDER HE GOT, ATTRACTING THE attention of a couple of bouncers. Hirsch had to drag Pittman out of the bar that evening. At their car, Pittman said, "You drive."

"Where are we going?" Hirsch asked.

"Jus' listen." Pittman belched. "Okay, keep going on this road." After a few minutes, Pittman pointed. "There's a gas station. Pull in across the street and back in, so the trunk is facing across the street."

"Pitt, what are you planning?"

"I'm gonna do the shooting. I'll show you how it's done."

"Not a good idea, man. You're hammered."

Pittman opened the door and almost fell on the pavement. He grabbed the doorframe, pulled himself upright and staggered the few steps to the back door. Hirsch jumped out of the car and helped Pittman get the shooting perch ready. Pittman squeezed his bulk through the opening. "Could you have made this smaller?"

"I made it for me."

"I don't think I can get back out."

"No problem. Let's call it a night, find someplace to open the trunk and you can get out that way."

"Fuck you. Get in the front and pick out a target."

Hirsch climbed back into the car and adjusted the rearview mirrors. He keyed the new walkie-talkie. "Pittman, can you hear me?"

"I can fuckin' hear you. Stop yelling, that's why we got these radios. Now tell me what's going on."

The back of the car bounced like someone was jumping on the trunk.

"What the hell are you doing?" Hirsch peered over his shoulder. All he saw was Pittman's large ass wedged in the opening.

"I'm set. Stop yappin'."

"There's a car pulling in from your right. A lady is getting out of the car. Do you see her?" Her brown wavy hair, the way she moved, reminded Hirsch of his soon-to-be ex-wife.

"Hang on." The car bounced again. "Yeah. Yeah, I got her. She's unscrewing the gas cap."

"Right. Be patient. Wait until you have a full-body target."

"Shut your yap. I know how to shoot."

"Patience ..."

The shot echoed through the car. Hirsch shivered.

It was after 9:00 p.m. when Brad headed to his car, calling it a night. Mentally and physically exhausted, he'd try to get some sleep, but knew he'd replay Monday's events over and over with the same questions. What had they missed? Why four killings in one day? Why those victims? Why those locations? Had they missed something, anything that could have prevented those shootings?

The police radio still buzzed with cops pulling over white vans. One cop told dispatch the guy they'd stopped said police had already checked him out five times. The officer suggested they put police tape on any van they checked so they'd be less likely to stop white vans that had already been checked.

Not a bad idea. You don't realize how many white vans there are until you focus on them. It looked like every second vehicle was a white van or box truck.

He crossed Eighth Street heading for home when dispatch announced, "All units, report of a lady down. A gas station, Kensington Road and Fourteenth Street NW. EMS is responding."

Oh shit. Brad's stomach sank. *No, not another.*

The radio lit up with cops answering. Brad reached for his mic, then realized he'd never find an opening to talk. He swung up Tenth Street to Kensington Road and sped up as he headed west. He arrived in the parking lot at the same time as EMS. Bystanders waved them to the north side. Several cruisers pulled in behind.

Brad jumped out of the car and shouted, "Everyone step away from the patient and go back to your cars."

He pointed to two of the first cops to arrive. "Make sure the witnesses stay in their cars. No one leaves until we interview them."

Brad grabbed his portable radio. "Dispatch, set up a tight perimeter around the gas station. We have enough units here on scene, so don't dispatch more. Then block all intersections within a ten-block radius. No one drives in except emergency vehicles, and no one leaves. Lock this area down. Get me Deputy Chief Archer, Detective Griffin, Sergeant Sturgeon, the Crime Scene Unit and TSU."

"Roger, Coulter."

Brad glanced around the scene. What if the shooter was still here? He might be bolder. With the cops and paramedics, there were a lot of targets. "Dispatch, I need TSU here." He pointed to a cop. "Move the ambulance close beside the paramedics." The fire department parked behind the ambulance. He hoped that would be safe. He headed over to Amir Sharma and Jill Cook, where they worked on the lady in her mid-forties. Her eyes stared unseeing to the sky. Her stomach was soaked with blood. She scared the crap out of them when she gasped.

Brad gasped, too. "She's alive?"

Sharma peered up. "We've stopped the bleeding, but we're getting out of here. We need an escort to the Foothills Hospital."

"Sure." Brad pointed at two cops. "You heard the paramedic—give them an escort. Have dispatch shut down the intersections between here and Foothills."

They nodded.

Cook and the firefighters wheeled the patient to the ambulance.

Sharma stood and pulled Brad to the side. "We've got a good chance with her. I don't think it was a direct hit. Her stomach is open—like a knife slash. No exit wound."

"She was knifed. A mugging?"

Sharma shook his head. "Hard to tell. I haven't seen a wound like this. It seems like a slash, but it's like she was shot across her body, not directly through mass, like the others." Sharma rotated toward the ambulance. "I gotta go."

"Will she be able to answer questions?"

"No, she's unconscious. She'll go straight to surgery. You won't be able to talk to her for at least twenty-four hours."

Sharma jogged to the ambulance and closed the back door behind him. Sirens blared as police cruisers and the ambulance left the scene.

Brad peered at a man, early thirties who had been holding the patient's head.

"I'm Detective Coulter."

"Rod. Rod Fradette."

"Did you see what happened?" Brad asked.

Fradette glanced at the car. "She was filling her car, then I heard a ping, then she fell."

Brad cocked his head. "A ping, not a gunshot?"

"The gunshot came right after."

It *was* a gunshot wound, not a stab wound. "What did you do?"

"I ran to her, saw she was bleeding, and yelled for someone to call 911. I tried to stop the bleeding until the paramedics arrived."

He nodded. "Was she conscious?"

"Yes. She was screaming and saying how her stomach hurt. Blood was pouring out. A guy gave me his sweatshirt, and I put it over her stomach and applied pressure. She kept asking what happened and saying she didn't want to die."

"Did she give her name?"

"Jolanda."

"Last name?"

"Nope. Then she stopped talking."

Brad used his flashlight to examine the back quarter panel of her car near the gas cap. There were lots of scratches and dings, but one scratch—more pronounced than the others on the door-post—flashed when the light shone on it.

A dark Suburban pulled into the gas station. Steele and Zerr exited and headed to Brad.

"Dispatch said you needed us here," Steele said.

"I had this uneasy feeling that maybe the shooter was still here. We protected the patient with the ambulance and a firetruck. But if he started shooting, I wanted you guys here."

"Where do you think the shot came from?" Zerr asked.

"I think it might have been a ricochet."

Brad faced away from the gas station toward Kensington Road. "It might be the same as the others. From across the street and maybe a hundred to a hundred and fifty yards."

"We'll check it out."

"Detective Coulter."

Brad faced one of the uniformed cops.

"You should talk to the guy who was helping the paramedics again. I heard him say he saw a van drive away."

"Thanks." Brad found the good Samaritan sitting on a bench and sat beside him. "Thanks for your help. You gave her a chance."

He stared at the car, gas pump and blood. "I hope she's gonna be okay."

Brad leaned back. "I heard you saw something else."

Fradette nodded. "While I was sitting here, I went over everything that happened. While I was trying to stop the bleeding, I heard lots of vehicle noises, but it's a busy road all the time. I'm not sure why I turned, but when I did, I saw two vehicles out on the street. One was a white van; the other was a dark-colored sedan, maybe dark blue or green, a four-door. They were heading in opposite directions."

"When did you see them?"

"I'm not sure. Time was both standing still and racing past. It seemed like forever for the paramedics to get here. Jolanda was fading fast."

"Before we got here or after?"

"I think before, or maybe about the same time."

"Do you see the car here?"

"Not the same car, but like that one." Fradette pointed at Brad's car.

CHAPTER TWENTY-SEVEN

Wednesday Day Eight

THE MAYOR INSISTED THE 8:00 A.M. PRESS CONFERENCE TAKE PLACE on the steps of City Hall. The archaic sandstone building made an impressive backdrop with the clock tower centered behind the podium. The new mayor, Roger Kearse, wanted everyone to know he was in charge, that he had his fingerprints all over the investigation.

That was the problem, Brad thought. The last thing they needed was a politician offering advice on a situation they had no experience with.

When Kearse was a news reporter, he'd always treated the cops fairly, but more was at stake—his reputation and his ego.

For the show, Kearse had pulled out all stops and cashed in favors. The chairs on the top step of City Hall were filled with federal politicians, provincial politicians, and aldermen. Deputy Chief Archer sat, arms across his chest with a sour look that shouted *hemorrhoid problems*. Archer had sent his staff to find Brad earlier in the morning. Luckily word reached Brad and he avoided them.

Brad stood off to the side, close enough to hear, far enough away to go unnoticed. Then Archer's dark eyes swept in Brad's direction. Even from this far away, he felt the penetrating stare. This might come back to haunt him.

Sergeant Llewelyn Carew stepped to the podium and tapped the mic. "Test. Test. Good Morning. As most of you know, I'm Sergeant Llewelyn Carew, Public Information Officer for the police. Mayor Roger Kearse has asked me to moderate this press conference and he would like to say a few words."

Kearse stood and approached the mic. Where Carew was tall and thin, Kearse was short and squat. He leaned toward the mic, his trademark smile in place. "Thank you, Sergeant, and thank you for the excellent job you are doing keeping the media informed."

Brad muttered under his breath, "*Gag*."

"I felt it was important to keep the media and the citizens up to date on the shootings and the investigation. I know we'd all like additional information, to know there were suspects, or that police had made an arrest. But remember, it is only forty-eight hours since the first shooting. It is unprecedented to have these many murders in our city. I ask that we are patient with the police. I know they are overwhelmed by the gravity of the situation, but I also have the utmost respect for them, and I know they will lead this to a successful conclusion. Arrests are imminent."

Oh, damn.

"I would also like to thank representatives from the federal and provincial governments who are here supporting us today and who have guaranteed that anything we need, I just ask. I can also say the RCMP has called and will assist in any manner required."

Double damn.

"Sergeant, I'll turn the time back to you."

"Thank you, Mayor Kearse." Carew surveyed the gathered media. "I can take a few questions."

Angus Ferguson bullied himself to the front.

"Sergeant. The five victims were adults. Yet many citizens are expressing concern for their children's safety as well. Are our children in danger?"

Uh oh.

"Children should continue to go to school and not be afraid. Starting today, we are placing police officers at the schools when the children arrive and when school is out. As well, the children are in the school all day, so I don't see how a shooter would be able to attack."

Brad closed his eyes and shook his head.

"Sergeant," Sadie Andrus called. "You said police are at the schools, morning and afternoon. Aren't you making the cops targets? If the bullet is a .223, will their ballistic vests stop that bullet?"

Carew leaned into the mic. "Our officers are well-trained and aware of the risks they take every day, not just this week. As we assigned officers to the schools, not one officer refused to go. There was no grumbling. The children are in good hands. A final note, the reward for information leading to the arrest and conviction of the shooter is twenty-five thousand thanks to the community. Information on the shooter must be called to the tip line. Please do not use 911 as our emergency lines are being overwhelmed with calls. Thank you, everyone, that is all for today."

Carew escorted the politicians back into City Hall.

Brad leaned against the wall. The question about the kids had his stomach rolling. It wasn't good enough having cops there. They weren't talking about a guy with a knife or a handgun. He was skilled and didn't need to get close. It was hard to know, but Brad felt the five shots had come from over a hundred yards away. Heck. Maybe two hundred and fifty yards. He glanced at the roof of City Hall and Police Headquarters. If you didn't know what you were searching for, nothing would seem out of the ordinary. But Brad spotted the police snipers he'd positioned, just in case. He spun to cross the street to Police Headquarters.

"Detective Coulter."

Dang, didn't leave fast enough. He rubbed his face and turned. "Good morning, Ms. Andrus."

"Sadie."

"Sadie."

"Detective, off the record, *are* kids safe?"

Brad grinned. "Off the record, I know that nothing is ever off the record."

Sadie laughed. "And I thought you were just a dumb cop."

"I spent years in the St. Louis Hotel, where Roger Kearse tried every play in the book to get information out of my TSU team and me." Brad smirked. "He never succeeded—even on the rare times he bought us a round of beer. Very rare. Have a pleasant day." He took a couple of steps.

"Detective … Brad."

He stopped.

"Kids aren't safe, are they?"

"I thought the shooting had ended Monday morning. Then there was a shooting last night. There's still no reason to think kids are the target." Brad sighed. "But I don't think anyone is safe. There's nothing in common with the victims."

"Do you think he'll shoot again?"

Brad shrugged. "I have no clue."

"He could target anyone, including cops."

"Including cops."

"If you could get a message out, what would you say?"

"I wouldn't say anything, Ms. Andrus."

"I promise your name will never appear."

His brain said, walk away. His gut said, take a chance. It might save lives. "I'd say everyone needs to change their routines. If you have to go shopping, park as close to the store as you can. Keep the car between you and the entrance. Minimize the time you are outside and exposed. At gas stations, fuel up at the inside pump with the vehicle between you and the street if possible. When it comes to kids, there are a few things that might pay off. Buses should drop kids off at the back of the schools. They should park with the bus door as close to the schools as possible. The bus will provide protection. If parents are dropping kids off, the same thing. Get to the back of the school or to a door that is not exposed to the street."

"Thank you," Sadie said.

Brad nodded and headed across the street. He'd either save lives or end his career. But hell, he'd ended his career a dozen times already.

When Brad got back to the zoo, Archer was leaning against a wall, arms crossed, jaw clenched. Archer, in a charcoal suit, dressed like he'd just stepped out of a fashion magazine. Griffin was sitting at his desk wiping donut powder off this blue suit jacket. "Just interviewed Jolanda D'Amore."

Brad set his jacket on his chair. "Great. What did she say?"

Griffin frowned and pulled out his notebook. "Not much that will help us. She said everything happened so fast. She was standing facing her car, watching her kids, when she heard a *ping* and then her stomach split open and she was overwhelmed by white-hot pain. She collapsed as the blood poured out of her. The next thing she remembers is waking up in the recovery room."

"The witness, Fradette, talked about a ping," Brad said.

Griffin picked up a file. "Sturgeon gave this to me. They've examined D'Amore's car. There's a recent long scratch on the rear quarter panel that leads toward where D'Amore was filling the car. Best guess is a ricochet. He will do additional tests today."

Brad scratched his chin. "How did he miss a stationary target?"

Archer peered in from the door. "Walk with me."

"Uh oh," Griffin said. "Coulter's in trouble."

Brad followed Archer down the hall. His gut did flip flops. Why did Archer want to see him? Had Archer talked to Dr. Keller? Was this it? He'd be suspended.

"What's up, Chief?"

Archer stopped and peered at Brad, his gray eyes mere slits. "How are you doing? And don't give me bullshit."

Brad shrugged. "I'm fine."

"Fine is a shitty answer."

Brad swallowed hard, failing to maintain eye contact. "I'm good." He focused anywhere but at Archer. "Griffin and I are all over the shootings."

"Your head is clear? You're dialed in?"

"Yeah."

Archer pursed his lips and nodded. "Tell me about your altercation at the domestic Saturday night."

Oh shit. "You know?"

"Of course, I know." Archer's voice rose, and his eyes bored into Brad. "You can't hide things from me."

"It was a onetime thing."

Archer's eyebrows raised. "You believe that?"

Brad licked his lips. Damn, why did he do that? This is what it was like being on the other side of an interrogation. "It took me by surprise, that's all."

"A flashback?"

"Something like that."

"Maybe you need to talk to Dr. Keller."

"Sure, but he's away until next week."

"Next week, then." Archer cocked his head and stared at Brad. "I'll let you get back to work."

When Brad entered the zoo, Griffin glanced up from the reports he'd been reading. "Coulter getting a timeout?"

"Funny."

Brad sat at his desk. Archer smelled a rat, and that made Brad nervous.

CHAPTER TWENTY-EIGHT

AFTER ARCHER LEFT, GRIFFIN HEADED UPSTAIRS TO COLLECT THE tips. Brad ignored the ringing phone as he stared at the city map on the wall. He'd marked the location of each shooting with a red pin.

The locations appeared random, except that they surrounded the city core. None in the core, but close, between Sixteenth Avenue to the north and Seventeenth Avenue to the south. The harder he stared, the less he saw. Too many shootings but no clues, no evidence.

"Detective Coulter."

Brad glanced over. "Yup."

Constable Mullen stepped into the office. "There's a phone call for you."

"Take a message." Brad waved Mullen away. "I'll call back when I can."

"The caller insisted, sir. I think you should take this call."

"Okay. Where's the call?"

"It's the flashing light on your phone."

Brad glanced at his desk. "Right. Thanks."

Mullen closed the door as he left.

Brad grabbed the receiver and punched the flashing button. "Coulter." Perhaps harsher than he'd intended.

"Detective, it's Sadie Andrus. Sorry to—"

"Ms. Andrus, I am swamped and—"

"Detective, you need to listen. I received a note at work. It's addressed to you."

"What?" Brad leaned forward.

"When I got to work this morning, there was an envelope on my desk. It says: *For Detective Coulter only.*"

"Did you open it?"

"Of course not. But someone did. Possibly a guy in the mailroom. The note is attached to the envelope by a paperclip."

Brad grabbed his jacket off his chair as he stood. "We need to meet. I'm coming to your office."

"Not here."

Brad paused, phone at his ear. "Where then?"

"Truckstop on Barlow. You know the one?"

"Yes." Interestingly, she picked one of his breakfast stops.

Mid-morning Brad sat in a booth at the back of the restaurant, eyes scrutinizing everyone who came in. He'd already checked out the half dozen patrons—nothing suspicious so far. He wondered if this was a set-up. Something to get him away from the command center. A way to get him alone and pump him for information. Had it even been Ms. Andrus? It sounded like her. He should have asked a test question. Jeez. Now he was overthinking everything. Better that than the alternative. He had told no one where he was going. First overthinking, now paranoia. He shook his head and sipped his coffee, his eyes seldom wandering from the entrance.

The door opened, and Andrus stepped in. Brad sipped his coffee as her eyes searched the restaurant, finally landing on him. She slid into the booth across from him. He stared at her hands clutching the envelope inside a plastic bag. Slender fingers, clear nail polish and her fingers—and fingerprints—on the plastic bag.

"That's the envelope?"

She held it out to him. It was addressed: *Saidy Andrews. CFAC.* The handwriting was sloppy, and her name was misspelled.

He waved to the waitress. "A coffee for the lady. Refill mine, please."

The waitress refilled his coffee, poured coffee for Sadie, and headed to the kitchen.

Brad sipped his coffee.

Andrus stared at her cup. "I just sit here and hold the plastic bag?"

Another sip.

"Look, before you make a bigger ass of yourself than you already have, I did not handle the envelope or note with my hands. As soon as I saw it, I grabbed a plastic bag and some tweezers. I put both the note and envelope in the bag. I figured it might be the significant break in the case."

"Or your opportunity for a national story." Brad squinted over his cup.

"Sure. That's my job. I'm trying to help."

He took another sip of coffee, then set the cup on the table.

"Angus Ferguson hasn't been a lot of help reopening wounds and questioning my abilities."

"I already told you I'm not like him."

Brad reached into his pocket, pulled out a pair of latex gloves, and slid them on. "I'll take that." He set the plastic bag on the table, with the note facing up.

Andrus grabbed two coffee creamers and two sugar, stirred the coffee, and took a drink. She sighed. "My, that is good."

"First coffee of the day?"

"No, third. I don't function without coffee. Especially in the morning."

Brad set his coffee to the side of the table. They had something in common. Coffee. He preferred his black. Andrus, two cream, two sugar. Just like Annie. A double-double.

Brad read the note.

Dear Policeman Colter
I am that I am
You will hear from me again
I only talk to Colter

"What does he mean?" Sadie asked.

Brad slid the note to the side. "Tell me how you found the note."

"When I got to work after the press conference, I immediately went to get a coffee. When I reached my desk, I saw the envelope and note propped up against my phone. I was about to grab it when I saw it was addressed to you." She held her coffee in two hands, took a sip, then leaned across the table. Her voice was a whisper as she said, "I scanned the office. I thought I'd be able to figure out who put it there. But I was the first one into the newsroom. The night guys left about 4:00 a.m."

"What time did you get to work?"

"About 8:45."

"And no one else was in the room?"

"Nope."

"What did you do next?"

She smiled. "What did I do next, or what did I want to do?"

"I know what you wanted to do."

"You bet. I wanted to grab that note and write the story of the decade. *Sniper Contacts City Cop.* I must have stared at the note and envelope for twenty minutes. I reached for it several times. I was arguing with myself. You know, the angel on one shoulder and the devil on the other."

"Who wins?"

She smiled again. "Sometimes the devil." She let that hang in the air for a few moments, then sat back and frowned. "The angel. That's when I put them in the plastic bag. I didn't have your direct line, so I had to go through the switchboard. After being on hold for close to fifteen minutes, I gave up."

Brad chuckled. 911, the hotline and the switchboard to Police Headquarters were overwhelmed by callers.

"Then I called the PIO's office. I got an idiot who wouldn't even take my name and number. I said I needed to talk to Detective Brad Coulter about the shootings. He said he works for the PIO and they have nothing to do with the investigation and I should call the hotline. I said all lines were busy. He said they were getting a lot of tips. I lost my temper and asked for his name. He said, Regis Allard. Why did I want that? I told him I needed it so when I saw you, I could tell you how people died because he was an idiot."

Brad stared over his coffee.

Sadie smirked. "That's when he transferred the call to dispatch."

Brad took a gulp of his coffee. "Sadie. Thank you for bringing this to me. But I've got to go." He grabbed the plastic bag and stood. "Remember, you can't print this."

Andrus followed him outside. "I brought this to you. It's my story."

"I'll call you when you can print it."

Sadie stood, hands on her hips. "Coulter, you don't have my phone number." She held out a business card.

He took the card and slipped it into his pocket. As he started to leave, Sadie coughed and held out her hand. Brad handed her his business card. She glanced at it and handed it back. "Your direct line, please."

CHAPTER TWENTY-NINE

Brad had radioed ahead, and when he sprinted into Archer's office, Sturgeon, Griffin, Devlin, and Archer were sitting around the conference table. Sturgeon and Griffin were drinking coffee and sharing bigger and better stories. Devlin was reading Sports Illustrated.

Archer set aside a report he had been proofing. "What's got you so fired up?"

"The shooter made contact."

"No shit," Griffin said. "How?"

Brad handed the letter to Sturgeon. "Fingerprint this right away. Make a copy of the envelope and note and get it to me."

Sturgeon nodded. "I can take photos right away. Give me ten minutes. The fingerprints will take longer."

"What does it say?" Archer asked.

Dear Policeman Colter

I am that I am

You will hear from me again
I only talk to Colter

"What the hell," Griffin said. "How do we know this is legit?"

"Good question," Archer said.

"Why not just deliver it here?" Griffin asked.

Brad scoffed. "If you were the shooter would you walk into a police station?"

"I would if I was a smug asshole," Griffin replied.

"So, you would, then." Sturgeon took the note and left the room.

"I've seen that saying before." Brad chewed his bottom lip. "Recently."

"With the shootings?" Archer asked.

Brad slowly nodded. "The picnic table."

"What?" Griffin asked. "Where?"

"The fourth shooting on Sixteenth Avenue. I was across the street at Peters' sitting at a picnic table staring back at the scene. When I glanced down, I noticed the top of the table was littered with carved names, dates, and hearts. But I also noticed this saying. Probably because it appeared newer than the rest."

Archer shook his head. "Let me get this straight. You saw the saying, I Am That I Am, carved in a picnic table at the murder scene Monday?"

"Yup. I thought nothing of it at the time, though."

"What the hell does it mean?" Archer asked.

"Not a clue," Brad said. "Unless it is a code so we'd know the letter is real."

"Exactly." Devlin leaned forward. "To me, that confirms the message."

"It doesn't tell us much," Griffin said.

"More than you think." Devlin leaned forward. "There's some good news."

"How do you figure?" Griffin asked.

"He's made contact," Devlin explained. "He may be bragging, but I think he wants to negotiate and has picked the negotiator: Brad."

"I'm not a negotiator, you are," Brad said.

"Sure," Devlin said. "I'll do the negotiating, but you'll be the voice. I'll guide you every step of the way."

"Why did he pick me?"

Devlin shrugged. "That's important. Carew has been all over the TV, but he picked you. Carew has been underestimating him. Maybe that pissed him off. He's not going to deal with politicians or Archer. He saw you on TV or read about you in the paper. You're the name he knows and cares about. He told us his terms. He will only talk to you, and that is important to him. We keep this information to our group and out of the press. We'll create a statement for Brad to make later today, so the shooter knows we received the letter and we want to negotiate."

"The press will want more," Brad said. "They'll think we're hiding something."

Devlin nodded. "We are hiding something. By changing the voice of the department and throwing Carew to the bench, we can set a fresh course with the media. Tell them we want to cooperate, be partners, that they are important in the shooter's arrest. They'll eat that up."

"One problem," Brad said.

"What's that?" Archer asked.

"Sadie Andrus of CFAC. She's the one they sent the note to. She brought the letter to me directly without running the story, and I told her she can't report this without our go-ahead. She wasn't overly happy."

"Fine." Devlin shrugged.

"Doesn't matter," Archer said. "Griffin. Find her and bring her here."

Griffin glanced at Archer. "What if she doesn't want to come?"

"Use your charm."

Devlin laughed.

Archer glared at Devlin. "Worst case, arrest her."

"If you arrest her, she'll be our enemy for life," Brad said. "That will be her ticket to the national networks."

"We don't want that." Archer shrugged. "I guess we're back to charm."

As Griffin left the office, Sturgeon came in with copies of the note. Archer and Devlin grabbed one and read.

Sturgeon pulled out a chair and shook his head. "While I was developing the photos of the note, we dusted the envelope for prints. The same two sets are on the edge of the note."

"That's how Sadie would have held it." She didn't tell Brad the complete truth. "The mail boy, too."

"We need to get their prints so we can eliminate them," Sturgeon said.

"Griffin has gone to collect her," Archer said.

"Collect her?" Sturgeon asked.

"He means ask nicely with persuasion," Devlin said.

"Oh, that kind of collecting," Sturgeon said. "Let me know when she's here. We'll take her prints."

"There's one more thing," Archer said.

"What's that?" Brad asked.

"The RCMP want to assist us with a profile of the sniper."

"Devlin and I don't work too well with the RCMP," Brad said.

"I'm painfully aware of that," Archer said. "I will have control, the RCMP have no authority here, but it's a good idea to work with them and use their resources. They will keep working on the profile. They'll be here in a day or two. They're excited about profiling."

"Like the stuff Tina was working on with Wolfe," Brad said.

Devlin's jaw tightened. Archer glanced at Devlin, then continued. "The profile is all I authorized them to do. The commissioner of the RCMP offered the use of their crime lab in Edmonton. Anything we need to be analyzed is a priority."

"Who do they have working on the profile?" Brad asked.

"Stinson," Archer replied.

"Ah, Chief," Brad said. "Not Stinson—"

Brad hated waiting. There were too many things to do. He needed to get back to the zoo. He checked his watch for the twentieth time. Finally, a knock at the door.

Griffin opened the door and Ms. Andrus entered. She stepped away from Griffin and glared at Brad.

Archer stood and extended his hand. "I'm Deputy Chief Archer and—"

"I know who you are."

"My apologies, Ms. Andrus. That was my error. Please." He nodded toward a chair.

Andrus accepted Archer's offer, then sat across from Brad. She glared at him with her arms folded across her chest. "Am I under arrest?"

Archer leaned forward and held his hands out. "Absolutely not, Ms. Andrus. I merely want to talk."

"Strange way of starting a conversation. Dragging me out of my station in front of the news staff. That will be the lead story on the news today."

"I apologize. It is urgent that I speak with you."

She glanced at Brad, and then her eyes flicked back to Archer. "Go on."

"It's about the note delivered to you."

"I have said nothing about the contents." She glanced at Brad again. "He told me I couldn't."

Archer nodded. "That's good."

"Obviously, it is vital to your investigation. But I would have had the scoop of the year."

"Perhaps," Archer said. "And perhaps with the release of the information there would have been additional shootings."

"Don't put that on me." Andrus leaned toward Archer. "What do you want?"

"Your continued silence about the note."

"I already gave that to Detective Coulter. I've kept my word." She sat back and crossed her arms. "What's in it for me?"

Archer sat back, his fingers steepled under his chin.

Andrus pushed away from the table and stood. "If I'm not under arrest"—she glanced at Brad—"or a suspect, then I'd like to go."

"I'll ensure you have the complete story, start to finish—when I can," Archer said.

Andrus cocked her head. "Everything?"

"Every piece of information we gathered," Archer said.

Andrus scrutinized Archer. "I don't mention the note, and I get the exclusive story? Including interviews with Coulter?"

CHAPTER THIRTY

BRAD SPENT HALF AN HOUR STARING AT THE NOTES ON THE WALL OF the gym containing at least fifty suspects. Every time they cleared someone, at least two additional suspects appeared. Following up on every lead was time consuming, and they didn't have enough cops. Maybe it was time to get the RCMP involved.

You don't realize the distrust there is in a city until something like the shootings happen. Everyone with a grudge with a neighbor, brother-in-law, co-worker, or boss took advantage of the opportunity to call the tip line and get that person in trouble.

Brad headed back to his office and pulled out the sandwich he'd picked up in the cafeteria. No sooner had he taken a bite when Constable Mullen knocked on the door and stepped in. "Sir, I have a tip here you might want to check."

"From where?" Brad set down his sandwich.

"It came on the tip line, sir."

"What makes this tip so important?"

"The lady who called is a receptionist for a chiropractor. She likes him, but she's scared. He was not in the office for at least some shootings. Then he comes back to the office a short time later."

"I'm still not convinced."

"She told me his schedule on the days of the shootings. His office is here." Mullen pointed to the map. His finger landed around the nexus of the shootings. "He started work at ten."

Brad snatched the paper out of Mullen's hand. "Excellent work."

Brad circled the block a few times and then found the chiropractor's car in a parking lot behind his building. His stall had a placard with the man's name on it.

"Nice car," Griffin said. "I'm in the wrong profession."

"Was there ever any doubt?" Brad asked.

"Only when I think about the cost of putting kids through college."

"You want them to be more better smarter than you?"

Griffin rolled his eyes. "You're the one in the wrong profession, letting a law degree go to waste."

"You'd miss me. Does Dr. Wilken have any traffic tickets on that fancy BMW?"

"Nada. Never been arrested. Never filed a complaint. Regular boy scout."

"Those are the ones you need to worry about," Brad said. "No witness mentioned they saw a BMW at any crime scene."

"Or he's smart enough not to use this car."

"Good point." Brad opened his door. "Let's go have a chat."

They crossed the street and headed up to the second-floor chiropractic offices. They entered and stepped to the reception desk. "Detectives Coulter and Griffin," Brad said. "We'd like to talk to Dr. Wilken."

The color drained from the receptionist's face, her eyes widening. "I … I'll get him." She used her desk to steady herself as she stood. As she headed down the hallway, she glanced over her shoulder. Then she was back with a tall man, at least six-foot-two and skinny as a rail. He stopped several feet from them.

"I'm Dr. Wilken. My receptionist says you two are detectives?"

"Right" Brad showed his badge. "Is there a place we can talk?"

Dr. Wilken glanced toward his receptionist. "We'll be in my office. Have my next patient wait."

Brad and Griffin followed Wilken down a short hallway. He entered his office, took a seat behind his desk, and pointed to two chairs. "Have a seat."

"We'll stand," Brad said.

"Uh, okay." Wilken sat back. His shoulders dropped. "How can I help?"

"We'd like to ask you a few questions about the shootings this week."

Wilken perked up, sat upright and swung his shoulders back. "Of course—fascinating, isn't it?"

Fascinating?

"That's an interesting way to put the murder of four people and attempted murder of one."

Wilken held his hands out. "I just mean things like this don't happen in Calgary. Maybe Vancouver or Toronto, just not here."

Brad nodded. "Do you own any guns?"

"Yes, I do. I'm an avid shooter."

"A .223?"

Wilken nodded. "That's my favorite."

Brad felt this was going too well, too easy. Something wasn't right, yet ...

"Can we see your gun?"

Wilken stood. "Sure, it's in the trunk of my car."

"Hang on a minute." Griffin nodded toward the hall. "I need to talk to my partner."

Griffin closed the door once they were in the hall. "So, Mr. Lawyer. What do we do? He said we could see his gun. He volunteered that. Do we check the gun and seize it, or do we get a warrant?"

"He was free with his answers," Brad said. "First, I think he's guilty as hell, then I think he's innocent or just stupid. To be safe, we need to get a warrant. He's blurted enough information getting the warrant won't be a problem. Go back and babysit him."

An hour later Brad was back at Dr. Wilken's office with the warrant. He opened the door and waved a piece of paper. "Dr. Wilken. I have a warrant to search your office, car and home."

"You didn't have to do that. I offered to show you the gun."

"I understand and you have been cooperative, Doctor, but this is a legal formality. Let's head down to your car."

Brad and Griffin followed Wilken out of the building to his car. He pulled out his keys and opened the trunk. Brad's hand automatically slid to his pistol. When the trunk lid swung up, Brad said, "Step back from the car."

Brad slipped on examination gloves, reached into the trunk and pulled out a gun bag. "When did you last fire this?"

"A couple of weeks ago."

A dark SUV pulled in behind them. Ames and Zerr got out. Brad handed the gun bag to Ames. "Test the gun immediately."

Ames placed the gun in the SUV.

"Dr. Wilken, will you to accompany us to the police station. We have additional questions."

"I'm cooperating. We can do it here."

"The station will be better."

"Okay. Tell my receptionist I'll be away for a while."

"Will do," Brad said. "Constable Zerr will take you to headquarters. We'll be there shortly."

Brad and Griffin searched Wilken's office and two treatment rooms but found nothing incriminating.

Brad headed down the hall to the receptionist. "Other than the office and two exam rooms, are there any extra rooms?"

She nodded. "There's a room next door he rents. It's his private office away from patients."

"Have you been in there?"

"Sometimes."

"When was the last time?"

"At least a month ago."

"Do you have a key?"

"Certainly." She opened a drawer, removed a key and stood. "Follow me."

Griffin fell in step behind them. She opened the door and stepped back. Brad took a step forward and stopped. "Ah, shit."

Griffin peeked over Brad's shoulder. "Mother of god."

The wall directly in front of them held a map of Calgary. He'd marked the locations of the shootings with red circles, with the number of the shooting inside each. A red arrow pointed to each crime scene. It was eerily similar to the map Brad had created. On the wall to the right, he'd tacked newspaper clippings for each shooting.

Brad and Griffin headed down the hall toward the interview room where Zerr was leaning against the wall.

"How's he doing?" Brad asked.

"He was quiet on the drive here. But then again, I told him he had that right. He hasn't said a word since."

"Thanks," Brad said. "I'll call you when we're done."

"Sure, boss." Zerr strolled back down the hall.

Brad swung the door open. "Dr. Wilken."

Wilken jumped at Brads's voice. They took seats opposite Wilken.

Brad leaned back in his chair, arms crossed, and stared. "We searched your private room. Interesting. Do you want to tell us about it?"

Wilken leaned forward. "I'm not … not a killer. I already told you. I found the killings interesting. Calgary is a quiet city."

"Being interested is one thing. But it appears you were planning your shootings."

"No, not planning, keeping track. Of *the* shootings—not my shootings."

"And for all five shootings you weren't at work. You were not at home."

"I was driving to work. I don't start until later in the morning, then work in the evening because a lot of my patients come after work."

"When we get ballistics back, is it going to confirm your gun is the murder weapon?"

"No—well, no. I don't think so."

"You don't think so?"

"I don't know how ballistics work. My gun fires a .223 bullet. I guess it might say a gun like mine is the murder weapon, like the cops said they're searching for on the news. Please. Can I tell you something?"

Brad raised an eyebrow. "Go ahead."

"I'm a hobby detective."

Brad swung forward. "What?"

"I'm a hobby detective."

"What does that mean?"

"I follow crimes. Not just here, but everywhere. I learn as much as I can and try to solve them. Sometimes I send my research to the cops in other cities."

"How many crimes have you solved?"

"Well, none, but it's a hobby."

Brad and Griffin stood at the same time and left the interview room.

A door at the end of the hall opened. Ames strode toward them, shaking his head. "No match on the bullet."

Brad frowned. "We've got the wrong guy."

CHAPTER THIRTY-ONE

LATE THAT AFTERNOON BRAD WAS LEANING BACK, HANDS BEHIND his head, staring at the map, when Devlin strolled in. He sat at Griffin's desk and sighed. "Kinda nice to be out of the noise."

"I could sleep right here." Brad closed his eyes.

"Not so, grasshopper," Devlin said. "I've got to teach you everything I know about hostage negotiations."

Brad swung his legs to the floor and sat up. "Where did the 'shoot first, ask questions later' Devlin go?"

Devlin snorted. "We both know things are different."

"I still like the hunt," Brad said.

"Me too." Devlin gazed past Brad. "But there comes a time when the player becomes the coach. You'll understand that someday if you coach football."

Brad grinned at Devlin. "Or get too old."

Devlin gave Brad the finger. "It's not about making one scoring play. It's about the strategy for the entire game. It's like a chess match. You against another chess master. You can't charge your way out of this situation. It's strategic. More cerebral."

"Wolfe must have hit you harder on the head than I thought. I can't believe what I'm hearing. Go ahead, teach me everything about negotiations. I've got five minutes."

"I'm serious."

Brad peered at Devlin. "There aren't any hostages."

"That's where you're wrong." Devlin leaned forward, his forearms on the desk. "If he'd stopped with the four shootings on Monday, life would have gone back to normal. But with the shooting last night, the entire city is on edge. We—you—screw this up, and people die."

"Nice. Put the pressure on me. Fire away."

"We learned a lot from the note."

"It was merely four lines."

Devlin set a copy of the note on the desk. "Four significant lines." He slid his finger under the first line. "He said, 'Dear Policeman Colter.' Using *Dear* and *Policeman* shows respect. For authority and policemen."

"Or sarcasm," Brad said. "Who is he mad at?"

"We don't know. I'm not sure what he means by 'I am that I am.' But he says, 'you will hear from me again.' He has opened the channel for conversation. This isn't over."

"He doesn't say how he'll communicate."

"True. We have to wait for him to make a move."

"Why'd he send the note to Sadie addressed to me?"

"I don't know. Maybe he saw you and Sadie at the news conference. Maybe he likes Sadie better than Angus."

"That's not much of a competition."

Devlin smirked. "Ah, so you've noticed."

Brad gave Devlin the finger.

"Last, he wants to negotiate with you. Who knows why? He thinks Carew is a dick. He wants to talk to someone in the investigation and your name is the one that's in the news."

"Carew said my name, I don't think they put it on the screen."

"Right, so either he heard it on TV ..."

Brad pointed the pen at Devlin. "Or radio."

"Excellent point." Devlin leaned back in the chair. "Whatever the reason, he picked you to negotiate with. I can tell you what to say, but he might ask for something we haven't discussed. I won't always have time to give you an answer. Delay too long and he will know something is up. Understand?"

"You can do it, how difficult is it?"

Devlin shook his head. "Laugh it up, funny boy. Negotiating is one time where lives are at risk. Screw up, and ..."

Brad twirled the pen in his hand. "Okay, give me the two-month course in ten minutes."

Devlin's jaw was set, and his eyes bore into Brad's. "A lot of this will be hard for you. You thrive on action and making things happen. In negotiating, the goal is slow everything down. Time is on our side, not his. It's important you let him know you understand his situation and his side of things. Say things like, 'I understand what you are going through.'"

"Empathy."

"Right. That will be new for you. You can't get caught in how horrific his crimes are. How evil he is. Try to understand it from his side. Why is he doing this? Is there some cause or ideology he's fighting for? No judgments."

"Oh, shit. How can any of what he's done have a purpose?"

Devlin vigorously shook his head. "See, that's how you can't think. Next is to get him to say no. He knows that during negotiations, you're playing him. Even the most inexperienced crook knows that. Most people think negotiating is about saying yes to minor demands, then you can get him to agree to bigger ones, like releasing a hostage. Turn it around. Ask something like, 'Do you want me to fail?' This is opposite to the way we usually ask questions and his defenses will drop."

"Okay, sure," Brad said.

"Above all, show respect. Treat him as an equal. Let him know he can help you as you are helping him. 'If you can help me out, that would be great. My boss is breathing down my neck.'" Devlin leaned back. "That's enough, but we have to think out all probable scenarios and have a prepared response. Remember, the goal is to drag this out as long as we can so we can arrest him with no additional shootings."

Brad nodded. "Got it."

CHAPTER THIRTY-TWO

Brad increased the volume up on the TV as the opening for the CFCN 6:00 p.m. evening news flashed on the scene. "Good evening. I'm David Todd and this is the CFCN News. We have a special update. Let's go to Angus Ferguson outside Police Headquarters with breaking news about the five shootings in our city."

Angus Ferguson's face appeared on the screen. "Thanks, David. In an exclusive to me and CFCN, we know the police received a note from the shooter this morning."

"Uh oh," Brad said.

"How the hell ..." Devlin covered his mouth.

"In a copy of the note shared with me by an anonymous source, the shooter reaches out to Detective Brad Coulter. The note is simple, with some grammatical and spelling errors."

The screen changed to a photo of the note.

Dear Policeman Colter
I am that I am
You will hear from me again
I only talk to Colter

"We don't know why the shooter has reached out to Detective Coulter. Perhaps they have a connection."

The screen moved back to the news anchor. "Have the police responded to this note?"

"Not yet. I expect they will have a press conference later tonight."

"Son of a bitch," Devlin said. "That stupid bastard. The shooter will retaliate. We've got a leak."

"No shit," Brad said. "Few people knew about the note."

"You know the saying. Three people can keep a secret if two are dead. Lots of people were involved. The note went to the Crime Scene Unit for fingerprints and photos. Cops know to keep this quiet, but we have support staff everywhere—copying, filing, making calls, logging evidence. Maybe it was Sadie."

Brad shook his head and chewed his lip. "No. We promised her the full story. She wouldn't give that up to a rival like Ferguson."

"We could pull Ferguson in."

"We could. Then we'd have a huge problem. Ferguson would make his arrest the story, not the shooter." Brad stood. "I'm going for a walk to clear my head and think this through."

Brad shoved open the back door of headquarters and headed down the alley. He had three hours until 9:00 p.m. when Archer said they'd do a press conference and Brad would be in front of the media. Archer had his staff working on the response.

When he thought back to where the morning started, it seemed days ago. Too much was happening too fast, it was hard to keep up. His brain was full. He jogged kitty-corner across Sixth Avenue and into the parking lot. As he slipped his key into the lock, he heard gravel crunch behind him. He swung around with his left hand on his gun. "Hello, Sadie."

"Sure, that'd be a glorious end to my day." Sadie motioned to his gun. She faced Brad, legs apart, hands on her hips with eyes that bored into his soul. "We had a deal. I knew I shouldn't trust you. But then you give the scoop to Ferguson and CFCN. If my boss finds out about this, I'll be doing the weather on Baffin Island."

"That would be easy," Brad said. "Minus a hundred, overcast and dark. What's so hard about that?"

"Damn you, this isn't funny." She glared at Brad, chin held high. "Do you know how hard it is to break into this profession? I needed that scoop."

Brad held out his hands. "Seriously, Sadie. We didn't tell Ferguson. I know you don't believe we did—you're smarter than that. Why in the world would I go to that jackass and hand over the information? Archer made a deal with you and we still have a deal. When it's time for the complete story to come out, I want it to be complete and accurate. I've seen your work. I trust you'll do it justice."

She sighed and stepped back. "What's the story with the chiropractor?"

"Nothing there either. He's just a weird dude."

"Can I quote you?"

"I'd prefer you didn't." Brad leaned against his car, arms crossed. "You can quote me when the time is right. Then we'll do a sit-down interview—you and only you get that information."

"Carew insists it's too early to change routines at schools."

"He's an idiot."

"Oh, that's an even better quote."

"I'm speaking freely because I believe you have ethics—you're not Ferguson. If you want to make a difference and be the hero, go with the information I gave you about kids and schools. Change routines, that stuff. That will make the most difference."

"Angus seems to think there is a story about you. Maybe I could get some inside info. The real Brad Coulter." Sadie spread her arms wide like unrolling a banner. "Not the shit Ferguson is making up."

"You can correct that when you write this story. You'll have direct police resources and the truth will make all those like Angus who made up shit appear like they should work for a supermarket tabloid."

She shrugged. "Nothing official. Maybe we end up at a restaurant in the same general vicinity, same general time. It is two-and-a-half hours until your press conference. I'm sure you're hungry."

"I'm starving. And so is my dog." Brad opened the car door. "It's not safe in the city. Can I give you a ride back to your office?"

Brad slid out of his comfortable chair, grabbed the dirty dishes, and headed to the kitchen. He set the plates in the sink, thought about washing them, then thought, screw it. Then he heard there would be a TV special report about the shooter. He increased the volume up and slid back into his chair. Lobo lay across his feet.

"We'll go to a special report from Sadie Andrus." The news anchor faded and the image of Sadie outside a school replaced it. It was dark out, but floodlights lit up the scene.

"Hello. I'm outside Ernest Manning High School in the southwest. It's quiet here, but tomorrow morning hundreds of students will flock to this school, and thousands more to schools across the city. There has been no direct threat by the shooter to school children, but a source within the Calgary Police Service has suggestions for the safety of the children."

The camera panned to footage of a school bus.

"For kids arriving and leaving school, there are a few things that might pay off. Buses should drop kids off at the back of the school. They should park with the bus door as close to the schools as possible. The bus will provide protection. If parents are dropping kids off, the same thing—get to the back of the school, or to a door that is not exposed to an open area. There is advice for adults. If you need to go shopping, park as close to the store as you can. Keep the car between you and the entrance. Minimize the time you are outside and exposed."

The screen centered back on Sadie.

"I'll be reporting from another school tomorrow morning. I'm Sadie Andrus, CFAC news."

Brad shut off the TV and headed to the door.

"Lobo, let's go."

CHAPTER THIRTY-THREE

Lobo lay beside the podium in the jammed briefing room. Devlin said some members of the press had been in their chairs since 7:00 p.m. Brad tugged at the neck of his open-collared shirt and thought about taking off his jacket. The room would get hotter when the lights of the cameras came on. But he did not want anyone focusing on his gun, magazines, or handcuffs. The jacket stayed on.

Brad set his notes on the podium and at 9:00 p.m. nodded. The room was ablaze with light. "Good evening and thank you for coming. Earlier today a letter was delivered to Sadie Andrus of CFAC and addressed to me. The note read: *Dear Policeman Colter, I am that I am. You will hear from me again. I only talk to Colter.*"

Brad swallowed. He flipped his notes over.

"Please understand we are doing everything we can to stop the shootings," Brad said. "When we receive a note like this, we need to confirm its authenticity and meaning. Irresponsible acts by a member of the press in the name of transparency or the right of people to know, or ego, puts lives in danger, and does nothing to mitigate risks."

Brad glanced around the room, then his eyes stopped on Angus Ferguson.

"Until we have completed our analysis," Brad continued, "I will not be taking questions about the note."

He pushed his notes to the side.

"My favorite class in high school was English," Brad said to the crowd. "I enjoyed writing short stories, comedies, and satire. However, despite my enthusiasm for writing, I would never portray myself as an expert writer." Again, he glanced around the room. This time his eyes landed on Sadie. She grinned and winked. He jerked his head back. "And, uh … nor should a reporter feel they know more about policing than I do."

He gripped the side of the podium.

"Today," Brad continued, "we followed a promising lead. Investigations like this take time. We are methodical. While we were investigating, a member of the press released the name of a suspect and showed photos of the suspect, his family, and place of work."

Brad glared at Angus. Other reporters followed his eyes.

"The investigation concluded when we found the suspect was merely interested in the crimes and had not committed the killings. He was released, and we appreciate his cooperation. However, as his name and occupation were made public, it is my opinion the reporter owes this man an open apology. I hope the irresponsible reporting will not affect this man's life. If this man pursues legal action against the members of the press who slandered his name, I would be honored to testify on his behalf."

Brad stepped out from behind the podium. "I'll take a few questions."

"Detective Coulter, Angus—"

Brad waved his hand over the gathered reporters. "Next question."

"Detective, Tony King, XL Radio. You refer to the villain as a shooter. Wouldn't the correct term be sniper?"

Brad nodded. "Good question. Let me talk about the terms shooter and sniper. It's a matter of opinion rather than one of definition. The origin of the word sniper comes from the Brits in India in the 1770s. Sniper referred to people who could accurately shoot a snipe, a tiny bird. A shooter refers to anyone who fires a gun. We think of a sniper as having specialized military service, or a style of hunting where the shooter, by stealth, gets close to the animal he or she is hunting. A great deal of skill and marksmanship is involved. To answer your question, the use of sniper is appropriate."

"If I may," Tony King said. "How and when will the sniper contact you?"

"I don't know how or when the sniper will contact me, but I want him to know I am open to any form of communication. A call to the tip line would be appropriate. Next."

Brad's eyes surveyed the group and stopped on Sadie. "Detective," Sadie said, "the RCMP have offered to assist. Do you feel it is time to invite the RCMP to take part in this investigation?"

"We have already been in contact with the RCMP and they are helping us with specific elements of this case. Did you have another question, Ms. Andrus?"

"What do you say to Calgarians who are scared to go out of their homes? Who are terrified to buy groceries or go to work?"

"I get it. Something like this has never happened here before. However, you have already reported on the precautions citizens should take and I support your reporting. It's reasonable to be scared, it's reasonable to take precautions such as the ones you mentioned in your report earlier this evening, but to shutter up the house and lock away the children and silverware?" He frowned. "The sniper wins if we do that. We're stronger than that. Look out for each other, go the extra mile for your neighbor, and we will come out of this a better city."

Brad stepped away from the podium, then swung back.

"A last note," he said. "The reward for information that leads to the arrest and conviction of the sniper is at fifty thousand, thanks to additional contributions from a local petroleum producer, Nickle Oil. They will match any funds collected from the community. Information on the sniper must go to the tip line. Please do not use 911 as our emergency lines are being overwhelmed with calls. That's the end of this briefing. Thank you."

CHAPTER THIRTY-FOUR

PITTMAN POUNDED THE DASH OF THE CAR. "THE FUCKIN' OIL companies upped the reward money?" He hit the dash again.

Hirsch switched off the car radio. "It's not a bad thing."

"What the hell does that mean?"

"We have their attention. Isn't that what you wanted?"

Pittman chewed his bottom lip and glared at Hirsch. "Those bastards. They don't have money to keep us working, but they can toss money out for a reward."

"If you expect the CEOs to make sense, you're crazy," Hirsch said. "It's not about the money. It's about them appearing respectable."

"The fuckin' cops are buying into this. We're not getting any respect."

Hirsch nodded and pulled into the parking lot across from the bars. "Not from that asshole, Carew, doing all the talking for the police."

"He's a jerk."

Hirsch shut off the car. "At least Coulter takes us seriously. I knew he was the right choice."

Pittman slumped in his seat and exhaled. "Maybe too seriously."

Hirsch shrugged. "It's clear the cops don't have a clue what to do."

"Don't they understand we decide who lives and who dies?" Pittman opened his door, slipped out of the car, and strode across the street. "I'm gonna call them."

Hirsch jumped out and raced to catch up to Pittman. "What?"

"Yup. I'm gonna call them and let them know we aren't taking any shit from them. We get respect, or more people die."

Hirsch grabbed Pittman's arm. "How are you going to contact them?"

"I'll use the tip line."

"Not a good idea. They'll have a trace on that line."

Pittman glared at Hirsch. "You got a better idea?"

"Call 911 from a payphone in the bar. Give your message quickly, then hang up. We're in another bar by the time the cops get there."

Pittman waited in the back hall of the bar as a guy staggered toward the bathroom, then he lifted the payphone receiver and dialed 911. Hirsch stood beside him, making sure no one could overhear the conversation.

"911. Please hold, we are experiencing a high call volume."

Pittman pulled the phone away from his ear. "They've got me on fucking hold. Can you believe that?"

Hirsch laughed. "What a bunch of idiots."

Pittman held up his hand.

"911. Police, fire, or EMS?"

"Uh, police."

"Please hold while I transfer your call."

"On hold again." Pittman rolled his eyes.

"RCMP dispatch. What is your emergency?" a female voice asked.

"Yeah, I want to tell you about the shootings."

"Where are you calling from?"

"Why does that matter?" Pittman asked.

"Sir, I need to direct your call to the right police agency."

"Fuck that. I'm trying to tell you about the murders."

"Sir, please don't swear. Now, where are you calling from?" RCMP dispatch asked.

"I'm not telling you that. I'll tell you about the shootings."

"The shootings in Calgary?"

"Are there other multiple shootings I don't know about?"

"Sir, I'm trying to be patient."

"Yes, damn it, the shootings in Calgary."

"Thank you. What is your name?"

"My name?"

"Yes, sir."

"I am that I am," Pittman said.

"I don't understand that. What are you saying?"

"I'm saying I want to tell the cops about the shootings in Calgary. It all started in Rocky Mountain House."

"I'm confused, sir," RCMP dispatch said. "Are you calling about the Calgary shootings or a shooting in Rocky Mountain House?"

"Calgary."

"The RCMP is not investigating that shooting. I'll forward you to Calgary Police Dispatch."

"No, wait ..."

Hirsch raised his eyebrows.

"On hold again." Pittman slammed the receiver down. "Those bastards are gonna pay."

CHAPTER THIRTY-FIVE

Thursday Day Nine

THE SUN WAS PEAKING OVER THE HORIZON AS JILL COOK FOLLOWED the narrow lane and parked at the side of the school. She slid out of her vehicle and surveyed the area. The turn of the century brick school was nestled against a thickly forested hill. The school building provided cover from the street out front.

Jill shivered as a blast of cold fall wind whipped across the parking lot. Zipping her hoodie, she headed to the passenger door. The other cars and buses unloaded kids. Parents grabbed their children by the arms and dragged them into the school.

Jill took Joel's hand as he stepped out of the car. He immediately ripped his hand from his mother's grasp. Jill smiled. A ten-year-old boy does not hold hands with his mom in public, no matter the danger. He allowed her to walk beside him across the playground and up the stairs to the back door.

With a quick, "Bye, Mom," he sprinted into the school.

Jill sighed. Now Joel was safely in the school. She should be relieved. Again, she shivered, but not from the wind. It was like a cold force had passed through her. She stood on the steps and surveyed the parking lot and playground, shaking her head. A few children were playing on the swings and monkey bars. She started that way, then noticed a lady motioning and calling to the kids. Her eyes roamed over the area once before heading back to her car.

She'd dressed for a jog—hoodie over a T-shirt, sweatpants, and sneakers. The jog from the school to Elbow Drive was about five blocks—then a jog along the Elbow River. Calming and relaxing.

She had just started stretching when a shot rang out.

Screams followed.

Paramedic instinct kicked in. She spun toward the direction of the shot and took several steps toward the trees. Where there's a gunshot, there's a victim. She frantically scanned the hill. Was the shooter still there?

"Oh my god, he's shot," someone yelled.

Jill swung to the voice and started jogging.

"Someone, do something." The voice was frantic.

Jill was in a sprint. Parents rushed toward her, some dragging children by the hand, others with their child tucked under their arm. She jostled as she headed toward the screams. She'd seen Joel enter the school. He was safe. She hoped. She shouted at a parent fleeing toward the school to call the police and lock down the building.

Jill glanced at the school's doors, but in the flood of people, she couldn't see him. She prayed he remembered her instructions: find cover.

She dodged a couple of cars and broke through the panic of

people. A half-dozen adults and kids grouped next to a child on the ground. Her first thought: *it's not Joel.*

Jill dropped to the ground beside the boy and dragged him behind a car. Her eyes glanced down his tiny body. He was Joel's age, with light-brown hair and freckles across his nose. The right side of his Pac Man T-shirt was blood soaked. With each gasping breath, blood flowed from the wound. Jill ripped off her hoodie, put it over his chest, and applied pressure with one hand.

He winced and let out a slight cry.

"I'm Jill. I'm a paramedic. I'm going to help you. What's your name?"

"Shawn." He gasped and stared up at her. Tears formed trails down his face, his brown eyes wide and scared. She checked his carotid pulse. Rapid and very weak. She grasped his trembling hand.

"It hurts so bad."

Jill squeezed his hand. "I know, baby. Can you be brave for me?"

Tears streamed down his face as he nodded.

She peered at the few adults nearby. She knew in situations like this you had to be direct and specific with your instructions. She selected a man, mid-fifties, wearing blue work clothes.

"Do you work here?"

He nodded. "Janitor."

"Good. I need you to run into the school and call 911. Tell them this boy has been shot. We need EMS and police."

He nodded and stared.

"Go, now."

In the seconds it had taken to give instructions to the janitor,

Shawn had paled considerably. Nothing more helpless than a paramedic without her ambulance.

"Oh my god, Shawn." A woman knelt next to him. "Oh my god, so much blood."

"That's not helping," Jill hissed. "Who are you?"

The lady nodded and chewed her lip. "I'm Sarah Park, Shawn's teacher."

"I'm a paramedic."

Sarah hesitantly reached out to Shawn and placed her hand on his shoulder. She sniffled, then her eyes focused, and her jaw clenched. "Sorry. What can I do?"

"Run to the school. Get the first-aid kit and get back here as fast as you can. Tell someone to call his mom and have her go to the Children's Hospital."

Sarah patted Shawn's shoulder. "I'll be right back."

Jill exhaled deeply and focused on Shawn. His tiny gasps were frequent. His eyes were heavy and closed. His pale face grimaced in pain.

Jill enfolded his tiny hand. "Shawn, can you hear me?"

His eyes slowly opened, and his head rotated toward her. His lips quivered and his shoulders shook. "I want my mommy."

Jill's jaw clenched. She swallowed hard and clutched his hand. *Damn.* It was cold. "We're calling your mommy. She'll meet us at the hospital."

"Mommy." His heavy eyes closed.

Where the hell was the ambulance?

All she could do was hold his hand, talk to him, and reassess. *Okay, the airway is open.* She controlled the bleeding on the chest. His skin was ghostly pale, and his hand was cold. She should check his back, but couldn't risk moving him. Faint sirens sounded in the distance. Help was on the way. She closed her eyes. *Please, faster.*

"I've got the first-aid kit." Sarah, out of breath, set it next to Jill.

"Open it." Jill glanced into the kit. *Son of a …* A couple of dozen finger-sized band-aids, safety pins, ointment that had leaked throughout, aspirins—expired—and a finger splint.

"Nothing useful there." Sarah's shoulders sagged. "I'm sorry. None of this will help, will it?"

Jill shook her head.

"Shawn. Shawn." Jill gripped his hand. He didn't respond. "Shawn. Open your eyes."

Through rapid breathing, he asked, "Am I gonna die?"

Sarah's hand covered her mouth as she gasped.

Jill stroked his face with a finger. "I will not let that happen." Jill's jaw clenched. This could have been Joel. Tears welled in the corner of her eyes. She clutched his hand again. "Remember how brave you are."

Sarah curled her legs under her at Shawn's head. She brushed a few strands of hair from his forehead. "Oh, Shawn. Please be okay." She wiped her nose with the back of her hand. "Precious little boy."

"What does he like?" Jill asked.

"He loves reading." Sarah chewed her lip and took a deep breath. "He always has a book or two on the go. He signs more books out of the library than anyone else." Sarah brushed her fingers through his hair.

"Shawn. What books do you like?" His hand was limp in hers.

Sarah glanced toward the street. "The sirens are getting louder. That's good, right?"

Jill nodded. Help was close. "Shawn. Shawn. Open your eyes." She glanced down his tiny body, his T-shirt soaked in blood. She checked the boy's pulse—weak and rapid. His breathing, shallow, gasping and fast. She spun at the sound of boots. *Shit.* Tactical cops with guns, not EMS.

"Ma'am, move back so we can assess the kid."

"I'm Jill Cook. A paramedic. I've assessed him. Gunshot wound to the chest. Any chance you've got a decent first-aid kit?"

"I'm Charlie Zerr." He pointed to his partner. "Sam Steele.

Zerr opened a pouch on his ballistic vest and tossed a package to Jill.

"What's this?"

"Trauma dressing." Zerr spun away and swept his gun back and forth across the hill.

Zerr glanced back at Sarah. "Who's she?"

"Sarah. She's a teacher here," Jill said.

Zerr did a double-take, pursed his lips, then stared across the schoolyard.

Jill ripped open the dressing, pulled her hoodie off Shawn's chest, then placed the trauma dressing over the wound. "What are you doing?"

"Looking for the shooter," Zerr said.

"You think he's still here?" Sarah's eyes were wide with fright.

Jill hoped not.

Zerr kept his gun pointed at the hill. "No reason to think he isn't."

Jill glanced at the back door of the school. *Oh, Joel, stay inside.* She twisted toward the hill. She'd forgotten about the shooter once she saw Shawn and dragged him to cover, but the protection of working in the car's shadow was minimal. *Shit. We've been a target for the last five minutes.*

The sirens were so loud it was difficult to talk.

"Shawn. Shawn." Jill leaned close and gently shook his shoulders. He didn't respond. She placed a hand on his tiny chest and her ear over his nose and mouth. The chest barely rose, but little puffs of air brushed her ear.

"What do you need?"

Jill glanced up.

"Oh, god. Dixon and Thompson. Am I glad to see you. Gunshot wound to his right chest. Shawn's about ten—unconscious, shallow breathing, rapid pulse. External bleeding on his chest is under control. I haven't checked his back."

Dixon nodded. "Thompson, get the ambulance ready."

"No time for that." Jill scooped Shawn into her arms.

Thompson sprinted back to the ambulance.

When Jill arrived at the ambulance, Thompson had the stretcher at the back bumper. Jill gently set Shawn on the bed and they lifted him into the ambulance.

Dixon swung toward her. "I need you with me."

"I can't. My son ..." She glanced back at the school. "I have to call my ex-husband to get Joel."

"Shawn needs you," Dixon said. "The cops will keep the school locked down. Call your ex from the hospital."

Oh god, Joel—please be safe.

Jill jumped into the back of the ambulance. She rolled Shawn onto his side, exposing a sizeable hole in his back—Dixon applied bandages. Jill glanced over her shoulder.

Sarah stood at the back door, arms hugging her chest tight. "Is he ... okay?" Her jaw quivered.

"Sarah, you're coming with us as his guardian," Jill said. "Get in."

A cop closed the back doors, and the ambulance sped away.

"Dixon, I need suction." Jill's voice was calm, but firm.

Blood bubbled out Shawn's mouth and nose.

Zerr watched the paramedic hustle to the ambulance with the boy in her arms. It didn't seem promising.

Zerr lifted his rifle to his shoulder and scanned through the scope. He swung it back and forth across the hill.

Shot a kid. Zerr ground his teeth. One shot. All he needed was one shot. A glimpse of a shoulder. An ear. *Come on, you son of a bitch—look at me.*

"See anything?" Steele swung his gun across the hill.

Zerr lowered his rifle but kept his eyes focused up the hill. "No. Had to have come from the top. I'd be above the trees on the hill."

"Why?"

"I'm a sniper. That's where I'd be. Where would you be?"

Steele glanced at the wet pool of blood behind them, merely twenty feet from a set of monkey bars. Deep frown lines creased his face. His eyes roamed from the blood to the hill. "Top of the hill."

Briscoe strode over with his new rookie, Caterina Toscana, at his side.

"Is the school locked down?" Steele asked.

"Yup," Toscana said. "First thing I did."

"It's pandemonium out front," Briscoe said. "Parents are

running in from all directions. I've got cops making sure the right kid gets with the right parent."

Steele nodded. "What about roadblocks?"

Briscoe swung his arm in an arc. "Everything out front of the school is blocked."

Steele rotated and pointed away from the school. "We need roadblocks at the top of the hill."

"Why?" Toscana asked. "We've got all the roads out front barricaded."

"He didn't shoot from the front," Steele said. "He shot from the hill." He stared at Toscana. "Tell me you ordered roadblocks at the top of the hill."

Briscoe watched Toscana's face pale. He slid off his cap and rubbed the bald spot on his head. *Damn.* He watched Steele and Zerr race up the hill.

CHAPTER THIRTY-SIX

BRAD SAT AT A TABLE IN THE GYM, POURING OVER THE STACK OF TIPS that had come in during the night. Around the room, dozens of cops worked through their own piles. He tossed a handful of useless tips onto the table, leaned back, rubbed his eyes, and took a deep breath. Mistake. Four days of up to one hundred cops working in the gym, around the clock, and forgetting about personal hygiene. The odor was worse than a locker room after a football game in ninety-degree heat. Garbage cans overflowed with coffee cups and take-out food containers. The only people not working this case were the caretakers.

Two detectives stood at the wall in front of the suspects list. One deleting suspects, the other adding additional names.

Spaced around the gym were TVs atop five-foot-high carts. A few were silent, the others on low volume. The closest TV to Brad showed the weather report—sunny but cool today and snow this weekend. Fall in Alberta.

Then a banner flashed across the screen. "Breaking News."

The screen changed from weather to an image of a school and an ambulance racing away. Dozens of emergency vehicles had parked anywhere they could around the front and side of the school. Cops, guns drawn, rushed from cars toward the back of the school.

Brad knew that school—Cliff Bungalow. He jumped up and cranked the volume.

"—student shot moments ago. Our news crew was blocks away and provided this footage." The newscaster put his hand to his ear. "We have an on-scene report. We'll go live to Sadie Andrus at the school."

The TV changed to an upper-body view of Sadie Andrus, with the school in the distance. "About ten minutes ago, a boy, ten-years old, was shot at Cliff Bungalow School in the Mission District. We understand a paramedic was dropping her child off and provided immediate aid."

"Oh my god." Brad stepped backward and dropped into his chair. He closed his eyes and his head dropped into his hands. "No. Not a kid."

They increased the volume from the other TVs. Brad glanced up. Everyone was standing, eyes on the TVs, jaws dropped. Other than Sadie's voice, not another sound was heard in the gym.

Brad stared at the TV but didn't hear a word. A boy, barely ten, shot. He rubbed the stubble on his chin. *We didn't do enough. I didn't do enough.*

His caution to Sadie and her news report hadn't been enough. He clenched his fists. *Son of a bitch. I'm coming for you, asshole.*

Brad grabbed his coat and sprinted out of the gym.

The ambulance bounced several times as it rolled over the curb and onto the street. Dixon started IVs in each arm. A cardiac monitor beeped at a rate of over one hundred and fifty.

Jill sat at the head of the stretcher, alternating suctioning of blood out of Shawn's mouth and nose and ventilating him with a bag-mask.

"It's getting harder to ventilate," Jill said.

Dixon nodded and picked up his stethoscope. He listened to each side of Shawn's chest. "Decreased on the right. He's developing a tension pneumothorax."

"Are you doing a needle decompression?"

"Not yet. I'm going to loosen the occlusive dressing. If that lets the air escape, we won't have to put another hole in his chest."

Dixon leaned toward the front of the ambulance. "Thompson let the Children's Hospital know we're coming in with an approximately ten-year-old child with a GSW to the right chest. He's gonna need a trauma team and a chest tube."

The cardiac monitor beeped wildly with a heart rate of one hundred and eighty.

Dixon glanced up, then peeled back the tape covering the gunshot wound. As he did, air escaped.

"It's easier to ventilate," Jill said.

The cardiac monitor slowed back to one hundred and fifty.

Dixon wiped his hands. "That will buy us some time. Hopefully enough to get us to the emergency room."

"Two minutes out," Thompson shouted.

"All right," Dixon said. "Let's get ready to move him out as soon as we arrive."

Jill switched the oxygen to a portable tank. Dixon removed the IVs from the hooks on the ambulance wall and attached them to an IV pole on the stretcher. He listened to Shawn's chest. "Breath sounds faint on the right again—he needs a chest tube. But we bought him some time."

Brad turned right off Fifth Street onto Twenty-Second Avenue. The street in front of the school was jammed with marked cruisers, cops, and news vans. *Shit. All the media is here.* Brad parked a block from the school.

Reporters shouted questions as he sprinted toward the police tape that surrounded the building. Several cops tried to stop him, but he flashed his badge as he elbowed past. He continued around the school to the back, heading toward Briscoe and Toscana, who were staring up the hill. Briscoe had his portable radio in his hand. Briscoe was telling dispatch they needed help with all the traffic from parents approaching the school. Toscana was on the radio, too. It surprised Brad when she mentioned roadblocks on Hope Street. That was at the top of the hill.

"What's happening on Hope Street?" Brad asked.

"Steele and Zerr figure that's where the shot came from."

"Shit," Brad said. "Where are they?"

Briscoe nodded toward the hill. "They headed up there about five minutes ago."

"I'm heading up there, too."

"I'll go with you," Toscana said.

"Boy scout can make it on his own," Briscoe said. "You need to make sure our roadblocks are in place."

"But I can help—backup. In case the shooter is still there."

Briscoe sneered. "He doesn't need backup. If Brad finds him on the way up, your gun won't clear your holster before he's got the gunman in his sights. We all have critical things to do. I need you to check on the roadblocks."

Brad drew his pistol, jogged into the trees, and keyed his radio. "Steele, Zerr. I'm on my way up."

His radio clicked twice in acknowledgment.

Trees and bushes completely overran the hill. Branches slapped at his face, and thorns snagged on his pants and jacket. The backs of both hands were bleeding. By the time he pushed through at the top of the hill, he was breathing hard, and blood oozed from dozens of lacerations.

He stepped out of the trees into a backyard and faced rifles held by Steele and Zerr. "I told you I was coming up."

"We can't be too careful." Steele slung the rifle over his shoulder.

"That hill is dense, like thousands of hands grabbing at you." Brad glanced at his bleeding hands.

"We made it up fine," Zerr said.

"You drove."

Steele laughed. "We took the path."

"There's a path?" Brad stared wide-eyed.

"You bet," Zerr said. "How do you think the kids get to school?"

"Ah, shit. Where?"

Steele shrugged. "About four feet to your left."

Brad's head dropped to his chest. "Are you shitting me?"

"No."

"How did you find it?"

Steele smirked. "We asked the kids."

"Did Briscoe know?"

Zerr nodded. "He sure did. Why?"

Brad shook his head. "No reason. Bring me up to date."

"The houses on this block all overlook the school," Zerr said. "The shot could have come from any of them." He pointed down the street a few houses. "That's where he shot from."

"That's where Zerr thinks the shot came from," Steele said.

"Where would you shoot from?" Brad asked.

Steele shrugged. "Same spot."

Brad rolled his eyes. "Have you been over there?"

"Not yet," Zerr said.

"Let's go." Brad followed Zerr and Steele down the street.

Zerr stopped in front of a house. "This is it."

Brad called to a couple of cops leaning against their car. "I need this entire block taped off. No one in or out. Get additional cruisers here and do a door-to-door canvass. I need to know if anyone saw anything suspicious this morning." He pointed to Zerr. "Lead away."

Zerr headed up the driveway, then to the right of the house, and followed a sidewalk to the backyard. He stopped where the yard dropped off. They stood at the edge, gazing down toward the school to where the boy was shot.

Zerr hiked along the edge of the hill. "Boss, I've found footprints in the dirt. He was here for a while. Right there."

Zerr planted his feet near the trampled ground and raised his sniper rifle. "I can see Briscoe's bald head in the crosshairs."

"Let me see," Brad said.

Zerr handed the rifle to Brad, who raised it to his shoulder and stared through the scope. It was directly in line with where the boy was shot. "This is it. Shit."

"He changed his plan," Steele said.

"He shot from outside the vehicle." Brad lowered the gun.

"There was planning—this specific location. You don't just find this. You have to scope it out. We need this area canvassed quickly."

Brad stared at the school. "I told parents to drive the kids to the back of the school."

"What?" Zerr said. "That's what Sadie Andrus said on the news."

Steele punched Zerr's arm.

"What? Oh," Zerr said.

"I told the shooter how to defeat the measures I'd suggested. They'd always shot from the front, from across the street. I told parents their children would be safe behind the schools. I screwed up."

"There are hundreds of schools in the city," Steele said. "There was no way to know they'd pick this school." Steele pointed toward the school. "If he used a rifle, the case would eject ..."

"To the right," Zerr said. "Let's find the case."

They spread out and searched. After fifteen minutes, Brad was ready to give up. "The shooter must have picked up his case."

"Bingo." Zerr pushed branches back with his rifle and pointed to the base of a tree. The case sparkled in the light.

The ambulance swung off Seventeenth Avenue onto Richmond Road, then quickly turned left and into the ambulance bay. A dozen gowned nurses and physicians waited. As soon as the ambulance's back doors were opened the stretcher was pulled out and rushed down the hall. Jill stood on the stretcher frame and used the bag-mask to provide oxygen to Shawn.

They passed reception and into the trauma room. Bright lights reflected off the white walls, giving the room an eerie otherworld feel. The stretcher was surrounded by trauma staff and Shawn was quickly lifted onto the trauma bed. A respiratory therapist took over from Jill and provided suction and breaths for Shawn.

"Shawn is a ten-year-old boy," Jill said. "Gunshot wound entered the upper right chest and exited his right back. External bleeding controlled. He developed a tension pneumothorax in the ambulance and Dixon released the pressure. Breathing is shallow, and we assisted with a bag-mask. Heart rate one hundred and fifty to one hundred and eighty. We could not get a blood pressure."

"Who are you?" the emergency physician asked.

"I'm a paramedic. I dropped my son at school, and I was there when Shawn was shot."

The physician's eyes widened. All heads in the trauma room glanced at Jill.

"Is he your son?" the physician asked.

Jill shook her head. "No. His mother was contacted—she should be on her way."

A nurse prepped the right side of Shawn's chest, then an intern inserted the chest tube.

Thompson pulled the stretcher away and out of the room. Jill and Dixon stood at the trauma room door. Nurses changed IV solutions for blood. The emergency physician put an endotracheal tube into Shawn's mouth and down to his lungs. A lab tech drew blood samples and brushed past them as she sprinted to the lab.

Jill turned to Dixon. "I have to call the school to make sure Joel is okay. Then get my ex to pick him up."

"You'll never get through," Dixon said. "Call dispatch and find out who we have on scene."

The emergency doors opened and a frantic woman entered, shouting, "Shawn? Where's my baby?"

Brad led them back toward the street. They waited at the front of the house for Sturgeon and the Crime Scene Unit to arrive.

"Boss, there's something you should know," Zerr said.

"What's that?"

"The boy's teacher. The one who helped EMS. You know her."

Brad spun toward Zerr. "What?"

"Sarah Park."

"Are you sure? She teaches high school."

"Then it was her twin," Zerr said. "And they're both named Sarah."

Brad's jaw clenched. Three years ago, he and Sarah dated for a brief time—a very brief time. Brad and TSU were in the middle of a motorcycle gang war. Every day the violence escalated. Then the bikers made it personal. They firebombed Brad's car, which exploded. The front of his house was damaged, and spears of glass and wood hit Sarah. After she recovered, the bikers went after her directly. Fortunately, she was rescued by the quick actions of a custodian. Sarah ended the brief relationship and moved to British Columbia. He hadn't heard from her and didn't know she'd moved back.

"She's here?"

Steele shook his head. "No, she went with EMS as the boy's guardian until his parents arrived."

"Sarah?" Brad started toward the hill. "You guys got this scene?"

"Sure, boss," Zerr said.

Brad nodded. "I'm going to the hospital."

Steele grabbed his elbow. "That's a terrible idea. I'll go."

Brad pulled his arm away. "I'll be okay. You two wait for Sturgeon."

CHAPTER THIRTY-SEVEN

BRAD SHOVED OPEN THE DOORS TO THE EMERGENCY DEPARTMENT. A flood of sounds and smells assaulted him. The urgency of voices. Medical staff racing from patient to patient. The chemical smell of cleaning fluid. Many body scents and the unmistakable odor of blood.

When Maggie died, he'd been injured as well and rushed to surgery. It wasn't until the next day he found out Maggie and their unborn child had died. The following weeks were a blur. The pain didn't go away, and he learned how to cope, to move onward, even if it was a minor step. Then suddenly something brought it all back—a teen assaulted, a woman raped, a child shot, the smells of the hospital.

He fought the gauntlet of activity toward the trauma room. Standing in the hall outside the trauma room were Dixon and a lady. She was familiar but she was out of place in a T-shirt and sweatpants. Not Sarah. The kid's mother? His brow furrowed. Had Zerr been mistaken?

"Dixon, where is he? How's he doing?"

"They've taken him to the operating room." Dixon shook his head. "The bullet entered the upper right chest and came out his lower back."

"The X-rays show several broken ribs, so the bullet bounced around," Jill said. "Probably lots of internal damage."

Brad cocked his head. "I know you, but—"

"Jill Cook. I'm a paramedic. The jogging outfit probably threw you off." She pulled a loose strand of hair back behind her ear.

Brad nodded. It was interesting how you recognized people by their uniforms and a location. Change the clothes and the situation, and you didn't have a clue. "I didn't recognize you out of your uniform."

Dixon snickered.

"Oops," Brad said.

"I know what you meant." The strand of hair was loose again. Jill tried to tuck it into her ponytail.

"How are you involved?"

"I was dropping my son at school when I heard the gunshot."

"Your son?" Brad's eyes were wide.

"No. No. My son's safe. I was stretching before my jog. I sprinted to the school and saw Shawn Fortin lying in the field." She grabbed one of Brad's scratched hands, examining it. "What happened?"

"I climbed the hill to see where the shot originated. It was a lot more tangled than I thought."

"Why didn't you use the path?" She glanced down, still holding his hand. She quickly let go.

Brad nodded. "Yeah, excellent point."

"Let me clean those cuts."

Brad held up his hands. "No. Don't bother."

Jill pulled some supplies off a cart beside them. "No bother." She took one of Brad's hands, poured some disinfectant on gauze then wiped his hand.

Brad hissed.

"Sorry."

"Just stung a little."

She took Brad's other hand. "I didn't have a lot to work with at the school. At least here I can clean this up properly."

"She's selling herself short," Dixon said. "She did what needed to be done."

Jill tossed the gauze in the garbage and washed her hands.

Brad glanced at the backs of his hands. "There're a lot of scratches. Thanks."

Jill shivered and crossed her arms, holding onto her shoulders. "Dixon was the one who recognized Shawn's breathing problem. He's the smart one."

"She makes an excellent point," Dixon said. "I'm a master at hiding my brilliance."

"Are you cold?" Brad slipped off his jacket and handed it to her.

She swung the jacket over her bare shoulders. "Thanks. I had to toss my hoodie."

"You were the lady taking care of Shawn?"

"Yeah. Why?"

Brad cocked his head and pursed his lips. "Nothing important. I was told it was another lady."

Jill nodded and glanced down the hall. "Oh, you mean the teacher, Sarah. She helped me. I left her in the staff lounge."

Zerr was right. "Sarah."

"You okay, Coulter?" Dixon asked.

"Um, yeah, I know her. Sarah Park?"

Jill nodded. "That's her name."

Dixon glanced at Brad. "Sarah? From the explosion?"

Brad strode down the hall toward the emergency entrance, then stopped at an unmarked door—the staff lounge. He opened the door.

Sarah was sitting in a chair to the right. Her elbows were in her lap, hands cradling a cup of coffee. She stared blankly at the cup.

He stepped into the room, but she didn't hear him. Her black hair was wild, and tears had smeared her makeup. Her light-colored dress had dark stains and drops of blood had dried on her forehead.

"Sarah," he whispered.

She sighed and glanced up from her cup. Her eyes widened, and her hands shook, coffee slopping onto the floor.

"Brad."

He sat in a chair across from her. "Circumstances suck, but it's good to see you."

She shook her head. "I wish I could say the same. The three worst events of my life all involve you."

Brad stared at his feet. "Oh. I didn't mean—"

"What happened to your hands?"

"Got some scratches from the trees."

She nodded, then had a faraway gaze. "I'll bet they hurt. But not like wood and glass is stuck in them."

There wasn't anger in her voice, no emotion. But his gut

tightened from the verbal shot. He fought against the memory of that night, but lost. It all came back in full color. Sarah and Brad on the couch in the living room. Neil Diamond playing. His car exploding. Sarah's screams as wood and glass embedded in her back. The hate in her eyes. He tucked his hands under his legs, embarrassed at how minor the cuts were.

"It was horrible, Brad." She sniffled and grabbed some tissue. "Shawn was lying there so scared. He wanted his mommy. The paramedic was outstanding. She kept her cool. I don't know how she did it. I was barely hanging on." She blew her nose, grabbed more tissue, and wiped her eyes. "I thought he was dying." She shook her head. "He was so tiny on that bed with doctors and nurses rushing around." Her chest spasmed and she gasped for air.

Brad stood and took a step toward her.

She held out a hand. "No." Her icy glare drove him back.

"I'm sorry about Maggie. I didn't know her, but ... I'm sorry."

Brad nodded. "I'm sorry to disturb you." This was a terrible idea. "I'm glad you're back in Calgary."

"Wait. Sit." After a moment, she said, "I didn't want to come back. Heaven knows there was nothing but horrific memories." She sniffled. "Teaching jobs were hard for me to get in British Columbia. But I finally got an offer here teaching grade five. I hope you catch the bastard who did this." She sat straight and smiled weakly. "I know you'll get him. We need people like you. You know, to keep the monsters away. It was ... nice to see you. Let's grab a coffee some time when this is over."

Brad forced a smile. "Sure, sometime."

CHAPTER THIRTY-EIGHT

Pittman and Hirsch sat in a corner booth in the pancake restaurant a couple of miles from the school where they shot the boy. Pittman surveyed the restaurant and scrutinized everyone who came in. Cops would like this place, but he figured they'd be busy for, well, weeks.

Hirsch stared at his coffee sloshing in his shaking hands. His jaw trembled and his stomach churned. He glanced around for the restroom in case he needed it. He mumbled words that made little sense.

Pittman reached across the table and grabbed Hirsch's shoulder. His lips were tight over his teeth. "Man up. You're the guiltiest bastard in the world. Either that or both your girlfriend and dog ran away." Pittman snorted at his joke.

Hirsch didn't move.

"Shithead. Buck up or we need to get out of here."

Hirsch glanced at Pittman. "It was a kid, for fuck's sake."

"Just a target."

"You don't know what it's like to kill a kid."

"You'd be surprised."

"What the hell does that mean?"

Pittman smirked, sipped his coffee, then said, "They had it coming. They mocked us. We warned them."

Hirsch felt his jaw tighten. He blew air out his nose. "How did you talk me into this?"

Pittman chuckled. "It was easy. You're the better shot. I couldn't make that. It had to be you."

"Oh my god. I shot a *kid*."

Pittman leaned across the table and glared at Hirsch. "Keep your voice down."

The waitress filled Pittman's coffee. "Breakfast, boys?"

"Yeah." Pittman smiled. "We'll both have the rancher's special. Eggs over easy. White toast and hash browns."

The waitress headed to the kitchen.

"I'm not hungry." Hirsch tried to sip his coffee but spilled it.

"You gotta eat, boy. You agreed to strike back. This is war. In war, you make tough decisions. They know we're serious."

Hirsch snorted and shook his head. "The first five shootings weren't enough?"

Pittman stared over his cup. "Apparently not. They didn't take our calls and that shithead Sergeant Carew didn't take us seriously. What did he think would happen when he said kids were safe? No one is safe."

They sat in silence, staring at each other and the people around them, the tension between them building until the food arrived.

The waitress set the plates on the table.

Pittman grabbed his fork in his fist and shoveled the food

into this mouth. Hirsch moved food around his plate but didn't take many bites.

"You gonna eat that bread?" Pittman asked.

Hirsch slid over the toast.

Pittman pushed the toast around his plate and soaked up the egg yolk.

CHAPTER THIRTY-NINE

Brad radioed Griffin to pick him up at the Children's Hospital. He waited outside. Seeing Sarah had gut-punched him.

"Brad."

He glanced up.

Jill held out his jacket and smiled. "Thanks for the loan of your coat."

A horn honked. Griffin waved to him. "Uh, yeah. No problem. Be careful."

"You too." She jogged back into the hospital.

Brad tossed the Subway wrapper at the still overflowing garbage can in their office. He leaned back in his chair and sipped his Coke.

Griffin hung up the phone. "Sturgeon confirms the case was

from a .223 and there's a partial print. Not enough to compare, but if we get a suspect, that partial will come in handy. They got some decent molds of the footprints you guys found, and they're following the trajectory trying to find the bullet."

Brad sucked up the last of the Coke with a slurping sound. "Great. Now, all we need is a gun to match to the case and a boot to match the footprint. Hell, we're ninety-nine percent there. We should have the sniper by four." He shot the cup toward the garbage can.

"Easy, buddy. Sometimes it's baby steps."

"There's no time for baby steps. He shot a kid because I told parents to use the back of the school. I put a target on that kid."

"You're not that important." Griffin snorted.

Brad stood and leaned on his desk. "What the hell does that mean?"

Griffin glared at Brad. "It means you're delusional if you think this asshat is taking cues from you. He's angry and we don't know why. Carew was the one who taunted the shooter, not you. You tried to protect the kids. And by the way, you'd better hope Archer doesn't figure that out. I don't want to know what arrangement you and Ms. Andrus have. Sure, the clues we got today aren't great. But solving these shootings is a puzzle, and we put it together one piece at a time. Every piece counts. You just don't know how many pieces you need."

"It was a kid." Brad dropped back into his chair. "A kid."

"Yeah, it was. And I might seem cold, but tonight get this out of your system however you need to. Go for a jog. Drink yourself into unconsciousness. Punch the speed bag until your hands bleed. Whatever. But get dialed in."

CHAPTER FORTY

BRAD WAS CALMER AND RELAXED AFTER A WORKOUT. AS HE arrived at headquarters about five-thirty, a stranger approached. The guy said, "The person who aimed the rifle and shot the kid raised my ire. I had to do something. Somebody knows the sniper. Maybe sold him a gun or bullets or drank beer with him when he talked about doing the shooting or after the shootings. I can't investigate this, that's up to you. But I'm giving twenty-five thousand dollars toward the reward. That should help bring people forward with information."

More reward money would bring additional crank calls, too, but this guy cared enough to do what he could. He could entice someone who knew something to come forward. Brad admired the man.

This shooting of Shawn was disgusting in the worst way. Jeter Wolfe had been evil beyond words. When Brad caught the sniper, and he would, Brad knew when he peered into the suspect's eyes, he'd see the same deadness, the lack of a soul.

He entered the zoo and halted. Paramedic Jill Cook was sitting at his desk talking with Griffin.

Jill jumped up. "Sorry. I took your chair."

Brad waved her to sit. "That's fine." He stood in the middle of the room, eyes glancing at one, then the other. "This can't be good."

Jill stepped around the desk and held out her hands. "Shawn made it through surgery."

Brad's breath caught. "He's alive?"

"Yes." She rushed to Brad and hugged him.

He was knocked back a step by the force of her embrace. Her arms locked around him and he gently held her, then eased back. "Um, that's fantastic."

"Oh, god." Jill's hand covered her mouth. "I'm so sorry. I ... I just got caught up in the excitement. I knew you'd want to know, and I didn't want to phone you, so I thought I'd stop here and tell you in person, I—"

Brad held up a hand. "No need to apologize. Anytime you need to get a hug out of your system, I'm here for you. That's fantastic news about the kid."

"I didn't think he had a chance," Jill said. "He's a tough kid. Making it through surgery was a miracle. He's got a long recovery and it won't be easy." She sidestepped to the door, keeping her distance from Brad. "Um, good luck finding the sniper." She slipped out the door.

Griffin leaned back in the chair and hooked his fingers behind his head. "Whatever you did for the past couple of hours, let me in on the secret. What the hell was that?"

"She saved the kid. She's excited."

"Uh-huh." Griffin nodded. "I'm not sure it was the kid she was excited about."

Brad flopped in his chair. "What'd I miss?"

"Good idea." Griffin smirked. "Change the subject. You didn't miss squat. Door-to-door canvass didn't turn up any witnesses on Hope Street. The roadblocks just created a mob scene with parents blasting through the barricades to get their kids from school. The rookies are still searching for the bullet. Oh, yeah. There was panic in every school in Calgary. It was rush hour traffic for hours in the middle of the day." Griffin spread his arms wide. "Oh, and one last thing. I've been busting my ass for four days and I haven't received a single hug."

Brad stood. "Ah, you need a hug?"

"Not from you, asshole."

"I feel terrible telling you this, but, um, have you gazed in the mirror lately? You are not hugging material."

"Sit." Griffin switched on the TV. "Six o'clock news."

Brad nodded, picked up a stack of tips from the hotline and ignored the news anchor. One by one, he tossed the tips into two piles—ridiculous and possible. Then the squeaky voice of Angus Ferguson caught his attention. He increased the volume.

Ferguson sat behind a desk in the TV studio. He wore a dark-green jacket over a pink shirt with his tartan tie.

"We are pleased to have with us tonight, from the ABC News studio in New York, Martin Freeburg, a former FBI Special Agent who was a hostage negotiator and profiler. Welcome, Mr. Freeburg."

Brad could have picked Freeburg out of a crowd. Thinning gray hair, clean-shaven, and wire-rimmed glasses. He wore the distinctive style of the FBI—conservative blue suit, white shirt, and a striped red tie.

"Thank you, Angus. It's a pleasure to be on your show. And please, call me Martin." He flashed a brilliant smile.

"Martin. You are aware of the recent murders in Calgary. We have discussed this off-camera. The murders are the work of a sniper and in three days, six people have been shot"—Ferguson's appearance grew grim—"including one child. In your experience, what are we dealing with?"

"In my many cases such as this, I believe the sniper is acting alone and has extensive military experience including combat." Martin frowned and shook his head. "He was likely outstanding in combat with a high kill rate. He likely volunteered for dangerous missions that put him in the position to kill multiple enemy targets. Now that he is out of the military, he still has that urge." Martin gazed at the camera. "I believe he is hunting as we speak."

"Wow." Ferguson sat back in his chair. "That's quite a statement. How do you account for the differences in the targets? Women, men, and a child?"

"In combat, he may have been faced with killing all three groups, within seconds of each other. His targets are of convenience. If I understand right from what I've been told, he has never been seen, and most times, where the shot came from is speculation. That backs my contention that he is a military expert."

"Let's switch hats for a moment." Ferguson folded his hands on the table and cocked his head. "If you were here and able to negotiate with the sniper, what would you do?"

Martin confidently faced the camera. "The first, most important rule, is never to discuss police tactics in front of the media. There is no doubt the sniper is watching the press—he's probably excited about the reporting. Where leads are taking the police, suspected vehicles, descriptions of suspects, all should be kept to a minimum."

"Doesn't that put the public at risk?" Ferguson's eyes were wide.

"It does somewhat, but this man is a professional. You will not find him because someone bumped into him at the grocery store. Police must not negotiate." He emphatically shook his head. "They must pressure the suspect into making a mistake."

"Won't that lead to additional shootings?"

"Angus, I fear the shootings will continue no matter what." He frowned. "Getting the sniper to make a mistake is the best chance of catching him."

"How will the police know a mistake has been made?"

"If I may, I realize the local police," Martin said, his voice becoming patronizing, "who have never handled a situation such as this, are far out of their realm. They may not recognize the error committed by the sniper. It would be advisable to get experts who have dealt with this type of criminal."

"Are you recommending the RCMP take over this case?"

"That is one option, although I'm afraid their expertise is lacking. Several big-city police departments such as New York and Los Angeles have expertise. There are several retired experts who could assist. Including the FBI," Martin grinned."

"Thank you, Martin Freeburg, a former FBI Special Agent, hostage negotiator, and profiler." Ferguson faced the camera. "One last note. Police received another community donation for the reward fund today. That means donations from the community are fifty thousand and Nickle Oil will match that, putting the reward at one hundred thousand dollars. If you have information, please call the tip line at the number at the bottom of your screen."

Brad shut off the TV. "Well, Griffin, it is my learned opinion that Martin is full of shite."

"He's an ass, no doubt. But he started okay and made some valuable points."

"His profile might make sense in the US, but there aren't that many of our military who get the experience he thinks the shooter has."

"You know the RCMP will come with the same profile," Griffin said. "Then they'll quote Martin Freeburg, FBI Special Agent, hostage negotiator, profiler and all-round giant prick. And that the RCMP should take over the case."

Brad flipped the bird at the TV. "Out of my cold, dead hands."

CHAPTER FORTY-ONE

THE SUN WAS SETTING AS BRAD PULLED INTO THE DRIVEWAY. LOBO came flying from behind the garage and sprinted circles around the car until Brad got out. "Hey, buddy. Glad to see you." Brad knelt and Lobo soaked Brad's face with kisses and drool.

Brad stood and headed to the house past Annie's car.

As he stepped into the house, he said, "This is the police, trespassers will be shot. Survivors will be shot again."

Annie appeared from the living room. "Like I'm scared. My dog would protect me."

"Whose dog?"

Lobo padded over to Annie and sat at her side.

"Traitor," Brad said.

"There's a plate of food in the fridge. I'll heat it."

"What are you doing here?"

"I heard about the shooting on the news. I knew it would be a rough day for you, and I know you don't exactly eat healthy since you have to cook for yourself. Plus, I miss Lobo and I knew he'd be here alone."

"He's never alone. Remember, he's got that pack of feral cats he hangs out with."

"That's just wrong. It'll take a few minutes to heat your dinner. Let's sit in the living room."

Brad dropped into his recliner and Annie sat on the couch with her feet curled under her. Lobo curled up beside Annie.

Brad reclined the chair. "Am I in trouble?"

"What makes you think that?"

"I used my detectiving skills."

Annie frowned. "That's not a word."

"I think it is. Try using it in Scrabble."

Annie rolled her eyes.

"I'm too tired for twenty questions, tell me what's on your mind."

"I'm worried about you. I'd hoped you could ease into work. But you're right in the middle of the biggest case ever. When I heard they shot the boy, I knew you'd be pissed. You don't go to counseling."

"Keller is on vacation." Brad stared out the living room window.

"And heaven knows you won't talk to any of the boys."

"Is this a long story?"

Annie swung her legs off the couch and leaned forward. "No more bullshit. Are you okay?"

Brad swallowed hard. She was right, damn it. He'd gone from low stress to one hundred percent in a couple of days. It felt right to be working. It was healthy to keep busy. He loved the challenge. But he was exhausted. He slid the chair upright.

"I will never be all right. But hanging around here with

Lobo, as much as I love that, it wasn't enough. Sure, it would have been great to ease into work."

"That's on Archer," Annie said. "Why'd he put you in Homicide?"

"There was an opening."

Annie's eyes went wide. "Oh my god, you asked to go there."

"No. He offered, and I didn't refuse."

"Idiot." Annie shook her head and sat back on the couch. "The case is all we talk about at college."

"Ah, the finest minds in criminal justice. And what does your Mensa group think?"

"They think the police have bungled the whole thing and the snipers have the cops backpedaling. Someone said you guys couldn't organize a piss-up in a brewery."

"And you agree?"

"There were mistakes."

"Sure. It's easy to peek back in time and say here's where you should have done something. But real world doesn't have the luxury of hindsight. You make the best decisions you can at the time with whatever information you have. Most of the time you are making split-second decisions based on little information and gut instinct."

"I'm not saying I agree with them. But—"

"Oh, here it comes."

Annie frowned and cocked her head to the side. "But the sniper is ahead of you."

"That's the way every case starts. We're playing catch-up. But we eventually catch up. We'll get the sniper. He'll make a mistake, and when he does, we'll pounce."

A bell chimed from the kitchen. "Your dinner is ready."

CHAPTER FORTY-TWO

Friday Day Ten

Brad slept in but needed the jog, and so did Lobo. While Brad showered and dressed, Lobo had curled up on his bed and was snoring. Brad figured he'd give Lobo the day off. On the way to work there was a coffee stop at Gerry's.

He took the stairs to the basement and down the hall to the zoo. The door was closed and the lights off. He smiled. Everyone must have slept in. They wouldn't know when he got there, so he'd have some ammunition for the day. He unlocked the door, flipped on the lights, set his coffee on the desk and flopped into his chair.

A stack of reports from detectives following up on tips sat neatly in the center of his blotter. He sighed, grabbed his coffee and started reading. The first dozen reports didn't catch his interest. The first report of interest was a guy who'd used cinder blocks to barricade his house. He blocked up the doors and windows. Apparently, he bought enough food and water to last a month.

The next two reports were of interest. After the shooting of Jolanda D'Amore on Tuesday night, a white station wagon had driven around a police barricade and nearly hit two officers. The description of the car and partial license number was put on the radio. Five minutes later, a dozen officers were aiming revolvers and shotguns at the car surrounded the vehicle.

They took the driver and passenger into custody and left them in cells while the detectives investigated further. The car was searched but they found no evidence of any involvement in the shootings. They obtained a search warrant for his house. During the search of his home, police came across a .223 rifle and ammunition. Both the rifle and ammunition were tested but did not match the previous victims. When the detectives finally interviewed the driver and asked why he'd dodged the cops, he said he had an expired driver's license and didn't want to get stopped and lose his license—the one he didn't have—because he needed his car to get to work. His license had indeed expired. The passenger, the first suspect's roommate, was on probation for theft and drugs, but nothing violent or firearms related. Based on the lack of evidence, they were released. However, the detectives had a feeling about these guys, so they were put under surveillance.

He tossed that report on the outgoing pile and grabbed the next report. This was the second police contact with the suspects in the white station wagon. Shortly after the Shawn Fortin shooting, the car again sped around a police roadblock, and again, the car was stopped, and the suspects faced guns and shotguns. And then the detectives who had the suspects under surveillance pulled up. They'd been following the suspects since

6:00 a.m., and the suspects hadn't been near the school when the shooting occurred. They were no longer suspects, but clearly assholes. Now they were in police cells thinking about their bad choices.

He picked up a report from Ames. He'd been to every gun store in the city. They'd given him the names of anyone who'd bought a .223 rifle in the past six months. He'd seconded a bunch of cops and they'd tracked every owner. They all had alibis for at least three of the shootings. Dead end.

That created a whole new list of questions. What if the guns were purchased over six months ago or the guns were purchased outside of Calgary? The RCMP could find out.

If the shooter was from outside Calgary, why did he come here to kill? Did Calgary mean something to him? Great questions and he didn't have a clue what the answer was to any of them.

He sat back and took a long gulp of coffee. *Shit.* He hated cold coffee.

None of the guys had come in yet. Might as well get something to eat. In this job, you never knew when you'd eat again.

It was the in-between time. 10:00 a.m. Too late for breakfast but too early for lunch. Brad sipped his coffee and stared at the menu he knew by heart. His brain argued: breakfast, lunch. Breakfast, lunch. What the hell. He waved down the waitress. "I'll have a BLT on white with fries."

"We're still on the breakfast menu."

"So, no BLT?"

She shook her head.

"Okay, I'll have three slices of white toast. Two sides of bacon. Sliced tomatoes, and if you can put some lettuce on the side, that would be great."

The waitress peered over the pad as she wrote his order on.

"Oh, yeah, and mayo on the toast."

The waitress rolled her eyes. "Right. One BLT. Do you still want the fries?"

"That would be great." Brad reached for his coffee. No quality leads in the shootings and soon he'd have to deal with the RCMP. He did not get along with the Mounties. No city cop anywhere did. He didn't even know why there was this rivalry, but he was happy to keep it going.

For Brad, it started when he and the team were hunting Jeter Wolfe. Unknown to Brad, the RCMP had undercover members in Calgary doing the same thing. When both groups ended up in the same location in the dark, they nearly killed each other. As it was, one RCMP member was shot, but likely from one of his own. There'd been bad blood ever since, especially between Brad and Stinson.

He stared out the window and wondered what his next step should be. None of the leads so far had produced anything other than clearing a bunch of outstanding warrants and nabbing a few parole violations. It was worth it to get some guns off the street, the ones the bad guys had.

The problem was that they'd taken firearms from law-abiding citizens. That didn't sit well with him. The people who registered guns, kept them locked up, and followed safety rules weren't the problem. The courts needed to be tougher on any crime where a gun was involved. Any crime where an illegal or stolen gun was found.

In his periphery, someone was approaching. Expecting his

BLT breakfast, his head turned as he smiled. Not his breakfast. Sadie.

"What are you doing here?"

She slid into the booth. "Imagine that. We're at a restaurant in the same general vicinity, same general time."

"Are you following me?"

"I'm an investigative reporter." She grinned. "I can find stuff out."

"Seriously, how did you find me?"

"I called headquarters and got a guy named Mullen. I told him I was supposed to meet you, but I didn't remember where. He said you'd gone out for breakfast. I asked where. He said either the Three Brothers or the truck stop. You weren't at the Three Brothers."

The waitress refilled Brad's coffee and poured a cup for Sadie.

"Your special order will be ready in a few minutes," the waitress said.

"Special order?" Sadie asked. "You must be a regular."

"Long story," Brad said.

Sadie leaned forward. "I've got time now."

"Sadie, what do you want?"

"Coffee and conversation."

"I'm sure your cameraman would love to have coffee with you."

"He's not much on conversation."

Brad laughed. "And you think I'll be great conversation?"

"You've got better stories than he does."

"That may be true, but I'm afraid I'm not sharing with you."

Sadie sat back and clutched her chest. "I'm so hurt."

Brad laughed. "You're fishing for a scoop. Not from me."

"Haven't I been fair in everything so far?"

Brad nodded. "That you have."

"Let's just talk."

"Go ahead."

The waitress placed Brad's meal in front of him.

"A BLT at ten?"

"I've got pull." Brad poured ketchup on the plate.

Sadie reached over, grabbed a French fry, dipped it in the ketchup, and popped it in her mouth. "Maybe I should get one of those."

"I don't think you've got that kind of pull here."

"But you do." She grabbed another fry.

Brad picked up half his BLT and ate.

"If I don't have pull here, maybe you'll share?"

"Not gonna happen." Brad waved at the waitress. "A breakfast special just like mine for the lady."

"You've got to be kidding me," the waitress said, then headed to the kitchen.

"You do have pull here. You eat. I'll start. I grew up on a farm in Pincher Creek. Farming wasn't so great, but I had a horse, so that made it endurable. I couldn't wait to get off the farm, so I enrolled in Lethbridge College and took journalism."

"No kidding," Brad said between bites.

"You wouldn't believe what a cutthroat business journalism is. I finally got a job in Lethbridge for a TV station. I made the most of it and then landed the job here in Calgary last fall. Your turn."

"I'm still eating."

Sadie stole a French fry off Brad's plate. "Okay. I hate football and hockey. I love golf. I like to jog and hike. Roughing it to me is a Holiday Inn instead of the Hyatt. I don't like cats, but I like dogs."

"Wow. At least we agree on one thing."

"Only one thing?"

"Yup," Brad said. "You met Lobo."

"That's right, you're a dog person."

"Of course."

Sadie shook her head. "German shepherd, too. You are one hundred percent cop."

The waitress set the breakfast special in front of Sadie and refilled their coffees.

"You'd better leave her a huge tip," Brad said.

"Aren't you buying?"

"Sure. Then the next one is on you and I will be hungry."

"Chivalry is dead."

"Women's lib and all that stuff."

"You're finished your special. You talk, I'll eat." Sadie grabbed half the BLT.

Brad sat back and stared at Sadie.

She glanced up. "What?"

"I'm trying to figure out your angle."

"No angle." She wiped her mouth with a napkin. "I was hungry."

"Nah, that's not it. You're waiting for me to blurt out something spectacular you can lead with on the news tonight."

"Is it that easy? That you'd blurt out something?" She took a bite of her BLT. "I doubt that. Do you have something spectacular?"

"Nice try."

She set the sandwich down. "Here's what I know. You grew up

in Calgary in the Bowness neighborhood. You were a high school football jock, then university football superstar. You became a cop and you're first-rate." She ate a couple of French fries.

"That's it. You've got it nailed."

"But you also have a law degree."

Brad shrugged. "I had to take courses when I was in university. Basket weaving and finger painting were full."

"Come on, there's more than that."

"True."

"You took economics and are a savvy investor."

"Change the topic."

"Okay. What do you think of the RCMP showing up today with a profile? Is that even a thing?"

"I love the RCMP, they are truly Canada's police force. I'm sure they will be of immense help in this investigation."

Sadie laughed. "You said that with a straight face."

"I meant every word."

"Seriously?"

"As far as our discussion goes, yes, seriously."

"You're not a lot of fun."

"Not anymore." He slid out of the booth. "Have a grand day, Sadie. Next meal is on you."

CHAPTER FORTY-THREE

After his late brunch, Brad stopped in the gym and flipped through the latest stack of tips—the most promising. *If these are the best leads, we're screwed.* If you owned a gun, and someone knew about it, you were reported. *Hell, this is Alberta, firearms are in their genes.*

Brad tossed a stack of tips into an overflowing box on the floor. Ames had drawn a blank in his tour of the gun shops. No city in Canada had experienced shootings like this. This was new, and they were fumbling their way through this mess. Archer said he'd contact some chiefs he knew in United States departments. A few promising leads went nowhere, and they quickly removed each suspect from the list.

If you owned a white truck of any kind, you'd likely parked it in your garage. You'd probably been stopped many times and even having the truck in your driveway meant someone would call the tip line. Looking for the white van was a waste of time. If the sniper had been driving a white van, he'd be stupid to keep using it with all the publicity.

Checking for vehicles stolen in the past five days might be an excellent idea.

He wandered over to the suspect list on the wall. The double doors to the gym burst open, like saloon doors. Brad wasn't sure what it was about those doors that encouraged people to throw them open. Four guys in cheap suits strode into the gym. The guy in the lead surveyed the room. Brad knew him, but from … ah shit. *Stinson.*

They'd crossed paths during the search for Jeter Wolfe. To say they didn't get along was mild. A couple of times, they'd come close to blows.

Thousands of Mounties in the country and this is the guy they send.

Stinson's eyes found Brad, and a sly grin crossed his face. He nodded to the other three members of his group and they headed over.

"Coulter."

Brad stepped closer. "Stinson."

"Looks like we're working together again."

"Looks like you're here to provide consultation."

Stinson smirked. "Consult. Partner. Same thing."

"I see you two have picked up where you left off." Archer glared at Brad, then Stinson. "Let *me* be clear. Shove your dicks back in your pants and lose the attitude. Until told otherwise"—he glanced at Brad—"I'm in charge of this investigation. You two report to me. We have more significant problems than you two stirring up ancient rivalries. Follow me." Archer led them up to his second-floor office.

Brad closed the door behind him and took a seat at the

conference table across from Stinson. He sighed. Archer was right. This was no time for personal vendettas. He may dislike Stinson, but Calgary had a sniper terrorizing the city. They had the same priorities.

"All right, Stinson," Archer said. "What do you have for us?"

Stinson opened a file folder and passed out a report. "This is the profile we've created for the sniper. I've talked to the FBI Behavioral Science Unit. They reviewed what we wrote and added their own information."

"How did you do a profile?" Brad asked. "You just arrived."

Stinson shrugged. "Chief Archer has been cooperative, so we know what you know. The press has their own sources, so they add to the information."

"What if we've interpreted the info wrong?" Brad asked. "What if we're on the wrong track?"

"That's where we come in," Stinson said. "With help from the FBI, we can weed out the baseless information, but also add to the profile. They've got data on hundreds of killers. Their profiles are accurate. We're trying to share information."

"There are a few other things you could help us with," Brad said.

"Name it," Stinson said.

"We've checked the local gun stores for anyone who bought a .223 rifle in the past six months. We need to know is how many are there in Alberta."

"Done," Stinson said. "What else?"

"It would be worthwhile to know if something like this has happened anywhere else in Canada or the US. And if there have been any known snipers released from jail lately, or on a federal watch list."

"No problem."

CHAPTER FORTY-FOUR

Brad leaned against the back wall of the briefing room. As crowded as it had been earlier in the week, there were at least another thirty people crammed in.

Right on the dot of 3:00 p.m., Stinson stepped up to the microphone. "Good afternoon. I'm Sergeant Stinson of the RCMP. I'm here to provide a profile on the sniper. This information is gleaned from the information about the patterns of the shootings and what the sniper may have done in his past, providing him with the skills to accomplish what he has. I've also consulted the FBI, who has a unit dedicated to the analysis of serial killers—the agents at the Behavioral Analysis Unit. Together we have come up with a profile. My partners are handing out our analysis. While they do that, I'll share our information."

Stinson opened a file folder.

"The sniper is a male," Stinson read, "has a highly aggressive personality, and is control-oriented, controlling and coercive. It is likely he has always been a bully and took pleasure in humiliating others. He views the display or even the idea of emotions as a sign of weakness. He does not like to be told what to do, is hypersensitive to negative feedback, and will carry a grudge until he has the upper hand."

Sounds like half the guys I've arrested.

"As mentioned, he is coercive and will become aggressive to others who get in his way. Others may do what he says out of fear. He is closed-minded and set in his ways. He does not like change and has extreme personal beliefs, which he will defend."

Set in his ways? Damn, could be me.

"He may be socially intolerant and inherently racist. An affiliation with an extremist group of white males is likely."

Brad sighed. The profile read like an horoscope for criminals.

"He is mean-spirited and has a callous disregard for others. He is particularly resentful of those in power, such as politicians, CEOs, and bank presidents. There is no doubt he has extensive experience with firearms, likely the military. In the military, it is likely he was in trouble a lot and possibly received a dishonorable discharge. It is not unreasonable to believe the sniper is an American, probably a Vietnam Vet who was disgruntled with the United States and moved here, to find he's again being persecuted. He grows stronger with each killing and has a powerful urge to kill that will not be extinguished."

Huh. Vietnam veteran. Brad considered this.

"If anyone knows someone who fits this profile, *do not* approach him. Do not ask probing questions. Call the hotline and leave the investigation to us. I will take questions. You, sir."

"Angus Ferguson, CTV News. You refer to the sniper as *he*. Could there be more than one sniper? Sniper teams? With the first four shootings occurring over two-and-a-half hours, maybe two units or more?"

"Good questions, Mr. Ferguson. We believe the shootings are the work of a single individual without a partner. And certainly, one man, not multiple teams." Stinson held up his hand. "Thank you for your cooperation today. I'll stay around for any of you who have additional questions."

After the RCMP press conference, Brad and Griffin headed back to the zoo.

"We need to talk about their profile," Griffin said.

Brad opened a drawer in his desk and rummaged around.

"What are you doing?" Griffin asked.

"I can't find my Magic 8 Ball, tarot cards or Ouija board."

Griffin chuckled. "Sometimes you kill me."

"I'm serious."

"You don't think they had some excellent ideas?"

Brad's eyes widened. "You do? Let's go through the RCMP's profile." At each point, he held up a finger. "One, he's male—no shit. Two, he's aggressive—obviously. Three, controlling—son of a bitch. Four, bullies and humiliates people—heaven help us. Five, hypersensitive to negative feedback—clearly."

Griffin pulled out his handcuffs. "You don't have to say anything. In fact, I'm encouraging that. I'm arresting you, Brad Coulter."

"Don't be a smartass, it doesn't look good on you."

"Ah, but it fits you like a tailored Italian suit."

Brad held up his index finger on his left hand. "Five, extensive experience with firearms—knock me over with a feather.

Six, military, dishonorable discharge, Vietnam—did Einstein work with them?"

"Excellent points. I'll arrest Ames, Steele, and Zerr. Maybe Sergeant Jackson, too."

"Seriously. How does this help?"

"You forgot racist and hangs out with white guys."

Brad threw his arms up in the air. "I give up." He leaned his head against the wall and hit his forehead on the concrete.

Griffin headed over and placed an arm around Brad's shoulder. "Your brain is mush, buddy. We're both beyond exhausted. If my wife asked me if I wanted rice or potatoes, I'd stare blankly at her. I have no brain power left. Let's get out of here."

Brad nodded. "I'll go home for dinner. I need to eat something other than takeout breakfast sandwiches, subs, and burgers. But I'll be back later."

"Stay home. Get a good night's sleep."

CHAPTER FORTY-FIVE

JUST AFTER 8:00 P.M., THE COUPLE STEPPED OUT OF THE PONDEROSA Steakhouse. Rain mixed with snow whipped around them. They wrapped their coats tight as they hustled across the parking lot to their car. They bent forward as the wind blew the sleet toward them like icy pellets. She waited as her husband pulled keys out of his pocket to unlock the passenger door. She heard a boom and glanced to the sky, thinking it was thunder. When she glanced back, her husband stumbled, took three steps, then fell onto his face.

Her first thought was he'd had a heart attack. She knelt next to him and rolled him onto his back. In the light from the overhead streetlight, she saw his shirt was torn and blood flowed from his stomach. Rain flowed over his exposed intestines.

She screamed.

At home that night, Brad and Lobo wandered around the farm. He still couldn't believe anyone would shoot a child. What mental illness or hatred could be so evil a child became a target? Brad's one wish was that he'd be the one to confront the killer. The one who could apply street justice. Now, instead of coming home to relax, his jaw clenched until it hurt, and a heavy weight pressed down on his neck and shoulders. He glanced at the old truck. He couldn't get the timing set. He might need to ask Zerr for help getting it going. They headed back to the house.

Brad reheated a roast dinner Annie had left. Lobo cleaned his bowl in a matter of seconds, then sat by the table, hoping against hope today would be the day Brad fed him dinner scraps. It hadn't happened in six years, but today might be the day. Lobo was ever hopeful.

Brad tried to relax. The victims and autopsies fought for his attention. He'd flipped through the TV channels. Tried to read a novel. He'd even tried to nap. Nothing worked.

At eight he headed back to work with Lobo snoozing in the back of the car. Brad didn't have the heart to leave him home alone. Who knew when Brad would be home again? Annie was great about caring for Lobo when Brad was stuck at work, but Brad missed hanging out with him. He felt safe with Lobo at his side.

Besides, it was raining, and if it became a thunderstorm, the big baby would hide out in the barn. Lobo had no problem with gunshots, flashbangs, or explosions. But thunder ...

The rain turned to sleet the closer he got to downtown. He followed the curve onto Ninth Avenue when the call came in. "Man down. Ponderosa Steakhouse. 720 Seventeenth Avenue SW. EMS on the way. The caller says man is in the parking lot. His wife is screaming he's been shot."

Lobo's head appeared over the front seat when Brad activated the siren. Red-and-blue lights reflected off the wet pavement. The radio was alive with units responding. The car fishtailed as Brad drove south on Eleventh Street. As he headed west on Seventeenth Avenue, several cruisers raced past ahead of him. He followed them. Four blocks later, they stopped on the street next to the parking lot. As Brad slid out of the car, an ambulance pulled in.

Brad cracked a back window. "Wait here." Lobo slipped his snout out the window and licked at the sleet.

He grabbed his raincoat off the passenger seat and slipped it on as he jogged to a handful of people by a car. The paramedics rushed over from the other direction.

Brad surveyed the scene. "There's few people here."

"Happening a lot," a cop said. "There are seldom bystanders when we arrive. People are scared and don't want to be exposed. There are a few potential witnesses in the restaurant."

"Go to the restaurant and don't let anyone leave," Brad said. "We need statements from them. Don't let them talk about what they saw."

Brad knelt next to the paramedics. Jill Cook was placing saline-soaked pads over the intestines. Sharma and two cops slid the stretcher beside the patient. Once on the stretcher, they rushed the victim to the ambulance.

As Brad watched the stretcher roll away, a hand touched his shoulder.

"Did you secure the witnesses?" Griffin asked.

"They're in the restaurant."

Griffin glanced at the ambulance. "How is he?"

"Not dead," Brad said. "But unconscious. This one is a gut shot. Either our shooter has lost his skill, or he is purposely making people suffer. Maybe our victim moved at the last second or the shooter was disrupted as he shot."

Griffin nodded. "You need to go with him. If he regains consciousness, even for a minute, you need to be there. I'll handle the scene."

"Lobo is in my car."

"No problem. Leave me your keys."

Brad opened the side door of the ambulance and stepped in.

"What are you doing?" Jill asked.

"I'm riding with you."

She placed a pad over the patient's stomach, then pulled a blanket over him. "Fine, but don't get in my way."

Sharma glanced back from the driver's seat. "Ready to go. Jill?"

"Yup. Fast and easy."

Sharma winked at Brad. "Yes, ma'am."

"And stop that shit," Jill said.

"Anything I can do?" Brad asked.

Jill peered over her shoulder, then hung an IV bag on a pole. "You a paramedic and a detective?"

"Nope."

"Then, I guess not." Jill attached an IV line to the needle she'd just inserted.

"You want me to squeeze the bag, get the fluid running faster?"

Jill slid into the jump seat at the patient's head. "Yeah, I guess that would be okay." She adjusted the oxygen mask that had slipped off the patient's face.

Brad grabbed the IV bag and began squeezing. He glanced at the cardiac monitor. "His heart is racing. About one hundred and thirty. Is his blood pressure low?"

Jill shook her head. "Yes, Dr. Coulter. It's low and sinking fast. Keep the pressure on that bag. You learn that from doctor shows on TV?"

"Paramedic show. *Emergency*!"

"Seems like you were paying attention." She leaned toward the front of the ambulance. "Let the Holy Cross Hospital know his blood pressure is crashing. He must have some significant internal bleeding. We're pouring the fluid to him, but it isn't helping."

Sharma reached for the mic, and over the whine of the siren, Brad heard Sharma repeat Jill's words to the hospital.

Brad rolled the top of the bag down and kept squeezing. Maggie had told him once—forever ago—that when the patient had internal bleeding, the paramedics couldn't stop, the one thing that would save the patient was surgery. The fluid the paramedics infused kept them alive, to a point, but eventually, the blood became diluted, flowed like Kool-Aid and didn't clot.

Sharma yelled back, "We're going straight to the operating room. They're holding an elevator for us. We're one minute out."

"Okay." Jill grabbed the nearly empty IV bag from Brad and attached a full bag. "Keep squeezing to the OR."

"Where do you think the internal bleeding is?"

"Hard to say. It appears the bullet went through. The shock wave of the bullet split his abdomen open. It could be anything and everything. Spleen, pancreas, liver, bladder, none of them or all of them."

"You said the bullet went through?"

She nodded. "I think so. A high-velocity bullet will go through the abdomen like a hot knife through butter."

The siren stopped, and a backup alarm sounded. As soon as the ambulance came to a full stop, the doors were yanked open. Several orderlies, paramedics, and nurses surrounded the back of the ambulance. Brad had to push his way past the group to keep up with the stretcher. The last thing he wanted was for the IV line to become dislodged. They jogged down a hallway to a waiting elevator. As soon as the stretcher was in, the doors closed. Seconds later, the door opened, and the jog was on again. At the OR doors, nurses in caps, masks and gowns waited. One took the IV bag from Brad as others pulled the stretcher through the doors. As the OR doors closed, the heart monitor gave a steady, low tone.

"Ah, shit," Jill said.

They stood in silence. Brad peered through the small glass window in the door until the patient was out of sight. He sighed and glanced at his hands. Some spattering of blood. He'd seen worse.

Sharma was the first one to move. "We've got one hell of a mess to clean up." He headed back to the elevator.

"It will be easier to clean and stock at the station," Jill said.

Sharma nodded.

"Can you drop me back at the scene?" Brad asked.

CHAPTER FORTY-SIX

Late afternoon Pittman and Hirsch sat in front-row seats in the basement of the York Hotel. Three days and each day a seedier bar. The York sounded promising, perhaps upscale. They were wrong. Their first clue should have been the tough hookers lined up outside the door. Their second clue was that they headed to the basement Spotlight Club—a stripper bar. The girls here were nastier than the ones upstairs. A few could kickstart a Kenworth.

Logan Hirsch's eyes flickered around the bar. He didn't like being upfront. If a fight broke out, they were trapped. He'd been in some low-end bars with rig workers, but none as rough as this place. Who knew what color the carpet was originally, but it squished from decades of spilled drinks. He wasn't sure which odor was stronger—vomit, urine, greasy cooking, or disinfectant.

A waitress came by, cigarette hanging out of her mouth, low-cut faded T-shirt and a too-short skirt on her eighty-year-old body. "What do you want?"

Hirsch said, "Tray of draft."

Pittman slapped Hirsch on the shoulder. "We're lucky to get great seats like this."

Hirsch stared at Pittman. *What the hell?* "Yeah, sure."

The stage lights came up and strobes danced across the floor. The husky dancer sashayed onto the stage. She wasn't wearing a lot, but the little she had was leather, including a leather Catwoman mask. When she snapped a whip, Hirsch cringed. Then the speakers blared *Whip It,* by Devo. *Oh shit.*

Hirsch was thankful when the aging waitress set a tray of draft on their table and he could focus on his beer.

The dancer mesmerized Pittman who whooped and cheered. Every time she passed in front of Pittman, he slipped another dollar or two in her G-string. The cash they'd stolen from the dealership was running lower and lower with every sashay of her hips.

Hirsch drank another beer. Thankfully the dance and the music stopped, with the promise of another dancer in ten minutes.

"This is fantastic." Pittman had an ear-to-ear grin. "A lot better than the peelers in the rig towns." He downed a draft and grabbed another.

"Hey," Hirsch said. "Uh, are we gonna talk about the RCMP's profile?"

Pittman laughed so hard he spilled half his beer. "What's to talk about? It's all smoke and mirrors."

"They were specific. Like about holding a grudge."

"Sure, that's why we're doing this. Call it what you want.

We're tired of being shit on. We're tired of gigantic oil companies making money, then dumping us when times get tough. The fuckin' CEOs are parasites feeding off us. Grudge, revenge, taking a stand. It's all the same. They're getting what they have coming to them." He glanced at the stage, then grabbed another beer.

"Why do they think we're military?"

Pittman smirked. "Cuz we're that damn effective."

Hirsch stared at Pittman and realized he didn't know Pittman's background. Just that he worked rigs. "Were you in the military?"

"You've seen me shoot. I can hit a moose at fifty feet, maybe. You're the one with an accurate shot."

Hirsch held up a hand. "Hey, I don't mean nothing."

"The Horsemen are in your head. That's what they wanted. Now you're buying into their bullshit." He jabbed a finger into Hirsch's chest. "I don't need no negative shit from you." Pittman finished his beer. "Maybe the cops need a reminder." Pittman slid a beer over to Hirsch and grinned. "Forget that shit. The next dancer is coming out."

CHAPTER FORTY-SEVEN

BRAD JUMPED OUT OF THE AMBULANCE, THANKED JILL AND Sharma, and jogged through the sleet to the restaurant. He ducked under the police tape and glanced at the spot where the victim had fallen. Nothing but puddles. All signs of the victim's blood were washed away. He wiped the moisture from his face. Not just water, wet snow. *Well, this screws up our crime scene.*

Inside the restaurant, he shed his raincoat and tossed it over a chair. Briscoe sauntered over, coffee in his hand.

Brad reached out. "Thanks."

"Get your own," Briscoe replied.

"You're dry," Brad said.

"Got my rookie to do the outside work. Toscana's out there coordinating roadblocks. We've stopped a dozen white vans, but no shooter. The Crime Scene Unit left for the hospital about ten minutes ago. Nothing for them to find in the rain."

"So, you're sitting here, drinking coffee, and watching witnesses."

"Hey, I'm the inside guy." He held up a clipboard. "I have the names of all the witnesses. I check off the names after they're interviewed."

"Sounds like a tough job. I hope they got you a comfy chair to go with the coffee and arduous task."

"Luckily, I'm up to it."

Brad peeked around the corner of the restaurant. Not many people there. "How many witnesses?"

"Thirteen."

"How many have been interviewed?"

"Eleven."

"How'd they get that many interviewed so quick?"

Briscoe sipped his coffee. "Griffin called for lots of backup. Every detective on duty is here. Sex Crimes, Drugs, Arson, Robbery, you name it."

Brad winced. "There's not gonna be a lot of consistency in the questions asked."

"True, but from what I overheard, no one saw or heard anything. Those who heard something thought it was thunder. When they were asked where the sound came from, they were confused and pointed to the sky."

"We're gonna get five buckets of nothing."

Briscoe nodded.

"What about outside?"

"What about it?" Briscoe wiped some sleet off Brad's shoulder. "It was raining, now it's snowing. Any evidence was washed away."

"Did anyone search for the case or the bullet?"

"Where the hell are we supposed to search? Besides, the bullet is in the body."

Brad shook his head. "Through and through."

Briscoe spread his arms wide. "Be my guest. You think you know where the case and bullet are, go for it."

Brad nodded and grabbed his coat. Before he headed outside, he ordered two coffees. At his car, he let Lobo out. "Heel." Brad headed back to the spot where the victim had fallen, Lobo tight to his left side.

Brad glanced up when Lobo growled. Sergeant Toscana was walking toward them. Brad held out a coffee. "Figured you could use this."

She took a sip. "I'm soaked to the bone and it's getting colder."

"I see Mr. Personality has you outside doing all the work."

Toscana snorted. "Most of the time he treats me like it's my first day on the job."

"I remember that. Once his rookie, always his rookie."

"You were his partner as a rookie?"

Brad rolled up the collar of his coat. "No. I'd been on the street four years, but that didn't impress him."

"Ouch, that had to hurt." Toscana wrapped both hands around the coffee.

"No different from treating a new sergeant that way."

"How did you cope?"

Brad smirked. "The key is to push back. He's waiting for you to prove to him you're strong. He hates weak cops. Next time tell him to stand in the rain."

Toscana snorted. "That'll get me bounced back to a constable."

"Nope. He'll bitch, but he'll do it." Brad sipped his coffee. "Your life will be better when you show him you won't take his shit."

Toscana toasted Brad. "Thanks for the advice."

Lobo stood and shook water over Brad. "Thanks, pal."

If the victim and his wife had finished dinner and were walking to their car, they were headed north. The injury was left to right. That means the shot had to come from the west. Maybe behind the victim, or it would have gone through the victim and his wife. Since it missed her, either she was a step behind, or the shot came from slightly behind. So, the shot came from the park to the southwest. He drew an imaginary line from the spot of the victim to the park and headed in that direction.

"Lobo, heel." They crossed Seventh Street into the park and stopped.

Brad pulled out a spare magazine and held it to Lobo's nose. Lobo sniffed the magazine. "Seek."

Lobo stood, with his neck extended, nose to the air. He shook his head a few times, rain and snow splattering Brad. Lobo glanced left, right, then left again and trotted diagonally across the park. He'd gone twenty feet when he slowed and his nose dropped to the ground. He rooted around. With a paw, he pulled back a branch and gawked at Brad, who shook his head. "Nope. Not a stick." He held the magazine to Lobo's nose again. Lobo sniffed the air, then headed to a tree and sat at the base of the tree.

The snow had gathered under the branches, but close to the tree was barren. Brad eyed the spot where the victim fell. If he'd taken a step or two after he was shot, the shooter would be …

Brad leaned against the tree and held his arms like he was shooting a rifle. If this was the right spot, the shooter had been closer than he'd been in the previous shootings. Less than fifty feet.

After the shot, the case would eject from the right side. Most of the time, the case flew at least a foot away. By now the snow would cover it. Once again, Brad held the magazine to Lobo's nose, then directed Lobo to the right. Thirty seconds later, Lobo stopped and sat, about two feet from the tree. Brad knelt and shone his Mini-Mag flashlight over the area. Nothing. Totally snow-covered.

He slid on an examination glove and carefully brushed the snow away, starting in an ever-widening circle. He found twigs, rocks, bottle caps—and a case. With his other hand, he pulled out an evidence bag and dropped the case in. "Good boy, Lobo." Brad pulled a couple of treats out of his coat pocket.

Brad headed back to the tree and again raised his arms in a shooting motion. He focused on the area to the northeast of the victim. "Lobo, heel."

As they crossed Seventh Street, Brad's gaze focused on a point to the far side of the parking lot. They crossed where the victim had fallen, then stopped. Brad held his Mini-Mag at his stomach and aimed it to the northeast. The beam lit a garage across the alley. They headed that way.

The garage was timeworn and pitted. If a bullet was there, he'd never find it. Maybe not even in daylight. But he'd have Sturgeon send a team back here in the morning.

His pager buzzed. He glanced at the message. From EMS. Their patient didn't make it.

Brad stared blankly at the pager. Jill said the injury wasn't that serious. But he knew it was impossible to know what internal injuries a patient had. The icy slush turned to large snow flakes. He stood beside the garage, numb. He wiped the snow from his face. The murders continued, and they were no closer to catching the sniper.

CHAPTER FORTY-EIGHT

Saturday Day Eleven

DESPITE THE COLD WIND, ICY SIDEWALK, AND EARLY MORNING, THE press was out in full force. Not only had they staked out the front doors, but they filled the back alley with TV vans with large satellite dishes. Reporters dressed in parkas, snow boots, gloves and beanies with microphones blocked the way. Brad fought through the mass of people and batted away microphones thrust into his face. He noticed two men, dressed in suit jackets, shivering as they held out microphones labeled ABC and CBS. Shit. *The American press was here.*

"Detective, what can you tell us about the shooting last night?"

"Have you identified the man killed?"

"Detective, was this the sniper?"

Brad headed into the crowd. Instinct from his football days

came back. He dropped his shoulder, clearing a path to the back door.

"Considering this shooting, do you think the RCMP profile is accurate?"

"Should the RCMP be in charge since they have this detailed information about the sniper?"

He swatted at microphones that were bouncing off his cheeks.

"Do you think the RCMP press conference yesterday frustrated the sniper, and that's why he struck again last night?"

"Detective, why does the sniper want to talk to you? Is it someone you know?"

He finally reached the back door where two uniformed cops stood guard. One of them opened the door as the reporters continued shouting questions.

Inside, he took off his coat and shook off the snow and rain, then took the back stairs to the basement, into the gym and met Detective Windsor by the coffee machines. Windsor supervised the command center for the night shift. Brad refilled his coffee cup and offered some to Windsor.

"Not for me. I plan on hitting the sack as soon as I get home."

"Busy night?" Brad asked.

"Nope." Windsor yawned. "Nothing happened, and even the tip lines were moderately quiet after the rush of calls following the RCMP news conference. No leads that made the high priority list. A few people confessed to crimes, everything from using their neighbor's garbage can to running over a cat. Day shift can check those out. I heard the Crime Scene Unit heading back to the Ponderosa."

Brad sipped his coffee. "This stuff is shit. I don't know why I don't buy a half-dozen decent coffees on my way to work."

Windsor grinned. "They stopped about a dozen white vans last night after the shooting, but no suspects. The cops put stickers on the vans so they won't get stopped again. You see those stickers all over the city. That's all I've got. If you're okay, I'm heading home."

"Night, Windsor." Brad headed to the zoo and plopped into his chair. He wasn't surprised it had been quiet overnight. After a shooting, 911 and the tip line lit up for four or five hours, then slowed to a trickle. Even the chronic complainers slept through the night. He spotted a file folder in the middle of his desk. He grabbed the folder and flipped it open—a report from Sturgeon. They'd analyzed the case over night but didn't find a useable print. Just a smudge. He tossed the folder on his desk.

Something Windsor had said was nagging at the back of his brain. *White vans.* For six days, they'd been searching for a white van and they had stopped hundreds. *Some five or six times until we started putting stickers on the ones we'd checked.* They'd found a dozen drivers with outstanding warrants for everything from failing to appear to assault. They even confiscated a few rifles. But not the right rifle and not the sniper.

Then they'd tracked through motor vehicle records for all white vans and cross-referenced it with people with criminal records. That netted another dozen suspects, but no sniper. They cleared up a few outstanding warrants.

Interesting that there was no buzz on the street. With hundreds of confidential informants on the street, not one had any information to trade for the reward growing daily. The snipers were ghosts, even in the crime world. How was that possible? He took another sip of coffee and immediately regretted it. He tossed the cup in the garbage.

CHAPTER FORTY-NINE

HIRSCH DROVE DOWN TWELFTH AVENUE SE AND PAST THE CRACK houses. The streets were quiet at this time of the morning. The crackheads came out after dark.

Pittman's fingers tapped rapidly on the dash. His right leg bounced to some unknown rapid beat as he chewed on his lip. "Can you believe those bastards? I figured Coulter was interested. He's as corrupt as Carew. Screwed us over. Our note was clear. We would call the Ponderosa at eight this morning. How could I be clearer? We don't have to use one of their lines where they can trace the call. I can keep it brief. Coulter and I negotiate." The veins in Pittman's neck bulged as his face reddened. "No one humiliates me. They think this is a game. Well, game on." He pounded the dash.

Hirsch slowed as he passed the Victoria Park bus barns, continued to the MacDonald Bridge, and swung a U-turn. He drove back even slower.

"Stop here." Pittman glanced over his shoulder. "There." He

pointed into the yard where dozens of Transit buses were parked. "Middle of the first row. See the guy smoking outside the door of the bus?"

"Yeah. I see him."

Pittman slapped his thigh. "Oh, how perfect. A bus driver."

"I'm not sure," Hirsch said. "We're exposed here."

"Pull the car ahead another fifteen feet."

Hirsch glanced over his shoulder. "I can't park the car so the back end is facing that guy. I'd be in the middle of the road."

"I don't care. Get out." Pittman slid out, headed to the back of the car and opened the trunk.

Hirsch raced around to Pittman. "What are you doing?"

"I'm shooting from the side of the car, not inside."

Hirsch glanced up and down the street. "Someone will see you."

"Not if you stand on the driver's side. Pretend you're searching the trunk for something."

"Pit. This isn't a safe place. You killed the guy last night. It was an expert shot. Leave it at that. Let this go."

"You're a maggot." Pittman swung on Hirsch. He pulled his handgun out of his coat pocket. "You want to die here?"

Hirsch's hands automatically raised, and he stepped back. "What the hell?"

"Get your hands down." Pittman's dark eyes burned through Hirsch.

"You're insane."

Pittman's lips curled. He slid the pistol into his jacket, reached into the trunk and slid the rifle out of its case. He leaned into the trunk, slapped in a magazine and chambered a round. "Any cars or pedestrians?"

"N-no," Hirsch said.

Pittman slid the rifle out of the trunk and swung it toward the buses. He spread his legs and leaned into the gun. The driver fell back against the bus, then the shot sounded. As the driver slid down the side of the bus, two more shots rang out.

Pittman threw the gun in the trunk. "Let's go." He slammed the lid.

CHAPTER FIFTY

AMIR SHARMA AND JILL COOK WERE DRIVING BACK TO THEIR station for 10:00 a.m. brunch with the firefighters after dropping their patient at the Holy Cross Hospital.

"Medic 2. Man down at the Victoria Park bus barns," dispatch said.

Jill grabbed the mic. "Roger, Victoria Park bus barns. Do you have any additional information?"

"Not a lot," dispatch said. "Other drivers can see a man in uniform lying beside a bus. They think it might be a heart attack."

"Anyone check to see if he's breathing?"

"Ah, no Medic 2. The drivers are inside the barns. No one wants to go outside in case it's the sniper."

"Understood." Jill replaced the mic. "We're gonna see more of that."

The mid-Saturday morning traffic was light. Sharma didn't use lights or siren but complained non-stop about missing breakfast. The gate to the bus barns was open. As they pulled into the yard, they saw the man on the ground by a bus. He appeared to be the driver.

Sharma parked between the bus and the driver. Jill jumped out and headed to the man. She carefully rolled him over and saw three bullet wounds. One in his right shoulder, one in his right thigh, and one in the center of his chest.

Then the driver coughed and spit up blood. Sharma set the paramedic kit by Jill.

"He's alive," Jill said. "Get the stretcher."

Jill opened the kit, grabbed handfuls of gauze bandages, and stuffed them into the driver's shirt.

Sharma dropped the stretcher beside Jill. "I called for backup, but no one is close."

She nodded. "Then onto the stretcher."

They rolled the stretcher into the back of the ambulance.

"I'll stop the bleeding and start IVs if I have time," Jill said. "How fast you can drive."

"One diesel infusion, coming up."

Jill jumped into the back, and as she shut the door, the ambulance accelerated way from the curb.

She administered oxygen. She stuffed gauze into the shirt, wrapped the wound in the leg and taped gauze near the shoulder. When the ambulance stopped, emergency staff were waiting and helped rush the driver to the trauma room. The staff surrounded the driver. Less than five minutes later the emergency physician held up his hands. "Time of death, 10:25 a.m."

CHAPTER FIFTY-ONE

BRAD PARKED OUTSIDE THE EMERGENCY DEPARTMENT, FLASHED HIS badge, and asked the security guard to watch his car. He pushed through the door and headed down the hall to the triage desk.

Again, he held out his badge. "Detective Coulter. Shooting patient, Trauma 1?"

The triage nurse shook her head. "Too late, Coulter. He's dead."

"What? I heard he was alive."

She shook her head again. "Died on the way here. He was pulseless and not breathing when the paramedics brought him in. Three gunshot wounds. One to his chest."

"Three?"

"Yes. The one to the chest killed him, but the one in his leg hit an artery, so that didn't help."

"Dang. Where are the paramedics?"

"In the coffee room."

"Thanks. I'll be back to get his belongings."

Brad headed down the hall, then turned back. "Has his family been notified?"

"Detectives are on the way to tell his wife."

He nodded, headed down the hall and opened the door. Jill was slouched in a chair, pale. Sharma glanced up as Brad entered.

"Heck of a way to start the day." Brad sat across from them. "What can you tell me about this one?"

Jill closed her eyes and shook her head.

"We got it as a 'man down' beside a bus," Sharma said. "On a Saturday morning that can be anything from someone sleeping off the party from the night before, a drug overdose, or maybe a cardiac arrest. When we arrived, no one was near the guy. The bus barn door was open, and a group of drivers were watching us. That was weird, but we drove over to the bus. That's when we realized he'd been shot. There wasn't time for backup, so we grabbed him and raced here. But he was dead when we got here."

Brad pursed his lips and shook his head. "Shit."

"Are you going to the scene?" Sharma asked.

"No. Griffin is heading there. I'll need a statement from you two."

Jill opened her eyes and nodded. "He was just lying there. No one helped him. They watched him die."

"People are scared," Sharma said.

"I'm scared," Brad replied. "Being scared is a reasonable response."

CHAPTER FIFTY-TWO

By early afternoon Griffin and Brad were back in the zoo comparing notes. Brad sipped a coffee as Griffin flipped through his notebook. "Nothing. No one heard or saw anything. They were drinking coffee in the bus barn when one of the drivers saw"—Griffin flipped through his notes again—"Harry fall to the ground. A few guys started toward him, but others warned them to stay back in case it was the sniper. So, basically, they watched Harry die." Griffin tossed his notebook on his desk. "Shit."

"Something isn't right," Brad said. "If the driver was standing by his bus, not moving, why three shots? The sniper has never fired more than one shot."

"Copycat?" Griffin asked.

Brad rubbed his three-day growth of beard. "Maybe. This was sloppy. Some shots are expert, others seem impulsive and imprecise. Either this guy has split personalities, or we may have to consider a two-shooter possibility." He threw his empty coffee cup at the overflowing garbage can. "For Christ's sake. Can't they empty that garbage?"

Sturgeon and Devlin, breathing hard, burst into the zoo.

"You two will have heart attacks if you keep running like that," Brad said.

"We found another letter," Sturgeon said.

Brad bolted out of his chair. "Where."

"They nailed it to a tree by the garage behind the Ponderosa. We found it while we were searching for the bullet. We have that, too."

Sturgeon handed Brad a copy of the letter. He read the letter out loud.

For Detective Colter, only. Do not open.

The second page read:

For you Detective Colter.

"I am that I am"

We have tried to contact you four times to start negotiations. But the incompatence of the cops is unacceptable.

1. *We don't trust the hotline, so on Tuesday we called 403-555-6660, the lady said we had to call the hotline and hung up.*
2. *We called 911 on Wednesday. The call went to RCMP Red Deer. The operator said the RCMP were not investigating. They said we needed to call Calgary Police as they were not investergating the shootings.*
3. *We contacted a preacher. We confessed. He didn't believe us.*

Brad pointed to the letter. "He makes it clear in the letter when he says *we*, there's at least two of them. A spotter and the shooter. That's what we'd do in TSU."

Brad continued reading the letter.

These people took our calls to be a hoax. The little boy didn't need to be shot, but you taunted us. You mocked us. That will cost lives.

If stopping the killing is more important to you than catching us, you will acept our demands.

1. *You will place 5 milion dollars in Bank of Western Canada travelers checks in a location we will specify.*
2. *Try catch us picking up money, and you will need more body bags.*
3. *From now on, we only communicate with Colter.*
4. *Will call Pondersosa restaurant at 555 897-1357 at 8 a.m. Saturday for farther information.*
5. *You have until 8 a.m. Saturday morning to get the money.*

"Oh, no. Shit." Brad hung his head and dropped into this chair. "The deadline has passed. That's why there was a murder this morning. They were waiting for us to answer their call."

Devlin sat in a chair against the wall, legs crossed and arms over his chest. "What's done is done. We couldn't have known."

"We screwed up."

"We made a decision." Devlin shrugged. "Now we make another one. How do we move forward?"

"You're pissing me off," Brad said.

"I hope so," Devlin said. "Because you need to make the decision that moves us forward. What are you going to do?"

The room was quiet. Brad stared at the letter.

"Griffin. You need to talk to Archer about the five million dollars and come up with a plan if we have to pay."

"He will not agree to that," Griffin said.

Brad shrugged. "We know that, but the snipers don't."

"They've been trying to contact us since Tuesday?" Griffin asked. "How did we screw that up?"

"Sturgeon, follow up on the phone call Tuesday."

"What can I do?" Devlin asked.

"Contact Stinson. I need a copy of that 911 tape and transcription. Then come back and help me with a press release."

"What are you going to tell the press?" Griffin asked.

"I'm going to read the letter," Brad said.

"Are you crazy?" Griffin shouted. "We'll appear like the stupidest cops in the world."

"There's a leak to the press and I think I know who it is. So rather than have the leak send out the full letter, we release part of the letter. If the leak thinks he's got the genuine thing, he won't dig for the one we have."

"That's crazy," Sturgeon said.

Devlin rubbed his chin. "No, it's brilliant. We can let some of that information out to the public. Just not the Ponderosa phone number. We've got nothing to lose. If the leak and the press believe it's real, great. If later the genuine letter comes out, well, at least we bought some time."

Brad put a sheet of white paper on the wall and started writing.

Things to do/Assign duties

1. Ransom—Griffin
2. Set up press conference for 4:00 p.m.—PIO
3. Press Conference—Brad/Devlin

4. Find Preacher—Brad
5. Find call to RCMP dispatch—Stinson
6. Trace phone number—Sturgeon (an internal number)

Brad stepped back from the board. "Okay. Let's get to this. Devlin. You ready to do a news conference?"

A few minutes before four, Brad and Devlin stepped into a meeting room at the Stampede Grounds. As much as he hated to admit it, Carew had done a decent job with little notice. At least fifty people occupied chairs facing a riser and podium. More chairs were being added. There was plenty of room for the news cameras. Best of all, the room was cool. Brad didn't have to worry about melting from the hot lights.

At four, Brad headed to the podium. Now, fingers crossed, they hoped the snipers were watching the news.

"I'm Detective Coulter. Yesterday evening there was another shooting. A thirty-seven-year-old male was shot outside the Ponderosa Steakhouse. He later succumbed to his injuries in surgery. This morning there was another shooting at the Transit barns in Victoria Park. The victim, a fifty-six-year-old male, was pronounced dead at Holy Cross Hospital."

Brad glanced at a sheet of paper on the podium and licked his lips.

"The sniper left a note at the scene last night, addressed to me. The weather affected our ability to locate it."

There was murmuring from the reporters.

"We are handing out a copy of that letter. I will not read the letter to you. I'm sure most of you can read."

Dozens of hands shot into the air.

"I will not be taking questions about the letter. I have a brief statement to make." Brad stared at the cameras. "To the people who sent me the letter, I did not receive it until this afternoon. Please be patient with us. No lives need to be lost. I want to talk to you. I will talk to you. I'm encouraged you have contacted me. What you asked for will take time. You know the number to call. Please call me at 6:00 p.m. today." Brad collected his notes and nodded to the room. "Thank you for your cooperation."

Brad quickly headed out a side door as reporters rushed the podium.

Hans Keller stood on the balcony and inhaled the warm air. His eyes panned the view—palm trees, beach, and dark-blue water. This was the life, but this was the last day of vacation. He flopped onto the bed. After ten glorious days in Hawaii, they had to leave in the late afternoon. It was the most relaxing holiday he'd ever had. It was just something about Hawaii. The people were friendly, the pace slower. It was something in the air. You couldn't help but relax.

Every day had been a different beach in the morning, with an activity in the afternoon. Sometimes on a tour, other times they rented bikes, or they just stayed at the beach. He never wanted to leave. He'd never been so relaxed in his life. His wife headed to the shower.

Absently, Hans grabbed the remote for the TV. That was another thing. They hadn't watched TV during the entire vacation. It was morning in Hawaii—afternoon in Alberta. The national news came on with "Breaking News." Surprisingly, the lead story was from Calgary. He sat up and increased the volume.

The screen faded from the national anchor to a press conference. Leading the press conference was Brad Coulter. *What the hell?* Hans's jaw dropped. *Coulter—a press conference?*

He increased the volume.

"I'm Detective Coulter. Yesterday evening there was another tragic shooting. A thirty-seven-year-old male was shot outside the Ponderosa Steakhouse. He later succumbed to his injuries in surgery. This morning there was another shooting at the Transit bus barns in Victoria Park. The victim was pronounced dead at Holy Cross Hospital."

There was murmuring from the reporters.

Brad glanced at a sheet of paper on the podium and licked his lips.

"The sniper left a note at the scene last night, addressed to me. The weather affected our ability to ..."

Coulter—at work? Sniper ... murders?

Hans's wife came out of the bathroom with merely a towel around her head. He barely noticed.

"Hans. Hans."

He slowly twisted toward her voice. He still didn't notice she was naked.

"Hans." Her hands were on her hips, her head cocked to the side. "What is it?"

All he could say was, "Coulter. Son of a bitch."

CHAPTER FIFTY-THREE

While Brad was at the press conference, Archer had arranged for the phone company to transfer the number from the Ponderosa to the zoo. This way, they didn't have to take over the Ponderosa at 6:00 p.m. and didn't have to worry about the press hounding them or somehow disrupting the call.

Brad sat at the desk, phone close at hand. Devlin sat at his side with a pad of paper, ready to give Brad information on negotiations. Archer sat across from Brad while Griffin paced the room.

The phone rang. Brad grabbed the phone. Devlin hit the record button and switched the phone to a speaker.

"Coulter."

Silence on the line.

"Coulter."

Again, silence. Then, "Uh, is this the Ponderosa?"

Brad started to say no, then shook his head. "Uh, yeah. How can I help you?"

"What time are you open until today?"

Brad glanced at Devlin, who shrugged. Griffin shook his head. Archer didn't make eye contact.

"Uh, we're open until nine."

"Great. Thanks."

Brad replaced the receiver and leaned back. "What was that about?"

"Now we know the Ponderosa phone is redirected properly," Devlin said.

The phone rang again. "Coulter."

Silence on the line.

"Coulter."

Again, silence. Then, "Uh, is this the Ponderosa?"

Brad rolled his eyes. "Yes, it is."

"What's the soup special today?"

"Chicken rice," Brad said.

"Oh, I was hoping for Clam Chowder."

"That's only Fridays." Brad hung up.

"That's only Fridays," Griffin mimicked.

"Why don't you make yourself useful and call the Ponderosa and get the right answers."

"Ah, but you were doing so well."

"Maybe you should answer with *Ponderosa*," Devlin said.

Brad glared at Devlin. The phone rang. "Ponderosa." Brad took reservations for a group of eight.

Griffin came back with the information, and Brad answered another twenty calls, including some reservations. He hoped the restaurant wasn't busy and these people would get a table.

For the hundredth time, Brad glanced at the clock. He swore time was going backward, at least standing still. His palms were sweaty, and his neck ached. His left fingers cramped, and his right knee bounced to some unknown rhythm at one hundred beats per minute.

The second hand clicked 55, 56, 57, 58, 59 … 6:00 p.m. Brad stared at the phone. Nothing. He let out his breath. Okay, so it wasn't exactly at 6:00 p.m. The second hand worked its way around the clock once, twice, three times.

The phone rang. A reservation.

6:10.

Three more reservations, one takeout order, and a wrong number.

6:15.

More reservations. Two wrong numbers and a crank call.

6:20.

Takeout orders were the main calls.

6:30.

"Why didn't they call?" Brad asked.

"Maybe they didn't get the message?" Devlin offered.

"Maybe they were never going to call," Griffin said. "Maybe they're watching the Ponderosa and figure we didn't show up. So, the call was off."

Archer sat quietly, his fingers steepled under his chin. "Patience. We wait."

Brad's voice became sharper with every call. He hung up on several customers. He glanced at the clock too often. Griffin paced and Devlin doodled. At 7:00, Archer stood. "It's not going to happen today."

Brad rocked back in his chair. Devlin tore up the doodles, and Griffin stomped out of the office.

"Now what?" Brad asked.

"Go over everything they've sent you again," Devlin said. "Start to finish. Notes and letters. Have the Crime Scene Unit talk to the phone company about the phone number. Check all phones in and around the Ponderosa."

"So, we wait?" Brad asked.

"We wait for their response." Archer headed to the door. "Whatever it might be."

The phone rang, Brad's feet hit the floor, and he rocked forward. His hand grabbed the phone. "Ponderosa—I mean … Coulter." He waited for the sniper to answer.

"Brad, it's Sturgeon. We're at the Ponderosa."

"Great, did you find something?"

"Nothing you're gonna like."

Brad's shoulders sagged. *A break. Was it too much to ask for a break*? "What?"

"The phone number the snipers gave you is not the phone number for the Ponderosa."

"What are you talking about?"

"The number the sniper gave you and said he'd call."

"Yeah."

"It's not for the Ponderosa."

Brad shook his head. "I don't follow you."

Sturgeon sighed. "I'll slow it down for you. The sniper said he'd call you at the Ponderosa, and then gave a number. We got the phone company to transfer the Ponderosa number to you at the office."

"I know that."

"The problem is that the number the sniper gave you is not the number for the Ponderosa. It is one number out."

"That doesn't matter. The phone company transferred the number we gave them."

"Uh, no. They didn't use the number we gave them, because they knew it was wrong. So, they transferred the right number for the Ponderosa."

"You think the sniper screwed up, gave us the wrong number. And while I was answering the Ponderosa phone number, the sniper called another phone number?"

"Right. I confirmed with the phone company that a call was made to the number the snipers provided at exactly six. But they don't know where it originated."

CHAPTER FIFTY-FOUR

THEY WERE GETTING READY TO HEAD HOME WHEN BRAD POINTED over Devlin's shoulder. "Turn on the TV. It's time for the news."

Devlin leaned back and switched on the TV. The opening music was just finishing.

"Good evening. I'm David Todd, and this is the CFCN News. We start with a special report on the sniper story from Angus Ferguson. Angus."

"I'm standing outside Stampede Park tonight. Today, police held a briefing led by Detective Brad Coulter. The citizens of Calgary are scared and have not been reassured by what the police have accomplished. There are no suspects, no arrests, and seemingly no leads. Today Coulter said he had received a letter from the sniper. There are some alarming statements in the letter."

Ferguson read from the second page:

For you Detective Colter.

"I am that I am."

We have tried to contact you four times to start negotiations. But the incompatence of the cops is unacceptable.

"The sniper details each of the times he tried to contact the police. All of those times were after the fifth shooting. If the police had taken the calls seriously, would they have shot additional people, including the boy who at this moment is fighting for his life?"

Ferguson's reading continued:

These people took our calls to be a hoax. The little boy didn't need to be shot, but you taunted us. You mocked us. God will not be mocked. That will cost lives.

If stopping the killing is more important to you than catching us, you will acept our demands.

Ferguson listed the demands.

From now on, we will only communicate with Colter.

Brad held his breath.

"Coulter made a plea for the sniper to contact him, although we do not know how that communication will occur."

Brad let out his breath. They'd held back the information about the Ponderosa. It worked. The authentic letter had not been leaked to the press.

"All of this brings up many questions. Will the police agree to the ransom demands? Again, the police are tight-lipped. The letter often says 'we.' Is there more than one sniper? More than two? Perhaps teams of snipers? The public has a right to know, yet the police are silent. Why does the sniper want to communicate with Detective Coulter?"

Devlin switched off the TV.

CHAPTER FIFTY-FIVE

Brad agreed to meet Steele and Zerr for a late dinner and beers. He pulled into the parking lot of The Place restaurant. As he got out of his truck, he noticed a few of the cars had bumper stickers that said *Not the Sniper*. Creative.

The guys were already at the booth in the corner, leaving him with his back to the door. He hated that. Every cop did. As he slid into the booth, he grabbed a beer. "For me, I hope." He took a long gulp and sighed. "I needed that."

"That's what we figured," Steele said.

"We saw the news," Zerr said. "Why did you release the note to the press? They will crucify you."

"Maybe," Brad said. "Someone close to the case is leaking information to the press."

"Why would a cop do that?" Zerr asked.

"Hard to say." Brad sipped his beer. "Either I release the note, or it would have been leaked."

"You held something back," Steele said.

Brad smirked. "Did you guys order?"

"Yup." Steele slid a menu to Brad. "The special today is lasagna."

"I'm in."

Steele leaned forward. "Me and Charlie have been thinking about the shootings and what we'd do."

Brad raised an eyebrow. "I like it, putting your evil minds to use."

"From the letter, there are two of them," Zerr said. "That's the way we'd do it. Ballistics suggests that most of the shots were on a flat trajectory. Meaning the shooter was level with the victim. So not in a tree, or on a wall, or from a building. We keep hearing about the van. That could make sense. You could build a platform in the back of the van. Either it has a sliding glass back window or some way of removing it. The shooter could lie flat and would have an excellent line of sight."

"Take the shot and drive away," Brad said.

"The driver might be the spotter like we do," Steele said. "He's picking the targets. It would be hard to be ready to shoot on a moment's notice and pick the victim, too."

"You two are evil geniuses." Brad smirked. "Cuz that's exactly what I was thinking."

The waitress set their dinners and three beers on the table. They started eating.

"We have another idea." Steele gulped his beer. "We think they're both shooting."

Brad set his fork on his plate and sat back. "Why do you say that?"

Steele took a couple of bites of lasagna. "The first four victims were killed with well-placed shots. Then D'Amore was seriously wounded, but she was hit with a ricochet. The kid, shit, I can't believe I'm saying this, was an excellent shot. Today's shooting was shit. Two terrible shots and probably one lucky one."

"We have a marksman and a second shooter who's not accurate." Brad nodded and sat back. "That's what I was thinking. But how does this help us?"

"We're just lowly tactical guys," Steele said. "You're the detective. You figure it out."

CHAPTER FIFTY-SIX

Sunday Day Twelve

BRAD LEFT THE CAFETERIA JUGGLING A TRAY OF COFFEES AND headed down the stairs to the zoo. He peeked into the gym. There were a dozen cops working, but all were facing a TV. It was a news clip he'd recorded earlier that morning.

His face took up the entire screen. "This is to the sniper. This is to the person who left me a message at the Ponderosa on Friday. You gave us a telephone number. Again, yesterday, I could not get your call. We want to talk to you. Please call again at the number you provided. At 4:00 p.m. today." He paused and took a deep breath. "I hope you understand I want to talk to you. Thank you."

Brad slipped out the door of the gym before anyone saw him and headed to the zoo. He slid into his chair, sipped his coffee, then noticed a note propped up against his phone. It said to call Ken at Nickle Oil. Brad grabbed the phone and dialed.

"Ken Nickle."

"Good morning. This is Detective Coulter. I'm returning your call."

"Ah, great. Look, I know you are busy, but I want to help."

"Your reward is bringing in a lot of tips."

"Right. Let's not bullshit. You're probably getting crap. I want to loan you something that might come in handy."

"What's that?" Brad sipped his coffee.

"A helicopter."

Brad spit his coffee. "A helicopter?"

"Yeah. Look, we got a few and they're not being used. Maybe it will help you, maybe not. One of my pilots flew in Vietnam. Damn experienced pilot."

"He must be," Brad said. "He's alive."

"He's agreed to be on call for you anytime you need him. But I was thinking you might need him urgently and there might not be enough time for him to get to you."

"Okay, what are you thinking?"

"He's gonna fly to the parking lot north of your headquarters. I think your police association has a parking lot and a pub there. He'll land the chopper there. If you have someplace he can stay where he's close to you, then he can get you anywhere you want, fast."

Brad stared at the phone. He didn't know what to say.

"Coulter, you still there? Do we have a deal?"

"You bet. I'll get his landing cleared with dispatch and have some guys bring some gear over."

"Outstanding. Good luck."

Brad dialed the phone.

"What?"

"Zerr, it's Brad."

"Boss, why are you waking me so early."

"It's nine."

"Like I said, early."

"I need you and Steele to get three sets of tactical gear over to the helicopter parked in our parking lot."

"A helicopter?"

"Yeah. Nickle Oil donated one. I need gear for the three of us in the chopper. Get some for the pilot, too. Oh, and clear his landing with the airport and traffic section. Do it, now."

Brad sat back in his chair and exhaled. At first, he was excited to have a helicopter. Now he was wondering what the heck he would use it for.

He reached for the first of two files on his desk. The phone number was the direct line to the Public Information Officer's office. *Carew*.

The file contained the interview with Carew's secretary. She remembered the call on Tuesday. Carew wasn't in the office, and he hadn't told her what to do if a call like this came in, so she thought it was best to tell the caller to phone the hotline. When asked by the detective why she hadn't just transferred the call, she said she was too busy to do that.

Mullen stuck his head in the door. "You're needed in the Deputy's office ASAP."

"Thanks." Brad took the stairs to the second floor. His stomach did a flip. Was he always going to feel that way when he went to Archer's office? Griffin, Devlin, and Stinson were seated at the conference table and drinking coffee. Archer was at his chair behind his desk.

"What's up?" Brad asked.

"Stinson has the tape from the 911 to the RCMP," Archer said.

Stinson set a tape recorder on the table and pushed the play button. There was static and then:

"911. Police, Fire or EMS?"

"Uh, police." A man's voice.

"Please hold while I transfer your call."

"On hold again."

"RCMP dispatch. What is your emergency?" a female voice asked.

"Yeah, I want to tell you about the shootings."

"Where are you calling from?"

"Why does that matter?"

"Sir, I need to direct your call to the right police agency."

"Fuck that, I'm trying to tell you about the murders."

"Sir, please don't swear. Now, where are you calling from?"

"I'm not telling you that. I'll tell you about the shootings."

"The shootings in Calgary?"

"Are there other multiple shootings?"

"Sir, I'm trying to be patient."

"Yes, damn it, the shootings in Calgary."

"Thank you. What is your name?"

"My name?"

"Yes, sir."

"I am that I am."

Brad felt the blood drain from his face and his pulse quicken.

"I don't understand that. What are you saying?"

"I'm saying I want to tell the cops about the shootings in Calgary. It all started in Rocky Mountain House."

"I'm confused, sir, are you calling about the Calgary shootings or a shooting in Rocky Mountain House?"

"Calgary."

"The RCMP are not investigating that shooting. I'll forward you to Calgary Police Dispatch."

"No, wait—"

There was silence in the room. Brad stared at his hands. *Wednesday. They called Wednesday.*

"How many other times do you think they called?" Archer asked. "How many times were they taken as crank callers. Oh, shit."

"This may still be a crank call," Devlin said.

Brad shook his head, stood and paced. "Nah, this feels right. He says 'I am that I am.' What does he mean, it all started in Rocky Mountain House?"

"I don't know," Stinson said. "I've got a constable in Rocky Mountain House checking their calls for the last few months."

"It could be anything, but my guess is someone died there," Brad said.

CHAPTER FIFTY-SEVEN

BRAD'S TASK FROM THE LETTER WAS TO FIND THE PREACHER THE sniper had confessed to. It was easier than they'd thought. First, the sniper was precise. It was a preacher, not a priest, so Brad started with non-Catholic churches inside the killing zone. That narrowed it down to six churches. On the third phone call, he found the right preacher at Knox United Church on Fourth Street SW. He said he'd meet with Brad at twelve-fifteen after he finished the morning service.

Brad stood inside the main doors and waited for the service to end. He had mixed emotions standing in the church. He'd grown up going to church and believed in God, heaven, and certainly hell. After Maggie's death last year, he had a hard time believing there was a God. How could an all-knowing being allow monsters to do horrible things to others? That couldn't be part of the plan.

Brad stepped back to the wall as people exited the church.

When the church was vacant, he headed into the chapel and found the reverend.

"I'm Detective Coulter. We talked on the phone earlier."

"Ah, yes. I am Reverend Branton. Walk with me."

Brad followed Branton to pews in the front and they sat.

"How can I help you?"

"I understand you received a call from someone saying they were the sniper."

"Yes, that is true. He called on Friday. It was a garbled phone call. He identified himself as 'I am that I am.' Which, of course, is a Biblical reference."

"Really?"

Reverend Branton nodded. "The quote is found in the Bible in Exodus 6:3. The Israelites were crying for deliverance, and God had tasked Moses to lead the Israelites out of Egypt. Moses asked God, what is your name? The answer, in Hebrew, is *ehyeh asher ehyeh.* It has been interpreted in many ways, and one of them is, *I am that I am*. The more accurate translation is, *I will be what I will be.* To keep it simple, it means that God will be whatever you need him to be. In Exodus, the Israelites needed him to be a deliverer, and through Moses, he was."

"Okay, I think I understand the interpretation. But why would the sniper use this line from the Bible?"

Branton stared past Brad to the cross behind the pulpit. "I don't know. My guess is two things. One, he wants you to know he is in power. Second, what he is may change."

"Change, how?"

Branton shrugged. "Today he's a sniper. Perhaps he will change to another crime."

Brad rubbed his face. "Back to the phone call. Tell me about it."

"He told me to write down a message," Branton said. "At the time, it didn't make any sense. He repeatedly talked about Rocky Mountain House. It all began there. It was a rant, and as I mentioned, I couldn't understand a lot of what he said."

"Why didn't you call us?" Brad asked.

"Frankly, I thought it was a hoax." Branton held a hand out and shrugged. "I know the police had been receiving a lot of false calls, and your system was overwhelmed. I figured it was someone playing a joke. It's not unusual to get crank calls."

"Was there anything about the voice that stood out?"

Reverend Branton shook his head. "I didn't hear an accent, but it was hard to hear him most of the time. His speech was simple. A common man, if that makes sense. Not an educated man. But that's just a guess on my part."

"Thank you. This was helpful." Brad stood and held out his hand.

Branton stood and gripped Brad's hand in both of his. "I will pray to Saint Michael, the patron saint of police officers. I will ask him to guide you, Brad Coulter, and protect you in your battle. Crime and personal." He bowed his head. "Please come visit me again."

CHAPTER FIFTY-EIGHT

Brad sat alone in the zoo. He glanced up at the glass wall. A half-dozen dispatch staff on break drank coffee and stared.

Brad swung back to his desk and checked the equipment. He had two radios, one for their assigned dispatch channel, the other to communicate with Air One. Next to the radios sat an audio recorder and finally, the tracing unit. When the snipers called, the tracing unit would automatically trace the call and first display the telephone number, then location. The key was to keep the sniper talking long enough.

Brad glanced at the clock. Two minutes to four. "Two minutes. Let's see if they call." Brad drummed his fingers on the metal desk and watched the second hand.

4:00

4:01

4:01:30

4:02

When the phone rang, Brad nearly jumped out of his seat. He

glanced at the dispatcher who nodded. Brad picked up the phone. "Coulter."

"Just listen. Another person died yesterday because of your incompetence. We don't know how we can make this clearer. Enough with the telephone tag games. You have tried our patience for the last time."

The dispatcher keyed his mic. "All units. We have them on the phone."

The radio clicked twice in acknowledgement.

"You have our demands. Meet them or pay the price. We wonder if you like finding bodies as much as we like killing. Coulter, you have one last chance. You know no one is safe. Not kids, cops, no one."

"Wait, I want to talk." It hadn't been enough time to trace the call. "Why ask for me?"

"Don't think you're anything special. The first guy on TV was obviously an idiot. You were the guy in charge. No sense dealing with a middleman."

"But you sent the first note to a reporter."

There was laughter on the phone. *"You're making this too complicated. She's hot and we weren't going to walk into the police station with a note for you. We aren't stupid. We know you are tracing this call. I won't use 911 or the hotline. Good luck finding us. Like the hot reporter said, we're ghosts."*

"Wait ..."

"Oh, and Coulter. Fuck you!"

The voice was gone, but it sounded like the line was still open. Brad stared at the tracing monitor. The phone number came up. Then the line went dead. Fifteen seconds later, the address appeared.

Brad keyed his radio. "All units. I have the location."

Steele and Zerr crouched low in the outdated motorhome in the parking lot of the school at Fourteenth Street and Nineteenth Avenue SW. They didn't want to take any chances with the black Suburbans that shouted *tactical team*.

Steele glanced across at Zerr, who wore a ball cap with a long-haired wig glued inside. "You're kinda cute in long hair."

"Screw you," Zerr replied. "I'm not sure a backward ball cap and Ray-Bans count as a disguise."

"Sitting next to you, it does."

"How long do you figure it will be until some mom with her kids in the park calls 911 about two perverts in a motorhome?"

"Not in this area. She'll rush them home and keep them there. Residents of this neighborhood don't like police parked outside their house. It gets the neighbors talking. One police cruiser in a driveway can ruin your uppity-up reputation forever."

"Now we wait," Steele said.

Zerr took a drink from a brown sandwich bag.

"What the hell is that?" Steele asked.

"Chocolate milk."

"Bullshit."

"Truly." Zerr held it out. "Learned that from Devlin. That was part of his homeless schtick when he was undercover."

"You could have got one for me, too."

"Do you think the boss is right?" Zerr asked. "That the snipers will phone from inside the area of the shootings?"

Steele shrugged and stared out the window. "It's as probable a theory as any. Brad thinks they're staying somewhere in this area. That's how they can shoot and disappear so fast."

"Makes sense."

"All units. We have them on the phone." the dispatcher said.

Steele clicked the mic twice in acknowledgment. Then they waited. Zerr tapped the steering wheel.

Then Brad came across the radio. "All units. I have the location. The 7-Eleven, Fourteenth Street and Fifteenth Avenue SW."

"Yee-haw," Zerr shouted as he wheeled the motorhome out of the parking lot and onto Fourteenth Street. "That's us."

Steele got air, then his seatbelt locked as the camper launched off the sidewalk onto the street.

Zerr jammed his foot down on the accelerator as the light changed to yellow. The motorhome continued at its slow pace.

"Oh, shit." Steele braced for impact.

Somehow Zerr zigzagged the heavy, unbalanced vehicle through traffic to a chorus of honking. He got air again as he wheeled into the 7-Eleven parking lot.

They both had their doors open before they stopped.

A white station wagon was parked in front of the payphones. A man fumbled around in his pocket, inserted a coin, and dialed. He glanced over his shoulder a couple of times but ignored Zerr and Steele racing toward him. He was whispering. Steele reached him first, dragged him away from the phone and tossed the man onto the ground. Steele held the man down with his knee and tightened the cuffs.

Steele heard a door open and glanced over in time to see Zerr pull the passenger out of the car and onto the ground by Steele's prisoner.

Sirens sounded from all directions, and cruisers skidded to a halt around them.

Steele and Zerr lifted their prisoners to their feet.

"You two are under arrest for murder."

Steele's prisoner protested. "No. See. Not true. Call my wife. She misses me."

"Oh, I forgot to say you should shut up."

They shoved the prisoners ahead of them. Before they reached the cruisers, the press swarmed the parking lot. If possible, more reporters than cops. They shouted questions.

"Are these the snipers?"

"What led you to this location?"

"Have they confessed?"

Pittman and Hirsch were at the pickup window at A&W when they heard the sirens. Police cruisers raced past. More cruisers arrived from the north.

Pittman pulled out onto Fourteenth Street, then drove south a block. He parked at the curb in front of the Sacred Heart Church.

They munched burgers and fries as the cops swarmed around two men on the ground.

They slurped some root beer and watched as the cops shoved two men into separate police cruisers. The cruisers raced away with an outdated motorhome trying to keep up.

Two officers unrolled police tape around the parking lot. Others put up barricades to the avenue.

Marvin picked chunks of beef out of his teeth with a fingernail, then used the end of the straw to catch the meat he couldn't suck out. "I don't think we can let this go unchallenged."

They spent an hour interviewing the suspects, then met in the hall outside the interview rooms and compared notes.

"I have nothing," Brad said. "My guy says they're from Newfoundland and came here searching for work. They do handyman jobs."

"My guy, the same," Griffin said. "When they get paid, they call their wives and talk to their kids."

"There weren't any weapons in their vehicle. Their licenses and registration are up to date," Brad said. "Neither have a criminal or military record."

Devlin headed down the hall toward them. "It's confirmed." He glanced at Griffin. "Your suspect was on the phone to his wife. RCMP out east confirmed it."

"Shit." Brad leaned his head into the wall. "TSU and cruisers were there within a minute."

Brad headed back into the interview room. "Was someone on the phone before you?"

"What?" the suspect asked.

"Before you used the phone, was someone else using it?"

"Oh, yeah." He nodded vigorously.

"Can you describe him?"

The suspect shrugged. "Just a guy."

"Tall? Short? Fat?"

"Not tall, not short. Not fat. Just a guy."

"Facial hair?"

"No. Maybe. I'm sorry. I didn't know I needed to remember him. I just wanted to call home. I was excited to call my wife. I just rushed up to the phone."

Damn. Brad hung his head. *We can't catch a break.*

CHAPTER FIFTY-NINE

After the interviews, Brad was back in the zoo trying to figure out what went wrong. Zerr and Steele were there in less than a minute and arrested the wrong guys. Sturgeon and his team were dismantling the payphone. They could do a better analysis in their lab.

He spun in his chair and stared at the map. He had been right—the snipers were staying inside the target area he'd marked. Not that the information had done them any good.

There was a knock at the door, and Mullen popped his head in. "Detective Coulter, call for you."

Brad nodded and picked up the phone. "Coulter."

"Detective. It's Sadie Andrus."

"I expected to hear from you."

"I just wondered—"

"I'm not your personal unnamed source."

"You sort of are." He imagined her smirk.

Brad leaned back and rolled his eyes. "Ms. Andrus. I apologize—my fault. I made the mistake of talking to you last week. Now you think we're friends, or whatever it is you think. I've got work to do."

"Does that mean the men you arrested are the snipers?"

"No comment."

"Ha, you know that a no comment means yes."

"No, it does not. I don't know how to make this clear. I have nothing to say either way."

"Okay. I'll go with the story as I have it: Police Capture Snipers. We've got excellent film footage from the arrest. A shame you weren't there."

Brad rubbed his temples. "Don't do that."

"Why not?"

"I'm busy, Ms. Andrus. I have snipers to catch."

Silence on the line.

"I just don't think that's the career-making story you think it is," Brad said.

"You said you're still searching for the snipers. You've said all I need to know."

The volume was down on the television in the zoo when Brad entered. When he saw the banner across the bottom of the screen saying regular programming would be interrupted, he increased the volume.

The CFCN and CTV logos replaced Grizzly Adams as he stumbled through the snow-covered forest. Like the weather here today.

"I'm Angus Ferguson. At 4:00 p.m. today, my cameraman and I witnessed the arrest of the snipers. In a lightning-strike raid, police descended on the 7-Eleven on Fourteenth Street and Fifteenth Avenue southwest."

The screen changed to a bumpy film out the front of a vehicle. Police cruisers raced past. The video bounced as the picture showed the parking lot.

"We could get these images as we raced to the scene. My cameraman kept filming as we jogged closer to the arrests."

The image switched to a tactical officer grabbing a suspect running away from a telephone booth. A second tactical officer pulled the other suspect out of a white station wagon.

"While police have released little information, it is apparent police were acting on reliable information and conducted this arrest with overwhelming police presence. The scene is taped off. They towed the white station wagon to Police Headquarters for examination. We will interrupt programming as additional information becomes available."

Shithead.

Brad switched channels to CFAC. He was treated to Charlie's Angels saving the world. Just as he was getting interested, the screen changed to the CFAC logo, then Sadie Andrus appeared.

"Earlier today, police arrested two men at a payphone on Fourteenth Street and Fifteenth Avenue in front of a 7-Eleven."

The video on the screen showed police cars converging. The sound of sirens came from all directions.

"Police quickly rushed the men away from the scene. While there has been no formal announcement from the police, other news outlets are reporting this is the arrest of the snipers."

The screen switched to a white car.

"Also, at the scene was a white station wagon. Those same news outlets are reporting the white van police have been searching for is a white station wagon. I have it on excellent authority these are not the snipers. Citizens should maintain caution until we have additional information from the police. Sadie Andrus, CFAC News."

Brad shut off the TV, slumped in his chair, and rubbed his temples. A tension headache had worked its way across his shoulders, up his neck and lodged in his temples. He opened his desk drawer and searched for Tylenol. He pulled out a bottle and dumped the pills into his hand. He popped two Tylenol in his mouth and swallowed. They lodged in his throat. He grabbed a cup of coffee, washed the pills down, then gagged on the cold coffee.

CHAPTER SIXTY

Monday Day Thirteen

By seven, Brad and Griffin were pouring over stacks of tips. Stinson knocked on the door of the zoo and glanced in. Brad waved him to a chair.

"We're on to something," Stinson said. "We figured out what the snipers meant about Rocky Mountain House."

Brad leaned forward in his chair.

"Ten days ago, an oil field worker was killed at a pump station near Rocky Mountain House. He'd been dead for hours before they found him. He'd been shot with a rifle."

"Why didn't we know this before?" Brad asked Stinson. "No one thought it was related to the Calgary shootings?"

"No, because we had a guy in custody."

"He confessed?" Griffin asked.

"No, but he was a suspect in several other shootings." Stinson slid a file over to Brad. "His name is Karl Vogel. We suspected him of sabotaging several oil and gas wells. He had a hate-on for oil and gas. He felt the wells were sour gas wells and were poisoning his drinking water and making his family sick. Not just his family, but that the sour gas was responsible for stillbirths, miscarriages, and deformations that started after they drilled the sour gas wells. He lost it in a bar in Rocky Mountain House when his granddaughter was born stillborn. He ranted that night about how the oil companies would pay. Three days later the oil well worker was killed. Karl was arrested that night and his guns seized." Stinson sat back in his chair and sighed. "They questioned him for hours. He didn't confess, but he didn't deny it. He sat and grinned at the investigators. Through a lawyer, he pled not guilty and they set a court date for September. Bail was denied."

Brad slid the file back. "Were any of his guns a match to our sniper?"

Stinson shook his head and rummaged through the file. "No, but the bullet is a match to your sniper."

"How did you find that out?" Brad asked.

"The evidence was bagged and tagged and sent to the crime lab. But there was no rush on the analysis because we had our man. Or so we thought."

"Oh, shit," Brad said.

"One of the Mounties in Rocky believed Karl was taking responsibility because it helped his cause, not because he did it. That made Karl a celebrity and hero in the community. The Mountie put a rush on getting the bullet analyzed. That's how we know the bullets match."

"So, the snipers were in Rocky Mountain House ten days ago." Brad grabbed the file and flipped through the pages. "Was this the first murder?"

Stinson shrugged and swallowed hard. "That's not all."

"What do you mean?" Brad's head snapped up from the file.

"There was a shooting in Airdrie later that same day —Friday."

"What the heck?" Brad glared across the desk at Stinson. "You're just telling me now?"

Stinson pushed his chair back against the wall. "Airdrie RCMP thought it was a robbery. The salesman was shot with a handgun, probably a large caliber pistol." Stinson shrugged and cast his eyes down. "He wasn't found until the next day when the dealership manager came to work. The credit card slips were on the floor and the cash was gone."

Brad knew he had to make this quick, there was a lot happening, but his gut told him the shooting at the Airdrie dealership was important. He could have phoned, but he wanted to talk to the manager in person. He headed up Highway 2 to Airdrie, swung onto the exit ramp, and stopped in front of the dealership. He had his badge out as he headed to the receptionist. "I'm Detective Coulter. I need to see the manager, urgently."

The receptionist pointed toward an office as a man stepped out. "That's me. What's this about?"

Brad strode over. "I don't have a lot of time. Tell me about your salesman who was shot last week."

"I already told the RCMP everything I know."

"I'm aware. If you don't mind, could you tell me as well?"

"Sure. Uh, on Friday afternoon I had one guy working, Roy. The new guy who was supposed to be working as well took off camping for the weekend."

"I'm short on time."

"Sure. All I know is that when I came on Saturday morning, the front door was locked. I found Roy dead on the floor behind the sales counter. I called 911. The RCMP and paramedics came fast. The paramedics said Roy had been dead for a long time. I showed the RCMP the credit card slips on the floor and told them the cash was gone."

"How much cash?"

The manager wrung his hands. "A few thousand."

"Anything else missing."

"Not that I know of." He shook his head.

Brad glanced at the cars in the showroom. "Did you do an inventory?"

"No. It was a robbery. They took the cash."

Brad nodded. "Perhaps. Can you do an inventory? I need to know if a vehicle is missing." Brad handed the manager his card. "This is critical information. If you could do it ASAP, that would be great. And it might stop other people from being hurt."

"We have over two hundred vehicles ..."

"I get it. I wouldn't ask if this wasn't crucial." He turned to leave, then stopped. "Can you check and see if you have an extra vehicle? One that doesn't belong here."

The manager tilted his head. "How did you know? There's a truck that I don't have a record for."

"Show me."

The manager took Brad to the back of the dealership and pointed to a GMC in the corner. Brad headed over to the truck and wandered around. It was a working man's truck—lots of scrapes and mud. Maybe a farmer or someone in construction. He slipped on a glove and opened the passenger door.

Brad searched the glove box, the center console, and under the seats. Not so much as a napkin or a nickel. He reached under the passenger seat and felt a bottle. He pulled it out. Liquid rolled in the bottom. He pulled an evidence envelope out of his jacket and inserted the bottle.

He glanced at his watch. 8:20. Shit. He headed to the driver's side and copied down the vehicle identification number. There wasn't a license plate. "Thanks for your help. I have to go." He sprinted to his car.

On the way back to Calgary, Brad radioed Sturgeon to send a team to Airdrie to fingerprint the truck and that he had a beer bottle to check for fingerprints.

CHAPTER SIXTY-ONE

MARVIN PITTMAN PARKED ON THE NORTH SIDE OF SEVENTEENTH Avenue with the back of the car facing the school. He used the side mirrors and the rearview mirror to track the students and staff entering the school. Parents dropped most of the students off at the back door. Still, some students arrived by city bus and wandered in groups across the front lawn. They were in no hurry, and despite a cop shouting for them to hustle it to the back of the school, they operated on their idea of hustle. Typical teenagers. They chatted without a care in the world. That was about to change.

Pittman keyed the mic on his radio. "You should have a clear line of sight. Check it out."

The car bounced as Logan got in position. "Okay. This will work."

"I can see two viable targets. They're standing still, not looking this way. Counting from your left, I think number three is your best choice."

Hirsch shuffled in the trunk. Then his voice came over the radio. "Are you sure?"

"From here, you can't miss."

"That's not the point." Hirsch's voice hesitated. "I take this shot, everything changes."

"We've tried to work with the cops. They jus' keep jerking us around. This time they'll get the message."

"They'll come after us with everything they've got."

Pittman laughed. "How did that work for them when you shot the kid last week?"

"Didn't change a lot."

"And the bus driver I shot?"

"You mean the one it took three shots to kill?"

"Fuck off." Pittman's voice had an edge. He was tired of pissing around. "Take the shot or get out and I'll do it."

"On it." Five seconds later, the shot echoed throughout the car.

Pittman yawned to get the air pressure out of his ears. He put the car in drive, and slowly pulled away from the curb.

Constable Conall Baines had his back to the sandstone brick building. Western Canada High School was one of the oldest schools in Calgary. Just south of downtown with a diverse student population.

Baines marched across the front of the school trying to get the students moving faster to morning classes. The yellow school buses headed to the back of the building where a half-dozen officers funneled them into the school. Out front, there was Baines and Sam Steele. They had been partners years ago. It was fun to be working with Steele again.

Some students arrived by city bus and wandered in groups across the front lawn. They were in no hurry despite school starting in five minutes at eight-thirty. Baines and Steele shouted for them to hustle into the school, but they operated on their idea of hustle.

Baines kept his bulk between the kids and everything in front of the school. Traffic was congested as parents drove into the congested parking lot.

It isn't enough having us here, Baines thought. *We need traffic control, too.* With morning rush hour, it was hard to keep track of cars as they dropped off kids. Most of the time two or three buses blocked the view.

He had no problem with this duty. He had three kids of his own. Not yet old enough for school and safely tucked away at home with their mom. His wife insisted she'd feel safer if no one could see into their house. Last night he'd put aluminum foil on all the windows. Not that anyone had been shot in their living room, but why risk it? She wasn't alone in that idea. As he drove to work early this morning at least half of the houses had their windows blocked. On a few, he even saw sheets of plywood over the windows. Just like Florida did before a hurricane.

The buses pulled away and a new flock of meandering students crossed the grass. Not a care in the world. His eyes stared past them, out toward the road.

He caught the glint of reflected sunlight off the back of a car. Maybe off the chrome bumper.

Baines stumbled to the ground, hit by something unseen. Then he heard a rifle shot. Some kids screamed, others continued their slow march to the school.

His ass hit the ground first. He put out his left hand to stop his fall, his right drawing his gun. He stared across the grass toward the strip mall. A car was pulling away. He squinted to identify the vehicle, then a wave of intense pain bolted through his body like an electric shock. He gasped and felt an incredible agony in his chest. His breath caught. Baines watched the car disappear. He dropped his gun to use his right hand to steady himself. No use. To him, his fall onto his back happened in slow motion, but when his head struck the grass, he felt his neck snap.

He fought to breathe through the pain. He tasted blood in his throat. His left hand went to his chest.

When he pulled his hand away, blood dripped from his fingers. He glanced around. Were the kids safe? His eyes were drawn back to his bloody hand. He was mesmerized by the drip, drip, drip of blood. Like a ticking clock, his eyes blinked with the drops then fluttered closed.

Steele heard the shot and immediately sprinted across the lawn toward the sound. Steele glanced across the street, then raced to Baines.

He slid on his knees. "Baines. Baines." No answer.

Steele keyed his lapel mic. "Officer down. Code 200, red. Western Canada High School. Front. Need EMS and lots of back-up." He flipped open his knife and cut away the uniform shirt. Next, he cut the straps on the ballistic vest and lifted it away. Blood bubbled from Baines's right chest. Sam pulled out a trauma dressing and applied it to the wound. Blood continued to ooze over his hands.

Cops, guns drawn, raced to Steele from the back of the school. One cop asked, "What can we do?"

"Get the kids into the school, now," Steele shouted.

The cops spread out and chased the kids into the school.

Sirens sounded in the distance. Zerr sprinted in front of Steele and Baines, dropped to a knee, and faced the street. Without glancing back, he said. "Sam, you got this?"

"Yeah. I got the paramedics on the way. I need your trauma bandage."

Zerr tossed the trauma bandage behind him.

"We could use better protection than your skinny ass."

Sirens wailed in the distance, getting steadily closer. *Not frickin' fast enough.* Steele adjusted his position on the brittle fall grass. The grass mingled with the coppery smell of blood and what was probably a breakfast sandwich with onions. He put one bandage on Baines' chest and a second on the bleeding hole in his back. Steele clamped down like a vice. Baines moaned but didn't open his eyes.

"Baines. Baines. Can you hear me? Baines. It's Sam. Open your eyes. What the hell were you thinking? I'm a sniper, not a paramedic. Shit. I thought you were smarter than that. If you're going to get shot, do it around the paramedics."

"Come on, Baines. Fight, buddy. Your kids need you."

Steele glanced at the ballistic vest. The right side, over the heart, was a shredded mess. Baines might be alive because of the vest. It didn't stop the .223 bullet but had slowed it.

"Baines. Hang in there, buddy. The paramedics are almost here."

Steele had never felt so useless.

Zerr stood and pointed to cops racing toward them. "Get some cruisers around us. Now. The rest of you beside me."

The cops formed up next to Zerr, creating a human wall shielding Baines. Later they might have second thoughts. Right now, there was no question. Their jaws were set, and their eyes roamed the street in front of the school.

As extra cruisers arrived, the cops took positions behind their vehicles.

"Where the hell are the paramedics?" Steele shouted.

Zerr called on his radio. "Dispatch, ETA on EMS?"

"One minute out."

Zerr peered at the surrounding cops. "I need a volunteer to head out to the street and tell the paramedics to drive next to Steele. Anyone?"

Every hand went up.

Zerr picked a lean cop built like a runner. "Off you go."

He took off like he was running the 100-meter final in the Olympic games. He crouched at the street. When he saw the ambulance approach, he flagged them down.

CHAPTER SIXTY-TWO

THE AMBULANCE BOUNCED ACROSS THE LAWN AND STOPPED BESIDE Steele. Jill Cook jumped out of the passenger side. In three steps, she was next to Steele.

"Just get the stretcher," Steele said. "Chest wound. We gotta go."

Jill knelt next to Steele and pulled gauze bandages out of her kit. "One thing at a time. I'm going to put additional bandages over the ones you applied. When I say release the pressure, slide your hands out. First, the one on the chest. Then put pressure back on over these fresh bandages."

"No." Steele shouted. "We have to go."

Jill put a hand on Steele's arm. "We will. Trust me. This is where I take over. You've done great. Sharma is bringing the stretcher. But we have to slow the bleeding, too."

Steele nodded. Jill applied the bandages as Steele removed his hands, then re-applied pressure.

Jill nodded to Steele. "Good work."

The stretcher plopped to the ground beside Steele. Several cops lifted Baines onto the stretcher, while Steele kept the pressure on the wound.

"You okay?" Jill asked.

Steele's jaw twitched. "This isn't my thing. You need Coulter back here."

"But I've got you. Keep that pressure on until we get to the hospital. Understand?"

Steele bit his bottom lip and nodded.

"You can't let up. Tell me if you get tired."

Steele glared at Jill. "Let's go."

They slid the stretcher into the ambulance. The back door had barely closed when the ambulance lurched forward. The siren wailed. They bounced across the front lawn and onto the road. As the back tires hit the road, Sharma hit the gas and tires squealed as the ambulance raced away. Steele saw flashing red-and-blue lights reflected through the front window. Cops were clearing the way for the ambulance.

Jill slid an oxygen mask over Baines's face, then tied tourniquets high on each arm. Despite the bouncing and jarring of the ambulance, Jill slid the needles into the veins, taped them in place, and had two IVs running.

CHAPTER SIXTY-THREE

On the way back to Calgary, Brad radioed communications and gave them the VIN from the truck. A few minutes later, communications had the information.

"It's a 1976 GMC Truck. Registered to Marvin Pittman of Drayton Valley." She gave the license plate number.

Brad scribbled the information as he drove. "Now check Pittman's name."

"I did. Not a lot on him. Date of birth, October 31, 1945. He doesn't show up in our records until about ten years ago. Then there are several trucks registered to him and addresses from across Canada. He's had a dozen traffic tickets over that time, mostly speeding. No criminal record."

"Okay. Put a BOLO out on that plate. Us and the RCMP. Thanks."

The BOLO had just come across the radio when dispatch reported a cop shot at Western Canada High School. Brad was south of Airdrie, fifteen minutes away.

Griffin and Sturgeon were closer to the shooting, so they headed to the school. Brad was assigned the hospital.

The police radio was jammed with angry voices. Brad finally broke into the radio chaos and told everyone to search for the truck's license plate. It could be on any vehicle.

Cops from all over the city converged on the high school. Dispatchers did their best to maintain control and set up roadblocks. Cops without assignments reverted to what they knew, and that was that the suspects were in a white van or truck. At least that's what they remembered under stress. So again, every white vehicle was being stopped whether or not the license plate matched.

They'd jammed the horseshoe entrance to the Holy Cross Hospital with vehicles—police cruisers, unmarked cars, and of course, the media.

Brad parked on the street and jogged to the emergency entrance. A sea of blue uniforms blocked the door. Then one cop recognized Brad. "Let the detective through." He pushed past the cops and into the hospital. He strode down the hall to the triage desk where Jill Cook was writing her report.

"How is he?" Brad asked.

Jill set down her pen. "They're stabilizing Constable Baines and then they'll take him to surgery. The bullet entered his right lung, and it's collapsed. He lost a lot of blood. Lucky for Baines, Steele was there. He controlled the bleeding with a trauma dressing."

"Will Baines make it?"

"He's still alive," Jill said. "Other than that, we wait."

Brad glanced toward the trauma room. He wanted to head there. Not that he could do anything, but standing here didn't feel right either. They finally had some clues, but the snipers struck before they could do anything with that information. They already had this shooting in the works.

"No sense standing here," Jill said. "Let's head to the coffee room."

Brad took another glance toward the trauma room and followed Jill.

He poured two coffees, handed one to Jill, and flopped into the seat across from her.

They sipped coffee in silence, then Jill said, "Are you okay?"

Brad chewed his cheek and stared past her. "This case is exhausting."

"Well, if it means anything, you look like crap."

Brad's eyes drifted to her. "I appreciate the compliment."

"It must differ from what we do." Jill said. "We go to the scene, street, house, wherever, and treat the patient. We take them to the hospital, do the report, and we're done on to the next patient. How do you keep your energy for days, weeks?"

"Apparently, not well." Brad rubbed the stubble on his chin. "I'm still not used to that. I prefer the action, but there is satisfaction in solving a murder and thinking, in some way, justice was served."

CHAPTER SIXTY-FOUR

BRAD TOSSED HIS JACKET OVER THE BACK OF A CHAIR AND FLOPPED into his chair. How the hell do they get ahead of this? A note propped against his phone caught his eye. It was a message from the Airdrie Dealership. He grabbed the phone and dialed. When the manager answered, Brad said, "It's Detective Coulter. What do you have?"

"We've confirmed the truck is not in our inventory."

"Great." I had that part figured out. "Thanks."

"Wait. We're missing a vehicle."

"What?"

"It's a dark-green Ford LTD. It was a former RCMP undercover vehicle. Can't imagine why they didn't steal a better car, though." He gave the VIN.

Shit. Brad felt his gut churn. He'd seen that car at crime scenes. He knew exactly why they didn't take something flashier. A Ford LTD blended in everywhere.

"Thanks for your help."

Brad hung up, called communications, and updated the BOLO to include the information on the green LTD.

When Griffin, Sturgeon, Stinson, and Devlin had gathered in the zoo, he told the group about the murder ten days ago and that the RCMP thought it was a robbery because a handgun was used, and the cash taken. Brad filled them in on his meeting with the manager that morning and the discovery of the truck and the beer bottle, along with the missing car—the stolen former RCMP undercover car, a green LTD, its license plate possibly from the truck. The vehicle's registered owner was identified as Marvin Pittman. He shared Pittman's known details. "Sturgeon will fill us in on any prints recovered from the bottle in the truck."

Sturgeon handed out a sheet of paper. "You'll be surprised. I got a match on the fingerprints from the beer bottle, but not to Pittman. They matched a *Logan Hirsch*."

"Who the hell is Hirsch?" Brad asked.

"An impaired is the lone record he has, which is unusual for the oil workers," Sturgeon said. "Usually, there's a fight or two in their record. We made some calls and discovered he worked in the oil patch in Drayton Valley but was laid off six months ago. There are no jobs for oil workers. Unemployment Insurance sent him to a course in Rocky Mountain House to determine his skills, write résumés, and practice interviews. But he stopped going to classes a week ago Wednesday. No one knows where he is. His wife left him months ago and moved to Whitecourt. She hasn't heard from him since she filed for divorce two months ago."

"Son of a bitch," Brad said. "Drayton Valley? Rocky Mountain House, then Airdrie?"

"We found other prints in the truck," Sturgeon said. "These, as we would expect, belonged to the registered owner, Marvin Pittman. Some digging showed he'd been working in Drayton Valley on the oil rigs, too."

"Oh, shit," Brad said. "We might have our guys."

"People we called say Hirsch hung around with a guy named Marvin Pittman at the unemployment class," Sturgeon said. "Guess what? Pittman is missing, too."

"Brad asked me to check into Pittman," Stinson said. "Something in Pittman's history wasn't right. This is where it gets interesting. Marvin Pittman didn't exist until ten years ago. There are no federal records, criminal, census, taxes, or residences for Pittman before 1970. I sent Pittman's fingerprints to Ottawa and got a rush on the analysis."

CHAPTER SIXTY-FIVE

WHEN THE NEWS OF THE COP SHOOTING WAS REPORTED ON RADIO and TV stations, the city went into a panic. Parents left work and homes, raced to schools and, in a lot of cases, physically dragged their kids out of the schools. Then they sped through the streets, ignoring traffic signals. Within an hour, reported traffic collisions were over one hundred.

Grocery and department stores closed. Businesses sent employees home. On city transit, passengers sat low in their seats with their heads well below the windows.

Hardware stores stayed open late because of the sharp increase in the sale of tarps and plywood. Around the city, homes were being fortified. All this, even though the shootings had occurred around the city core.

Brad sat at his desk in the zoo, planning their next steps. They'd need a press conference to talk about the school shooting. How could they use the information they had on the identities of the snipers? Maybe luck was on their side for once, and the information on Pittman would help find him.

Just before noon the door to the zoo swung open. Archer stepped in, his eyes ablaze his lips pursed. Brad wondered if there had been another shooting.

"Hey, Chief, everything okay?"

Dr. Hans Keller followed Archer into the room and leaned against the wall, arms crossed.

Brad's gut lurched. "Hey, Keller. Good to see you."

"Hello, Coulter." Dr. Keller's voice was flat.

"Nice tan. How was Hawaii?" Brad stood, shoulders back, chin high. He needed to control this conversation. "Did you hang ten?"

"Coulter, shut up," Archer barked. "Dr. Keller just told me a fascinating story."

Brad's chest tightened at Archer's tone.

"He didn't clear you to return to work."

Brad's eyes narrowed as his head swung toward Keller, then back to Archer. "Chief, I can explain."

"There's nothing to explain," Keller said. "The situation is simple and—"

Brad interrupted, "You don't understand."

"I'm an educated professional psychologist," Keller spat.

Brad snorted. "Combined with your vast experience as a police officer? How's that working out for you?"

"Based on clinical psychology."

"Ah, book smart."

Archer raised his hand. "Watch your mouth, Coulter."

"I was going crazy stuck at home," Brad said. "You kept stonewalling me, Doc."

"I wasn't stonewalling." Keller pushed off the wall and took a couple steps toward Brad, then stopped. "I made an unbiased clinical decision that you were not ready to return to work. You needed to deal with issues in your past."

"I'm not dwelling on the past." Brad glared at Keller. "I lost someone I loved. I don't deny that. My work, it's all I have. I had to do *something*."

"So, your big plan was to steal and lie?" Keller asked. "Exactly the kind of irrational behavior I predicted."

Brad rolled his eyes. "Oh my god, that's a bit dramatic."

"That's enough, Coulter." Archer's nostrils flared. "You've danced the line several times, but you've never stepped over. Never, to my knowledge, have you committed a crime."

Brad's face reddened. Being accused of a crime hit hard. "Technically, yes. But, Chief, can't you see—"

"Technically!" A bright redness started at Archer's shirt line and quickly moved up his neck to his face. "You mean, according to the Criminal Code of Canada!"

Brad feared he wasn't going to be able to talk his way out of this.

The muscles of Archer's jaw flexed. "You took property, a doctor's letterhead, that wasn't yours. That's theft. Keller did not dictate, write, or in any way create correspondence clearing you for duty. You wrote and signed the note, that's forgery. Presenting the note to me, fraud."

Brad's eyes darted to Keller, then back to Archer. "Chief. Doctor Keller. I didn't think my actions through. It was a mistake. I apologize."

"The better-to-ask-forgiveness method may have worked in the past, but not this time." Spittle flew as Archer spoke. "You don't leave me any choice."

"Chief, not now." Brad pointed to the charts and photos on

the walls. "I've got it narrowed down. We've identified the snipers."

Archer shook his head and frowned. "You're part of a team. It's not about *you* nailing the snipers. The team will handle this case just fine."

"I'm going to break this case. I can feel it." Brad held up a finger. "One break. A mistake by the snipers, and I'll have them. It's only a matter of time."

"You're done." Archer glared at him. "You are suspended until further notice."

That was a gut punch even though Brad knew it was coming.

Archer stepped toward Brad until they were inches apart. They stared, eye to eye. "Stay away from this case. Get your personal shit together."

"My *shit* is together, sir. It's a complicated case. Has anyone suggested I'm not handling this case appropriately? Do you have concerns about my progress? We fucking identified the snipers."

The veins in Archer's neck pulsed. "You need to understand the seriousness of your actions, Coulter. I sympathize with your reasoning, but that doesn't mean it was acceptable or excusable. Detective Griffin will lead the team."

Brad held his hands wide. "How about we deal with this after I arrest the snipers?"

"Your immediate suspension stands."

Brad cleared his throat. "You can't do this. The snipers will only talk to me."

"Griffin will figure out how to deal with that." Archer glanced at the notes, charts and photos on the walls. "None of these leaves with you. Later this week, we'll have a serious discussion regarding the viability of your career and future with the service. That's the position you've put me in, and honestly, I'm not sure I can get you out of this." He shrugged. "Do I even want to?"

"Chief, you have to let me continue." The reality of his situation hit him like an avalanche. Sticky wetness dampened his armpits. His jaw clenched, and his heart raced. This wasn't the way for it to end. He had to make Archer understand. "I'll break the case, then you can suspend me, demote me, or fire me. Heck, I'll resign. But I have to see this through to the end."

"Pack your personal stuff. I'll get someone to escort you out of the station." Archer reached for the phone on Brad's desk, then turned back. "Since you screwed up your relationship with Dr. Keller, he will assign you to another psychologist."

"Great. Hopefully, it'll be someone who knows his shit with real-world experience and understands policing." Brad grabbed his jacket and headed to the door. "You're making a mistake, Chief. A huge mistake. I should be here to see this through to the end."

"Get your stuff before you leave," the chief shouted.

"I have nothing here worth taking." He brushed Keller's shoulder as he stomped past. "Your tan makes your skin appear like leather. You should get it checked. Could be skin cancer."

Brad slammed the door behind him.

Shortly before 1:00 p.m. Griffin stood off to the side of the briefing room. He rubbed his wet palms on his trousers. What the hell was Archer thinking? Sending Coulter home was one thing, but assigning the press conference to him was insane. Griffin glanced at Devlin. "You should do this."

Devlin grinned. "Gee, I'd love to, but Archer assigned you."

Griffin glanced around the room. "A lot of reporters."

"There are," Devlin said. "We kept it to merely fifty for you."

Griffin swallowed hard. "Only fifty."

"Not counting about ten TV stations."

"Ass." Griffin tugged on his shirt collar and headed to the podium. Just as he reached to adjust the microphone, the blazing lights from ten TV cameras flared in his eyes. His hand hit the mic, knocking it from its stand.

"Shit," echoed throughout the room.

He fumbled with the mic and eased it back into the holder and coughed.

"Well, we know that works." He waited for the laughter from the reporters to die down. "It's 1:00 p.m. so let's get started. I'm Detective Griffin." He licked his lips. "I, uh, have two items to present. First, at 8:30 a.m. today, Police Constable Conall Baines was shot outside Western Canada High School. Baines is recovering from surgery. His wife and children are at the hospital with him. Constable Baines is an exemplary police officer with ten years of service. When he was assigned to the school, he willingly accepted the assignment. That's the kind of cop, and man, he is. Please give the family privacy. I, well, someone, will update you as we get better information."

Griffin gripped the sides of the podium.

"Detective Coulter is unavailable, so I was asked to give this message to the snipers." He paused, glanced at his notes, and wiped his brow with the back of his hand. "In the past several days, you have tried to contact us. We could not hear everything you said. The audio was unclear. We want to get everything right. Call us at 6:00 p.m. at the same number you used before. We are waiting for your call."

CHAPTER SIXTY-SIX

Mid-afternoon Constable Mullen knocked on the zoo door. Archer glanced up from behind a desk. "What?"

"Sorry to interrupt, sir. Sadie Andrus wants to see Coulter. She said it's urgent."

"Coulter is not here," Griffin said. "Take a message."

"Sir, that won't work. I've dealt with her before. Easier to talk to her straightaway than deal with her later."

"Fine, bring her in," Archer said.

While Mullen went to fetch Andrus, Griffin found Devlin and brought him back to the office.

Mullen again tapped on the door. "Chief, Ms. Andrus."

Griffin stood and stepped away from his chair. "Have a seat."

Sadie took the chair. "Chief, I asked to see Coulter."

"He's not here," Archer said.

She sat back and crossed her arms. "I'll wait."

"He's not on the case," Archer said. "Whatever information you have, you can share with us."

Her eyes widened. "Is he okay?"

"He's fine," Archer said. "Just on, uh, administrative leave."

"Well, then, you've got a problem." Sadie held out a note in a plastic bag. "After Detective Griffin's press conference, someone gave my cameraman a note."

"Does your cameraman know who the guy was?" Griffin asked. "Did the guy give a name?"

"No, he was putting a camera away, and the guy said, 'Give this to Andrus.' My cameraman thought nothing of it, except that some guy was passing notes to me. He forgot about it until we were back at the TV station."

"Let's see the note," Archer said.

Sadie slid the plastic bag across the desk.

Devlin and Griffin stepped behind Archer and read the note.

Dear Police
We were clear, we only talk to Colter.
If <u>HE</u> does not answer our call at 6 p.m.
Expect another shooting.
I am that I am

"Ah, shit," Archer said. "Where's Coulter?"

"Not a clue," Devlin said.

Griffin shrugged.

"Well, find him!"

Devlin slammed his car into park and slid out. He limped as fast as he could across the grass between the tombstones. Since the beating from Wolfe, his leg hadn't healed properly, so the limp was a permanent companion.

He stopped at a stand of trees and pulled out the map from the cemetery manager. He had to be close. He glanced at the headstones, but none were Maggie's, and the dates were wrong. Then he saw another stand of trees, two hundred yards away. Shit.

He worked his way around one row of tombstones, then headed to the next. He found Maggie's grave. Two bouquets lay crossed at the foot of the headstone. Devlin knelt and picked up one bouquet—fresh. Brad had been here. Devlin set the flowers back. He wasn't particularly religious, but he knew he was in a sacred place. He closed his eyes and thought of Maggie. Brad's life was darker with Maggie gone. All their lives were. She brought light to everyone around her. Then the fire was extinguished.

In the late afternoon, Zerr's SUV bounced up the lane to Brad's house. He jammed on the brakes, dust swirling around the truck. He jumped out and sprinted. As he rounded the side of the house, he faced a shotgun.

"Whoa, Annie." Zerr held out his arms.

Annie's eyes were wide—the shotgun shook in her hands. "What are you doing racing in like that? You scared the shit out of me."

"Easy, Annie." He kept one arm outstretched, palm out. "Lower the shotgun."

Annie glanced at the gun, then lowered it. "What's going on?"

"Brad is missing."

"What do you mean, missing?" Annie cocked her head. "Why isn't he at work?"

"Archer suspended him."

"What? Why?"

"Not important now." Zerr took Annie's hand. "I have to find him."

"Is he in trouble?" The pitch in Annie's voice rose. "Did he go over the edge? Is he going to kill himself?"

Zerr squeezed her hand. "Slow down." He took a deep breath. "Brad forged his papers allowing him to go back to work. Archer found out and suspended him."

"I-I still don't—"

"Annie." Zerr shook her shoulders. "I don't have time for this. Is Brad here or not?"

"No."

Zerr let go of Annie's shoulders. "Where's Lobo?"

Annie glanced across the yard. "He must be with Brad."

"Do you know where Brad is?"

"No. I came here to drop off some food."

"Where does he go when he's upset?"

Annie's eyebrows scrunched. "If he's feeling low and needs someone to talk to, he'd go to Maggie's grave."

"Devlin didn't find him there. Would he go drinking? I've got Griffin checking the St. Louis."

"That hasn't been how he's handled stuff this last year. For sure he wouldn't go to the Cuff and Billy." Annie chewed her lip, tapped her foot, then snapped her fingers. "Bowness Park."

"That's a gigantic park."

"Not the main park. At the east end, past the Eighty-Fifth Street Bridge. Where the lagoon joins the Bow. He always took Lobo there, and then it became his and Maggie's place. I don't think he's gone there for a long time. But if he's nowhere else. It's worth a try."

Griffin opened the back door to the St. Louis Hotel bar. He stepped inside and let his eyes adjust to the dim light. Dense smoke swirled around the lights and a musty odor oozed up from the carpet leftover from another century. The place was doing a roaring business for late afternoon in Calgary. These were the people who let nothing like a sniper interfere with their trip to this bar. Then again, they'd likely been here since the doors opened and had no clue what was happening outside. Everyone ignored an outdated TV in the corner of the bar.

But there was a healthy sampling of three-piece suits drinking cheap beer, eating chicken and chips, and hiding out until the city was safe. They'd probably tell their wives they were stuck downtown until the cops arrested the snipers.

"Hey, Griffin. Join us."

Griffin followed the voice to a table with Mayor Roger Kearse and a couple of city council members.

"Grab a chair." He pointed to the table. "More important, grab a beer."

Griffin slid into a chair next to Kearse. He leaned close and whispered, "Have you seen Coulter?"

"Coulter," Kearse boomed. "In here? Ha. Not since he became a lawyer. Too snobby for us, I guess." He glanced at the council members, who laughed.

"I need to find him."

Kearse leaned over to Griffin. "Between you and me. I miss arguing with that son of a bitch. It was good sport."

Griffin stood. "Thanks. If he shows up, tell him to contact me right away. Then you two can debate."

Griffin loped across the parking lot. Next stop, The Cuff and Billy Club.

Brad sat against a rock in east-end Bowness Park and watched Lobo dig for stones in the river. From the moment Brad inherited Lobo from Curtis, the dog had a fascination with rocks. Not just any rocks, the same stone.

Brad closed his eyes and thought about the meeting with Archer and his world crashing down. Bloody fantastic that Keller saw Brad on TV from Hawaii. *What are the chances?* Apparently, one hundred percent. Brad was lucky the charade had lasted this long. What the hell had he been thinking? Now that he had crossed the line, would it be easier to cross the line again? If the criminals didn't follow the rules, why should the cops?

Archer was right. Brad had brushed up against the line—the line that divided right from wrong. Ethical from unethical. Moral versus immoral. He had never stepped so far over, no matter how tempting it was to say *screw the rules,* just to do what needed to be done.

Following the rules got friends killed and others hurt. He did everything by the book and Jeter Wolfe killed Maggie. Was this some punishment? *Am I cursed?*

In trying to save children, he got Shawn injured. He couldn't locate the snipers, then they shot a cop. If he wasn't making a difference, then what was the point?

Lobo knew the pure joy of splashing in the river, fetching rocks, and chasing squirrels. He didn't care how cold the water was. He was always happy and loved unconditionally.

Brad had no idea what made him happy. He worked out not because he liked it, but as a form of punishment. When emotions slipped to the surface, he forced them back down. He liked his friends, but the joy of banter and closeness wasn't the same with Maggie gone.

Other than Lobo, he didn't feel close to anyone, nor did he want that. When Maggie died, the ground was ripped out from under his feet. He was powerless to save her—or Curtis or Tina.

He desperately wanted to go back in time, reset the clock, to return to when work was fun, when he laughed with friends and came home to Maggie. His jaw clenched. He swallowed hard, and his shoulders tightened. None of that was possible. What was the point?

He glanced at the river where Lobo lay beside he chilly water. Lobo was in his prime at six years. However, a large dog's life expectancy was ten to twelve years. Then what? Another dog? He could no more replace Lobo than he could replace Maggie.

Twigs snapped, branches rustled, and heavy footsteps sounded. Lobo jumped to his feet, standing between Brad and the sounds. Lobo's growl was low, then fierce barking. In reflex, Brad's left hand reached for his pistol.

Whoever it was, they were not quiet. While Brad seldom saw people at this end of the park, it wasn't exactly a secret.

Lobo snarled and sprinted down the path. Lobo's growls stopped. Brad stared in the direction Lobo had gone.

Then Sam Steele came around the corner, Lobo at his side, tail wagging.

"What the hell, Sam. You made enough noise for ten people. Didn't I teach you better than that?"

"If I'd come up quietly, I would be leaking valuable blood."

"Excellent point. How'd you find me?"

"We listed your favorite hideouts, and I got this one."

"Who is we?"

"Zerr is at the farm. Griffin is checking the downtown dive bars in case you decided to slum it. I think he headed to the St. Louis first, but he's probably having a drink with Mayor Kearse."

"Why are you searching for me?"

"We heard from the snipers again."

Brad relaxed his hand and shrugged. "That doesn't involve me. I'm off the case. You guys take care of it."

"They sent a note to Sadie Andrus."

"Good for her. Now she gets the scoop she's been seeking."

"What is the matter with you?"

"I screwed up, and it's cost me my career." Brad snorted. "I was angry and pissed at Archer, Dr. Keller, and at a God I'm not sure I believe in. But none of them can help. None of them can change what's happened this year. Half an hour ago, I was ready to completely give up. Accept that I was a danger to everyone around me. I was thinking Lobo and I could pan for gold in the Klondike."

"What are you talking about? Did you steal drugs from work?"

"No. Reality set in."

"Well, fuck that. Archer needs you back on the case, as much as it pains him. Like before. The snipers will only talk—negotiate—with you."

"No shit?"

"Archer wants you back post-haste." Steele spun and stalked away, Lobo at his heels.

If I believe I have nothing left, then I have nothing left to lose. Fuck it. He would bring these snipers to their knees.

CHAPTER SIXTY-SEVEN

Brad stepped tentatively into the zoo. The room oozed with exhaustion and tension. It didn't have the best of smells on a normal day. Now Griffin, Devlin, and Sturgeon, three tired men, after many days of long hours, unhealthy food, and little sleep, stunk up the room.

"Well, look who came back." Griffin was at his desk, leaning back, feet up. "When I didn't find you at the St. Louis, I was tempted to stay and have beer with Mayor Kearse."

"That would work," Brad said. "As long as you were buying."

"I think Kearse misses you." Griffin swung his feet off the desk. "Good to have you back."

Devlin was sitting at Brad's desk, staring at a file folder.

Brad tossed a box of donuts on his desk. "Here's your dinner." He glared at Devlin. "I'm gone a few hours and you move into my desk?"

Devlin snatched a donut."You're timeout was short."

Sturgeon sat in a chair facing Devlin, hands clasped behind his head, eying the donuts.

"You missed the fun," Devlin said. "Griffin had to do the press conference. He nearly ripped off the top of the podium, he was gripping it so hard."

"He was sweating like it was a hundred degrees," Sturgeon said.

Griffin frowned. "Yeah, well, it was Coulter the snipers wanted."

Brad glanced at Devlin, then Sturgeon. "Maybe one of you should do the next news conference."

"How about Sturgeon," Griffin said. "With his Scottish accent, they'd never understand a word he says."

Sturgeon glared at Griffin. "Arse."

Brad took the last chair. "Anything new?"

"Stinson found some additional information on Pittman," Griffin said.

Brad leaned forward. "What'd he find?"

"Remember Sturgeon saying Pittman just appeared about ten years ago?"

Brad nodded.

"Well, there was a reason for that," Griffin said. "He's dead."

"What the hell does that mean?" Brad asked.

"Marvin Pittman was born 31 October 1945 and died four months later. He's buried in Sarnia, Ontario."

"Then who the hell are we searching for?" Brad asked.

"The guy we know as Marvin Pittman is actually Virgil Knowles. He was born in Lexington, Kentucky, on 23 January 1945. He's thirty-seven years old. In 1964 he enlisted in the US army and served in Vietnam. In 1967, while on leave in the US, he disappeared. There is no record of Knowles in the US after

1967. He was an infantryman, a marksman, and saw lots of action. He was involved in some questionable firefights where entire villages were wiped out."

Brad sat back. "He deserted and came to Canada."

Sturgeon nodded and opened a file folder. "In 1970, a new birth certificate was issued in Windsor, Ontario, for Marvin Pittman. From then on, there is a trail of driver's licenses, banking, and so on. He even pays taxes."

"What's his address on his tax returns?"

"Drayton Valley," Sturgeon said. "He hasn't been at that address for over six months."

"Shit. That doesn't help us."

"No," Devlin said. "But we know who we are dealing with. Stinson was right on his profile."

"Please don't say that," Brad said.

"You might have to admit Stinson's profile wasn't all hokey pokey."

Brad grimaced. "Maybe in this room. But if any of you say that to Stinson, I'll deny it."

"Does this mean Pittman—Knowles—is the accurate shooter?" Griffin asked.

Devlin tapped his fingers on the desk. "That would make sense. Also that he's the leader."

"Now we have to decide what we do with this information," Griffin said.

"If we go to the press and say we're seeking Hirsch and Pittman, will they run?" Brad asked. "Are we sending them to be the problem of another city?"

"Or will they go on a final rampage?" Griffin asked. "They move from target to target, location to location. It seems random, but it isn't to them. I think they're following a plan. It wasn't about who they shot, except for the Shawn Fortin and Conall Baines shootings, but they had locations in mind. If they get pissed off, they'll grab the list and start shooting."

"What if Pittman and Hirsch were just a coincidence?" Brad asked. "Another false lead? Sure, Pittman, or rather, *Knowles* fled the US to get away from the US army. Lots of guys did that in the 1960s and 1970s. They'd been laid off, lost property, family in turmoil and were in a bullshit government course. Two guys who went hunting or fishing to get off the grid. That's enough for me to head into the hills."

"Or go on a rampage?" Griffin said.

"There's that," Brad said.

"I don't know about the rampage," Devlin said. "Why try to contact us if the goal is to keep killing?"

"You think they're after the money?" Griffin asked.

"They came here to shoot people," Devlin said. "Maybe they feel they've done what they needed to do. Now they want a simple life—on a beach in the Caribbean. To do that, they need cash to live off. Five million would do that."

"I'm not sure," Brad said. "They've made their demand but haven't pushed it. I feel that beyond 'we want money,' they don't have a clue what comes next. They selected the first victims. Now they're reacting to us. We said kids were safe, they shoot the kid. We miss a meeting, and they killed a bus driver. We screw up surveillance, and they shoot a cop."

"Were there two sets of snipers?" Griffin asked.

"But they may take turns," Brad said. " The first shootings were one shot and dead. Then the next couple weren't as accurate."

Devlin glanced at the clock. "We need to prepare for the press conference."

Archer joined them in the zoo and glanced around the room. His eyes stopped on Brad.

Brad jumped out of his chair. "Thanks for bringing me back in, Chief."

"Don't thank me." Archer leaned against the wall as his eyes bored into Brad. "Your suspension still stands. Once this case is over, you're out." He pointed to the others. "One of you bring me up to date."

Sturgeon told him what they had learned about Pittman-Knowles.

Archer paced back and forth across the racquetball court. "We have to be careful about the wording. I don't want these men ruined if we're wrong, like we were with the chiropractor or the workers from Newfoundland."

"The information from Stinson is excellent," Devlin said.

"We need to be blunt," Griffin said. "We can't sugarcoat this. Why not, 'Wanted—Persons of Interest in Sniper Shootings?'"

Archer shook his head. "That's what we'd say if we knew they were guilty."

"The press will be all over that," Brad said.

"We won't tell the press," Griffin said.

"Keeping stuff from the press hasn't worked so far," Brad said. "We've got a leak."

"It seems there are two leaks." Archer glanced at Brad. "One set of information is getting to Ferguson. Different information getting to Ms. Andrus."

Brad peered away but didn't argue his innocence. He knew he was on rocky ground. He glanced at Griffin.

"Don't look at me, buddy." Griffin took a big bite of a donut. "She doesn't come pining for me."

Brad pulled the box of donuts over and took his time selecting a double chocolate.

Devlin cleared his throat. "No matter what we write, we need to understand it will get to the press," Devlin said. "We can't make this perfect. It's cliché, but: just the facts."

"How about, 'Wanted for Questioning'?" Griffin suggested.

"We're overthinking this," Archer said. "Keep it simple and to the point."

"What Griffin said." Brad took a bite of donut. "Wanted for Questioning. Witnesses to Shootings. Use their pictures from the motor vehicles branch. Add the description of the car and license plate."

"It might cause panic," Archer said.

"After Baines was shot, the city panicked," Brad said. "What other choice do we have?"

CHAPTER SIXTY-EIGHT

THE MINUTE HAND CLICKED ON THE TWELVE, THE HOUR HAND ON the six as they waited for the call. Griffin sat in a corner operating the tape recorder and talking through headphones to the telephone company who would trace the call. Devlin sat next to Brad so he could give Brad advice depending on what the snipers demanded. Archer paced the hall.

Brad leaned back in his chair and closed his eyes. Every part of his body sagged. His energy level was low. Part of him wished they had left him alone at the park. Just him and Lobo. Forget about the world. Someone else could be the hero.

The office was quiet. No one dared talk. This was an urgent call. Could they end this madness tonight? What did the snipers want? They had received a lot of publicity. Their egos had to love that.

The phone rang, and Brad sprung forward in his chair. Griffin started the tape, talked to the phone company, then nodded.

Brad picked up the phone. "Coulter."

"Coulter, your bumbling has cost you."

Brad started to reply, "You need to know—"

Devlin glared at Brad, eyes wide, and mouthed, *Zip it.*

"Shut up! Listen."

"I'm listening."

"We warned about trying to catch us, but you traced our call. We watched you arrest the wrong men. Another person died because of your incompetence."

There was silence for a moment. Devlin nodded to Brad. "I hear you. I hear the frustration in your voice. We haven't made it easy for you to contact us. That's on me."

"A little late. Those deaths are on your head."

"My boss isn't happy with me because of that."

"Like I give a shit about you or your boss."

"We're talking. I don't know why you wanted to talk to me. Other than we're guys trying to do the right thing, but the system keeps knocking us back."

"What the hell do you know about me?"

"I don't know you, but I get that we frustrate you, that the system has let you down. That part I can relate to."

"Sure, we're practically best friends. Let's get a beer sometime and talk about our troubles."

"We keep talking. If you can help me, that would be great. Can you agree to stop the shootings?"

There was laughter on the speaker. *"Sure, we'll stop the shootings for ten million in travelers checks. You have until Tuesday at 10:00 a.m."*

Brad's eyes went wide. But before Devlin could give advice, the sniper spoke.

"Thanks for the talk, Coulter. By now you must have traced this

call. We'll call and tell you where to drop the money. Targets are already selected. No one is safe, not kids, cops, media, no one. If police are at the drop site, you'll need a lot of body bags."

"Wait, I'll need time—"

"Negotiate. Coulter, last chance."

The line went dead.

Brad stared at the receiver. "Wonderful talk." He hung up the phone.

Griffin shook his head. "The call came from a payphone in an industrial park in the deep south. We don't have anyone close."

"The snipers knew we would trace the call," Brad said.

"They learned from the last time. They picked a location far from anywhere we know they've been. I'll bet they're watching to see if we show up."

"If Pittman and Hirsch are watching to see if we traced the call and show up, they'll be in their car, not around a TV set," Devlin said. "We should do the press conference immediately."

Griffin tossed his headphones on the desk. "If they're in their car, they might hear it on the radio."

Devlin shrugged. "That's a chance we have to take."

CHAPTER SIXTY-NINE

THE SECOND-FLOOR BRIEFING ROOM AT HEADQUARTERS WAS PACKED. Sweet perfumes and aftershave mixed like a stroll down the makeup aisle at The Bay. At 6:15 p.m., Brad approached the mic. "Thank you for attending on short notice. Constable Conall Baines is in ICU after successful surgery. We expect him to make a full recovery, but it will take several months. We ask you to honor Constable Baines and his family's privacy during his recovery. Questions can be directed to the Public Information Officer."

Uniformed officers circulated among the members of the media, handing out packages.

"You are receiving packages of important information. Through our investigations, we have identified two people of interest in this case. They are Logan Hirsch and Marvin Pittman. We believe they are from the Drayton Valley area and may have been taking employment training in Rocky Mountain House before arriving in Calgary."

Brad's eyes roamed across the gathered reporters, stopping briefly on Sadie. "We believe Mr. Hirsch and Mr. Pittman may have information vital to our investigation. As a caution, consider them armed and dangerous. Information on these two should be called to 911."

Brad paused. This was the first time they had sanctioned the use of 911 for tips. They had contacted every dispatch center in Western Canada and even Montana and Idaho, in case a 911 call went to any of their dispatch centers.

"They are driving a dark-green Ford LTD, possibly with the following license plate number." Brad gave the number, and it appeared on the projection screen behind him. "If you see this vehicle, do not approach. Immediately call 911." Brad folded his notes. "I will not be taking questions."

Uniformed officers formed an escape route for Brad. Reporters fired questions as he left.

Back in the zoo, Brad flopped into his chair. "Now we wait."

"For them to be spotted or for another shooting?" Griffin asked.

"Yes," Brad said.

Stinson knocked on the door. "We're getting calls from the Drayton Valley area. People who know Pittman and Hirsch from jobs in the area. I've got members checking them as fast as they can. But one thing is coming in clear. Hirsch was a decent guy who had a whack of awful luck. I've got members heading to talk to his wife in Whitecourt. Pittman, on the other hand, was uniformly hated and was an ass."

"How did Hirsch get hooked up with Pittman?" Griffin asked.

"Pittman targeted him," Devlin suggested. "Pittman saw a guy down on his luck with everything getting worse. When

Hirsch was served divorce papers, I bet that was the last straw. He would be putty in the hands of Pittman." Devlin frowned and glanced around the room. "Pittman has a doesn't-give-a-shit-about-anything attitude. He's probably been a bully all his life. Someone will tell us he likes to hurt animals and people."

"Isn't he the shooter?" Brad asked.

"Not initially." Devlin stood and pointed to the pictures of the first victims. "These four were near-perfect shots. I think Pittman wanted in on the action. But he couldn't let Hirsch know he was a marksman. He got pleasure out of making Hirsch a killer. He took a calm, honest family man and made him one of our worst murderers."

"It'll be a pleasure to get my hands on him," Brad said.

"I bet you won't," Devlin said.

"Get pleasure?"

"Not that. You won't take him alive."

CHAPTER SEVENTY

Constable Mullen raced into the zoo. "A trucker called about three minutes ago, at 10:30 p.m. and says he saw the car—the LTD, matching the license plate. It's across the highway from the ski hill on the west city limits. The car is partially hidden by some camping trailers."

Brad jumped out of his chair. "Mullen, tell Gary Schantz to start the helicopter." Brad buckled his gun belt, slipped on a ballistic vest, then followed Steele and Zerr out of headquarters into the dark, full-moon night. The icy wind hit their faces like hundreds of tiny needles as they sprinted to the parking lot.

As they approached, the helicopter's motor whined, and the blades turned. When they reached the helicopter, the engines were at full throttle. They ducked under the rotors and into the seats. Brad took a position next to Schantz, and Steele and Zerr jammed themselves into the back. Zerr set the case for his sniper rifle across his knees and slid out the gun.

The engines whined, the helicopter shuddered, and gained

air. Once Schantz had altitude, the nose dropped, and they sped down Sixth Avenue, gathering speed as they headed west.

Brad slid the headphones in place and twisted toward Schantz. "Body armor suits you."

Schantz grinned. "Brings back memories for sure."

Brad gave him a thumbs up. "Patch me into police dispatch on the secure channel."

Schantz nodded and adjusted the radio dial.

"Dispatch. Coulter, Steele, and Zerr are in the air heading west. We will use the call sign, Air One. Tell responding units to secure the area but hold back. Have Tactical Support Units meet us on Sixteenth Avenue, east of the ski hill. We'll coordinate from there."

"Roger Air One," dispatch said. "We have units coming from the north and Two District cars are coming down Sarcee."

"No one approaches."

"Message relayed," dispatch said.

"What's the plan, boss?" Steele's voice came over the headset.

"We'll go on foot. We'll be about a mile out. It won't take us long to jog in there."

"You sure you're in good enough shape, boss," Zerr said.

"Be sure you keep up," Brad replied.

They watched the Bow River flash below them.

"Zerr, get your rifle ready. If they get spooked, take out their tires."

"And if they shoot back?"

I'd like them alive. "None of us die tonight."

"Roger that," Zerr said.

The helicopter swung away from the river and followed Sixteenth Avenue. Ahead, the red-and-blue lights of at least a dozen cruisers flashed in the night. The helicopter rotated and prepared to land.

"They're on the run," an excited voice came over the radio.

"Unit, identify," dispatch said.

"Uh, 322. We, uh, got too close. They saw us as we drove past. They veered down Bowfort Road."

"Don't land," Brad shouted. "Get us back in the air."

The engines whined, and the helicopter appeared to stall a few feet off the highway, then slowly Schantz gained altitude.

"Follow Bowfort Road." Brad pointed.

Nose down, the helicopter raced between the hills into Bowness.

"They turned left," Brad yelled over the noise of the helicopter. "Dispatch, seal off all roads out of Bowness."

Schantz swung left. They were over the dark-colored LTD. The driver killed his headlights, which did little to hide them. At Forty-Eighth Avenue, the LTD turned left again.

"We're in your former hood," Steele said.

"Yup," Brad said. "Can you get in front of them?"

"No problem." The helicopter gained speed and then rotated to face the speeding car. Zerr slid the side door open and leaned out, bringing the LTD into his scope. "I've got him, boss."

"Wait, see if he slows."

The LTD swung hard to the right and into Bowness Park.

"We've got them," Brad shouted. "Dispatch, Air One. Have units seal off the entrance to Bowness Park. I'll need units to head to the river from Forty-Eighth Avenue and Eighty-Fifth Street and at the Woods Home."

"Roger, Air One."

"We're in my backyard," Brad said to Schantz. "There's a field to your right. Put it down there."

The pilot circled the field once, then set the helicopter down.

Zerr was out first and covered the area with his rifle. Brad and Steele grabbed rifles and joined him.

"Okay," Brad said. "They didn't come this way, so they've headed west. Spread out."

Steele jogged to Brad's left and Zerr to the right. They set off at a comfortable jog. They passed by the canoes, across the site of the deserted carnival and to the concession. No sign of the snipers. They cleared the cook shelters as they went. No sign of the LTD yet. Steele jogged farther left and followed the lagoon. Zerr followed a path over to the river.

They were close to the west end of the park when wood splintered on a tree next to Brad. The shot echoed throughout the park.

"Shit." Brad dove to the ground. "Either of you see where that came from?"

"Not positive, boss," Steele said. "Seemed straight ahead."

"All right. Let's move. Stay low."

They moved forward, crouched low. An engine started, and headlights flashed at Brad. They blinded him. "Shit, I can't see," he shouted.

"I have him," Zerr said.

Two shots rang out from Brad's right. He heard the hiss of one tire, then another. The car, fifty feet away, headed toward him.

Two shots from the left. One headlight blew out. The second shot hit metal—steam hissed.

Bullets struck the ground around Brad and hit a few trees. The barrage was steady.

Steele and Zerr returned fire.

The shooting stopped. "Boss, you okay?" Steele asked.

"I'm fine. Let's get these assholes. I'll shoot from here. You two come in from the sides."

Brad raised up on his stomach and fired at the grill of the car. In his periphery, Steele and Zerr flanked the vehicle. Steele threw a distraction device inside. There was a bright flash and bang. Brad was on his feet and sprinting for the car.

When he got there, he saw the disappointed faces. "They're not here, boss," Steele said. "They have to be close."

"Spread out, stay low, and keep cover. There's an open area left—then it's into heavy woods to the Bearspaw Dam." Brad took a few steps. "Wait."

"Zerr, go back to the helicopter. Fly over and use the spotlight." Brad keyed his mic. "Dispatch, have units seal off the east end of the park, but stay well back of west end where the river fills the lagoon." Brad nodded to Steele, and they set off. As they reached the end of the park where the lagoon ended and the path headed into the woods, they heard the helicopter overhead, and a spotlight lit up the area.

Brad keyed his mic again. "What do you see?"

"Nothing yet. But they're not right in front of you, so keep going."

"Coulter. It's Toscana and Briscoe. Where do you need us?"

"Go to my farm, there is a path to the north. Follow it down to the river."

"We won't find that in the dark," Toscana said.

"Shit. Lobo knows the way."

"Uh, that might work," Toscana said. "You left Lobo behind when you left, so Briscoe coaxed him into the van."

"He went with you?"

"Sweet talk and a ham sandwich, and he happily jumped in the van."

"Perfect. How long until you're there?"

"Not long, five minutes at the most, despite Grandpa Briscoe not seeing too well driving at night."

"Okay. Stop in my lane. Straight north is the path. Once Lobo finds it say, 'river,' and try to keep up."

"Roger, that." Brad heard Briscoe complaining as Toscana replied.

Brad led the way at a steady jog. The path was too narrow for them to run side by side.

"How far to the dam?" Sam asked.

"Fifteen minutes at this pace."

"We should catch them. From their pictures, they don't seem like athletes."

The helicopter circled above their heads as they followed the path.

"Hard to see anything," Zerr said. "The trees are too thick. Now and then I see you guys, but even knowing which way you're heading doesn't help a lot."

They weaved through the hundred-year-old trees. The path, though well worn, was narrow. The full moon provided some light, but the light didn't make it through the dense trees. The spotlight from the helicopter was useless.

Ahead, they heard a twig snap, then another. Brad and Steele slowed to a walk.

Bark sprayed their faces as the crack of a rifle shot echoed through the trees.

Brad and Steele dove to the ground.

"Shit, they set up an ambush," Brad said.

"Did you see where the shot came from?" Steele asked.

"No."

Zerr came over the radio. "You guys okay? Looked like a gun flash from ahead of you."

Brad keyed his mic. "Caught us off guard. We're fine. Where was the flash?"

"I don't know where you guys are."

Brad glanced at the sky. "You're right over us."

"Then about one hundred yards ahead and to the south."

"Can you see them?"

"Nope, but we're gonna circle above them and give them some sunshine."

"We need the light, but it will make you a target."

"Yeah," Zerr said. "We discussed that. We'll light up the area for a few seconds, then shut it off and move."

The light blazed into the trees ahead.

"I see them," Zerr said.

A half-dozen rifle shots sounded from ahead. Brad and Steele took cover behind a vast pine.

Bullets hitting metal and ricochets echoed throughout the valley.

"We're okay," Brad said. "Zerr?"

"We're not," Zerr replied. "We've got some red lights here on the panel. We'll head north for a minute and figure out what problems we have."

"Roger that," Brad said. "We're gonna split up and move ahead."

The radio clicked twice in acknowledgment.

Brad tapped Steele on the shoulder and pointed to the right, toward the river. Steele nodded. Brad headed into the trees to the left. The underbrush was thick, and progress was slow. Each step had to be placed carefully. Branches whipped at his face. Ahead he saw a shadow—a rock outcropping. Perfect place to set up a sniper nest. He veered farther to the left until he was past the outcropping, then headed toward the rocks. In close, his rifle was not the best choice of weapon. He slung the gun toward his back and drew his pistol. He crouched low as he eased toward the rocks. He squinted as he stared into the darkness. No movement, no shapes. He shuffled forward, then stood. No one hid behind the rocks. He crouched low, took out his penlight, covered the light with his hand, and clicked it on. He moved the narrow beam across the ground. The light created several glints among the rocks. He reached down and grabbed a shiny object—a .223 case. They had shot from here.

He ducked behind the rocks and keyed his mic. "Steele. I found where they shot from, but no one here. I'm moving farther west."

"Roger, I'm at the river and following it west to the dam."

"Zerr, what's happening?" Brad asked.

"Pilot says we're done here. We're heading back to the airport. Stand by."

Brad gazed into the sky and picked out the running lights to the north. The lights headed east.

"Sorry, boss," Zerr said. "I tried to get him to put me on the ground, but he's worried he wouldn't have enough power to lift off. I'll be back as soon as I can."

Brad clicked the mic twice. Two on two. Those odds were okay. Even if the asshats had the advantage of being ahead of them, however, they were being hunted by predators. He'd bet on Steele and him any day.

Brad crawled around the rocks and peered west. No movement and no sounds. He holstered his pistol, swung the rifle back into his hands and headed west. After about fifteen feet, he found the path and decided he'd follow it, keeping as close to the trees as he could.

The path weaved through the thick forest. Ahead, the grim shadow of the dam loomed. Brad slowed just before the trees ended and the ground opened to shale and gravel—the area had been razed when the dam was constructed. He knelt behind a Douglass Fir and scrutinized from the dam to the trees and back again. No movement. No sound. A hundred yards in front of him, where the trees began again, there was nothing but darkness.

To his right, he could make out the shape of the dam spillway and the churning water at the base. The only sound was the flowing, splashing water. Ahead, and to the left, were the sand caves he'd explored as a kid.

Not caves—indents in the sand. If you went in one side, you'd come out another opening in about six steps. Still, it was above Brad's position and would be another excellent location to lay in ambush.

Brad stared toward the caves. He let his eyes adjust to the darkness. Still, he saw no movement. He calculated how fast he could cross the clearing. On a good day, ten to twelve seconds. More in the darkness. If he fell, he'd be an easy target.

Flashes came from the cave, and gunshots echoed in the darkness.

Brad rolled behind the tree. Branches snapped overhead. He rolled out from behind the tree, dodging the falling branches, aimed his rifle at the caves, and watched for the flashes.

When the shots started again, he fired toward the cave. He heard the ricochet of the bullets on rocks. Then, in his periphery, he saw a figure sprinting to the right.

"Steele, suspect heading your way. East of the spillway heading into the open."

"Roger. I'm nearly there."

Bullets thudded into the trees around Brad. He crawled to a thick stand of trees. Then he worked his way through the thick overgrowth to the west. Maybe he could sneak past the shooter and come up from behind. It was slow fighting through the branches and trying to stay quiet. He glanced toward the river and saw the suspect was ten feet from the water. Steele would be on him any moment. The suspect planned to swim to safety. He was far enough from the spillway and out of the churning water that he might have a chance if he was an excellent swimmer. Well, to make it he'd have to be an Olympian.

Steele yelled, "Stop."

Brad swung to the sound of Steele's voice and saw the suspect turn toward Steele and fire.

Brad's gut flipped, his eyes widened, and icy chills swept through his body. "No."

As Steele crouched, a bullet slammed into a tree above his head.

The suspect lowered the rifle and aimed.

A dark shape raced toward Steele and drove him to the ground as a second bullet hit the mossy earth where Steele had been.

Brad swung his rifle toward figure by the river and fired. The suspect stumbled backward into the river.

A steady stream of gunfire from the cave hit near Brad. He ducked back behind the trees. With his back to the trees, he glanced at the river.

He heard a splash and saw a dark shape bobbing in the river.

Lobo swam to the suspect who was floating, face down, ten yards offshore.

Brad leaned around the tree and fired at the cave. He needed to keep the shooter distracted to give Lobo time to drag the suspect to shore.

Brad kept a slow, steady stream of bullets at the cave. When his thirty-round magazine was empty, he quickly switched out the empty mag.

He glanced to his right and saw Lobo was at the shore, and Steele was wading out to them. Steele grabbed the suspect by the jacket collar and dragged him into the woods.

"Who is it?" Brad asked.

"Logan Hirsch," Steele replied. Shots thudded the ground near Steele and Hirsch.

Brad spun to return fire, but the gun flashes were coming from farther away.

The shooter, who must be Pittman, had moved out of the caves and into the valley that wound its way toward Brad's house. Brad fired a burst of three shots and then rolled to his left.

Bullets struck the ground where Brad had been. The shooter was on Brad's turf. If he could keep herding him up the hill, Brad would catch up to him in the open.

Also, the uphill climb favored Brad, and he barely lost a step in his sprint up the trail.

Steele's voice came over the radio. "Thanks, boss. I've got Hirsch. Pittman is all yours."

Brad clicked the mic and headed up the hill. He heard shouting from ahead, and then a half-dozen shots. He raced toward the shots. Two more shots rang out, followed by swearing.

Brad rounded a corner and nearly knocked over Toscana. She was on her knees with her hands on Briscoe's gut.

"What happened?" Brad asked.

"We were coming down the hill," Toscana said. "We had slowed so Briscoe could catch his breath when a guy came around the corner and fired at us. We dove into the brush and then returned fire as he raced past."

"Not sure if we hit him." Briscoe grunted. "Bastard got me, though."

"Where are you hit?" Brad asked.

"Took one in the gut. Hurts like my innards are on fire."

Brad slipped off his pack and opened a zippered compartment on the side. He pulled out trauma dressing and applied it to Briscoe's gut.

"Toscana, keep the pressure on."

"Roger that. I've got EMS on the way."

"Kinda sucks, huh," Brad said.

"What?" Briscoe asked.

"You finally wear your vest, and you get hit in the gut."

"Biggest mass," Toscana said.

"Stop gawking, rookie." Briscoe twisted toward Brad. "Get that motherfucker."

Brad squeezed Briscoe's shoulder. "Hang in there, old-timer."

CHAPTER SEVENTY-ONE

THE HELICOPTER SHUDDERED, AND ADDITIONAL LIGHTS FLASHED ON the console. Warning alarms sounded. The chopper vibrated from the failing engine. Zerr watched helplessly as Schantz held tight to the cyclic stick that had a mind of its own.

After the rifle shots struck the helicopter, Schantz said they were okay—they'd make it to the airport.

A few seconds later, Schantz said, "We won't make it. I need to put it down. We're over a residential area. There's no place here. Too dangerous."

Schantz swung the chopper hard to the right.

"What are you doing?"

"Heading to the river."

"Can you land on water?"

"Of course, I can." Schantz glanced at Zerr. "Just not safely and we'll sink."

"Then what?"

"Unless I see a field large enough in the next minute, at least ditching in the river won't put others in danger."

"And us?"

"Make sure your seatbelt is tight." He keyed his mic. "Dispatch, this is Air One."

"Go ahead, Air One."

"We are declaring an emergency. We won't make it to the airport. We're ditching in the Bow River—west of Crowchild Trail. There's an island in the middle of the river. I'll try to make that. Notify fire and EMS."

"Roger, Air One. Fire and EMS notified."

"Dispatch, this is Zerr, TSU."

"Go ahead, Zerr."

"I need you to do one more thing."

"Anything, name it."

Zerr made his request.

CHAPTER SEVENTY-TWO

SHARMA AND COOK STOOD IN THE DARKNESS BESIDE THE ambulance at the boat ramp near Louise Bridge. A light rain that threatened to turn to snow quickly covered their jackets. Cook shivered. "Why can't we get better coats?"

Sharma snorted. "Budget, my dear, budget."

"We need gear like the firefighters have."

"Sure. That would be fun squeezing into a bedroom wearing that gear. We would appear like the Michelin Man."

The fire department was backing the rescue boat into the river.

"Can't they do this quicker?" Cook slipped on her life preserver.

"Read my mind," Sharma said as he did the same.

Finally, the boat engines roared to life. Two firefighters rushed over and grabbed some of their equipment. "Let's go," one of them said.

The firefighters assisted Sharma and Cook into the boat, the engines rumbled, and they backed away from the launch. The boat swung around, the engines thundered, and they were thrust back into their seats.

Cook worked through the problems in her head. Dispatch said a cop was shot, and so was a suspect. Sometimes these situations were complicated. Training said to treat the most severe first. The cops on the scene would want their own taken care of first, no matter how severe the injuries to the suspect. She played the scene both ways in her mind, then stopped. She'd know the right thing to do when she got there.

The boat skimmed the water as it fought against the current. Occasionally the pilot made a quick turn, throwing them against one side of the boat or the other. Cook saw little in the darkness. The sky and water merged into a continual cloud of black.

Somehow the boat pilot and the spotters navigated the river. They passed Twenty-Ninth Street, the road to Foothills Hospital, past Shouldice Park and under the Bowness Bridge. Then they swung to the west. The river was straight, and they accelerated.

On the right, Cook saw red-and-blue flashing lights on the parallel Bearspaw Dam Road. The red lights of two ambulances followed behind. They would wait on the north bank. Cook and Sharma would need to assess and treat the patients and prepare them for the quick boat ride across the river to the ambulances.

The engine slowed as the pilot guided the boat to the shore.

Cook jumped off the boat and into the water. She couldn't wait. Steele stood on the shore over a handcuffed man lying on his face.

"He's shot, but it's minor."

"I'll check him," Cook said.

"No." Steele glared at them. "Briscoe is shot. He's first."

"I'll go," Cook said. "Sharma can stay here."

Steele glanced at Cook. "Fine."

Cook called two firefighters. "Come with me."

She led them across the gravel shore to an opening in the trees and followed the well-worn path. They zigged and zagged through the trees. Ahead, she heard voices. They rounded a curve and came upon Toscana at Briscoe's side, holding a trauma dressing on his stomach.

Immediately Cook called to a firefighter. "He can't walk. We'll have to carry him out. Get a Stokes stretcher."

The firefighter called for help on his radio. Cook knelt beside Briscoe. "Shit, Briscoe. What happened?"

"We bumped right into the shooter. He got a few shots off and hit me. Dumb luck."

"One shot?"

"With a rifle," Toscana said. "Split the skin and muscle open."

"Did you see intestines?" Cook asked.

"No," Toscana said. "Lots of bleeding. Coulter stopped and gave me the trauma bandage. I think the bleeding has stopped—well, slowed at least."

Cook slid her paramedic shears out of the hip holster and cut the uniform shirt. She opened the Velcro closures and slipped the chest plate of the ballistic vest off. Finally, she cut away the T-shirt—the trauma bandage was soaked. She got another trauma bandage from her kit, then removed the blood-soaked gauze.

A firefighter stood over them and directed a flashlight beam toward the injury. In the light from the flashlight, she saw the bullet wound. More like a knife laceration across the abdomen. Deep enough to penetrate skin, fat, and muscle, but not deep enough to hit the intestines. She placed the fresh bandage over the wound and taped it in place.

As she finished establishing IV lines, four firefighters came around the curve. They set the Stokes stretcher next to Briscoe. They helped lift Briscoe into the basket stretcher. Cook covered Briscoe with blankets, and they set off, a firefighter at each corner of the cot.

CHAPTER SEVENTY-THREE

BRAD SPRINTED UP THE PATH, MORE DETERMINED THAN EVER. Briscoe was family. As the anger brewed, he sprinted up the hill at a pace he had never achieved before. His jaw was set, his mind clear. The shooter would die.

Brad crested the ridge, but Pittman was not in sight. Had he been so determined to get up the hill he'd passed the shooter? But surely the Pittman would have shot as he passed. No, he was still ahead. Brad darted past a fence post and then found himself at the lane to his house.

Not on my land.

Then he saw the Pittman stumble in the glow of the yard light—he spun toward the house. "Dispatch, shooter is headed toward my house."

Brad put everything into the sprint up the lane. As he rounded the corner, he saw Annie's car in the driveway. Then the screen door slammed shut.

"Dispatch, Pittman is at my house. Hostage situation."

"Coulter stand down. TSU is on the way. Coulter. Coulter."

Brad ripped the screen door off its hinges and leaped through the entryway into the kitchen.

The sound of a gunshot blasted through the house, then a second shot.

Fuck!

Brad raced through the house and stopped at the door to Annie's room. She sat with her back against the headboard—smoking shotgun pointed at Brad.

"Whoa, Annie, it's Brad."

She stared, frozen in time.

Brad inched toward the bed. Annie didn't move. Brad reached for the gun and took it from her hands.

He glanced toward the end of the bed. A man lay slumped against the wall. Blood oozed from holes in his chest. Most of his head was splattered on the wall behind him. The close-range shotgun blast had obliterated his face. Brad knelt and took a .45 caliber Colt M1911 Automatic out of Pittman's dead hand.

Brad keyed his mic. "Dispatch, Coulter. Suspect down. Repeat, suspect down. My house. Send detectives, Crime Scene Unit, medical examiner, and Deputy Archer."

"Coulter, dispatch. Say the number of casualties."

"One DOA," Brad said. "No other injuries here. Has EMS reached Briscoe yet?"

"Roger, Coulter. EMS on scene with a fire rescue boat."

Brad sat on the bed. Annie still stared at the bedroom wall. He leaned in front of her and whispered, "Annie. Can you hear me?" She didn't move. "Annie. It's Brad. Can you hear me?"

Her head slowly rotated toward him. "Is he dead?"

"Yes."

"I did it?"

"Yes." He put his arm around her shoulder. "You had no choice."

"I was so scared." Annie leaned into his chest.

"How did you know to be ready?"

"Dispatch called me."

Brad pulled back. "What?"

"Charlie was in the helicopter and heard you were chasing the shooter up the hill." She sniffled and wiped her eyes with a sleeve. "He had dispatch call me and say to stay in my room. I thought of the shotgun and took it with me."

"Smart girl," Brad said. "We might owe Charlie beers for the rest of our lives. But don't tell him."

There was a loud thump from the back of the house. Brad drew his pistol and aimed it at the open door.

Lobo flew through the opening and onto the bed. He climbed onto Annie's chest and licked her face.

CHAPTER SEVENTY-FOUR

SHARMA WATCHED COOK AND THE FIREFIGHTERS HEAD INTO THE woods. He focused on his patient, but all he could focus on was Steele and his rifle.

Sharma glanced up at Steele. "Can you lower your gun?"

Steele stepped back a couple steps but kept the rifle ready. "Sorry, but you'll have to get used to it."

"He's hurt."

"I know." Steele shrugged. "Brad shot him."

Sharma was surprised at the matter-of-fact way he said it. "At least take off the cuffs"

Steele shook his head and pursed his lips. "Nope, not gonna happen."

"It's difficult to assess him this way."

"Then don't assess him. I don't give a shit."

Sharma held out his hands. "What if he dies?"

Steele raised his eyebrows. "Then hell has another occupant."

"Please."

"I know you have a job to do." Steele's shoulders sagged. "I get that, I do. But they killed at least six people and critically injured three others. I have no sympathy for him. He's a murderer and I will not risk injury to you. His days of killing are over. If you treat him, whether he lives or dies, doesn't affect me."

Sharma knelt by the patient in the gravel. His clothes were soaked, and he shivered uncontrollably. His face was scrunched into the gravel.

"I'm a paramedic. My name is Amir."

"Let me die."

"I'm not gonna do that. What's your name?"

"Logan." He spoke through gritted teeth.

"Okay, Logan. I'm going to roll you onto your side. It will be uncomfortable because of the handcuffs."

Sharma glanced at Steele. "It's okay, I got it." Sharma rolled Logan onto his side, trying to keep him from going over onto the cuffs. "Where are you hurt?" He shone the flashlight over Logan.

"My left shoulder." He tried to turn his head to see Steele behind him. "Bastard shot me."

"Not me," Steele said.

"Okay, Logan. I see a wound in your shoulder. Anywhere else?"

"My right arm." He tried to move his arm closer to Sharma, but the handcuffs stopped his motion. "Fucking dog bit me and dragged me here."

"The dog?" Sharma glanced around.

"Yeah. They sent a dog after me."

"That's kinda close to the story," Steele said. "He shot at me.

He missed. Coulter shot him. He didn't miss. Shithead here fell into the river and was floating away. Lobo saved his life and dragged his sorry ass to the shore. He would have drowned if it wasn't for Lobo."

Sharma sat back on his haunches. "Where is the dog?"

"I don't know." Steele shrugged. "Possibly searching for Coulter. He raced off after he pulled this shithead out of the river."

"Your wounds don't appear serious," Sharma said. "The bites are easily treated. I'll clean your wounds, bandage the shoulder, and put your arm in a sling. You'll be fine."

"Fix him up so we can get out of here," Steele said. "I need him checked at the hospital, then to jail where he'll rot for the rest of his sorry-ass life."

Sharma ignored Steele and treated Logan. "He's ready to go. I'll take him to the boat."

"Not yet," Steele said. "He can wait. Briscoe is the first one to cross."

"They'll be up there for a while. They have to carry him out. We can be across and back before they get Briscoe out."

"Maybe, but we'll wait."

Sharma glanced up, preparing his argument, but when he saw the fire in Steele's eyes, he decided they could wait.

About ten minutes later, firefighters carrying Briscoe broke out of the trees and headed to the river. They lifted the stretcher into the boat. Toscana and Cook climbed in after him.

CHAPTER SEVENTY-FIVE

THE RUNNING LIGHTS OF THE HELICOPTER REFLECTED OFF THE WATER as they spun wildly. Schantz fought the cyclic control without success. It appeared the tail of the chopper was in charge. The spinning increased, and Zerr shook his head to get rid of the dizziness.

"Brace for impact."

Zerr eyeballed the cockpit. Nothing to grab to brace. He hoped the seatbelt held, and the chopper survived the impact. They were spinning faster and dropping like a rock. He had no idea how high they were when the engine gave its last sputter.

They hit the ground. It felt like thousands of pounds pushed down on him, his head pressed on the spine, spine collapsed, his entire body shoved into his pelvis.

Metal screeched and sparks flew as the rotors struck the rocks. The windshield exploded. Then he was flung to the right, and pain ripped through his shoulder and neck. The chopper rocked several times before coming to rest on its side. In the dim light, Zerr saw Schantz, motionless in his seat, held in place by the seatbelt.

Then pain. His neck was electrical shocks of pain. His right hip sent waves of agony across his lower body. He couldn't feel his right shoulder or arm. Zerr could not move. He fought to remain conscious. He was vaguely aware of the sounds of traffic and sirens, then darkness.

CHAPTER SEVENTY-SIX

BRAD AND ANNIE STOOD OUTSIDE AS COPS UNROLLED POLICE TAPE in a large circle around the house. His house was a crime scene. Again. Annie leaned close, and Brad put his arm around her. He felt her chest heave with the sobs she was trying to hold in.

His gut twisted into knots. He wasn't sure if he was relieved or angry. He'd come so close to another person in his life dying.

Lobo rubbed against Annie's leg, his way of providing love and support.

Archer had responded when the report of the snipers first came in, so he was at the farm in minutes and took command. The Crime Scene Unit wasn't here yet. They would be busy with the house, the location of Briscoe's shooting, processing the car, and probably another half-dozen locations. Brad wanted to see the car. How did they do the shootings? He also wanted to get Hirsch in an interview—alone. He wasn't sorry Pittman was dead, but a few minutes alone with him would have been therapeutic.

Archer strode over to them. "Annie, I'm sorry you had to shoot Pittman. But you did the right thing. There is no doubt about that."

Annie squeezed tighter to Brad but didn't reply.

"When you're ready," Archer said, "go to headquarters. Detectives need to interview both of you. Normally we'd separate you, but in this case, it's unnecessary."

Brad nodded. "Give us a few minutes, then we'll go."

"Take your time." Archer headed back to the house.

Then a voice came over Brad's radio. "Air One is down in the Bow River. EMS and fire department responding."

Brad parked Annie's car near the nurse's residence, about two-hundred yards from the emergency entrance. That was as close as he could get. Ambulances and police cruisers occupied every available parking spot anywhere near the emergency entrance.

Annie was out of the car and dashing to the entrance. Brad sprinted to catch up. Dozens of cops stood outside emergency. *That happens when a cop is shot.*

Annie forced the automatic doors open and rushed to the triage desk. "Where is Charlie Zerr?"

"Are you family?"

"No. Yes. I'm his fiancée."

Brad swung his head to Annie and raised an eyebrow. *Fiancée*?

"I'll have a nurse come to talk to you." The triage nurse went back to her paperwork. "Please have a seat."

"No, I need to see him this instant."

The triage nurse pursed her lips and glared over her glasses. "I'm sorry, but we're swamped. Wait and—"

"I'm not—"

Brad grabbed her arm and pulled her away. She struggled to break free, but Brad held firm.

"Let me go," she shouted.

"Trust me," Brad whispered.

Annie stopped fighting and allowed Brad to hustle them down the hall away from triage, then turned right. The sign said X-ray.

"Is he getting X-rays?"

"Quiet."

They passed a door labeled X-ray on the left. Past a door on the right, then stopped by the second door on the right.

"Is he here? Let's go in."

Brad held out his hand. "Whoa. He's here, but they lock the door."

"I'll pound on the door."

"Just wait."

Annie fidgeted as she stared at the door.

"You need to calm down. You're not gonna help Charlie, and you're not helping anybody here if you rush in and raise a stink. Follow me, keep your mouth shut, and I'll find out what's going on. Do you understand?"

Annie nodded.

Then the door burst open and an orderly raced past. Brad grabbed the door before it closed, and they slipped into the hall outside the trauma rooms.

Briscoe occupied the third trauma bed. The closest two were empty.

Annie put her hand to her mouth and choked. "Oh, no."

Brad put his arm around her. "Let me find out. Charlie might not be here yet."

Brad spotted Griffin across from Briscoe. "How is he?"

"He'll be okay. The bullet missed his vest but hit his stomach."

"Most likely helped that he had some extra padding there."

Griffin glanced at Brad. "What about you? Are you okay?"

"Yeah."

"That's a change." Griffin's lips quirked.

"Older, wiser." Brad snorted. "What's the word on the helicopter crash?"

"Paramedics are still on scene. The rescue boat from downtown was out at your thing. They had to bring a rescue boat from the south, and that took time."

"Any word on injuries?"

Griffin shook his head. "But dispatch sent two ambulances."

"Ah, shit." A cold chill passed through him. He could not lose anyone else. Charlie was like a brother. "There were just two on board."

Griffin nodded.

"Thanks for the update." He headed back to Annie and told her what Griffin said.

"Oh my god." Her legs collapsed. Brad caught her and eased her into a chair.

"Don't get ahead of yourself. He is alive. He's getting great care by paramedics. They will be here soon. We wait."

"I can't wait."

Brad shook his head. "You don't have a choice. When you're ready, let's go talk to Briscoe."

CHAPTER SEVENTY-SEVEN

FIREFIGHTERS CARRIED THE SPINE BOARD TO THE RESCUE BOAT. Thompson and Dixon jogged behind, carrying equipment. They jumped into the boat. As soon as they had the spine board strapped in place, Thompson said, "Let's go."

The water bubbled and roiled as the powerful boat backed away from the island—a firefighter on shore assisted by giving the vessel a push. The transmission clunked, and the boat lurched forward.

"Easy," Thompson said.

In less than a minute, they were across the river to the north bank. Another group of firefighters were waiting and carried the board to the back of the ambulance where they set the spine board on the stretcher. Thompson jumped in. "I need one of you in the back with me and another to drive."

Firefighters slid the stretcher in and closed the back door.

A firefighter climbed in the side door, removed his coat and sat at the head of the stretcher. The ambulance pulled forward, and the siren sounded.

Thompson handed him the bag-valve-mask device. "You know how to use this?"

"You bet." The firefighter began ventilating the patient.

Thompson strapped the patient to the stretcher while Dixon hung two IV bags on the stretcher pole. Dixon applied tourniquets to each arm and started the large bore IVs.

Thompson checked the splints on the legs. He'd done the best he could on the island, but he was worried. When the helicopter crashed, his patient's side had taken the full force of the impact. Thompson was sure both legs were broken in multiple places, and the pelvis was crushed.

The ambulance swung left and Thompson was tossed against the wall and landed on the bench seat. "Easy."

The ambulance braked hard, then the back doors opened. A line of paramedics and cops scrambled to assist.

Annie brushed her eyes with the back of her hand and stood. "Let's go see the old man."

Brad followed Annie to Briscoe's bed. The heart monitor beeped a steady hundred and ten beats. An IV pump clicked, infusing fluid into his veins. An oxygen mask covered his face.

Brad took one side of the bed, Annie the other. She put her hand on Briscoe's. "Hey, old man. You too slow to dodge bullets?"

"No sass. Respect your elders."

"How are you?" she asked.

"Just a flesh wound. The doc said I have add-di-post tissue."

"It's called adipose," Annie said.

"The bullet made a mess of my six-pack abs."

"I was thinking more like a keg," Brad said.

Briscoe glared at Brad and focused on Annie. "Why did you bring this asshole?"

"He's my chauffeur."

"You need one with a better attitude."

"I know. But he's all I can afford."

"Griffin says you're going to surgery soon," Brad said.

"Yeah. They're waiting for the surgical team to get here."

Brad nodded. "They'll patch you up good as new."

"Better," Briscoe said. "I told him they could take out all that extra padding while they were there."

Brad grinned. "Good thinking."

"Jerry!" a voice shouted from down the hall.

Elaine Briscoe raced to her husband. Brad stepped back and made room.

"Oh, Jerry, are you okay?" She glared at Brad. "Are you to blame for this?"

"Well, I—" Brad stammered.

Briscoe coughed. "This time, it wasn't the rookie's fault. All mine. Too old and slow."

"We'll leave you," Brad said.

Elaine gave Brad a hug. "Thank you for being with him. And thank you for sending a cruiser to get me."

As they left Briscoe, the emergency doors swung open.

Paramedics and firefighters rushed a stretcher down the hall to trauma bed three. Cops followed, blocking Brad and Annie from the room. They pushed as close as they could. The trauma team lifted the spine board onto the hospital bed. The patient was immobilized entirely, his neck encased in a plastic neck brace, and his face covered by lacerations. He was unrecognizable.

They heard Thompson giving a report. "Unconscious on our arrival. The firefighters, my partner and I had to cross the river to get to the helicopter."

"Do you have a name?" a nurse asked.

"No," Thompson said. Then, quieter, "Too many lacerations. I can't identify him."

Annie gasped.

"We were able to lift him out of the chopper: bilateral upper and lower leg fractures and suspected pelvic fractures. Breath sounds are decreased on the left. Left pupil is fixed and dilated."

While Thompson gave a report, other members of the trauma team performed their assigned duties. A central line was placed and blood infused. A chest tube was inserted. The portable X-ray machine stood by. A resident stepped to the head of the patient and prepared to intubate. Before he could insert the tube into the trachea, blood gushed from the patient's mouth. Bright-red blood flowed into the chest tube, then slowed to a trickle.

Monitor alarms sounded. The emergency physician gave curt, direct orders. Those outside the trauma room were silent, knowing the clock was ticking on a life. Fifteen minutes later, the emergency physician glanced at the defeated faces of the team. "Time of death, 0025 hours."

Annie grabbed Brad's arm and shook uncontrollably.

CHAPTER SEVENTY-EIGHT

SHARMA AND COOK HAD TRANSFERRED BRISCOE TO THE EMERGENCY staff when they got the call for the helicopter crash. They'd raced down the hill in time to see an ambulance heading to the hospital.

They parked close to the river. Firefighters met them and helped with equipment. They took the rescue boat to the downed chopper. On the way over, a firefighter shouted over the noise of the boat engines. "The helicopter landed on its side. We were able to lift the first patient out. It's difficult with this guy. The cockpit collapsed around him. We have guys cutting the chopper. By the time we arrive, they should be done."

The boat swung next to the shore. Cook was out of the boat and racing to the chopper. She rounded the front, her boots crunching on broken glass. A gas engine roared as the firefighters used the Hurst Tool to cut the cockpit door.

She waited until a firefighter gave her a nod, then she

climbed into the cockpit, her fingers going to the patient's neck. She felt a fast but weak pulse.

Sharma leaned over her shoulder. "Weak," she said.

She slipped her hands around the head, down the neck to the chest, abdomen, and pelvis. She glanced over her shoulder. "No obvious fractures or bleeding. From here, I can't check his legs."

"I've got it," Sharma said.

Cook took out her stethoscope and listened to the patient's chest. Breath sounds were hard to hear and shallow. She called to the firefighters. "Full spinal immobilization. Let's get him out of here." She asked Sharma, "How are the lower extremities?"

"Left leg is okay. I'm not sure about the right leg. Possible lower tibia-fibula fracture or ankle fracture. Or all of the above."

She nodded. "He's got a broken right arm."

Within minutes, the patient was out of the chopper, immobilized, and on his way to the boat.

Once in the ambulance, Cook applied oxygen then started one IV in the patient's left arm.

Sharma immobilized both legs.

The ambulance pulled into the hospital and the back doors were thrown open before the ambulance had stopped. Then the patient started talking.

The emergency doors flew open, and another stretcher surrounded by cops and firefighters rolled into the emergency department. Sharma saw Brad. "It's Zerr."

"What?"

"Charlie Zerr. He just woke up."

Annie pushed away from Brad and fought like a bobcat to

the stretcher. "Charlie, Charlie. Are you okay?" She grabbed his hand and held tight as the stretcher rolled to trauma bed one.

"I'm sore. It's been a while since I was in a helicopter crash."

"What? You crashed before?"

"Just once."

"Do you hurt?"

"Everywhere."

She leaned forward and kissed his forehead. "Why are you strapped to this board?"

"Makes the paramedic feel like they did something. Gives the firefighters someone to carry. Works out for everyone."

Cook gave her report to the trauma team while they worked on Zerr.

When she'd completed, Brad pulled Cook aside.

"How is he?"

Cook grimaced. "They landed hard. I'm worried about a compressed spine. Maybe spinal fracture. He's in a lot of pain and has some numbness and tingling. Likely a right lower leg and right arm fracture. We can't rule out a concussion, either. We'll have a better diagnosis after we do X-rays and a CAT scan."

CHAPTER SEVENTY-NINE

Brad found Griffin and Steele in the coffee room. Steele's jaw was clenched, and his neck muscles were taut.

Brad flopped into a chair. "It's finally over."

"Not soon enough." Steele stood by the coffeepot, stirring his coffee vigorously.

"He's pissed because his girlfriend got hurt," Brad said.

Griffin sipped a coffee. "Yeah. It seems they got some kind of bromance going."

"Screw you two. Those bastards shot at my best friend in the helicopter and it crashed."

"He's gonna be okay," Brad said.

Steele glowered at Brad. "How do you know? The docs don't even know."

Brad shrugged. "I just know."

"Well, aren't you telepathetic." Steele's spittle sprayed. "Maybe Saint Coulter can lay his hands on Charlie's head and cast out the demons."

"You're the one possessed by demons." Brad held out his hand. "I'd enjoy slapping the demons out. We did what needed to be done. We stopped the snipers."

"He's pissed he didn't kill the guy who shot at him," Griffin said.

Brad shook his head. "You don't need another demon in your head, Sam. Trust me. Go see Charlie. Maybe he's back from the scans."

Steele stomped from the room.

Brad sighed. "They're like brothers."

"Sure, if you say so." Griffin grinned.

"Close brothers," Brad said.

Griffin jutted his chin and nodded. "The take-a-bullet kind."

"Something like that." Brad poured a coffee.

"How's Annie?" Griffin asked.

"She's upset, but the shooting hasn't hit her yet. She's focused on Charlie. When she knows he's okay, then it'll hit her."

"Like a ton of bricks."

"Yup."

"You'll be there for her?" Griffin asked.

"For as long as it takes." Brad sipped his coffee, they made a face. "This is terrible."

"She's had a tough go of it." Griffin stared at his hands.

"Yeah, but it makes her who she is. She's come a long way in four years."

"She had a decent role model," Griffin said.

"She loved Maggie." Brad leaned back, head on the top of the chair.

"I don't mean Maggie."

"Not me. " Brad frowned and shook his head. "I wasn't there when she needed me."

"No, but she was there for you—made her stronger."

"Maybe."

"No maybe. She'll get through this and she'll be unstoppable. Then you'll have a genuine problem on your hands."

Not my problem, Brad thought. *Did she really mean she was Charlie's fiancée, or was she bullshitting the nurse like she knew I'd do?*

The way they were headed today, or later, he was fine with that. Except he wasn't ready to share, not yet. But that wasn't his choice.

"You should go. Get some sleep," Brad said.

"I'm waiting until Briscoe goes to surgery. He kind of grows on you."

"Like a bad rash," Brad said.

"We've got an interview to do." Griffin crumpled his coffee cup and tossed tin the garbage.

"I've got it." Brad refilled his coffee.

"You sure about the interview?" Griffin asked.

Brad slid back into the chair. "No problem. I need a few minutes to decompress, then I'll head to HQ."

"Okay." Griffin stood. "Page me if you need help. I'm worried about Briscoe. I'm going to check on him."

Brad sat alone in the coffee room. Every hospital staff member was working on the traumas or the usual mix of ailments and injuries. He closed his eyes and his other senses took over. Hospitals had a unique odor. Floor disinfectant and bleach mingled with blood mixed with a pinch of vomit and shit. The smell of blood was strong.

The night replayed like a movie. The race to the helicopter, the gunshots, the foot pursuit, the ping of lead hitting the helicopter. Briscoe shot, the panic for Annie's safety, the blood on the wall and a missing face.

How many times had he and Maggie sat in a hospital coffee room? The awkward, "Hey, so you're a paramedic," and her sarcastic reply. Briscoe making sure they found each other after they had separated when Maggie went to Banff and Brad to leading a TSU team. Back together, they grew close and had plans.

The problem was Jeter Wolfe had different plans. Maggie was rushed to the hospital first. Brad wanted to wait until she was out of surgery before he had his leg repaired. However, the doctor said Brad couldn't wait. He never got to say goodbye to her. He never got to give her the ring he carried in his pocket.

No one knew it, but he'd planned to ask her to marry him as soon as they had Wolfe. Even though Brad couldn't attend her funeral, Sam made sure she was wearing the ring.

He hoped he made Maggie proud today.

Brad stepped out of the coffee room and headed to the exit. He started to mentally prepare for the interview with Logan Hirsch. It would be a long process. The automatic doors opened, and he was blinded in the glow of bright lights.

"Detective Coulter. Did you arrest the snipers?"

"We heard one was killed? Did you shoot him?"

"Why did the helicopter crash?"

"How is Sergeant Briscoe?"

"Can you confirm the helicopter pilot is dead?"

Brad held up his hand. "I will make a statement. No questions, no interruptions. If you do, I walk away."

"But first, Detective—" Angus Ferguson said.

Brad spun to the cops mingling at the entrance and pointed at Ferguson.

"Remove him from this area."

The cops grabbed Ferguson and dragged him away.

Ferguson yelled over his shoulder. "You can't do this, Coulter. I have a right to know. You can't arrest the press."

"Anyone else have anything to say?" Brad asked.

Silence.

"At 10:15 tonight we received a call that the vehicle we were searching for had been spotted across from the Paskapoo ski area. Cruisers were dispatched and I responded with TSU members by a helicopter provided by Nickle Oil."

Brad paused and took a deep breath.

"As we arrived, the suspect vehicle raced away. We trapped them in Bowness Park. A foot chase ensued. During the foot chase, a sniper shot at the helicopter, causing substantial damage. As you know, the helicopter crashed on an island in the Bow River. The pilot has died from his injuries and the passenger, a TSU member, has undetermined injuries."

He clenched his jaw.

"The first chase progressed westward toward Bearspaw Dam," Brad continued. "One suspect was shot, but not seriously injured. The second suspect continued his escape from the dam south and up the hill toward a farmhouse where he was fatally shot."

Several hands went up. He ignored them.

"During the pursuit up the hill, a police officer was shot and will be taken to surgery soon with non-life-threatening injuries. The suspect who was shot has been released from the hospital and will be interviewed. Our investigation will continue, and we will have further comments at a later time. Thank you."

Brad parked in the dark alley behind Police Headquarters. First, he needed a large coffee, and then the interview would begin. He willed his feet to keep moving, one step after the other, moving on their own.

"Detective."

Brad stopped.

"Brad?"

He glanced up. "No, Sadie. Please, I have nothing to say."

"I … I don't have questions. I want to say I'm sorry your friends were hurt. Truly, I am." Her eyes lowered. "I hope they recover soon. That's it. I'm glad you're okay."

Brad nodded. "Thank you. I appreciate that."

Sadie pulled a few loose strands of hair behind her ear. "This is a one-time thing, you know. I'll be riding your ass for a scoop again soon enough. Maybe the next time we find ourselves at a restaurant in the same general vicinity, same general time."

"I look forward to it."

CHAPTER EIGHTY

Brad grabbed two coffees from the coffee pot behind the desk sergeant, tossed a dollar in a Styrofoam cup, and headed to the interview room. Deputy Chief Archer leaned against the wall outside the interview room.

"Good work," Archer said. "I'm going to join you in the interview."

"I can handle this."

"I know you can. But there should be two of us, and Griffin is still at the hospital. You're stuck with me. I won't interfere."

Brad peered at Archer. "Yes, sir."

They entered the interview room. The suspect was dressed in green hospital scrubs, his blond hair a wild mess, and a patchy beard. His left arm was in a sling, and his right forearm was covered with bandages. He stared at his hands, handcuffed to the table.

Brad set the coffee in front of the suspect. "Hirsch, right? Logan Hirsch?"

"Yeah." He eyed the coffee but didn't reach for it.

"I'm Detective Coulter, and this is—"

"Detective Archer," Chief Archer said.

"Yeah, Detective Archer is sitting in with me." Brad slid the coffee closer to Hirsch's right hand. "I'll be conducting the interview."

"Do you understand your rights as read to you by Constable Steele?"

"Sure."

"You're under arrest for the murder of five people and the attempted murder of three. I have no clue how accurate those numbers are. They don't include the shootings tonight."

"I didn't—"

Brad held up his hands. "I'm not here to argue the charges. That's between you, your lawyer and the prosecutor. We can do this two ways—I can ask about five hundred questions, or you can tell us a story from the beginning."

"If I just tell the story, will you go easy on me?"

Brad leaned forward. "Unless you tell me you never fired a shot, then I'll be honest, there's not a lot I can do. I'll tell the prosecutor you were cooperative, and it will be up to them how they view what you say."

"I'll never leave prison, will I?" Hirsch was slouched, his eyes red and on the verge of tears.

"I doubt it," Brad said.

"What about my kids?"

Archer was ready to say something, but Brad subtly shook his head. "That's between you and the prosecutor. Which way are we doing this, Logan?" Brad leaned back and clasped his hands in his lap.

Logan leaned down to the coffee and drank. He stared at the

liquid and then drank again. Hirsch stared over Brad's shoulder like he was talking to someone else. "I got laid off from the oil patch months ago. I met Marvin Pittman in a retraining class in Drayton Valley. I don't know why we hit it off. I think he talked to me first. He looked okay. Older than me by about ten years, and he'd been through the oil patch layoffs and downturn before." He sipped some coffee. "My wife was pissed I didn't have work, then she served me divorce papers. I was mad at the oil company, my wife, the retraining program, and a government that didn't give a shit."

He continued his stare past Brad, but a grin formed.

"We skipped training one day and went shooting," Hirsch said. "I'm a perfect shot. I shot since I was nine. It was therapeutic, like stress relief, you know."

Brad felt the same about shooting.

"Marvin had a plan to get back at the oil companies." Hirsch's grin disappeared, and he hung his head. "It doesn't make sense now. But at the time, I was excited, angry, vengeful, and when Marvin talked, it made sense. The more he talked, the angrier I got. He had this plan all along. He just needed someone he could control and who could shoot. He found me. His plan was to take some practice shots—kills—in Rocky Mountain House and Airdrie. I shot the oil worker in Rocky Mountain House, and he killed the salesman in Airdrie with a pistol. I did the first four shootings in Calgary. Then Pittman decided he wanted to shoot. He shot a lady at a gas station and the bus driver. He was a shitty shot. I was surprised he even hit them."

"What about the kid and the cop?"

"I'm not saying anything about them."

"With the cop, you missed deliberately," Brad said.

Hirsch stared blankly at Brad.

"What about your efforts to contact us?" Brad asked.

"At first, he just wanted to taunt the cops. But he couldn't get through. He called the jackass public information guy, Carew, but his assistant was an idiot. Calling the RCMP was even worse. But what set Pittman off was when he couldn't get ahold of you." Hirsch pointed at Brad. "He said you were a straight shooter, but he decided to taunt you with the notes. But then he figured you were messing with him with the missed calls and he was pissed. Some of the killings were because you were dumbasses."

"And the ransom?"

"A distraction, so you'd think we wanted to negotiate, to quit the shooting."

"But you weren't going to quit?"

"No. When the oil company upped the reward, Pittman went insane. He worked on a better plan."

"What was that?"

Logan sat back. "I'm not gonna say—I ... I didn't know." Hirsch crossed his arms over his chest. "That's all I got to say."

"When we publicized your identities, why didn't you get out of town?"

Hirsch leaned forward. "What are you talking about?"

"We told the press we were searching for you and Pittman. We showed photos of you to the press. They broadcast it on every news show. We gave the car description and license plate."

Hirsch shook his head vigorously. "I—we ... didn't know. No way. How?"

Brad grinned. "Good detectiving."

"You couldn't know."

"Yet, we did."

Hirsch sat back again. "I won't say another word until I see a lawyer."

CHAPTER EIGHTY-ONE

While Brad was conducting the interview, Sturgeon left a message for Brad to come to the police garage.

He crossed Third Street and into the garage. In the far corner, Sturgeon and his team were working on the LTD.

"What's up?" Brad asked.

Sturgeon showed him the set-up in the trunk and back seat. "Limited span of vision, but otherwise a perfect sniper nest."

Brad wandered around the car and climbed in the back seat. "Would have worked for a van, too. But who'd suspect a police LTD. Several witnesses told us about an unmarked police car before the shootings. I wrote it off as one of ours and that witnesses were mistaken when they said that's the type of car they saw. Heck, I even thought they were describing my vehicle."

"Brilliant in its deviousness. There's more." Sturgeon headed to the driver's door. "They'd removed all the plastic and padding on the inside of the door."

"Why would they do that?" Brad examined the door.

"In case they were stopped by cops. The driver could shoot through the door and have a better chance of hitting the cop. That would take a powerful gun."

"Shit. Pittman has a .45 caliber Colt M1911. He probably kept it under the driver's seat."

"That would do it." Sturgeon led Brad to the passenger side. He leaned into the car and opened the glovebox.

Brad whistled. It was full of boxes of ammunition for the .223 and the .45.

"They also installed an oversized rearview mirror."

Brad slid into the driver's seat. "The driver had a full view and could call out the targets on the radio."

"There's something you need to hear." Sturgeon led Brad over to a tape recorder sitting on a table. It was covered with fingerprint powder. Sturgeon pushed the play button. A voice began speaking. Not Hirsch. Pittman.

"We wanted the oil companies to feel our pain. But even killing people in their stations didn't affect them. They offered reward money to catch us. Money they couldn't afford to pay us but could freely offer to show what good guys they were. The only time anyone reacted, the only time people were upset, was when the little boy was shot. When the cop was shot, the cops were mad, but the public was blah. So, kids were your Achilles' heel. You know that a busload of children were killed today. Gone down in the safety of the yellow school bus.

Do we have your attention? Do we have your fear? Do we have your respect?

If killing a busload of kids wasn't enough to get your respect, what about the reporters killed at the press conference you called after the kids died?

The ransom is twenty million. From each of the following compa-

nies: Nickle Oil, Heritage Oil and Gas, Western Oil Exploration, Bison Oil, and Rocky Plains Oil and Gas.

Payment due in two days. Kiss your children goodnight."

"Oh my god," Brad said.

"They were planning to shoot up school buses and kill reporters," Sturgeon said. "You stopped them just in time."

Brad sighed. "No. Eleven shootings too late."

CHAPTER EIGHTY-TWO

One Month Later

LAWN CHAIRS CIRCLED A FIRE PIT AT BRAD'S FARM. STEELE MADE sure everyone had at least one beer and brought a hot chocolate to his pregnant wife, Emma. Annie had a long table loaded with buns, salads, and condiments. Brad barbecued burgers and hotdogs and glanced at his friends.

Griffin and Devlin relaxed in lawn chairs with Briscoe in Brad's oversized stuffed chair they'd hauled out from the house. Briscoe complained that a lawn chair would be detrimental to his recovery. They drank beer and told bigger and better cop stories.

Annie and Charlie sat on a bench together. Charlie had been lucky to some degree. His spine had absorbed the shock of the crash, but he didn't have any permanent damage. His right leg and arm had been broken. He'd get the arm cast off next week, but the leg cast would stay for another two weeks. Charlie drank beer with his left hand, and Annie served him piggies-in-blankets.

Sergeant Bill Sturgeon and his wife, Susan, arrived. Bill headed over to Griffin, Devlin, and Briscoe to add his own stories.

Susan caught up with Elaine Briscoe, who was watching her boys—seventeen-year-old Grant and fourteen-year-old Smitty—toss the ball for Lobo. Susan's girls, Stephanie and Heather, joined the boys.

Sam brought Brad another beer and Emma stood next to him. "What's with that smarmy grin on your face?"

"I've missed get-togethers like this," Brad said. "I didn't realize how much I need all of you."

"Not like we didn't try to stay in contact."

Emma jabbed Sam in the ribs. "Play nice."

Brad sipped his beer and stared out at the kids and Lobo. "I know." He sighed. "It's not easy moving forward."

Sam put his arm around one shoulder. "We know, buddy."

Brad rubbed his chin, then said, "Burgers and hot dogs are ready. Come and get them."

Despite being out in the field, Briscoe's boys were the first in line.

The sun had set, the fire roared, and the beer still flowed. The kids had settled and were roasting marshmallows. Lobo sat at Brad's feet.

"What's happening with Hirsch?" Briscoe asked.

"Gerry." Elaine punched his arm. "Not here."

Brad leaned toward the fire. "I'm working with the prosecutor's office to figure it all out."

"What he means is, he's spending a lot of time with the crown prosecutor, Jenni Blighe." Griffin smirked.

"Really?" Elaine asked.

Briscoe snorted.

Brad ignored them. "We know which murders Hirsch did and which ones Pittman was responsible for. To date, Hirsch has been charged with five counts of murder and three of attempted murder. His trial would be sometime late next year."

"Turns out Pittman was responsible for a string of murders across Canada," Griffin said. "The killings started after he deserted from the US army, then every year or so as he crossed the country. The RCMP are still linking cases to him."

"No one claimed his body," Sturgeon said. "May he rot in hell." He raised his beer and the others did the same.

"Don't forget, Mayor Kearse said you guys are heroes," Annie said.

Briscoe rolled his eyes and scoffed. "I think he meant the Three Musketeers—Bradthos, Steelthos, and Zerramis."

Griffin spewed his beer. "Oh my god, that is perfect."

"Deputy Chief Archer is less than thrilled," Brad said. "I have a meeting with him Monday and since the case preparation is wrapped up for now, I'm back on suspension. Possibly forever. I have no idea."

"You just can't stay out of the principal's office, can you," Devlin said. "What's this, like your third detention?"

Annie glared at Devlin. "You're not helping."

"I hear the Mayor and Archer are searching for a new Public

Information Officer after Kearse demanded Carew's resignation," Zerr said. "Apparently, Carew was the leak to the media through Angus Ferguson."

"Maybe pretty boy and his awesome press conferences should take that job." Briscoe glanced at Brad.

Devlin laughed and pointed his beer at Sturgeon. "We voted for Bill because no one would understand him."

Sturgeon let loose with what everyone figured was cursing in Scottish.

Brad leaned back in his chair and sipped his beer. "I heard yesterday that Carew and Ferguson are co-authoring a book on the snipers. They've already signed a huge book contract, including a North America tour."

"For Christ's sake," Briscoe blurted.

Elaine punched his arm again. "Not in front of the boys."

"The story with Carew gets better," Brad said. "They also signed a contract for a made-for-TV movie."

"Maybe Tom Selleck can play your role." Annie glanced at Brad.

"If that's the case," Sturgeon said, "Sean Connery would have to have my role."

"Maybe Danny DeVito could play Briscoe," Griffin said.

That brought laughter, and then everyone was selecting actors to portray them in the movie.

"If Angus Ferguson is going on tour, who is replacing him at CFCN News?" Devlin asked.

"Ask Brad." Steele smirked.

"Yeah." Zerr tried hard to suppress a grin. "He's got the inside track on information like that."

Brad gave Zerr and Steele the finger.

Susan glanced at Zerr. "What do you mean?"

"Perhaps there were two leaks to the media," Zerr said.

"Yup, someone's career took off when she published the story, start to finish," Steele said.

Devlin and Griffin glanced at each other. "Sadie Andrus?"

TO THE READER

Brad Coulter is Back! Thank you to everyone who made the launch of ***Wolfman is Back*** in November 2019 a success and propelled it to the bestseller list—twice!

I loved the emails from so many readers, those who loved the novel, those who wanted to kill me because of the ending, those who disagreed with the decision initially, but later jumped to my thinking. As I mentioned in the Afterword to ***Wolfman is Back***, the ending was an emotional experience for me.

After a break from Brad for a few months to write ***Speargrass—Opioid***, I returned to the Coulter thrillers and realized I'd painted myself into a corner with the way ***Wolfman is Back*** ended. I was also thoroughly exhausted from writing the final scenes with Maggie, Annie, Lobo, Brad, and Jeter Wolfe.

How could Brad recover? I struggled with that for quite a while. Then I realized he couldn't recover—he could never be the same. But that didn't mean the stuff at his core wasn't there—he'd have to work hard to find it and get his mojo back.

Before he could come back to work, he needed clearance from a psychologist. The counseling wasn't going well, so Brad crossed the line, and forged a back to work letter. In the real world, Brad might be fired or criminally charged for that.

I try to keep the plots realistic and I strongly encourage writers at writing conferences to write realistic scenes (genre dependent, of course). This was the first time in the Coulter thrillers I deviated. I hope you weren't distracted by Brad's transgression.

Back at work, they pair Brad with Homicide detective Don Griffin and Brad says the 'Q' word ('quiet'), an unforgiveable sin in emergency services. As usual for Brad, the quiet doesn't last long.

The idea for ***13 Days of Terror*** is based on the Beltway Sniper case in and around Washington, DC, in 2002. I had researched that incident for months when I discovered a retired FBI profiler was speaking on that topic at the YouthLink Interpretive Calgary Police Centre. I was too late to get a ticket. But my wonderful editor, Taija Morgan, attended and took awesome notes. When it was time for Taija to edit the novel, she understood the original event, and suggested changes to my novel.

13 Days of Terror introduces new characters like Jill Cook, a paramedic, because, well, I needed to replace one. Sorry.

One more point: ***The Title***. While Brad and the city weren't directly affected for the full 13 days, Pittman and Hirsch started planning their killing spree on Day 1 (and one may argue Hirsch was terrorized the full 13 Days by Pittman). And, ***13 Days of Terror*** sounds better than 8 Days of Terror.

You won't have to wait long for Brad Coulter #5. ***Goddess of Justice*** will be launched in March 2021.

13 Days of Terror is my second novel released this year. Perhaps there will be three or four novel releases next year!

Credits:

I have an exceptional team ...

Valerie West

Valerie has supported my writing right from when we met. She's always my first Beta Reader and provides just the right amount of critique and encouragement. When I hide out in my writing cave, she understands that I am in the zone. Or she thinks I am! I might not make it out of my office for hours and sometimes I will write late into the night. I'd be so lost without her love and support.

Jonas Saul

Jonas and I have been friends for 2 ½ years. We met at the Creative Ink Festival in Burnaby, B.C. Jonas is an outstanding thriller writer and New York Times bestselling author of the Sarah Roberts series. Jonas is a prolific writer and by Christmas will have written nine novels and published seven this year. I am no where near the production of Jonas, but he is continually pushing me to work harder and meet daily goals. I'm not as consistent as his 5,000 words a day, but I have had a few 6,000++ word days and can easily write 2500 to 3,000 words in a day. As I write this in October 2020, I am writing my seventh novel, with eight and nine in the early stages as well. Thank you, Jonas, for mentorship and friendship.

Taija Morgan

Taija is a huge part of my writing success. Her edits are so well thought out, suggestions are bang on, and she takes the opportunity to teach me. The fact I don't always catch on. is on me! My goal is to have her say "I didn't see that coming." Or "Nice twist." And especially, "I laughed out loud."

At times, well, often, I think she knows the story better than I do. She is excellent at noting times where I have forgotten a detail from a previous novel. Thank you, Taija, for your awesome edits, but also for teaching me to be a better writer.

TRAVIS MILES, PROBOOKCOVERS

Travis created all my book covers. Before anyone gets to my writing, they have seen Travis' work and are impressed. His designs are outstanding and stand out form other novels. He has created a vision for both the Coulter and Speargrass series.

BILL STURGEON

My good friend Bill Sturgeon was a classmate of mine at the police academy. For reasons neither of us understand, we became friends. Sergeant Bill Sturgeon of the Identification Bureau made his first appearance in ***OUTLAW**^MC^*. He assists Brad in ***WOLFMAN IS BACK***. And while he isn't getting his own series, he play a key role in the next two Coulter novels.

SHEILA CLAYDEN—MOM

My mom is my biggest fan. My fondest memories were of her reading to me, then teaching me to read. I've had a book or seven in line for reading since I discovered the Hardy Boys. I don't know if it was natural progression, but she had prepared me for writing by sharing her love of reading. She has a copy of the first draft of ***CRISIS POINT***. She hopes someday it will be worth a lot of money.

JENNIFER COCKTON, ONLINE FOR WRITERS

Jennifer keeps the web page up to date, manages all things social media, and reminds me when the newsletter is due.

MICKEY MIKKELSEN OF CREATIVE EDGE CLIENT GROUP HANDLES MY PUBLICITY.

Beta Readers

I have a great group of Beta readers that give me early feedback on the plot and characters. Each provide their unique perspective, which collectively gives me the direction I need.

Bill and Susan Sturgeon—Bill, a retired Calgary Police Sergeant, and Susan, retired RCMP, provide feedback on policing. Susan, as well, provides advice on Brad's love life and with each novel threatens me if I do something she doesn't like. (There were many threats after ***Wolfman is Back***!) Of course, I make sure to add those to the novel. Susan is my second biggest fan and shouts out to everyone she knows (and some she doesn't) that they should buy my novels.

Craig Ilott, as always, pointed out plot errors and out-of-character character responses to situations. I'd be lying if I said his comments didn't make me cry. He'd tell me suck it up and make the changes.

Bob Modray, has been a Coulter fan right from ***Crisis Point.*** He offered to read an early version of ***13 Days of Terror*** and offered outstanding suggestions.

Rod Fradette, good friend and golfing buddy, allowed me to use his name as a rescuer coming to the aid of a gunshot victim.

A Final Note to My Readers

This summer I attended several Farmer's Markets and Fairs. It was such a thrill to have readers who bought novels from me last year, track me down to either pick up the latest in the Brad Coulter series, or ***Speargrass—Opioid.***

At one fair, a lady was a hard sell. I spent a lot of time trying to convince her she'd like the novels. We made a deal. She would buy ***Crisis Point,*** on the condition that if she liked it she could come back and get the deal I was offering that day, for all three novels. I agreed and as she left, I said, "See you in two weeks." She smirked.

Two weeks later as the market opened, there she was, back for ***Outlaw*** ^{MC} and ***Wolfman is Back***.

A guy was flying past my booth, on a mission of some kind, then came to a screeching halt. He said, "I bought two books from you last year. Do you have new ones?"

I said, "I have two new ones."

He said, "I'll take them." Then rushed off.

Experiences like that are so thrilling. I am overwhelmed and touched that you like my novels and how enthusiastic you are in your emails. I even like the pressure you put on me to get the next novel out. At times, I'm obsessed with writing.

On days when the words aren't cooperating, an email from you reminds me why I'm doing this, and I forge on.

Thank you from the bottom of my heart. You are awesome!

ABOUT THE AUTHOR

Dwayne Clayden combines his knowledge and experience as a police officer and paramedic to write realistic crime thrillers.

His first novel, **Crisis Point**, was a finalist for the 2015 Crime Writers of Canada Arthur Ellis awards.

The Brad Coulter Thriller Series includes **Crisis Point**, **Outlaw**^{MC} , **Wolfman is Back**, and ***13 Days of Terror.***

In 2021,The Brad Coulter Thriller Series continues with ***Goddess of Justice*** and ***Bonded Labor.***

Dwayne released the first novel in a new Modern Western Thriller Series, ***Speargrass-Opioid.*** If you like Longmire, you'll love ***Speargrass-Opioid***.

Dwayne's short story, **Hell Hath No Fury**, was published in **AB Negative**, an anthology of short stories from Alberta Crime Writers.

His vast experience working with emergency services spans over 40 years and includes work as a police officer, paramedic, tactical paramedic, firefighter, emergency medical services (EMS) chief, educator, and academic chair.

Dwayne is a popular speaker at writing conferences and for writing groups, providing police and medical procedures advice and editing to authors and screenwriters. The co-author of four paramedic textbooks, he has spoken internationally at EMS conferences for the past three decades.

DwayneClayden.com

dwayneclayden@gmail.com

Made in the USA
Coppell, TX
08 November 2020

40985305R10223